Pr

"A must-read . . . The sex is imaginative considering the constraints Page has placed on the heroine. Fortunately the two hunky supernatural heroes are more than up to the challenge!"
—*Romantic Times*

"The power of love is at the very core of this immensely erotic and thrilling love story. The characters are intense and decidedly sexual, but at the same time their vulnerability is what makes them stand out. The ménage component of this story is exceptionally well done."
—*Coffee Time Romance*

"Ms. Page is a great storyteller, and she always manages to draw me in from the very first page. This story had enough surprises to keep me on my toes." —*Just Erotic Romance Reviews*

"A New Queen of Erotic Romance"
—*Romantic Times*

Praise for **BLOOD RED**

2007 National Readers' Choice Award Winner for Erotic Romance

"A blazing path into forbidden dreams . . ."
—*Romantic Times BOOKreviews*

"Ms. Page weaves an erotic and suspenseful tale that . . . puts you on a sexual roller coaster and doesn't let you off. . . . If you're a lover of vampire romance, curl up on a cold winter night with *Blood Red* to warm your heart!"
—*Just Erotic Romance Reviews* (Gold Star Award)

"An erotically charged tale . . . a wonderful action-packed story that combines suspense, intrigue, horror, bondage, and yes, a whole lot of sex."
—*Coffee Time Romance*

Praise for **BLOOD ROSE**

"Page's *Blood Rose* has scorching love scenes to make you sweat and an intriguing plot to hold it all together."
—*New York Times* best-selling author Hannah Howell

"*Blood Rose* is an action-packed, sexy paranormal overflowing with suspense, horror, and romance. Sharon Page is a master of the ménage—prepare to be seduced!"
—Kathryn Smith, *USA Today* best-selling author

"The female protagonist is completely believable, and the two vampire-slaying heroes . . . are simply hot! This is a thoroughly entertaining read." —*Romantic Times*

"Buffy the Vampire Slayer meets Regency England! Two sexy, to-die-for heroes, a courageous heroine, and a luscious ménage make *Blood Rose* a sinful treat."
—Jennifer Ashley, *USA Today* best-selling author

"A chilling tale of vampires with loads of suspense and intrigue combined with searing erotic heat . . . the magic of pure sexual steam that can only mean one thing—it's another winner from Sharon Page!" —Renee Bernard, *USA Today* best-selling author

"Intriguing paranormal romance along the same lines of Laurell K. Hamilton's early work . . . magic, mischief, and ménages."
—Fresh Fiction

Praise for **SIN**

2006 National Readers' Choice Award Winner for Erotic Romance

"How do you have an orgasm without sex? Read *Sin* by Sharon Page! . . . Thoroughly wicked, totally wild, utterly wanton, and very witty in its execution, *Sin* is the ultimate indulgence."
—*Just Erotic Romance Reviews* (Gold Star Award)

"Strong, character-driven romance . . . extremely sensual and erotic." —*Romantic Times BOOKreviews*

"Sinfully delicious. Sharon Page is a pure pleasure to read." —Sunny, *New York Times* best-selling author of *Over the Moon* (anthology) and *Mona Lisa Awakening*

"Sharon Page blends history, emotion, and hot, hot, hot sex within an amazing love story. Blazing erotica!" —Kathryn Smith, *USA Today* best-selling author

"An erotic page turner that must be read only in an air conditioned room as the book is hot hot hot . . . Sharon Page is now on my 'must be read' list." —*Romance Junkies*

Praise for **BLACK SILK**

2008 Romantic Times' Reviewers' Choice Award for Best Historical Erotic Romance

RT TOP PICK 4½ Stars: "This wonderful, well-written Regency has emotion, blindingly hot sex, complicated characters, and a surprise ending." —*Romantic Times BOOKreviews*

"I can sum this novel up in one word: wow! . . . Not only were the encounters burn-your-fingers-hot but also emotional and romantic." Gold Star Award! —*Just Erotic Romance Reviews*

Praise for **HOT SILK**

"With an interesting plot, likable characters, suspense, sexual adventure, and romance, this story satisfies." —*Romantic Times BOOKreviews*

"A delightfully sensual story of love . . . Outstanding read!" —*Coffee Time Romance*

Books by Sharon Page

BLOOD WICKED

BLOOD DEEP

BLOOD RED

BLOOD ROSE

BLACK SILK

HOT SILK

SIN

"Midnight Man" in WILD NIGHTS

Blood Wicked

SHARON PAGE

APHRODISIA

KENSINGTON PUBLISHING CORP.
http://www.kensingtonbooks.com

APHRODISIA BOOKS are published by

Kensington Publishing Corp.
119 West 40th Street
New York, NY 10018

All Kensington Titles, Imprints, and Distributed Lines are available at special quantity discounts for bulk purchases for sales promotions, premiums, fund-raising, and educational or institutional use.

Special book excerpts or customized printings can also be created to fit specific needs. For details, write or phone the office of the Kensington special sales manager: Kensington Publishing Corp., 119 West 40th Street, New York, NY 10018, attn: Special Sales Department, Phone: 1-800-221-2647.

Aphrodisia and the A logo Reg. U.S. Pat & TM Off.

ISBN-13: 978-0-7582-5094-0
ISBN-10: 0-7582-5094-0

First Kensington Trade Paperback Printing: March 2011

10 9 8 7 6 5 4 3 2 1

Printed in the United States of America

Prologue

Dartmoor, 1820

"This is the pool, milord. The one yer brother looked in afore he vanished."

Heath Winthrope, Earl of Blackmoor, swung off his mount. Ahead Tom, the moorsman who had led him here, pointed down to a tiny pond, encircled by a ring of granite boulders.

A full moon hung blue-white and plump in the sky. They stood high on the moors, alone, surrounded by quiet, dark hills of waving grass. Heath's jaw tingled as it always did before his fangs erupted. So as he crossed over the granite stones in long strides, he kept his face turned away. No point in letting poor Tom find out what he really was.

Heath rested one foot on a large rock and looked down at the small pool. Ripples on its surface sparkled beneath streams of silvery light. "You claim that the reflection seen in this pool will be the next person to die."

Tom pulled off his cap, twisted it in his hands. "Aye, milord. That's the legend, it is. If you look into the water you will see the face of the next person who will die. Young Mr. Winthrope was a bit foxed, milord, and determined to prove the legend to be just a myth."

Christ, he was going to have to take a look. Heath leaned over and frowned at the reflection he expected to see.

It was his face. Unchanged for the last ten years. He still looked to be a man of eight-and-twenty. His face was unlined, his features sharp and cleanly cut, his silvery-green eyes bright and cocky with eternal youth.

Tom stayed far enough back so his face would not reflect. Heath stared at the image of his unsmiling face. The magical powers of this pool were, as he suspected, nothing more than myth—

The water to the right of his image bubbled suddenly. The turbulence stopped and a woman's face appeared beside his in the pool. A bewitching face. Blue eyes, large yet full of intelligence and lively delight. The face was oval, the cheeks smooth and ivory. The hair was like spun gold pouring over slim shoulders.

Through the shimmering veil of it, he could see her neck, a long, smooth column of white.

It was like the sight of a bottle of port to a drunkard, or the scent of opium smoke to a fevered addict. His fangs burst forth.

He could see more of her now. She was naked, possessing two perfect ivory breasts, topped with peach-pink nipples. A smooth belly. Generous hips.

He was hard with desire and fiercely hungry for her throat. . . . Then he blinked. Bare breasts and a bare neck reflected beside him?

Heath jerked around. His normally slow heartbeat became a hard pulse in his throat. Tom, lurking behind a granite boulders, looked up fearfully. Around, the Dartmoor hills stretched, empty and still. Up here, he could see for miles—right to where his estate house sprawled, surrounded by a stone wall, lichen-covered trees, and the little white dots of slumbering sheep.

There was no nude woman behind him.

Tom peered at him, uneasy and curious. "Whose face did you see, milord?"

How could he see the face of a woman who was not even there?

Right, Heath. And how can you be a vampire—cheating death and surviving by drinking blood? "I looked into a moonlit pool of water. I saw my own face, of course."

Tom gave a strangled grunt of dismay.

Heath groaned. "Bloody hell, man, I am not going to die next. I can assure you of that. Your tale is nothing more than a faery story, meant to frighten and entertain."

Of all the men in England, he was the least likely to have a sudden and untimely death. He'd already done that bit and had escaped the final reckoning. He was now immortal. The undead. Nosferatu.

But the woman . . .

Cold unease gripped his heart. How could he be seeing her reflection? Had he actually seen someone who was going to die? Who was she? He didn't know, so he couldn't warn her to be careful around carriages, firearms, and unknown plants.

Then his throat tightened. In the reflection, the woman ran her hand down his chest as she lowered to her knees in front of him. Her hands deftly released his cock from his trousers. And Heath had the astounding experience of watching from a distance while a beautiful woman sucked his cock deeply down her throat. Hell . . .

The water bubbled again. This time his reflection disappeared. The woman was now reclining on a chaise, her hand draped over her curvaceous hip. There was a man standing beside her. But it wasn't him. It was his brother Raine, who had been missing for a fortnight. His brother was gazing at the beautiful blond woman as though he loved her.

Was he looking at the reflection of a woman who had harmed his brother? One who had also disappeared? He didn't know who she was, so why had he seen her sucking him?

Whoever she was, he had to find her.

1

London, Two weeks later

As a mortal man, Heath had adored women's breasts. They seemed to be a stroke of genius. Plump, bouncy, and tempting, and all the fun of playing with them pleasured the woman, too.

As a vampire, he found them irresistible.

For the ten years he had been Nosferatu, one of the undead, he'd been plagued with the yearning to sink his fangs into a woman's breasts and taste her succulent blood that way.

He'd resisted. But hell, it had been hard.

And now, he was standing in a brothel's salon while some foolish woman thought to tempt him by baring her generous bosom. Henna-red curls bounced around her face. She flashed a coquettish look to him beneath thick lashes, pursed her scarlet lips, then let her silk wrapper slide from her shoulders.

He knew he should look away. The gesture would annoy her and she would move on to other prey. Half the men in the room were watching that scrap of silk as it fell from her shapely shoulders and snagged on the swell of her generous bosom. She gave him a wicked smile. Then she shimmied to make the fabric fall free. Two stunningly large breasts popped into view—full, ivory white, and topped with nipples rouged to an erotic scarlet.

Blinking, blazing hell.

The two vampires who sat in front of the courtesan traded lusty smiles, then bent to the two full breasts on offer. But neither men suckled the aroused nipples; each drove their teeth into the plump sides of her breasts. What they wanted was blood.

The seductive, coppery tang of it filled the salon.

The woman gave a sensual moan of pleasure. Her head fell back. The vampires knew how to take enough blood to give her a thrilling sexual sensation. They wouldn't kill her. They would show her unfathomable delights by lightly drinking her blood, while stroking her nipples and her hot, wet cunny.

Years of abstinence reared up inside Heath. His cock reared in front of him.

No. He would not let himself give in to temptation.

Watching two men experience his fantasy had him taut as a bowstring and ready to snap. His hand closed too tightly on the glass of brandy in his gloved hand. With a delicate *ping*, the glass shattered. He dropped the remnants to a table and glanced around. Where in blazes had Julian gone? He needed to get out of here.

With her red-blond curls, this woman was not the one he was looking for.

He had made it to the door when the madam of the place, a demoness of some sort, sashayed out of the shadows and planted her buxom body in his path. "Ah, my lord. Have you only come to feed tonight, or do you wish to indulge in other pleasures as well?"

"Neither." Heath cleared his throat, hiding the two weaknesses that tried to claim him. Lust and hunger. "I've come in search of my brother."

Her plucked brows drew together in a frown. "But your brother is not a vampire, is he?" The stout woman was about forty. A stomacher crushed her belly flat and pushed her enormous bosom upward in a shelf of whitened flesh. That was the specialty of this brothel. The women within possessed the largest breasts in London.

"He is now. A mistake on my part—" He stopped. Christ, there was no need to explain his private hell to a madam. Swiftly he gave a description of Raine.

The woman shook her head. "No, he has not been here. But you must feed, my lord. I can sense the anguish within you." She reached out for his arm.

And though he had immeasurable power, Heath jerked his forearm back like a frightened boy. "I do not need it," he said curtly. "I wanted to find out about a woman. One who was involved with my brother. Blond—her hair is a dark gold. Very lovely. Blue eyes. Large ones."

"That could describe many of my girls. You shall have to look through them, my lord."

He glimpsed the madam's thoughts. Visions hit him. A thousand personal, useless visions—of gowns, jewels, the location of the keys to her locked drawers, the bare chest of a footman she slept with. Then one image came forth and pushed all the others away. A man's face—with auburn hair, laughing green eyes, a spray of freckles across his cheeks. *Raine.* And then he saw himself, with his brother.

Raine had followed him here once. A year ago, while his young brother had still been mortal and had no idea what he'd been walking into.

In her thoughts, the madam would naturally conjure up the last time she had seen Raine. Which meant what she had told him was the truth.

He saw images of several blond women in her head. Her

thoughts flowed easily to him. *He wants a blonde. Sally? She has blue eyes. If he wants a specific girl . . . how can I tempt him to choose one of mine instead?*

Heath drew back from the madam's thoughts, the shutters in his mind falling back into place like iron doors. *Clang. Clang. Clang.*

"Come." She moved to his side, a bright smile on her crimson lips. "Let us find the woman you are searching for tonight."

He knew the game. She wanted to give him a reason to stay, to peruse her voluptuous, half-naked tarts in the hope he would find one he couldn't resist.

"No, thank you. I'm not looking for a woman to fuck, but for one to question."

"How . . . odd. My lord, I sense great agony in you. I know you do not wish to feed, but I fear it is becoming painful for you to deny yourself any longer. How long has it been since you took blood?" she asked sympathetically, but he knew her concern was feigned.

"A week."

"That is far too long. Dangerously so. Surely you know that, my lord."

"I have gone longer." Three months. That had been the longest. And he'd been left so weak, he'd thought he was going to die. Then a servant had wakened him, had told him Raine was dying. That had forced him to leave his bedchamber, drink enough blood to regain strength, and then race to his brother's side to give him eternal life instead of lose him forever.

It had been months since he had come to a place like this—a brothel where the negotiations for blood were as common as those for pleasure. He had sworn he never would again. Not after the last time, when he had lost control.

The longer he tried to go without blood, the more violent the hunger became. It was irresponsible of him to walk amongst the human world without slaking his thirst for blood in the . . . kindest way he could. He should accept the offer here, where he could ensure the safety of the woman who let him take her blood. But he turned away and strode for the door.

Julian, come out from wherever you are. We are done here.

And he cursed the vampire council for sending Julian Tremaine with him. Tremaine was supposed to be his overseer, but Heath spent most of his time looking after the lad.

The madam chuckled behind him. His preternatural hearing easily picked out the sound, even as he heard Julian Tremaine's footsteps racing down a hallway. "You will be back," she murmured to herself.

No, he'd drive a stake into his own heart before he weakened.

The last time he had fed at this brothel, he had escorted a voluptuous lass to the bedchamber. The girl had flopped on the bed, swept back her hair to bare her throat, and waited for him with dead and resigned eyes.

He'd never lost an appetite so quickly in his life. This became an addiction for the women, like gin or opium. They needed to be bitten, to know the pain, to feel the earth-shattering pleasure of climaxing while being fed upon. The prostitute had told him, with whimpers, that her last client had been brutal and rough. She had clutched his arm, despair in her eyes. She was terrified, but she *needed* him to take her blood.

He had done it, despite his revulsion—with this world, mainly with himself. The girl had cried while he did it, and her emotions flowed to him, making her blood taste sharp as vinegar, foul as rotting fruit. He had paid her extra, a few gold sovereigns he had tucked in her closed fist, and placed against her heart. Since then he had fed from animal blood. It left him weak, unsatisfied. But it meant he did not have to touch a woman who truly did not want to be touched.

Heath shook off the maudlin thoughts and strode to the

bottom of the stair. He was here only in his search for Raine and for the woman he had seen in the pool. He grasped the banister and barked up the stair. "Julian, get your arse down here. I'm gone."

A servant hastily opened the door to him. Heath jumped down the front steps and strode away from the house. Three brothels along this street catered to the "nocturnal brotherhood"—the male vampires of London who chose to slake their thirst with the willing and leave their meals alive.

"Heath, wait—" Julian came running out of the brothel, retying his cravat, though the placket of his trousers still flapped where one button was undone.

Heath rubbed his temple. "Your trousers."

"Oh, right. I was in the middle of something. Could you have given me a few more minutes?"

"You were in the middle of *someone*. And no, I could not give you more time."

Julian licked his lips, flicking away a trace of blood. "She tasted good, but I hadn't got to the best part, where I got to be deep in her while I was drinking and she was coming around me."

"Another time."

Julian scowled. He was a youth. Only two-and-twenty. A pup within the nocturnal brotherhood, he had not even spent a full year as a vampire. "You promised me I could. And in return I agreed to look the other way about your activities tonight. This is not one of our five crime scenes."

This had to be the vampire council's sadistic idea of a joke. Julian had been assigned to ensure he completed his mission: find a succubus who had killed five English peers. But Julian was young, rebellious, and obsessed with sex. Julian was so like Raine, Heath had been forced to spend every moment of those nights reliving the mistakes he'd made with his brother.

They were supposed to be examining the places where the

men had died, questioning other men who knew the victims for a description of mistresses and lovers. Track the succubus down, in other words. But he had to find Raine.

The vampire council would have him destroyed if he did not unearth the demon before the next full moon. But the council had also issued a death warrant on his rogue brother. And his brother's existence came first.

Julian's lower lip protruded in a pout. He did up his trousers and drew out a cheroot from a pocket. "What exactly are you looking for?"

"A woman."

"They had those back there."

"Not the one I wanted."

"How can you be so certain?" Julian protested. Holding a match to the cheroot stuck between his lips, Julian looked longingly back toward the brothel. "We should have stayed there longer, to ensure we explored all the women and made sure none of them were the succubus we're supposed to find."

"I was able to determine that without wasting time, Julian. And for the love of Hades, don't make that pouting expression again."

He couldn't let Julian know the truth. Tonight he wasn't searching for the succubus. He was looking for the woman he had seen in the pool. And he had to ensure the council did not find out what he was doing. He couldn't reveal any clue that might lead them to Raine first.

Most vampires feared the vampire slayers who worked for the Royal Society for the investigation of Mysterious Phenomena. But Heath feared the vampire council more. The slayers knew it existed but since it destroyed vampires they left it alone. But it had grown more dangerous.

"What is a succubus exactly?" Julian puffed his cheroot. "The old vampires on the council never told me."

"A woman who can drain your soul while she's fucking you."

The lad stared, still holding the lit match. "Blast!" He waved out the flame as it burned his finger.

Heath shook his head at the naive shock on Julian's youthful, good-looking face. "You should be careful whom you drop your trousers for."

"What would a succubus want with us, Blackmoor? We've got no souls to drain."

It was a good point. He had no idea what happened when a succubus made love to a vampire. The council would know. They filled themselves on rules and legend and lore. "Let's make our way to another brothel. This one is a scene of one of the crimes—" He stopped. A soft sound floated to his preternatural hearing.

A second gasp of fear rippled from the shadows of an alley. A street flare threw light upon a sign. Derwent Lane was the name bestowed upon the narrow space that could barely let two people pass by each other. The light annoyed Heath; it prevented him from seeing as well as he could into the dark length of the alley.

The sound had come from a woman. A subdued, frightened cry of pain.

He doubted it would be the woman he was looking for; he'd scoured London for a week searching for her. He would hardly stumble upon her so fortuitously. But becoming the undead did not mean a man left his honor behind.

Heath stepped into the opening of the alley.

"Come 'ere, love." The harsh, raspy male voice broke in on Vivienne Dare's tumbling thoughts as she hurried down stinking Derwent Lane, rushing further into the depths of Whitechapel.

She looked up just as a brute of a man stepped out of a doorway and blocked her path. He was huge, large enough to fill the narrow lane. A leather apron splattered with dark stains covered him. He crossed his arms over a massive barrel chest and leered as his piglike eyes swept over her. "Ye smell pretty, lass. How much for a quick swive against the alley wall here?"

The stench of blood and butchered meat hung around him. It turned her stomach. But what frightened her most was his size. Vivienne knew what a man that big could do.

She felt for the pistol in her pocket and wrapped her hand around the smooth handle. She wore a long cloak with the hood pulled low. A tangled gray wig hid her blond hair. She had drawn wrinkles on her face with kohl. She should look like a wizened crone.

But the butcher seemed to know otherwise, despite the shadows, her makeup, and her stooped walk.

This kept happening to her, no matter how she disguised herself. Five times already, on her journeys to the apothecary, five different, large, dangerous strangers had pursued her. Each time she'd had to fight for her life. But she'd never faced a man *this* big.

He licked his lips, moving toward her. His apelike arms swung at his sides. "Come on, dearie." Smirking, he ran his hands over the front of his apron, mimicking the shape of an erection. "I've got a long pole and it's all for you. Now be a good girl. I don't want to have to hurt ye."

But he did. Want to. She knew it. She could see it in his lecherous, mocking grin. In the wild excitement lighting up his small, ugly eyes.

Just stay calm, girl, and think.

She had escaped this world. Had pulled her way out of the slums and into Mayfair's glittering ballrooms with her wits, not simply her tits. She had become London's most exclusive—and expensive—courtesan. Then she had walked away from that world. For her daughter's sake. For *Sarah's* sake.

She had vowed she would never let a brute touch her—or hurt her—again.

And she did not have time to waste. She pulled out the pistol, extended her arm, and took a bead on the stained apron. "Step aside and let me pass."

His eyes took on a wild, hungry, fanatical gleam. "Put that toy away and let me 'ave at ye."

Toy. Was he mad? Dear God, she had thought this would make him retreat. She did not want to shoot him. But she couldn't lose time, precious time Sarah might not have—

The ape of a man lunged for her in her moment of distraction. Her finger was nowhere near the trigger, so the pistol was pulled from her hand with more ease than taking off a glove. All because she couldn't kill him. Now he would rape and kill her. And Sarah would never get the medicine and she wouldn't live through the night—

No.

Vivienne slammed her fists against his wall of a chest. They bounced off, but it gave her momentum to hit him again. Her gun flew from his grasp and clattered across the cobbles. She kicked at him, driving her sturdy boots into his shin.

"Shit! Whore!" he shouted. And his fist came at her like a brick and snapped her head back so sharply, she fell against the wall. Tears sprang to her eyes. She'd never known pain like this.

And his fist was coming again—

She slithered down the wall and his hand smashed into solid brick. He howled in sheer fury. He was going to kill her and he might not pause long enough to swive her.

Vivienne darted to the side, but he caught her stupid cape and hauled her back. Her wig plopped to the ground, and he leered at her.

"Ye're a pretty one. My, my, this is going to be fun—" Silver flashed. He'd whipped a knife out of a pocket on his apron. The tip of it pressed against her cheek. And bit in.

She lifted her knee and drove it into him. Drove it into his male parts and the knife cut into her as he jerked downward with pain. His other hand dropped to cradle his wounded balls. And his eyes went wild with fury.

The blade slid down her face, opening a slash that leaked hot, wet blood. Stinging pain rushed from her cheek. Her legs wobbled, but she hit at his arm to push the knife away.

Suddenly her attacker took flight.

He soared through the air, down Derwent Lane, and landed with a thud in the unfathomable dark. His knife had gone with him.

And she was staring at the bricks across from her, frozen in place, even as she knew another man was now standing beside her. A man who had just picked up her attacker, who must have weighed fifteen stone, and threw him down the alley. And the man who had rescued her was not even breathing heavily.

Her knees threatened to dissolve like sugar in water.

"So I save your life, and you won't even look at me? Not even to reward me with a pretty smile?" His voice was soft, deep, cultured, gentle—the sort of voice a rich peer used when he wanted to coax a woman into his bed. Far different than the harsh, clipped, cold tones they used when they wanted to shove her out.

It was a tone of voice Vivienne knew too well. And right now, it made her shake. She kept her face away from him in the shadows, her gloved hand at the gash in her cheek. She had to play sweet and demure and rescued, but she had to get away. "Th—thank you. Thank you for saving me. I apologize there will be no smile. And no payment. But I must go—"

"I don't expect payment, little one." His hand braced against the wall near her head. "Rescue is a service I perform free of charge. Or obligation."

Suddenly she felt a spurt of dizziness, and her vision blurred. It vanished almost instantly, leaving her blinking, trying to get control of her thoughts.

The man stared at her as though she had two heads. He reached for her chin but she jerked her head away. "Who are you?" he growled. "*What* are you?"

He was blocking her way out. She looked down the alley to the butcher, who was still sprawled on the ground. Not moving.

"Struck his head rather hard," her savior remarked. Out of the corner of her eye, she saw a tall, glossy beaver hat. Crisp cravat cinching a stark white collar. Many-tiered great coat. He exuded wealth and the casual arrogance that went along with it. "If he's fortunate, he'll wake up in a few hours with a bad headache. If he's not fortunate, he won't wake up at all."

She swallowed hard.

"Now, tell me what you are—"

She twisted away and ran down the narrow lane toward the inert body, guessing he wouldn't expect this. Not for her to run toward the man who had tried to attack her. She tried to jump over the fallen body, but couldn't. Her boot landed on his arm and she lost her balance and fell forward.

A strong hand wrapped around her wrist and she was pulled hard against his male body. Sandalwood. Leather. Horse. Man. She smelled all those things in the dizzying moment she was clamped against her rescuer's chest, her face buried against him. "How?" she gasped.

"I'm a vampire, little one. I can move with great speed when I want to. And when it is necessary, I can fly. But you must know that. You've blocked your thoughts to me."

"I *what*? Y—you're mad," she cried, her voice muffled. Dazed, shocked, she reared back and looked up at the elegant beaver hat, the snow-white collar points.

He was smiling at her, smiling as though she was a tasty morsel he intended to devour. Suddenly the smile vanished. His gloved hands closed roughly around her arms. "What did you do to my brother?" he barked at her. "And where the hell is he now?"

"W—who?" she gasped.

Silver eyes. His eyes were a strange, reflective silver, and they dilated as he took in the sight of her face. She could taste the blood from the cut, tracking slowly along her lips. His lips were beautiful, she noticed madly. Perfectly shaped. His lower lip was very full, and his face was exotic and sensuous and filled with fury and suspicion.

"My brother," he growled. "I know you were his lover. And I know you aren't mortal."

"I don't know what you're talking about!" She shoved at him.

He blinked down at her. His hat hadn't even wobbled.

He moved her, pressed her back to the brick wall, and leaned in as though preparing to push his mouth onto hers in a kiss. "No!" she jerked her head to the side, turning her stinging, bleeding, cheek to him. She was not going to let him have her mouth.

His tongue came out as his face neared hers. Gently, the tip of it touched the top of her wound. A strange flow of heat began there, flooded her skin, and seemed to flood her brain. He traced the entire length of her cut, setting her skin ablaze in his path. She didn't understand why. She didn't *want* his touch.

He stopped where the wound did. On her throat. And he suckled there. Vivienne had to let her head drop back against the wall. Sensation roared up. She felt something she hadn't felt for years and years. Need. Desire. Hunger.

No. Sarah needed her. And the thought of Sarah, at home and sick, speared Vivienne like a blade. She fought him and he let her go. And smiled softly as he settled his hands against the wall on either side of her shoulders, trapping her. "There. All better. You are far too beautiful to be marked up like that."

She drove her knee up but something stopped her, pushed it down. It had to have been his hand, but she hadn't seen it move—his hands were still braced beside her head.

Icy fear rippled down her spine. The cut no longer hurt. She put her fingers to her cheek, took them away. There was no blood. But the wound hadn't scabbed over. Her skin felt perfectly smooth. There was no sign there had even been a cut.

"As perfect as I imagine you were to start with," he said softly.

"How did you *do* that?"

"Vampire. I can heal. I can move so swiftly you will not see it. Some of the benefits, of which there are, sadly, very few. Now tell me about my brother. You saw what I did to him." His chin jerked toward the unconscious butcher. "You had better start talking to me."

His mouth became a harsh line. The silver eyes narrowed, and she knew she was looking at a man who could become very cruel when he wanted to.

She'd seen enough of that to know. She knew men. Other courtesans always had their eye on the prize: they looked at the jewels. Vivienne had always looked at the gentleman's eyes as she received his gift. What was there? Joy? Pride? Guilt? The look a man got when he was preparing to run? All gifts were bribes. Either to ensure a woman was thoroughly snared, or to buy a man's way out of trouble. She had survived, flourished, rescued herself because she wasn't a courtesan who stared at her own face in the mirror. She looked at the man.

That was how she knew when a man was angry. Or when he was stripping off his masks, letting his cruelty show. Preparing to be violent.

"Let me go. *Please*," she begged, even when she knew how futile it was to beg a man. "I don't know anything about your brother. I have to get to an apothecary's. My daughter is sick, she is dying. Please, won't you just let me go?"

He shook his head, the selfish bastard. "I can't, my love. Not until I find out the truth." His gloved hand closed roughly around her arm.

"She's dying, you bastard!" she shouted at his handsome face. "Dear God, let me go."

"I've discovered God is not very dear, love. And I can't let you go."

Sheer panic gripped her. Then boot soles clicked sharply on the cobbles and she saw another man enter the mouth of the alley, framed by the meager light. "She's telling the truth about her daughter, Heath. I can tell."

"Can you, Julian?" Her captor's voice was tight and filled with suspicion.

"I saw it in her thoughts." The blond man was completely serious even though she knew he must be speaking utter rubbish. No one could read thoughts.

"She is really afraid for her daughter's life, Heath," the man called Julian went on. "And she is telling the truth: she is on her way to an apothecary's."

"Indeed." Heath, the man who had her captured, spoke so coldly it made her shiver. "All right, I will escort you to get your medicine, then take you home. After that, we can have a little discussion." His eyes looked cold as ice shards.

Suddenly his words penetrated. "Go with me! But that's impossible."

"No, love. It's your only choice."

"Heath—"

"We will help the fair lady with her task, Julian. I believe she needs our protection."

"And the investigation?"

"Can wait for a little while. I think a sick daughter is more important."

"You are supposed to be working for the council, not helping some damsel in distress by healing her child."

Vivienne gaped at Julian. She could see now he was a tall, handsome man in his early twenties. With pale blond hair, and large eyes, and the beauty of an angel. But his eyes were reflective, too. She swung around to the other man. Heath. "You could heal my daughter, like you healed the cut on my cheek?"

"I don't know. There are some things even a well-meaning vampire can't cure. Let's get the medicine first, my dear, and then get you home to your child." He turned to the other man, Julian. "If I can heal a young mortal girl, I have to do it. All you have to do is keep it quiet from the council."

Vampire. He must surely be *mad* to think he was Nosferatu. They were the stuff of faery stories, tales meant to frighten people. Vampires did not really exist.

But he had done three completely impossible things with her. He had effortlessly heaved an enormous man down an alley without even disturbing his hat. He had made her wound disappear with his tongue. He had moved so quickly she had not even seen him.

How had he done it?

There were illusionists in London. Could he be one of those? No. He had actually done those things. They weren't tricks.

And after she got her medicine, he expected her to take him home. To let him inside, so he could ask about his brother.

Heavens, what if his brother was one of the men she had been forced to seduce? One of the five peers who had mysteriously died afterward?

Julian hesitated. "All right. I had a young sister who died of scarlet fever. I would have given anything to save her. Try to help this girl; I won't tell the council."

It sounded as if the younger man should be in command, but Heath obviously was. And Heath suddenly grasped her by the elbow.

"Come, my dear. Lead the way. Julian and I will ensure you get there safely."

And Vivienne knew, once again, she had no choice but to let a man take charge and obey his command. But she'd learned a thing or two. She would let him *believe* he was in control, until she had her chance to break free.

No sign hung from the front of the shop. No name was painted upon the dirty window. But through the layers of grime, a few bottles could be seen. One lamp burned low, which meant Mrs. Holt was there.

Waiting for her, no doubt. Vivienne had never seen anyone else come in.

She stopped and turned to her rescuer. Heath had frightened away two other ruffians who had approached her. She might not have reached here at all without him. "You will have to wait outside. I do not know if Mrs. Holt will serve me if you come in with me. And I have to get this medicine."

"Why wouldn't she serve you? I'm an earl. I'm not accustomed to shopkeepers wanting me to stay outside."

An *earl*. "Oh dear God, please."

"And I believe you intend to slip out the back."

"Oh," she sputtered. She shoved him aside and stalked toward the door. His boots cracked sharply against the floor behind her. A tiny bell tinkled. And the door in the back opened, and Mrs. Holt shuffled out. "You are late, my dear. What has kept you?" The woman peered from behind tangled curls of gray-brown hair. "Ah, I see what has. Well, my lord, you may wait in the corner."

Mrs. Holt knew this man was a peer. She shivered, but charged forward. "I need Sarah's medicine."

"Of course." Cackling, Mrs. Holt took the vial out from a small glass-fronted case behind the counter. It was the same size as the others. Only three days' worth of doses.

"Could you not give me more? Please, *please*. I'll pay anything."

Gnarled hands pulled a shawl tighter. "Three. Or none at all."

"What is the price for the next one?" Like a canny whore, Mrs. Holt always demanded to be paid in advance of the drug. Equally intelligent, Vivienne had refused at first. Then Sarah had gotten so sick with a fever that climbed and climbed. Sarah had been about to die. And Vivienne had raced back here and promised to pay *any* price for the drug.

Mrs. Holt had not asked for money or jewels. Instead, she had demanded Vivienne seduce the young, handsome Earl of Matlock.

The woman had to be mad. But that night, distraught with fear for Sarah, Vivienne had put on a revealing gown, had found the young man in Covent Garden, and she had dazzled him until he couldn't remember his own name. She had vowed she would never be a courtesan again, but she had seduced a man she didn't even know, and their first encounter had been up against the theater wall.

Mrs. Holt had given her enough of a dose for one day. And outlined the "arrangement" they would have. If Vivienne slept with the man for a month, Mrs. Holt had promised, she would be given enough medicine for three days at a time. At the end of each vial, if not more often, she had to take her lover to carnal ecstasy—the price for the next allotment.

It seemed madness. What possible payment could this be?

What could Mrs. Holt gain from her sexual adventures with a string of young gentleman?

But she had done it. Now those men—the five men who had been her lovers—were all dead. And an earl wanted to know what had happened to his brother.

She wished she knew what the medicine contained. But she had taken it to a dozen apothecaries in London, and none could determine what was within it.

Mrs. Holt inclined her head. "The price is the same as always."

"Who—who will it be?"

Mrs. Holt glanced at the man waiting in the corner. And crooked her finger so Vivienne had to move closer. "His name is Lord Blackmoor," she rasped. "This particular man will be very hard to seduce."

Vivienne lifted a brow. She had yet to find the man who could resist her. She knew every erotic trick there was. Once upon a time, she had wished she could engage in them for love. But all that mattered now was Sarah. She slipped the vial into a secret pocket inside her bodice. "I am very, very good at seduction. Where will I find this gentleman?"

"Oh, this one you won't find, dearie."

Vivienne gritted her teeth. "Then how do I seduce him? Mrs. Holt, do not play with me, not with Sarah's life at stake. If she dies, I—" Her heart screamed with pain. She was tired of this witch's games. She *hated* this woman who controlled her like a puppet by dangling Sarah's life in front of her eyes.

"He will find you. I believe, in fact, he already has."

2

He had been transformed into the undead by drinking a quart of blood from a stranger's neck, had been given a demonic curse, and condemned his brother to endless darkness, yet *this* almost knocked Heath off his feet.

The voluptuous blond woman was supposed to seduce him, as payment to this old crone for the vial of medicine. And the blonde was the seductive beauty he had seen in the pool with Raine. The one who had slithered down his own body in the reflection and taken him into her hot mouth.

With his heightened vampiric senses, he'd heard the entire conversation from the corner. Heard the blonde's cool, crisp voice become angry, desperate, frantic, frightened. And the old woman answer her, brimming with power, confidence, and the damn perverse amusement he'd discovered permeated the demon world.

The old woman wasn't mortal. She could shield her thoughts from him.

Just as the blond beauty he'd rescued could. He'd tried to open the gates to her mind and read her thoughts, but he had seen nothing but a void. Which meant her thoughts were blocked to him, and apparently not to Julian.

None of this made sense. But as the blonde shoved past him and ran out the door, Heath had time for one swift glance back at the apothecary's mistress. She smiled at him, a smile that flashed surprisingly white teeth. He moved to her in the blink of eye, but when he reached her untidy counter, she was gone.

What did this woman know about him? Obviously a few things. Why else would she warn he would prove hard to seduce? After all, he carried a curse—one that prevented him from ever gracing any woman's bed twice.

He'd heard the blonde ask what the price would be this time. Did it mean she had seduced other men for the medicine? Was it too mad to speculate she could be the one who seduced and killed the five peers? That his two quests were connected?

"Let me go!"

He jerked around as the blonde kicked wildly at Julian's shins. He had to intervene. Julian, the pup, didn't yet know his own strength, and he'd grasped the woman's arm so hard, she had dropped to her knees. The younger vampire was white faced and looked ready to rip out his own heart in remorse.

Heath stalked out the door, letting it slam in his wake. He could return to the apothecary later. "Let her go, Julian. And love"—he turned to the blond woman—"don't try to run. I warn you it will be a futile gesture. I'll catch you again. Easily. You told me you're desperate to return to your daughter, so I'll take you there. In my carriage."

Her chin went up, but her eyes flicked around, seeking escape. Her mind was still eerily closed to him. And he didn't know why.

"I have a carriage. I do not need your help."

He bowed before the trembling blonde. The woman must know she had no way out, but was only looking more fierce as a result.

"This has nothing to do with help, my dear. You may not have noticed, but you are now my prisoner. Until I get the truth out of you, I'm not letting you go."

Her eyes widened with fury, snapping at him with blue fierceness. The same eyes he had seen in the reflection. "And who in hell do you think you are?" she demanded, all explosive fire.

He didn't play with fire anymore. He moved in the night, eternally cold, eternally dark, eternally deadened. "Ah, little one, you have no idea how apropos your question is. But haven't you guessed? I'm Blackmoor. The man you are supposed to bed. Now, tell me who *you* are."

The girl in the giant bed looked fragile. Like one of the porcelain dolls his daughter had treasured.

Heath knew pain again, a swift, sharp slice of it. He knew what it was like to lose a child. *Meredith.* His daughter. Someone he had vowed to keep safe forever, to protect from everything. When he'd first held his little girl in his arms, he had vowed she would never even have anything to pout about.

And now she was gone.

All he had were memories, but they were laden with pain and guilt, like thorny briars twisted around his heart. Memories, for a vampire destined to live for eternity, were tenuous things that slowly drifted away.

The blonde pushed past him, crossing the bedroom with soft, swift steps. She sat on the edge of the bed and tenderly stroked her daughter's pale face. Real lines dragged at her lush mouth, not ones she had painted on. "Sarah? I have your medicine, dear. Let's help you to sit up so you can drink it."

Heath folded his arms across his chest. Retreated into shadow. He'd sent Julian back to the apothecary after he'd learned the blonde's address. So he was alone here with the woman, her daughter, and her sleeping servants.

He watched her. Ariadne used to touch their daughter this way, with a mother's unique combination of love and firmness. It hurt like blazes to watch, but he couldn't look away.

"No," came the plaintive cry from beneath a heavy counterpane and snow-white sheets. "It's horrid. Don't want anymore. Hate it. Hate it."

Her mother tried for a soothing smile. But her lips wobbled. Tendrils of blond hair cascaded down her neck. She was a beautiful woman. At this moment, holding her daughter's hand, she shimmered like an angel.

"Well, we do not have a choice, Sarah." He heard the sharp rise in her heartbeat. She was terrified for her child. "You must take it. To get well."

To stay alive.

He could not hear the thought, but he could guess it. She hadn't given him her real name when she had finally given it to him in his carriage. *My name is—is Mrs. Tate,* she had said. She had been too distracted, too filled with fear for her daughter to lie convincingly.

On their way up here, he'd let her go ahead while he examined invitations left on a table beside the door. She was Vivienne Dare.

He remembered there had been a beautiful courtesan known as Miss Dare. Bosomy. Elegant. Lovely. The type of enticing, voluptuous temptress who made a gentleman so desperate to get her, he would sell his soul to have her in his bed. Or, at the very least, bankrupt his estate.

One night with her and a man was said to be addicted to her forever. No other woman could ever measure up. Heath had been married then, faithful to his wife, and he had been traveling the world. So he hadn't paid much attention. But he could understand why Miss Dare was said to be so addictive. She had a demon's lure.

Now she had a dying daughter. And from the look of the

young girl's elegantly appointed bedchamber, Vivienne Dare possessed fantastic wealth.

So what had she wanted with Raine? She wouldn't have gotten a soul from him. Or even expensive gifts.

"Come on, angel." Miss Dare helped her daughter sit up. She clucked and coaxed like a mother hen.

He liked this view of Miss Dare. Her skirts were tucked beneath her generous bottom. In profile, her nose was an adorable little curve, her cheeks softly sculpted. Her mouth was truly enticing. It never stayed still.

Miss Dare poured fluid from the vial to a silver spoon and replaced the stopper. Her daughter was an ethereal beauty. Long golden hair spilled around the pretty, faery-like face. She had big blue-green eyes, a button of a nose, and funny little pointed ears that made her look like a wee elf. But she must be at least sixteen, if not older. She was so thin, he'd thought her younger at first.

Miss Dare wrapped her arm around the girl's shoulders. Her face took on the lines of a mother's sorrow, even as she forced another soft smile to her lips. "It won't be so bad. A quick swallow. Then we'll give you a cup of chocolate, and you'll have something sweet to drink."

"Don't . . . want . . . chocolate. Want . . . want sleep. Darkness. Please." The girl clutched her mother's arms. Stared up with blank, stricken eyes.

He heard Miss Dare's heart skip a beat. Whatever her daughter meant, she had not said these words before. And Miss Dare was scared.

"Open up and one quick swallow and it's all done." Miss Dare slipped in the spoonful of medicine.

The girl struggled. Sputtered. But, with maternal firmness, Miss Dare held her daughter's jaw closed, so the child had no choice but to swallow. Then she put her palm to her daughter's pale forehead.

"I'm not so cold anymore, mummy," the girl whispered.

"Oh, that is so good, my love," Miss Dare whispered on a sob. She hugged her daughter.

Heath's heart gave a twist in his chest.

Outside the bedroom, in the hallway, footsteps whispered. Heath jerked his attention to the door as Julian appeared on the threshold.

"Did you get the crone from the apothecary?" he asked softly.

Julian shook his head. "She was gone when I got back there. The shop was locked up, Heath. I broke in—"

"Broke in. Hell, the woman will know that when she returns."

Julian's lower lip went out. "I was careful. I picked the lock, and I didn't touch anything. She won't know. Place is grungy and disgusting. There were jars of stuff she must use to make her medicine."

"Anything unusual? Eye of newt? Any animals in any state of evisceration?"

"There weren't any animals. Just powders and liquids." Julian nodded toward the bed. "What's wrong with the girl?"

"I don't know. Can you sense she's dying?"

"I can hear her heart." He gave a young man's jaded shrug. "It's weak and slow. Can you heal her?"

"I don't know. But I am going to try." A young girl's life? It wouldn't begin to balance the evil he'd indulged in as a vampire, but it would be a start. "I'm going to need some time alone with the lady and her daughter."

Julian frowned. Then he gave an abrupt nod. He turned on his heel and left, his greatcoat flapping around him like a bat's wings.

Vivienne sat with her back to Heath. She'd discarded her gloves—funny, he hadn't noticed her do that—had thrown them on the floor.

She held her back straight and tense even as her hand flowed over her daughter's long curls, stroking, reassuring, loving. Her gaze never left her daughter, she never turned, but he knew she was aware of him.

He waited while she felt the girl's forehead again. She pulled up the bedclothes, smoothed and fussed, and tucked her daughter in securely.

It was hard to imagine this woman had once been known for her ability to drive a man mad with her clever use of a riding crop, her tongue, or even just her smile.

Harder to imagine she was a demoness.

She crept backward, carrying her candle, and only when she had retreated past the bed did she turn to him. Raw hope blazed in her large blue eyes. "Can you do anything, do you think?"

"Come. We need to go somewhere private. Quiet. Where we can speak of what is wrong, what could be done . . . and what you've already done."

Sarah was safe again. Safe for a few days. And now Vivienne had to pay the price for this temporary miracle. That price was striding behind her into her drawing room, exuding all the masculine smells she knew so well. Sandalwood soap that had been lathered over his bare skin, witch hazel slapped to his cheeks after a shave, the polish rubbed into his leather boots, the rich earthy scent of his sweat.

She remembered his mad claim that he was a vampire. But he smelled like a live, healthy, carnal man.

Vivienne moved shakily to the brandy decanter. She wanted to ask him about Sarah, but she had to seduce him first—though all she yearned to do was fall onto the rug in front of her, shut her eyes, and sleep.

"Would you care for a drink?" she asked, keeping her tone throaty and sultry.

A chair creaked slightly as Heath settled into it. He stretched his endless legs out straight before him. His friend Julian had left the house. "Don't trouble yourself, love. Warmed brandy and fluttering lashes won't work. I've resisted some of the best."

There was *no one* better than she was. "Perhaps it is a thank-you for the rescue on Derwent Lane. Perhaps I want nothing more than to serve you, please you in this simple way."

"You've a pretty voice and you are a delectable woman, Miss Dare. But I don't believe you want to thank me for that."

Miss Dare. He'd used her real name. How had he known?

"I know you were with my brother. And now he's missing."

Before, when he'd demanded to know about his brother, he had grasped her arms hard and she'd expected violence. Even that had not been as terrifying as the way he kept his voice restrained now—like thunder before a storm that could fell a mountainside.

"I don't know *anything* about your brother," she repeated on a frustrated rush of breath.

"Indeed. Lord Matlock. Did you sleep with him?"

She jerked and brandy splashed to the inlaid table. How had he known about Matlock? "Yes," she answered, feigning composure. "Though that is none of your business."

He fired four more names at her suddenly, watching her with a steady, penetrating, unblinking gaze. *Lord Wentworth. Cavendish. Beltane. Avers.*

She had retreated behind the table, her gloved hands clutching the decanter, and his gaze settled on her grip. He must know she was holding it like a weapon.

"Were they your protectors?"

"No," she whispered. Then she saw a way out. "Yes. And they were all peers—so it is obvious I never bedded your brother."

"The pattern of the deaths has intrigued me. You sleep with

a man for a month. A fortnight later, on a full moon, he dies of an attack of the heart. Matlock died in a boxing ring. Wentworth in a gaming hell. The third, Cavendish, in a brothel." He counted on his long, elegant fingers. "Fourth during a horse race. Fifth in his wife's bed." Even in the dark, his eyes gleamed. Two silver disks, glittering like a predator's eyes.

The last one made her blush. She had normally taken unmarried protectors. But with the last man, she'd had no choice. No matter how much she had protested, Mrs. Holt had been unmoved. "I have done nothing," she said. "And I've hurt no one." But was that entirely true?

"So you expect me to believe it's a coincidence that five of your lovers are dead?"

"They all died naturally. Their hearts gave out. Men do die, my lord. They drink excessively, they live hard, and they die." She set the decanter down with a harsh clank. "Who is your brother, my lord? How could you think I've had anything to do with him? I do not even know who he *is*."

"His name was Raine. Raine Winthrope." Pain vibrated in his voice. "Brother to the Earl of Blackmoor." He took a deep breath. "He looks like me, only he is more handsome." He grinned at that, lines cascading around his sensual mouth. But his eyes threw light back at her, cold and untouched by his brief show of amusement.

Fear slithered through her veins. What would happen if she could *not* pay Mrs. Holt's price? "Why do you think I had anything to do with your brother? Or his disappearance?"

"I saw you."

Her hand tightened on the glass decanter. "You could not have done. It is impossible. I have never been with him. I do not know any man named Raine. And I have never before seen any man who looked like you." Which was true. All her lovers had been delectably handsome, but none had eyes that shone like moonlight in the shadows or a smile that made her legs jelly, or displayed a lithe, animal grace even without moving at all. She'd never seen a man with dark auburn hair and a strong chiseled jaw. With such sharp cheekbones and oddly slanted auburn eyebrows.

"Then how could I have seen you standing at his side?"

"Quite possibly because you are mad?" she threw at him. Inwardly she cursed. Hardly a way to begin a seduction. "I didn't mean that," she said softly. She moved to him, letting her hips sway, using the walk that was said to mesmerize men. And he stared at her every step of the way. "Not after what you have done for me. Of course it has not escaped my notice either that my former lovers were killed. But *I* didn't do it."

One tug of his hand ripped his cravat in half. His collar points fell away from his throat, exposing pale skin, skin that seemed to glitter in the light. She watched him swallow. "And you believe I'll accept that?"

"Why would I have done it? I would gain nothing by killing those men. They were . . . friends. I cared for them. I didn't get any money when they died. I had no reason to hurt them."

Light fell over her, cast by his reflective eyes. "So who do you think did it?"

She had the sense he was playing with her. "I don't know. Perhaps they could have been poisoned. Perhaps that was why all their hearts gave out. They were titled. Someone benefited from their deaths."

"True. Who is Sarah's father?"

She blinked. Why on earth would he ask that? "You can't think Sarah's *father* killed those men out of jealousy. I was a courtesan. Men didn't love me. They possessed me for a little while, until a shiny, new temptation came along."

"You said you *were* a courtesan. I thought, pretty one, you still are."

"I—I'm not. I accepted nothing from those men. I didn't ask them to buy me."

She could feel his gaze. She poured brandy, but for herself. "Why not?"

"I have everything I need." *Except Sarah's health. Except the certainty my daughter will live.*

"You seduced them to pay the old crone for her medicine. Why would she ask that of you?"

"I don't *know*. Don't you think I've asked that a thousand times? And she says nothing in answer!"

She stood only a couple of feet from his boots now. She moved around them, to the side of his chair, and she lowered herself to her knees.

Men liked submission. Just doing this, this one simple gesture, and she would normally have a man. A little bit of submission could put a woman in control.

He shook his head, a rueful smile quirking his lips. "There is no point trying to seduce me when you look like you're going to collapse with exhaustion, love. Go to bed. Go to sleep."

She had to do this. Had to. But he got to his feet so swiftly, she didn't see him move. "Come to bed with me?" she asked desperately.

"I don't sleep until dawn, my dear. You will want to be up in the day with your daughter. I'd love to fuck you until you're screaming for mercy, but we're not going to do anything tonight."

Fuck you until you scream for mercy. She bristled at the coarse words. Hated the way her body grew hot at the sound of them, the way they rumbled in his deep and arrogant voice.

"Go to bed, Miss Dare. Brave, daring, Miss Dare." Then, again moving like a ripple of wind through air, he scooped her into his big, hard arms.

She wasn't brave. Desperate, perhaps, which made a woman do crazy things. Her hands closed on his waistcoat lapels. She'd intended to struggle, but he moved as though she weighed nothing. And strangely, she didn't want to fight. She wanted to press closer to him.

She *must* coax him into her bed. She rubbed her cheek against his elegant waistcoat. And purred. "Please, please bed me."

Men loved this. A woman humbled by need. Need for *them*.

"Ah, I can only do it once, love. I'd much rather do it when you're awake enough to ride me hard and fierce and rip your nails into my skin when you come."

And with that echoing in her head, she saw her door fly open, pushed by his boot; saw her bed loom toward her.

He lay her down with infinite gentleness. "I need to undress."

"That I can do, Miss Dare," he murmured. Small buttons on her gown popped free, and he drew it down from her. She saw his jaw tense as he revealed her corset, her thin shift, the way her pink, round nipples strained against the fine muslin. "You are a temptation in every way, aren't you?" he asked, his smile rueful.

"They are yours to play with however you wish. I've had a child, after all. If you like, you can be rough with my nipples. And I will enjoy it."

His throat moved as he swallowed hard. "Another night. When we know enough about each other to actually like each other. How's that?"

Then he unlaced her corset with speed, drew it over her hips. He tucked her feet beneath her sheets, pulled her counterpane right up to her chin. Suddenly the sleepiness fell away from her. "Sarah—" She hadn't meant to speak aloud. Was Sarah safe around a madman?

"You are afraid for her. You don't trust me."

"I want you to stay in my bed." She pushed down the sheets he had so conscientiously tucked in, exposing her naked breasts. Most men could be distracted from anything by the sight of breasts bouncing, swaying, jiggling, or simply lying there, nipples waiting for a mouth.

"Ah, I see. That way you will know where I am. And your daughter will be safe." He pulled off his boots—boots sewn to fit like a glove to his muscular calves—in the blink of an eye. Normally it took a boot boy and a lot of struggling. Then his brow cocked up and he eyed her with an astuteness that cut like a blade. "All right. How naked do you want me to be?"

"Completely," she instructed boldly.

Without countering, he took off his tailcoat. Beautifully tailored, but he dropped it to the floor like he would a rag. With a flash of moonlight on silk, his waistcoat followed. Then his shirt. White linen fluttered through the air like a disoriented ghost.

Moonlight splashed on his body, glancing off his straight shoulders, pouring over the pronounced curves of his pectoral muscles. His nipples puckered at once. Soft hair, also auburn, sprinkled the muscles and shot down toward a rock-hard belly.

His trousers came down next, of course, and he had to bend to yank them off. So for one breathless moment she couldn't see—

Then she could. He wasn't aroused. No, his member was soft and lay to the right, but even in its sleeping state, it fell quite far along his thigh. Good heavens.

"It grew," he remarked casually. "When I became undead, interestingly, that was the one part of me that changed. A remarkable and often inconvenient four inches." Then he winked.

He must be crazy to think he was a vampire. But he was a beautiful, strong, very well-endowed madman. She did not think his length inconvenient. It was rather intriguing.

But he climbed into her bed, on the side opposite her, as

though they were an old married country couple and he expected to come to bed for sleep and warmth, not sex.

Nerves shot off inside Vivienne like a barrage of cannons. She had learned to take care of herself with any man, but with the attacker she'd encountered in the lane tonight, she had proved she wasn't as invincible as she'd tried to become.

She rolled over toward Heath. She was so tired, but she reached out to his naked body. Why now, after years of being with men, should she feel awkward?

She was bedding a stranger. One with a title, but a stranger nonetheless. She always took care to know as much as she could about her lovers before she even allowed them to grace her bedroom. In the stews, she had seen what a man could do. Even gentlemen. The ones who smiled, who dressed well, and called a woman "love," just before they would hit her in the face.

There was danger in this. Real danger. A woman could end up dead like this—and she was supposed to protect Sarah. And she'd grown up watching her mother having to have fleeting moments of sex with strange men for a few coins, to keep a roof over their heads.

Now she was doing it. Because she had to. To keep her own daughter safe.

She touched his waist, marveled at the solid feel of his muscles behind his soft skin for one breathless second; then he caught her wrist. He moved her hand back, where she wasn't touching him.

"Tonight, love, you should sleep," he insisted. "We touch when we're ready."

Ready? For what? She was quaking inside. Hot, bubbling, confused, yearning. And afraid. "Can you really cure my daughter?"

"I don't know, and it's too close to dawn. Let the medicine work tonight, and tomorrow night I will try."

Tomorrow night. To pay her price she must seduce him night after night. But she'd never encountered an unwilling man before. He pillowed his arm beneath his head and smiled at her. And apparently intended not to lay a hand on her. But he made her feel anticipation and need, things she hadn't felt for years and years.

Without even touching her, somehow, he was seducing her.

Vivienne expected to lie awake all night. Instead she must have gone to sleep the moment her head landed on the pillow for she found herself in Hyde Park on a sunny spring afternoon, in the hour before the ton went there. When courtesans came to flirt with gentlemen who would later be seen in the park with their wives.

She couldn't be there in reality, so she knew, as dreamers did, that none of this was real. Arousal wound up in her, tighter and tighter, like silk stretched to a point where one more tug would snap it.

Even in her dream, she knew she had come here to seduce the Earl of Blackmoor. Something whispered that in her mind. And warned she would have to be scandalously daring to do it. . . .

Dawn dragged him down into sleep. Heath had drawn the drapes in Miss Dare's room to protect his skin from the sun. Then he had realized what she would do first thing in the morning: fling them open. So he'd left her bed and found a dark corner of the attic in which to give in to the day sleep.

One moment he had been staring into the dark, seeing every detail of the roof timbers, every flicker of dust in the air. Then he had been staring at the ripple of green leaves as sunlight dappled them.

He heard the clop of hooves, the nickering of horses, the shouts of gentlemen, and the tinkling laughter of young ladies.

He looked around in disbelief.

Hyde Park.

How in blazes had he got here?

He hadn't. He had to be dreaming.

It wasn't the fashionable hour. The pretty women were courtesans. The gentlemen were here to peruse the lovelies and select new lovers. He wasn't riding. He was walking, bathed in sunlight, swinging his walking stick, aware of the swell of so many tempting breasts spilling over tight, low-cut bodices.

But the one thing that really aroused him? The feel of the sunlight on his skin, the way it made sweat trickle down his collar. The way it tempted him to strip naked and have his way with a bountiful woman on the soft grass.

A hand stroked down his back from behind, and as the hand slid down, his cock stood up. He turned, smelling a bouquet of sin: jasmine, roses, something sultry and exotic, and the rich, luscious smell of a woman's arousal.

Miss Dare stood there.

He inclined his head. "Ah, you're supposed to seduce me. Well, then, shall we find somewhere private?" In a dream, he couldn't turn into a demon. Anyway, he couldn't turn into one on the very first time. . . .

"Why waste precious time hiding behind a tree," she countered, saucy, sweet, tempting as the promise of eternal life when a man was dying in the dirt.

She rested her hand on his chest. And this time her body moved down first, while her hand slowly followed. It took him a minute to fully comprehend. She was sliding down his body, just as in the pool's reflection. And all the men around him watched in astonishment.

"I want you. And I intend to claim you, my lord. Very publicly." On her knees before him, she watched him. Her eyes widened, blue as sapphires, as the skies above Heaven, and she licked her lips. "I was warned you would be hard to seduce. So

I had to think: how was I to tempt you into madness, when I was certain you've done *everything*?"

This was madness. This couldn't be real. But she was gazing hungrily at his rigid cock.

"So I had to think very, very hard, my lord."

He was very, very hard. Hard enough to be as thick as two short planks. He should have stopped her. The entire crowd had stopped—talking, walking, breathing—and watched. Watched her undo his trousers and pull them down, and bare his backside to the cream of good society. And he didn't care. Didn't care that his tensed buttocks were on display to all and sundry. He couldn't because her fingers stroked his ballocks until he had to let his head fall back and growl to the heavens.

Then her mouth moved in for the proverbial kill.

Her wicked little tongue just rested against the crown of his cock. The barest bit of sensation, and it drove him mad.

"Now to pleasure you everywhere, my jaded lord," she whispered.

He forgot to breathe as those lush lips parted and she took him in. His cock plunged into heavenly, unbelievable heat.

Then she sucked him. Sucked him hard enough to drag his brains out through his cock. He had to bow his head in submission, for her tongue was heaven and hell all wrapped up into one blissful package.

He could be the most controlled man when it came to sex.

Not now.

First he panted. Then he groaned. And as she took him to the hilt and licked and suckled him, he howled, like a wolf confronted with a big, blood-red harvest moon.

He heard the fast breathing of every man around him. He felt their envy like blades pricking his skin. He reveled in it. And she looked up at him, brimming with innocence. Hell, she was smiling around his rock-hard, swollen shaft, smiling knowingly.

He was her slave.

At this moment, if she'd asked for the moon, he would have started to build an impossible iron bridge.

God. Then he was on the brink. Knew he couldn't hold back. Hastily, he took her hand and stopped her pleasuring him. He cupped her cheek and eased her back.

Her smile fell. "But you didn't—"

"Not yet, Flower. I think you should be the one to come first." He pulled her to her feet and dropped to his knees before her. His turn to supplicate before his goddess. He shoved up her skirts and two quivering cream-white thighs confronted him. Along with gold nether curls, already damp with her arousal.

He grasped her bottom and jerked her abruptly to him, burying his mouth in those springy curls, burying his face in her sweet-scented, eager little quim.

She tasted so very, very good.

He gave her one lick with his tongue before her hands gripped his head and she pushed his mouth hard against her. She screamed in ecstasy, jerked and jolted helplessly, and ground her juicy quim into his face.

His orgasm took him at the same instant. Took him and made him shout, jerk, and howl as his heart and soul seemed to burst, as his cock most definitely exploded, and the climax whipped him thoroughly and left him collapsed and gasping on—

The floor.

Vivienne cried out. She jerked up in her bed, covers tumbling away. She was dizzy with pleasure, her heart racing, her lungs fit to burst.

The dream had been so very real she could taste Heath's earthy flavor on her lips. And she had truly climaxed.

Then she knew, even before she looked. The bed was empty beside her. He had gone.

"Well, Flower, I definitely was correct about you. You are no ordinary courtesan. No wonder every peer in London was mad to have you."

The voice came from her doorway. He stood there completely naked, leaning on her doorframe. Arm propped, ankles crossed.

She stared at him. "What are you talking about?" His face was flushed and he was breathing hard.

"You, my dear, are a succubus. And if you will excuse me, I have to return to my sleep. Which you woke me from, Miss Dare, with your luscious dream. You are not to go anywhere, love, until I'm awake and can join you again."

3

Succubus.

He had not told her what he meant by it, what the word even meant. No, brimming with arrogance, Lord Blackmoor had turned on his heel and vanished after tossing that word into her bedroom like a flaming cannonball.

Vivienne jumped out of her bed and snatched up a robe. She dragged it onto her naked body as she charged out into the empty hallway. The door to the servants' stairs stood open. She raced up the back stairs in the pitch black. She missed steps, bumped her shins, and arrived at the top. She searched the attic rooms for him, finding one locked.

Damn. She'd run after him, but he had gotten here so far ahead of her, he'd had time to lock the door.

He was sleeping in a dark, ignored part of the attic. Faint snores came from the servants' bedrooms that filled the rest of the space. She tried again to turn the knob. It didn't budge. She rattled it. She didn't dare pound on the door or shout; she'd wake everyone else.

This stranger had barred her own door to her.

She braced a foot on it and pulled. But it stayed shut. This was *her* door; why should it obey his blasted command? She had to admit defeat and trudge downstairs. Rage made her eyes burn, and sheer stubbornness held the tears back.

But, in the morning, when she tried to leave her own house, a rough-looking, thick-necked brute stopped her.

She stood on the threshold of her doorway, unable to take another step without walking into a wall of a man. She was afraid, but she tried to drown that with rage. "Who in blazes are you? And what do you mean, I am not to leave the house?"

He touched his cap. Never had she seen such enormous hands. "Orders from his lordship, ma'am," he said. "I work for him. And his lordship insists you stay in the house until nightfall."

Fury crackled. "This is *my* house. *I* am the voice of command here."

The enormous man shook his head. "His lordship insisted this is for your safety, ma'am."

She threatened the man with everything she could think of, from her pistol to a dozen years in New South Wales after he was transported, but he merely turned his enormous back on her and crossed his arms.

"I will have you bodily removed," she roared at his back. People passed by on the sidewalk below, umbrellas over their heads to shield them from rain, all oblivious to the insanity of her situation.

"That would be a hard thing to do, ma'am. Lord Blackmoor hired me from my previous position as doorman in a gaming hell. I'm used to having to stand me ground."

Wonderful. There was no point sending any of her servants out to deal with him. He was obviously accustomed to cracking heads.

Fuming, she stalked to the back of the house. Another enormous man stood there, smoking a cheroot. Within minutes, she learned "his lordship" had positioned men all around her house.

She stomped up the stairs, but quieted her footsteps as she retreated to Sarah's room. Warm spring sunlight spilled in and a soft breeze batted lacy curtains. Her daughter was still sleeping. Vivienne settled onto the chair she kept always at the bedside.

How had this happened? A dozen years of pain and submission and saving and enduring, and she was back in a man's power *again*.

At dusk, rain, soot, and fog all conspired to turn the East End sky black as coal, making it safe for a vampire to emerge. Especially one in a heavy, hooded cloak. Heath stopped in front of the apothecary and held up his hand as Julian, also cloaked, headed for the door. "Wait," he warned.

He wanted to take a few moments and take in all the details of this place he'd ignored before.

Yesterday, his attention had all been on Vivienne. He had observed the apothecary only in his peripheral vision. Now, through the window, he saw dust, grime, and a jumble of ancient bottles.

He stepped back from the sidewalk. Fog billowed down the lane; the cobbles were slick and shining from the mist. Clopping hooves echoed from another street. The store was a narrow one, squashed between an empty building and a cobbler's shop.

Julian rattled the door. "Locked again."

"You expected otherwise?"

"It was open last night, when we came with the courtesan."

"Miss Dare," Heath corrected. "She's no longer a courtesan." He drew out a slim lockpick and had the lock sprung in a second.

"I did it faster."

"And clumsier. You left scratches on the plate. Scratches

which may or may not have been noticed. We have to be careful about this, Julian. And quiet."

"Why? If there are demons here, they don't need sound to know they're being invaded."

"True. But the place smells empty."

"I can't smell anything but the stink of chamber pots and rot. Same as yesterday."

"That's how I know there's no one—mortal or not—inside." The door gave a soft groan. Heath moved through the dark to the counter. Behind it Mrs. Holt had dispensed Vivienne's needed drug. On the wooden shelves, bottles were crammed in.

"I've already searched through here. What exactly are we looking for this time?"

Heath glanced up. Julian frowned at the counter, his lip curled in distaste.

"I want to know what Mrs. Holt is. What she wants. And who really is making magic potions in this chemist's. There have got to be some answers to be found here. Let's go to the back."

Vivienne had been instructed to seduce him. *Why?* If he kept thinking about the mystery behind it, he wouldn't slip and think about letting Vivienne kiss him, touch him, then finally, when he was about to howl with desire, mount him—

Hades.

A dingy curtain concealed a set of narrow, crooked stairs. Heath moved up them so swiftly, the steps had no time to creak. He found himself in the room in which the apothecary prepared medicines. On one side, a wooden counter ran the length of the tight space. Bowls and pestles littered the worktable. Faint light crept around the curtains and glistened on the surface, revealing stains, powder residue, and slick things that had long dried. Astringent scents filled Heath's nose, along with the heavy smell of rotting flesh. There were barrels along the wall beneath the lowest shelves.

"Body parts," he muttered.

"Christ Jesus!" Julian's shout had Heath spinning on his heel. "They weren't there before."

As he spat out the words, Julian jumped back. A stack of enormous jars swayed, tottered, and Heath jumped over the table to reach them—

His hand caught them and steadied the pile. Eyeballs sloshed in a yellowish fluid. Julian pointed to the counter and grinned sheepishly. "*Those* weren't there last night either."

Heath noted a tag attached to one. DRIED ELEPHANT PENIS, it read. "Poor buggers."

A stack of books rested at the end of the counter. Heath looked at the first, a treatise on herbs and plants for medical treatments. The next two were texts on human anatomy. Normal, acceptable books for a place that sold cures.

"There are three bedchambers beyond this room," Julian explained. "The largest is at the back and is the only one being used. The other two are empty."

"Many chemists are more successful than this one appears to be," Heath mused. "Most raise families within their shops." There was something wrong, something missing. . . . "Stairs."

"Over there," Julian said.

"No. I mean there should be stairs up to another floor. These narrow stores all have three floors. We're only on the second, and I saw no stairs that led upward. So they must be hidden."

He began tracing his way along the walls, tapping, until his fist made a hollow sound. The plaster appeared unbroken. So how did the door to the stairs open? Magic, obviously. With a spell he didn't know. So he raised his boot and slammed it through plaster and laths.

Julian jumped. "Hades, I thought we were supposed to be quiet."

Ignoring the younger vampire, Heath kicked a hole large

enough to climb through. He found himself on the landing of another narrow stair. There was no sound, only the soft flutter of bits of plaster settling. Then he charged upstairs. The stair opened onto a room that took up the entire floor, decorated like a gentleman's study with an ornate desk of black wood and large leather chairs.

It took only moments to know the room was devoid of demons or apothecaries. Heath searched the desk first. He ripped open drawers and found them also empty—except for the last, which held a heavy seal. He turned and lifted it to look at the pattern.

He knew the design well. It was a thick cross decorated with curves and loops. The sight of it shot his thoughts back into his past. He remembered the flame of a campfire, howls of wolves, and the barking of frightened dogs. A man wearing furs lifted a brand from flame, and the raised cross had glowed red.

Heath remembered searing pain, the stench of his own burning flesh, as his sire's servant had branded him while the ancient vampire placed the curse on his head.

"What is it?" Julian asked.

"Nothing."

Now he knew how Mrs. Holt had known who he was. The vampire who used this room was his sire. Nikolai, the five-hundred-year-old vampire who had made him, who'd cursed him.

What was Vivienne's part in this? As her payment for her medicine, was she supposed to unleash the demon in him?

Night had settled by the time his lordship bothered to come downstairs. Vivienne knew from stories that vampires had to stay out of the light and sleep in the day. But they slept in coffins. And vampires did not really exist.

She watched him with pursed lips as he prowled into Sarah's room, all long legs and mobile shoulders. He appeared oblivious to the anger stewing inside her, the arrogant wretch. He was dressed in trousers and a shirt, but he moved on bare feet. Silent, graceful, stealthy.

He paused at the end of the bed and studied Sarah with his head cocked. He took a deep breath as though he scented something in the air.

Vivienne opened her mouth, but he spoke first. "Does she normally sleep so much?"

And with one question, he probed the deep fears boiling inside her. "She has never slept a whole day before. She must have been very tired—"

"She must be getting weaker and the medicine isn't helping. That's what you fear."

She watched, hands fisted, as he approached Sarah. She flinched as he touched Sarah's throat with two fingers until she realized he was checking the pulse.

"If I try to help your daughter, it will mean she will have to drink my blood. Are you willing to let me do that?"

"N-no. That's preposterous—" She stopped. Doctors had come and had bled Sarah. And it had done nothing. "You licked my wound and it went away. Is that what would happen if Sarah drinks your blood?"

"It's not as simple as that. I can't feed her enough at one time to banish whatever this illness is. Not without taking the risk that I turn her into a vampire. I assume that's not the future you envision for your daughter?"

"No!"

"Then we start slowly. A little at a time. She will build a tolerance. We should know in a few days if it is working."

A few days. "And do you intend to keep me a prisoner all that time?"

"I intend to keep you with me, Miss Dare. Until we find my brother."

He might call himself a vampire, but he was as pigheaded a

man as any of her protectors had been. But she couldn't fight now. Or even protest her innocence. If believing she knew his brother kept him here to help Sarah, she'd hold her tongue. "That name you called me. Succubus. What does it mean?"

She had prided herself on the library she built, for she wanted Sarah to be well read. But none of her books defined that word.

He had been studying Sarah. He looked at Vivienne. "There is a way to prove what you are, Miss Dare. But it will mean you won't be making love to anyone—in your dreams or out."

"Your dream can't have been the same as mine," she challenged. "That's impossible."

A slow grin spread. "You dropped to your knees before me in Hyde Park." He spoke softly so Sarah could not hear. "You sucked my cock until I was on the brink of climax. And what did I do then?"

She flushed. "You lifted me up to my feet and knelt before me and—"

"You see. The same dream. Was your climax as good in your dream as it was in mine?"

But he had left her then and drawn a blade out of the waistband of his trousers. A long, thin knife. He drew it along his wrist, leaving a dribble of blood.

The sight of it brought back vile memories. Her mother's—Rose's—blood dripping from her nose after she had taken a man's blow. Vivienne shivered. Every maternal instinct screamed for her to protect Sarah. And to resist this man who had invaded her house, who was battering her defenses with something far stronger than violence. *Hope*.

With shaky fingers she touched her healed cheek. She had to try this. Was his promise any more far fetched than the crone's medicine? Yet Sarah looked so small and defenseless. Was she betraying her daughter? With a heart heavy as lead, she asked quietly, "Should I wake her?"

He shook his head. He tipped his hand to smooth the line of his wrist and send the blood oozing faster. "No. All I need to do is touch the blood to her lips. She will take over from there." Another rueful smile played over his mouth. "Like a babe at the breast."

But as he lowered his powerful body to sit on the edge of her daughter's bed and flicked back his sleeve, Vivienne ran to the fireplace and grasped the poker. In her mind's eye, she could see the leather apron–clad butcher flying through the alley. This would hardly stop Heath.

But it was something.

Heath murmured to Sarah. Vivienne couldn't hear the words, but his tone was soothing. She found her grip loosening on her weapon. She shook sense into her head and held it hard. There had been *gentlemen*—cads and scoundrels who had pursued her to get close to Sarah. She was not naive.

Heath held his wrist to Sarah's lips. "N—" Vivienne began in protest, but to her amazement, Sarah fastened her lips to his wound. Her daughter's eyes were still shut, but she drank fiercely. Suddenly Sarah's hand shot out from the covers and gripped Heath's arm to hold him there.

Heath motioned Vivienne to come to him. Holding the poker, she did.

"See how strong her grip is. Is it always like that?"

"Heavens, no." Vivienne's tongue felt thick and clumsy. "She is always so weak."

"This is a good sign then." He looked up at her. His auburn hair fell across his face, disheveled, red as flame. The sympathy, the hope in his strange, reflective silver eyes stunned her. She was a stranger to him. Why should he care about Sarah's fate, about hers?

And if he thought she had hurt his brother, why did he look at her so gently?

Transfixed, she watched Sarah drink. It should horrify her,

but pink began to bloom in Sarah's cheeks. It had been months since Sarah's skin had been anything but ashen.

"That's enough, little love," Heath whispered.

Her daughter's eyes flew open, desperate and angry, and she clung to him harder.

"No, Sarah," Vivienne tried, "you must stop—"

But Sarah ignored her. Heath spoke strange words. "*Arnum aria enta.*"

It sounded like Latin, but nothing Vivienne recognized. Sarah dropped away from his wrist and fell back onto the bed. Her eyes were closed. But her skin, instead of looking parchment thin, actually glowed.

"Is—is she all right?" Guilt and fear were a crushing weight on her heart.

"She needs to sleep. She has to digest whatever it is in my magical blood that heals." He stood, reminding Vivienne of his size. His head brushed the tasseled trim of Sarah's bed canopy.

"She looks so much better." She hugged that hope to her heart, desperate not to lose an ounce of it. Before her tear-blurred eyes, Sarah's face looked as pretty as it once had, instead of haggard and ill. Then her tears spilled. "The medicine never did that to her."

His sensual mouth twisted sardonically. "I suspect the medicine was only intended to keep her barely alive. Not to cure her."

"But why? I paid the price." She gaped at him before she thought to brush away her tears.

His gaze fixed on her wet cheeks. "And if Sarah was cured you would stop paying the price. A succubus steals part of a man's soul each time she beds him. Mrs. Holt didn't want you to stop."

"I am not a succubus. I do not steal men's souls. If anything, men have taken *mine*."

"I don't believe that." He looked around. "You care too much for Sarah to have no soul. I think, if anything, men made your soul stronger."

That was utter madness. And she was about to throw fierce words at him, when he smiled lazily. He grasped the poker and tugged it out of her hand.

"A woman with a weapon is always a dangerous thing. You know, there is a way to prove whether you are a succubus or not." He ran a considering hand over his jaw. "For the details, there is a book I must consult."

"Then go and look at it. And leave me alone." She stopped. "I'm sorry. I didn't mean—"

"Of course you did," he said softly. "Now, you will have to get dressed. The men I've employed can watch the house, and I assume you have your servants watch over Sarah."

She glared at him. "I'm not leaving my daughter."

"Yes, you are—for a few hours. I have to go out. I want to get that book. Then I need to find my brother, and I need to find out who has been using you to drain the souls of England's peers."

Vivienne could not even count all the dangerous things she had done within the last day. And now she was walking into a dark house with a well-built, muscular gentleman who called himself a vampire. She had no weapon, nor anyone to protect her. Servants surrounded her, but they were in his employ.

He had helped Sarah.

Heath had given her a miracle. And for that alone, she knew she had to do what he asked.

The door thudded to a close behind her, the heavy sound echoing in the massive foyer of his town house. She froze at the sound, her hands clutching the sides of her cloak.

"What is wrong, Miss Dare?" Moonlight spilled in from a

skylight, glancing across his face like a sword's blade. In the bluish glow, his eyes were silver. Unearthly. "There's nothing to fear in my foyer."

Oh yes there is. You. "Why did you help my daughter when you believe I am capable of murder? When you suspect—wrongly—that I made your brother disappear?"

"Your crimes are not your daughter's crimes."

"Do you intend to let me go home to her?"

"I want to find my brother." He watched her carefully. "However, I don't plan to take revenge. Revenge is a bloody useless thing to want and a dangerous thing to pursue."

She refused to show how much he scared her. "Do you have a portrait of your brother in this dark house? I should like to actually see the man you accuse me of seducing."

He paused. "I told you what he looks like."

"Yes. Like you only more attractive. I would prefer to see for myself."

With gentlemanly aplomb, he offered his arm. Given she was essentially his prisoner, the gesture seemed absurd. He felt no noble consideration to her. "Come," he said.

She sighed and touched him. Her hand slid along his forearm. Rock. Iron. Solid as stone. A sizzle rushed up her fingertips, then rippled in her tummy like waves in a pond. She'd never felt so giddy at a man's touch.

It must be the strain.

"The gallery is this way."

She had to hurry to follow his long stride. They stepped through a doorway, into a black, silent space. She felt cold as he moved away. He whipped back the drapes and silvery light fell in.

He raked his hand through his hair. She had survived by reading masculine emotions—all gentlemen revealed them. Men were far more expressive than women, and more honest about what they felt. Women only got into trouble because they tried to ignore what they saw. In Heath, she saw great pain.

He pointed to a life-size portrait behind her. "That is my brother and me," he said huskily. "He is named Raine."

Two young men stared down from the painted canvas. Heath was seated; she could tell at once it was he. The same sweep of auburn hair, but in the picture, it was caught back with a velvet bow. An identical proud nose and full sensual mouth, but his eyes were green. He sat back in casual repose but looked ready to leap out of the frame. His brother, Raine, looked thinner, more uncertain. His hands lay on the chair as though he was holding his brother and drawing strength from him. He looked very young. And despite their youthful faces, they wore elegant blue tailcoats, with pristine collar points and cravats.

"This picture was painted a long time ago," she observed. "Yet you have hardly changed."

"It was painted before my marriage. And I will never change, love. Never grow old. My soul has crumbled to dust. On the outside, you would never guess I was supposed to be dead. You would never see I was different at all."

His marriage. He said it casually, but he had said nothing about a wife. "And your brother?"

"He changed. He has aged since that picture. He only became a vampire a few months ago."

Vivienne stared intently at his brother. She tried to envision Raine looking older—more grizzled, more lined, more dissipated, or whatever ravages age had bestowed upon him. "I've never seen him. That is the honest truth."

"I believe you."

She jerked around. Shadows moved across him as though trying to caress his body. "Why do you believe me now?"

"You're angry. If you weren't innocent, you would be scared. Now you are just getting frustrated with me."

"Yes," she agreed. "Very. I don't know what happened to your brother. And I don't know *why* those peers died. Or what Mrs. Holt wants."

"You don't believe you take their souls?"

"Of course not. I don't believe in magic—black, white, or otherwise."

"It's interesting. You are a very jaded woman, but you are filled with hope. It glows from you. I can almost taste it exuding from you."

Hope. Vivienne flinched. Hope should not have existed for a girl whose mother was a tart, working for brutish whoremongers and living in grimy flashhouses. It should have been beaten right out of her. Yet he had given it to her.

Hope had always been her little secret. That and determination. *I will give us something better*, she would say to her mother. And Mama would stroke her hair and let her say it over and over—until gin became a substitute for hope for Mama and she'd stopped listening altogether.

"You said you were married. Where is your wife?"

His eyes changed; they turned black. Pure black, as though his pupils had gobbled up all the color. "She died nine years after we were married."

"How long ago was that?"

"Ten years. The tip of forever. I don't want to speak about it. She is in Heaven and I'm in eternal damnation, where I belong."

"Why do you believe that?" She stepped toward him, but he retreated from the light.

"We're here so I can question you."

"Well, I have another question for you. What have you done to try to find your brother? There are men who can be hired to do such things—former Bow Street Runners. Private investigators."

"My brother is a vampire. Too hard to explain, even to those willing to do almost anything for money. I've searched London for him—and for you, because I saw you standing next to Raine in a reflection in a pool of water."

"That's impossible. I've never been near him."

"It is a magical pool, high on the moors. It is said that it shows the face of the next person to die. In it I saw you and my brother."

"Surely you are joking. If you look into a pond, aren't you going to see your own reflection?"

"That is what happens to most people who do dare to try it. Then each one, according to legend, has died shortly after. Probably so damn nervous, they brought about their own deaths. And yes, when I looked in, I first saw my reflection. But of course, I'm not going to die. Then I saw you. You were reflected with me, as though you were . . . uh, standing behind me. Then my image vanished and I saw my brother. I could see, from the way he looked at you, that he cared for you and desired you."

"You believe this? Magical pools and wild predictions! You were probably foxed and imagined it all!"

"Vampires don't get foxed. Let us go to the library." He held out his hand.

Startled, she realized he intended to lead her through his house by holding her hand. She placed her hand on his forearm instead. To walk handfasted seemed too intimate. His auburn brow jerked up, but he said nothing. And stayed as quiet as his tomb-silent house as he led her through the darkness.

Silent men had always made her nervous. Like the dark sky, some men became very, very still before they exploded into a storm. Drunk ones were the most frightening. Any man who did not blather like a fool when he got foxed was a man to avoid.

What of a silent vampire? It unnerved Vivienne. Her half

boots creaked upon floorboards, her breath huffed in the quiet as they walked through the house. Heath moved without any sound at all.

"This is the library." He left her in the pitch black, and she shuddered. A moment later, she saw a blue spark in the middle, smelled a waft of sulfur. A flame caught to one wick after another. Soon a candelabra glowed, and a brilliant halo of light fell over a long, wooden table. It threw light over Heath's strong forearm and the glow turned his hair to red flame. Gilt lettering glinted as he walked along the shelves, which seemed to stretch endlessly into the dark.

"What can you prove from these books?" There must be thousands of them. Tens of thousands. She'd had affairs with rich and powerful gentlemen. None had possessed so many books.

He ran his finger along the titles, but held the light behind him. Apparently he did not need it to see. "That you are a succubus. Come here. Look at the books on this shelf." He set the candelabra on the floor.

The shelf in question was ten feet long. Books were packed side by side. She tentatively reached up. One of the volumes in front of her looked ancient. The other books gripped it so tightly, it would not come free. "These are all about that word you used? Succubus?"

"A succubus is a female demon who appears to men in dreams, naked, beautiful, and carnally skilled. Flower, I suspect every vampire hunter alive has either written a book about succubi—or would like to."

A female demon?

Gently, he eased out the book and opened it. In the light she could see an image on the yellowed paper. A woman with flowing hair, large bare breasts, and fangs was straddling a human male. "This *can't* be me. I don't have fangs. I don't bite men."

"I think you might. Under the right circumstances." He

moved behind her. His hard, taut thighs brushed along her bottom. She took a step forward, away from him. "A succubus steals a man's soul when he climaxes inside her. The fangs are not necessary."

She took a deep breath. "If I was one of these, how could I have been born to my mother and lived my life in England? I am a normal woman."

His voice softened. "I suspect you are an extraordinary woman."

Madness, but she felt a quiver of pleasure at his flattering tone. She quickly quelled it. "I am *ordinary*." Another picture leaped out at her. A blond woman had her mouth to a man's throat and his member in her hand while he writhed beneath her in pleasure and pain. "I was not a succubus. I was a whore." She hated saying the word. She heard the anger in it, vibrating like a blade of fine steel when it whipped through the air. "I was cursed, but not in the way you seem to think."

"I have to search a brothel tonight. You won't understand why I'm right unless you go there with me."

Dear heaven, she never wanted to set foot in such a place. She had escaped being forced to work in a whorehouse by the skin of her teeth. "No."

He inclined his head. "You don't have a choice. I am taking you with me. When we return, before dawn, I will feed your daughter again."

"You are wrong. I *do* have a choice—" She stopped. She knew what he would do. It was what any man would do to get what he wanted. Be vicious, ruthless. "You won't help Sarah unless I agree."

He recoiled as though she'd hit him. "I would never use your daughter as blackmail. Never. I meant merely that I could do this—"

A scream shot out from her lips as he came to her in a blurred motion and lifted her. The shelves raced by as she flew through the air, then flopped over his shoulder. His hand clamped firmly on her bottom.

"There, darling. No choice. You have to know temptation without release. Until you experience that, you aren't going to know what you are."

She had no idea what he was talking about. She hammered her hands on his back, wildly kicked her feet. He tightened his grip, and the most shocking erotic sensation raced from where his fingers pressed into her derriere. She should *not* be aroused by this.

This was what men did. When they couldn't win in any other way—not with money or words or power—they used their size and their strength.

She could never let herself forget that.

And she would never let herself feel hot and erotic and wanting at his touch. Not ever again.

4

Heath dangled a set of iron shackles in front of her eyes and Vivienne froze on the velvet seat of the carriage. Then she gathered her wits and her fury. "Just *what* do you plan to do with those?"

He merely grinned. Naughtily. "I intend to subdue a rebellious succubus. I assume you've enjoyed some bondage encounters. Your skills with a riding crop are legendary."

Enjoyed. He truly had no idea. Through pursed lips, she warned, "I have tied men up. I never let them do so to me. Those are my rules and I never—"

With a blur, he caught her wrist and drew her arm back with surprising gentleness.

"Let me go! I refuse to be bound!"

The only thing her fury succeeded in doing was to widen his grin to a completely dazzling smile. Deep, seductive lines bracketed his mouth. "You have a problem with trust."

"I *don't* trust you—" She broke off as something soft brushed over her wrist. A long, sensual caress that sent her shoulders quivering foolishly and made the fine hairs on her nape tingle. "No, don't do this. *Please*."

"You *can* trust me," he murmured and the silky wash of his voice over her cheek brought a nonsensical flood of heat to her cunny. "I would never hurt you. But darling, I have to ensure you don't run away."

The lock engaged with a soft *click*. What man with shackles in his hand would actually listen to a woman? And she was captured.

The iron band was lined with velvet. It circled her wrist snugly enough to make her nerves explode with awareness but it wasn't tight enough to hurt. These cuffs were obviously meant for erotic play, not enforcement of the law.

And what had she done while he'd clasped it around her captured wrist, fool that she was? She'd whimpered with arousal. Instinctively she did trust him, after how gentle he'd been with Sarah.

"I never take advantage of a woman, Miss Dare. No matter what the circumstance. This is just to ensure you are still here when I get back."

She tried to pull free, lashing out with her booted feet at the same time. She kicked his shins. He didn't even wince. He merely fed the other cuff, and the chain that attached them, through a large metal eyelet fixed to the wall of the carriage.

"What is that for?"

"I've had to capture things before," he said carelessly.

"Unwilling women?"

"No, something less dangerous. Bloodthirsty demons."

With lightning speed, he efficiently snapped the cuff around her other wrist. The chain was only a foot in length, which meant her arms were secured back behind her head. She wrenched furiously, trying to break free.

He cocked his head, admiring his work. With her arms drawn back, her bosom was thrust ahead, straining against the demure gray silk of her dress. "You can't pull the back of the carriage off, Miss Dare. Demons have tried. I learned how to reinforce the vehicle after a few of them escaped."

"But why do you capture demons? Aren't you one yourself?"

"Not yet," he answered, which was hardly an answer at all.

He had spoken of demons. She had her own—and being trapped, unable to defend herself was one.

She was completely dressed, and her pelisse buttoned up to her throat. But she felt exposed and vulnerable. As well as wicked—and terribly aroused. She must be ten times a fool to feel anything but infuriated.

She expected him to fondle and stroke her because she couldn't stop him, because she felt as though she was served up for his pleasure.

But he didn't. He had put her in this position, entirely his captive, and all he did was bow. "Stay still a moment, love. I have to talk to Julian. He followed us here." His silvery gaze held hers. "You will have to be careful around Julian, love."

Careful around Julian!

"If he finds out you are the succubus the vampire council has been looking for, he'll take you to them. And you don't want that, believe me."

Vampire council? This was insane. "I hate *you*," she whispered. But she feared it wasn't him she hated; it was how much her body desired him. "I hate needing you for Sarah. But I am indebted to you forever for helping her. So if you want me locked up in your carriage, I have no choice but to do what you want."

He winked, the wretch. Then he disappeared out the door. The carriage rocked as he jumped down to his drive.

Heath found Julian in his study, sprawled in a leather chair and smoking a cheroot. Naked, because Julian had shape shifted and flown there.

Heath held up his hand before the vampire could question him. "I know. You want to know what I'm doing, because you must report to the council. Very well. Tonight I am going to go to the brothel in which Lord Cavendish died."

Julian blew a smoke ring. "And you're taking Miss Dare. She's thinking some very ripe curses about you right now."

It irked him no end that Julian could read her mind and he couldn't. "There's no need for you to be concerned about Miss Dare. She is of no significance to them. She is just a former courtesan with an ill child." He tried to impose his will into Julian's mind. Normally he could do it with a lesser vampire. But Julian's mind resisted. The lad was more powerful than he looked.

The younger vampire eyed him suspiciously. "She's the succubus. I know she is; I saw it in her thoughts. She wanted to seduce you. And she's slept with the five men who died."

Raw panic shot through him. "Whatever she is, she didn't know it. She's being used by someone, and I need time to find out who. If you turn her over to the council—"

"I'm not going to do that. I don't like that bunch of old, arrogant vampires any more than you do, Heath. I have to take orders from them. Doesn't mean I do everything they ask."

Julian wore a rebellious pout, but Heath couldn't accept his apparent disloyalty at face value. He still had to be wary. "I have to go, Julian. You're free to drink my brandy to your heart's content, but you're not allowed to drink from my maids—"

"But you think Miss Dare had something to do with your brother's disappearance."

"She denies it. And I believe her."

Julian smirked. "Do you? Are there two reasons? The plump, round ones up on her chest? Or the curvy ones of her backside, equally tempting?"

"Christ," Heath muttered. He knew it was an odd curse for a vampire. "There is more to women than breasts and rumps, Julian."

"If this Miss Dare is a demoness and a murderess, what's going to happen to her? In the mortal world, she'd be hanged. I don't know what the council would do to her, but it wouldn't be pretty. It seems a shame to destroy such a beautiful woman. And her poor daughter would be left alone."

There were times Julian amazed him. The lad saw right to the heart of matters. "I believe she's an unwitting accomplice," Heath said. "I need to find out more about that apothecary." And about the seal that bore the design of his brand. Did it mean his sire was in London? Nikolai was not supposed to be able to leave the Carpathians. . . .

"You aren't going to send me there again instead of letting me go to the brothels, are you?" Julian asked.

"No. Keep away from there. Go to the brothels."

"Are you going to let Miss Dare seduce you?" Julian studied him. "You might learn a lot that way. You want her, don't you?"

"Shut up, Julian. I can't bed her. It is as simple as that."

The lad gave a sly grin. "You could bed her once, old man. It takes two tumbles in the hay before you unleash the curse."

"*This* is a brothel?"

Heath watched Miss Dare open her eyes wide as she took in the opulence of the foyer. A fountain bubbled in the center. The walls were covered in crimson silk. Glasses of champagne were whisked through the crowd on silver trays carried by elegant footmen, while prostitutes draped in transparent veils struck enticing poses.

Either she was a magnificent actress or she had never been here before. Her blue eyes were saucer wide. She had forgotten to glare at him, which she had done when he'd returned to the carriage and set her free. Apparently she did not like being taken prisoner, even though he had acted the perfect gentleman.

She was afraid to give up control. Afraid to trust. She must have been hurt in the past.

"Lord Cavendish died in here." He saw her flinch.

But her gaze did not dart around like a frightened creature seeking a way out. She faced him with pride. "There was no point in bringing me here. I'm innocent—" Then she saw something behind him that brought her hand to her lush mouth in shock.

"Oh goodness!" she gasped.

In front of her, a woman wearing nothing but a black corset spanked a second woman's bare arse with a riding crop.

Heath lifted Vivienne's gloved hand and bestowed a teasing kiss. "I brought you here because this is the perfect brothel for what I have to show you."

Vivienne sipped from the gold-rimmed champagne flute Heath had brought her. Bubbles exploded against her lips and danced on her tongue, but it tasted like vinegar mixed with her fear. A terrified voice whispered in her head, *What if he was right? How else did those men die?*

She was walking at Heath's side through a surprisingly empty hallway. In brothels she'd heard of, there were always drunken men and women stumbling about, and women were always shrieking and fighting.

But this place looked like a ducal residence. She'd glimpsed two bedrooms through open doors. Neither had been in use, and the beds within looked like fairy cakes. She suspected the linen was clean, which never happened in the brothels of the stews.

The women here were not of a type she'd seen before. They

weren't cool, calculating Incognitas. Or drunk penny whores, boldly painted, raucous and crude, but with as much real desire for sex as Vivienne had. Which was not very much.

"This is utterly pointless, Blackmoor." She stopped in the hall. "I don't see how being here would prove anything. I am not a demoness born in hell, unless you believe London's East End is the fire-and-brimstone-filled lair of Satan."

White teeth flashed at her as he smiled. And she saw the elongated ones on the sides of his mouth, like a wolf's fangs. "You are a remarkable woman, Miss Dare. Making quips when you're afraid of what I'm going to show you."

"I'm not afraid." But she was. After the miracle of what Heath's blood had done to Sarah, she couldn't continue to insist magic didn't exist.

"If I *am* a succubus, what is my daughter? Is she supposed to be one, too? What does this mean for her?"

She cringed at the frightened, desperate sound of her voice.

He stopped, concern in the way he gazed down at her. His hands touched her hips. And his devil-may-care charm was gone. "I don't know, Vivienne," he said softly.

"Can succubi have children?" she demanded.

Moans came through the closed door beside them. A crescendo of groans and cries and sobs was followed by one feminine shriek. With Heath's palms resting on her hips, she half-turned and stared in surprise at the door.

"I believe the lady was enjoying herself."

She turned back as his mouth suddenly claimed hers. She tried to pull away, but his kiss held her captive. He moved his mouth gently over hers. It wasn't a kiss of passion; it was the sort of kiss she would brush on Sarah's hair. And it made tears sting in her eyes.

He broke the kiss and whispered, "The books don't say anything about whether a succubus can have a child. Most books on the occult and demon world were written by men. Men with little scientific knowledge and a lot of superstition. It's possible. But I have no idea what it would mean for Sarah."

"It isn't possible," she said fiercely. She pushed his hands away, spilling the last of the champagne.

"Are you willing to come with me and find out?" Heath asked. He watched her bite her lip. Even without entering her mind, he knew she wanted to say *no*. And run from this. But she lifted her chin. "All right."

"First, though, I have business to take care of." He led her down the hallway. "I need to know more about Lord Cavendish. I need to know what he was like as a man."

She jerked her head up.

"I'm asking you because to find out what happened to him, I need to know who he was."

"He was quite tall. About six feet and four inches. Very muscular. Powerfully built. He had dark hair, very black. And green eyes."

"I've seen his portrait, love. I know what he looks like. But I suspect you knew quite a lot about him." They'd reached the end of the hall and he rapped on a blue door. It opened at once, and he led a wide-eyed Vivienne inside. The room looked like an artist's studio, and gentlemen did use it for painting. They either worked on canvases of luscious nudes or on the ladies themselves, doing naughty things with the brushes.

Several voluptuous women posed. Two of the lovelies were flitting through the crowd of gentlemen, bestowing kisses and rubbing their curvaceous breasts against male chests.

Heath glanced toward Miss Dare. She could not draw her eyes away from the giggling girls. She met his gaze. "They are remarkable actresses," she said dryly. "They truly appear to be enjoying themselves."

"At this particular brothel they are. And don't change the subject, or I'll invite them over here to kiss and fondle you."

Her brow arched. She ran her tongue with knee-weakening slowness over her lips. "Perhaps I might like that."

Lust hit him like a blow. But he couldn't let her see that. Victory crept into her blue eyes, and he knew she was deliberately tormenting him.

"Cavendish." The name rasped out of his tight throat. It had been so long since he'd made love. But what he hungered for was the laughter and joy and play that came with pleasure. He missed that so much, and he'd been too big a fool to understand how precious it was when he had it.

Vivienne was not going to seduce him. She no longer needed to. And he should be relieved, not filled with longing like a lovesick boy.

He slid his arm around her and led her to a shadowy corner of a room crowded with men and courtesans. Everyone was too intent on sex and temptation to notice them, but he wanted Vivienne to feel a sense of privacy.

"Cavendish was my lover for only two months." Vivienne frowned. "I never discuss one man with another."

"I'm not your lover. I won't be bedding you, so I don't need to hear I'm the best, the largest, or the only man who has ever made you come." He grinned at her surprise. "We males are not as easily fooled as you might think. Now, tell me what Cavendish was like—as a man."

She pursed her lips. "He liked wild adventure and he liked to take risks."

"What sort of risks? Risks in your bed?"

"No. He—"

Who would have thought an experienced courtesan would flush?

"He was always on top," she said. "He liked to hold my arms above my head and trap me beneath him. Half the time I couldn't breathe. I struggled to survive until he was finished." She cast a jaded eye on the giggling girl. "If these girls are cheerful, they can't have had much experience with men who buy them for sex." Her eyes looked so empty—the way he felt most of the time.

Madly he wanted to kiss her again. He wanted to tease her lips and show her what she could feel. But he'd taken a risk kissing her once. And all it had done was stoke his desire. "All right. What risks did he take?"

"He gambled heavily. But he generally won, so I would not count that as a risk. He liked to explore. Africa and India, mostly." She sighed deeply. "I don't think I can tell you anything about the man that will help you. His heart always appeared to be sound in my bed. And if I took his soul . . ." Tears glittered in her eyes. "I didn't know it."

"What did it feel like when you made love to him?"

"I was struggling to breathe. He was large and heavy. It was hellish."

"When he climaxed, did you feel heat? A rush of power? Colored lights before your eyes?"

"Sometimes I saw stars from lack of oxygen. I asked him not to crush me into the bed during lovemaking. He refused to listen. I was expected to let him have what he wanted."

"But you told me he wasn't paying you."

"He wasn't. But he knew I had been a courtesan. I had no right to ask anything of the great Earl of Cavendish, did I?" Bitterness made her voice sharp. "I didn't remember feeling anything in bed with him. I was doing it to pay the price for Sarah's medicine."

"Poor dear."

"Don't pity me, Heath. I am neither poor nor a dear."

He caught hold of her elbow and drew her farther into the corner. Two naked girls were now playfully spanking each other's bottoms in the center of the room. No one was looking anywhere else. "Did anyone have a reason to want him dead? Help me, Vivienne. It's the only way I can help you."

Vivienne knew what he must mean. Sarah. She owed that miracle to this man. "He held some debts of other peers. Some of the vowels represented vast amounts of money."

"Do you have the names of the gentlemen who wrote the vowels?"

"No. That sort of thing would not be a mistress's business."

"So one of those men might have had a reason. Or his heir. Anyone else?"

Vivienne shrugged. "He didn't talk very much to me. I think the only thing he wanted from me was to struggle beneath him while he pounded into me." Tears were burning in her eyes and she hoped Heath didn't see them.

He caught her by the elbow and led her around the room, toward a chaise where a naked blonde reclined. An artist was painting a picture of her. A gentleman stood behind the artist, watching the picture swiftly develop. In the painting, a man with an enormous cock had been added. Obviously it had inspired the gentleman, for he was stroking the front of his trousers.

Then Vivienne felt a nudge, and Heath led her around in a circle throughout the generous salon. She saw how his intense gaze landed on each courtesan and each gentleman and studied them, and how he watched her.

Finally he stopped by an older prostitute and began questioning her about Cavendish. Swallowing hard, Vivienne heard Heath say it was in this room Cavendish had died. Then she heard Heath ask, "And the lady with me—you've never seen her before?"

"No, my lord."

As he led her away, Vivienne turned on him. "You're questioning them to find out if I've ever been here?"

"I have to, though I don't believe you lied about it. You seemed too genuinely surprised by the place when we first came in."

She shuddered. "And Cavendish died in here."

"Don't think about that right now. I will do more questioning later. Right now there is a room I want to show you. And I assume, by this time of the night, the particular act you should see will be in progress."

A few minutes later, Vivienne found herself standing in front of large double doors painted dark burgundy. She didn't know what he was trying to prove, but she was nervous.

"This is a scene I think you'll enjoy, love. A woman in command of several men who will do anything to please her."

Vivienne frowned at his twinkling, reflective eyes. "A woman in command? It may look like that, but I very much doubt it's true."

Heath pointed to the curtain. "Feel free to peep there, where the curtains join."

His arrogance annoyed her. She knew he was daring her, so she stalked forward and looked. It took her several moments of blinking to really see it. . . .

A naked couple were making love on an oval-shaped bed in the center of the room. The woman, a redhead with enormous breasts, was on top. But they weren't alone. A man with chocolate-brown hair knelt behind her, his hand wrapped firmly around his erect shaft. The man could barely fit his hand around his cock, and she knew how big a man's hand was. He was even more generously endowed than Heath.

The man tipped a vial over the woman's rump and a stream of golden fluid slowly flowed out. It was viscous and lazy, like oil. It struck the top of her derriere and slid between the cheeks.

The brown-haired man inched forward, then stroked the tip of his enormous appendage in the golden oil. He massaged the girl's bottom with his penis. Then he began to slide his erection inside her arse.

Vivienne caught her breath. She had heard of . . . *this*. Of a man going inside a woman's bottom. She had never done it. The woman, trapped between two men, moaned loudly. Given she was already riding one man, how could another one fit, even in her bottom?

Another inch went inside the woman. The second man lifted both his hands and used the rocking of his hips to direct his cock inside her. A little more. And more. And more.

The woman cried out as he gave one last thrust. His groin pressed tight against her plump bottom. "Ooh, that feels so wonderfully full," she cried.

The man with the chocolate waves laughed. "We've only just begun." He bent forward and lifted an ivory rod from the surface of the bed. Such wands were intended for a woman to insert inside herself—for her own pleasure, or to stimulate a man who wished to watch.

It glistened in the light. Obviously it had been oiled already.

The man withdrew a few inches, so his engorged shaft could be seen until it disappeared between ivory cheeks. Vivienne could barely breathe. It looked so erotic.

The man pressed the tip of the wand to her stretched opening, beside his aroused cock.

"Ooh, my lord," the woman cried. "What are you doing?"

"Showing you what full really means, my dear."

Like an obedient servant, the girl nodded. But she screamed as he eased it in. Her hands became claws on the chest of the first man, who had coal-black hair. He smiled up at her. "Too much?"

Her face was scarlet. "No. No, not too much. I *want* this."

The second man's eyes gleamed with anticipation. As Vivienne watched with wide eyes, the wand slid into the girl, past its thickest circumference.

The girl gasped. "Oh, I did feel the pop."

"So did I," he murmured.

"Dear heaven," she whimpered. "I am crammed. You are both enormous to begin with."

"But you aren't completely stuffed, are you, love?" He thrust forward.

The girl shook her head.

Vivienne gasped. His flat abdomen collided with the end of the wand. His cock and the slim rod of ivory slid up the girl's rump. Withdrew. Slid again.

Vivienne knew her hands were in fists, like the girl's. Her head buzzed with heat. Her cunny throbbed. Even her derriere tingled at the thought of being so filled. . . .

The first man laughingly called, "Come out, Bedowin. We need a cock for her mouth. And bring the clamps for her nipples."

It all happened so swiftly. A third man—a blond—strode out from behind a curtain. He was aroused, a silvery stream of fluid already leaking from the engorged, purplish head of his cock. He carried small clasps attached to leather straps. Swiftly he fixed those to the girl's thick brown nipples and handed the straps to the other two men. Then he straddled the head of the man on the bottom and thrust his erection into the girl's eager mouth.

The three men thrust wildly, but the girl writhed and thrust and pounded as though possessed by demons. Her cries were muffled by the blond man's erection. But the girl suddenly arched her back and clutched the arse of the blond. She clung to him, his thick cock still buried in her mouth as she jerked helplessly between the other two men.

Those men laughed with delight and thrust hard, ruthlessly fucking her. The girl came again and again, and Vivienne's chest was tight with the building tension filling the room.

She realized what the men were doing: desperately hanging on. No one wanted to be the man who came first. The one with the least stamina.

Finally the one with the dark brown hair shouted, "Hades, I can hang on no longer." He shoved his hips forward, slamming everything he had into the climaxing girl's bottom, and he roared, "Oh God," at the top of his lungs. Vivienne was taken aback. Men usually grunted. Or panted. Orgasm often proved to be the one time they *were* silent.

Not this man. His head jerked forward and back as he came. He growled, roared, smacked his groin hard against the red-headed girl's rump. The other two men surrendered to pleasure rapidly, but neither were as thrilling to watch in climax. They grunted a bit, tensed, and relaxed.

"Ah, Molly, but you are the most spectacular lass in England," groaned the brown-haired man. Gently, he withdrew the wand, then himself.

He clapped his hands. A footman hastened forward, holding a basin of water and with cloths draped over his arm—warmed ones of rich, white linen. Steam rose from the basin and the linen.

The man cleaned himself swiftly with a towel. He selected another, dipped it in water, and gently cleaned Molly. The other men withdrew from her, then left the bed without a word. They vanished behind the curtain.

Vivienne's heart beat erratically as she watched a man she did not know clean his lover so tenderly. It was thoroughly astonishing. And Molly giggled throughout.

This certainly was not what she had expected.

"Did you find it arousing?" Heath closed his hands on her shoulders.

Vivienne jumped. He had not touched her—not at all—as they watched. He had stood in the shadows behind her and made no sound. And now, with his hands on her, she was almost ready to purr beneath his touch—

No, she wasn't. She was ready to spin around, claw his clothes off, and attack him sexually like a tigress.

"There's more." He smiled wickedly. "Your night is only beginning."

She sputtered. "If you want to arouse me, your job is done. But I was willing to bed you yesterday, without all—all this."

"You were willing to *sacrifice* yourself by bedding me to satisfy the crone in the apothecary's shop."

She whirled on him. "What is all this for? Did she arrange for you to do this?"

"I don't take orders, love. Not even from men who would happily stake my heart if I didn't."

To discover if Miss Dare was actually a succubus, Heath knew he had to ignite her. He had to give her enough carnal temptation to have her climbing the walls.

"Come, Miss Dare. Your night of sensual education is only beginning."

Darkness. It was so dark around her.

Vivienne opened her eyes wide. But she was plunged in blackness and she couldn't see. She wasn't in the brothel anymore. She had seen scandalous things. Mad, arousing things where groups of people made love, with men sticking their erections in every orifice imaginable—

Suddenly, her heart screamed in her chest. She sucked in deep breaths. She started to panic, but she couldn't slow down her breathing. Pain pounded in her head, wrapped around her heart, lanced her sides. She was cold, like she had fallen into the Thames on a winter's night.

She tumbled out of the bed. She was breathing so fast. Too fast. And even though she was gasping for air, she couldn't take any in. What was wrong? Why wouldn't it stop? She must be—

Strong arms lifted her and she was swept off her feet and pressed tightly against a warm, naked male chest.

Heath.

She struggled to look up at him. But she was seeing him through a crimson haze. A blurry veil the color of blood . . .

"What's wrong, love?"

She fought to speak. Her chest was getting tighter and tighter, like an iron band was being cinched around it. "I—"

His hand suddenly cupped below her left breast. He must be able to feel her heart gallop through her nightdress.

"I—can't breathe." She flinched as another jolt of pain sliced through her head. "You—you've turned red." Shivers wracked her. Vivienne no longer felt the heat of his body, even though his massive arms were wrapped around her, pinning her to the powerful muscles of his warm chest. But she was getting so cold she could no longer move.

"Sarah," she croaked through numb, frosty lips. Was she going to die and leave Sarah alone?

"Christ," Heath growled. "What have I done?"

And next thing she knew, her bed canopy was above her, she was flat on her back, and Heath had shoved up her nightdress. His hands parted her freezing legs. His breath flowed over her bared abdomen. So hot. She needed more—needed to fight the cold. She tried to grasp his shoulders and hold him close, but her arms wouldn't move.

Then he bent his head and his tongue, hot and wet, slicked over her cunny.

5

His plan had been damn idiocy.

Heath pressed his mouth to the soft curls between Vivienne's legs. She lay limply upon her enormous bed, and his heart, his long-dead heart, lurched at the sight. Whimpers of pain escaped from her trembling lips. Shivers wracked her ashen-white, voluptuous form. She looked so vulnerable. So weak and hollow and terrified.

He knew what death looked like. And she was on the brink of it.

It was his damn fault.

For being arrogant again. For thinking he was right.

He'd thought denying her would make her desire explosive. He'd never expected she would be in pain. That she would grow so cold. It was like her life force was flowing out of her. He could almost see it in the gloom of the ill-lit bedchamber, hovering like golden faery dust around her.

He had to stop it. Had to save her.

He slicked his tongue over her quivering cunny. Her taste—salty, rich, earthy, ripe—exploded on his tongue. Her nether lips felt like silk coated with cream. But even here, in her most intimate place, she was turning cold.

He didn't have time for finesse. Or for a long, slow session where he took his time devouring her and made her scream.

He gently licked her clitoris. Her shocked, thrilled cry echoed in the room, and her little nub plumped and hardened in his mouth. But she was afraid, too. He could sense that with her every heartbeat. She had no idea what was happening to her.

He flicked his tongue hard and fast across her, and she arched up on the bed. A wash of her juices flowed from her, drenching his mouth.

God, she tasted so sweet. He ran his tongue over his lower lip to savor the essence of her. For just a fraction of a second, before sweeping his tongue over her blushing, erect clit once more. *Her* taste could addict him.

He knew it, knew he had no choice but to risk the temptation. Risk craving something he could never have again.

Placing his lips around her clit, he suckled. Her hips launched off the bed. Color flooded her skin as she grew warmer. Her flesh was losing the terrifying whitish-blue cast.

His mouth tingled, heated, and he backed away as his fangs exploded forward.

He had to control himself. He couldn't bite her.

He had to pleasure her.

It had never been like this.

Vivienne clutched the crumpled bedsheet beside her. Once, when she'd been very young, she'd tried to fly by jumping out of the window of the flashhouse she lived in. She'd soared for mere seconds, then had fallen like a stone—fortunately into a cart of rags.

She was soaring now. Whirling through pleasure and delight. Heat flooded her cold body. Her skin felt alive, aware, *aroused*. Where the hem of her nightgown brushed against her belly. Where the lace around her bodice tickled. And especially when she stroked her fingers over her breasts.

Then a bolt of pain lanced her, and her hands froze on top of her bosom.

Heath suddenly gripped her hips. He rolled onto his back, pulling her with him, so her quim landed upon his mouth. She squeaked with shock. "What are you doing? I shall squash you being on top of you like this."

His tongue slid over her clit again, lavishly, thoroughly, and she had to shut her eyes.

"Love, you don't need to worry about me. Now quiet, my dear, and let me make you come. Let me begin my onslaught."

The words made her quiver.

Another playful lick of his tongue made her moan. She swiftly understood what he meant by "onslaught." He splayed his hands on her bare derriere and lifted her. Lifted her to open her nether lips to him so he could suckle her clit. Each gentle pull and tug flooded her mind with pleasure and pushed away every other thought.

Heavens, he stroked between the cheeks of her bottom. He touched her tight entrance, and sensation, dazzling sensation, rushed through her. She gasped. In shock. In astonishment at the pleasure. He didn't try to penetrate, he just stroked her.

She'd never let anyone touch her like that. It felt so amazingly good.

And pain vanished.

He slid two fingers into her cunny, while his tongue made mind-numbing spirals over her clit. Her passage clutched and squeezed as though begging for his cock. She'd never been so wet. She'd never felt so empty inside.

She needed him. Ached for him.

She was wantonly grinding her face on him. She stopped. She must be hurting him.

But his hand tightened across the cheeks of her rump, pulling her tighter to his face. He must like her being rough. He clamped her so her cunny was pressed tight to his mouth. His fingers slid out of her quim, but his index finger still played merry havoc with her tense, aroused anus.

It was so good. She'd forgotten pain. And warmth blossomed inside her. Warmth fired by the intense heat in her quim, the heat of Heath's hands on her bared bottom, the heat of his breath blowing across her most intimate place, and the slick fire of his tongue licking her.

His every caress felt intense, as though she'd never been touched before. Certainly no one had ever licked her quim while dallying with her bottom. Then, to her shock, he slid his finger slightly inside her rear. Withdrew. Did it again.

Her body resisted. But she liked it, and that resistance made it all the more thrilling.

Then he did everything to her at once. He flicked her clit with his tongue, slid two fingers inside her hot quim, and pushed two fingers inside her welcoming bottom. A scandalous two in a place she'd never allowed a man to touch her. Never had she guessed it would feel so good. His fingers in her quim made her rump feel so tight, and his fingers filling her derriere made her cunny so wonderfully full.

It was too much. So much pleasure, racing from everywhere at once.

Her body went off as though he'd touched a trigger. She came. Exploded. Her cries rang up to the ceiling, and she rocked madly on him. He held her while she went wild upon him. Moans filled the room—her moans, as her orgasm kept exploding inside her. It seemed it was never going to stop.

He kept licking her. Taking her beyond what she'd ever known before. It was delicious. Unbearably thrilling. Rather . . . frightening.

She'd never come without it being at her touch. She alone

knew how to pleasure herself to make herself climax, and even with a protector, she would cleverly touch herself to find her pleasure.

Heath had stripped her control away. And coming that way, with it being entirely at his touch and his command had been . . . exhilarating.

The pleasure was fading. And she was still on top of him. She stretched her hands, her toes, stretched languorously and squirmed and moaned in delight.

He lifted her and set her back across his shoulders. "How do you feel, love?"

She gazed down at him. His lips and cheeks glistened slightly in the lamplight. Heavens, her juices coated his mouth and chin. He licked his lower lip, smiling cheekily, tasting her.

"Good," she managed to whisper.

"No pain?"

"Heavens no." And she realized. "No. I'm not cold—" An agonizing pain spiked through her heart. She clutched her chest. Collapsed on him.

Through the roaring in her ears, she dimly heard his voice.

"Damn, it wasn't enough. But I can't do it, Vivienne. I can't put my cock inside you." His voice was hoarse and she whimpered. The pain had doubled. She had curled into a ball on top of him.

"I can do everything else," he whispered. "Anything else we can imagine."

She felt the thud of his heart. How she could feel it so acutely, she didn't know. She was half draped over his hips, her belly pressed to his long, hard erection. Some instinct drove her to rise on him. To slide her hands over the powerful muscles of his chest. Then go lower, over the hard plane that was his stomach, and take hold of his thick, rigid shaft through his trousers.

"Please," she whispered.

Do this and live. Take him and live. She didn't know where the words came from. They seemed to well up from her soul. She had to make love to him. She had to make him fill her with his scalding hot cum and stop the cold from freezing her to death.

She tore wildly at the fastening of his trousers.

It wasn't enough.

Heath knew it. He had ignited the demon inside Miss Dare. And the demon craved a man's pleasure. Her orgasm wasn't enough to satisfy her. She needed his climax or she would likely die.

What man wouldn't love it: a woman who would do anything to make him come? But it broke Heath's heart.

"No, love." He grasped her hands and drew them away from his throbbing erection. His oversized, vampiric penis was straining and pulsing in his trousers, seeking her heat—her hot mouth, her hand, her scorching, sweet cunny. But he couldn't make love to her.

Wrong. He couldn't make love to her *twice*.

She gently gyrated her hips on top of him. The simple movement almost blew the top of his head off. Her nightgown was still fastened, but the swell of her breasts rose up from the neckline in two flushed mounds. Her cheeks were pink. And she was still panting from the orgasm he'd given her.

There was nothing as erotic, as arousing as a woman still gasping from an explosive climax.

Damnation.

This was all his blasted fault.

She tried to wrench her wrists free of his grasp. "I want you. I need you. Please—I've never wanted anyone the way I want you now."

"It's a craving you can't control," he whispered. "If you don't make love to me, your body won't survive." Once was all right. He could still taste her on his mouth, and he wanted her.

"I know you're not doing this because you want to, but I swear I will make it good for you—"

She stroked his face. Her caress was so sweet, it touched his heart. And that heightened his desire even more.

"You're wrong," she whispered. "It's not just a craving. It's not just need. Ever since I watched you help my daughter, I've desired you. I've tried to fight it. I don't want to anymore."

She leaned over, letting her sinfully beautiful hair tumble over her and over him. Her lips touched his.

Such a kiss. Soft and loving, slow and passionate and heart melting. It was the kiss of a woman who admired him.

He knew she was driven by uncontrollable lust. Knew she had seen him do two good deeds: one for her, one for her daughter. She had no idea what a blackguard he really was.

And right now, he couldn't tell her. He just had to fuck her, make her come, and explode in the climax of his life.

He kissed her back hungrily. He reached up and cupped her generous breasts. Then he playfully jiggled them, making them bounce and slap his hands. She moaned in the middle of the kiss. A demoness like her would play fierce.

He tugged open the fastenings of her nightgown. Her breasts tumbled into his hands, plump, gold, and topped with blushing pink nipples. What more could a man want? These were breasts that could addict a man. And he only got to enjoy them once.

He flicked her nipples with his thumbs. Savored her fevered moan. Savored the sensation of velvety flesh hardening against his fingers. He delighted in the way he could make them grow thick and eager with just light brushes of his thumbs.

She was so hot and responsive. It had to be her demoness instincts taking charge. Before tonight, she had acted like a woman who didn't like sex, who had been taken roughly and was haunted by those memories.

He smiled up at her. God, she was exquisitely beautiful. Her eyes were luminous blue, glowing in a way that could remind him of the sun he'd never see again. She had a face that any man would want to watch for his entire life, for it changed every moment and it was impossible to look away. She cocked her head, letting silken hair spill over her smooth, creamy shoulder. "Please?" she whispered.

He hadn't made love to a woman like this, with deep smiles, with his heart pounding hard, for a long, long time.

"All right, Vivienne," he murmured. "But for our safety, let me be the guide."

Her brows made two golden arches. "Our safety?"

"I'm a demon, love. We can't forget that."

Softly, she added, "As am I."

He gave her a smile. "Tonight, I intend to make love to you like a demon." For their one and only time together.

Vivienne had no idea how a demon would make love. But she suddenly found herself lifted in the air and deposited onto her back. Her soft bed jiggled beneath her. It was like being made love to—fucked—upon a cloud.

Heath yanked his trousers down, displaying his remarkable, rigid, enormous cock to her. Aroused beyond belief, she reached out and touched. She stroked his chest, let her hands coast over his tight waist, his flat, hard stomach. She caressed the flares of his hipbones, stroked his deeply indented haunches. His cock stood tall, pointing to the ceiling. Evidence he wanted this as much as she.

She grabbed his hips and tried to pull him down to her.

With a smile that made her heart flutter, he gripped his cock in hand and lowered between her legs. One long, confident thrust took him inside her. "Ooooh." It was a long moan of pleasure. She'd been slick from her orgasm; she was now even creamier from lusting for *this*.

He took control. It astonished her how she wanted him to. With Heath, she had no fear, no fierce need to resist as he captured her wrists and held them above her head. He moved so smoothly in her, so controlled, it was like heaven. He stirred her tight, wet cunny with his massive cock. She wrapped her legs around him, determined to keep him inside her forever.

He thrust deep, the head of his thick member nudging the entrance to her womb. And each push gave her a jolt of pure pleasure.

"This . . ." Her voice died. Her legs were entwined around him, sitting above those delicious hips of his.

"This is my hard cock filling you," he rasped. "This is me driving deep into you. This is pleasure and sin. This is what being a demon is all about, my love."

"Yes," she whispered. She savored the lovely, slick kissing sound as his groin collided with hers. He was moaning, too, breathing hard with his thrusts. The bed groaned beneath them, the canopy swayed. She'd never had a man move so fiercely in bed, thrust so hard. He was almost lifting the bed off its legs.

And she loved it. Heath didn't scare her—not even when he was wild with lust and hungering to fuck hard. He braced himself over her, thrust deeply in without hurting her. He wanted it to be good for her. He looked after her, even as he drove madly to pleasure.

Her cunny was tugging at him, tightening around him. Tension built inside her.

Her eyes opened wide. Something heavenly burst inside her. Her fingers clutched his. Her back arched. She came with such intensity she had to scream, "Heath. Heath. Heath!"

"God yes, Vivi. Come for me. Come around me. Grip my cock and squeeze him tight."

She had to giggle, even while gasping for breath.

He laughed with her, a sharp, curt sound. Then his head bowed suddenly and his body shuddered. And he came, too.

With her.

She could barely savor his ecstasy for the wonderful waves

of *her* pleasure. He held himself above her, and she watched the fierce agony on his face.

He gave a low, harsh groan. "Vivienne, love . . . it's never been like this."

And he captured her mouth with his, kissing her deeply, kissing her with a passion she'd never known before.

Damn, he was hungry.

Heath paced in the dark, fighting his hunger for blood and listening to Vivienne sleep. Her breathing was soft and relaxed. Making love to her had worked; his explosive orgasm had satisfied her need for a man's pleasure.

Too bad it could never happen between them again.

All he had to do was open her window and he could fly anywhere he wanted. It would be easy to find an unsuspecting mortal and slake his thirst for blood.

He could hear the heartbeat of everyone in the house. It was a constant, rhythmic sound. It was temptation. If he was at home he could use some of his other sources of blood. He acquired animal blood from the slaughterhouses.

He should have drunk blood while he had taken Vivienne to his library. If he tried to push himself much longer, he'd break.

Through the window, he spied a dark shape. It flew across the night sky, soared over the roof of Vivienne's house.

Heath left the window. It was Julian.

6

She truly was a succubus.

Vivienne sat up in her bed. Moonlight crept into her room where her curtains didn't meet. She could see the gleam of her white escritoire, the curved shapes of two chairs drawn by the fireplace. Her bedroom looked blessedly normal. And she was not.

Last night, she had been in pain and terrified. She'd been consumed with the need to have sex with Heath. She had been determined to bed him. Even if she'd had to tear his trousers off and . . . and force him.

Fortunately, he'd been willing.

Sex had made the pain go away. It had banished the cold. Did that mean she could actually die if she didn't have sex? Why had she never felt such pain before? How could she be a succubus and not know about it?

Vivienne sobbed softly in the dark.

Heath had told her he didn't know what this meant for Sarah. What if Sarah was so sick because she was a succubus, too? Or a half succubus, if there could be such a thing? Sarah's father had been a vicious brute of a man, a fact Vivienne had never told her daughter, but he had been human, despite his cruel behavior.

Sarah was eighteen. She had been seventeen when she bore Sarah. Everything Vivienne had done had been to ensure her daughter never had to endure the risks and horrors she had. She had been determined Sarah would never have to sell her body for survival.

But what if Sarah was like her? What if Sarah had to sleep with men to keep herself alive?

There was only one person she could turn to for answers. And he had already left her bed.

Low masculine voices spoke outside her partially open bedroom door. Heath. And he was speaking to another man. Drawing on her robe, she opened the door to see Heath stalk across the hall to Julian, grasp the younger man's chin, and forcefully turn his face.

Vivienne swallowed a gasp. Julian's lips were stained red with blood. And a small rivulet of it dripped from his mouth.

"You fed," Heath said flatly.

Julian pushed the hand away. He adjusted his clothing. She knew the gesture: his pride was insulted, and he was now posturing against Heath's obvious dominance. "I'm a vampire. I don't intend to starve myself like you do."

She gasped slightly. She had not seen Heath bite anyone. Vampires were supposed to drink blood. But Heath had not bitten her. Or Sarah.

"Who did you feed from?" he snapped at Julian. "Did you leave them living or dead?"

She didn't understand. If he himself was a vampire, why did he sound so angry?

Suddenly, Heath roared, grabbed Julian by the shoulder, and hauled the younger man across the hallway. As she stared, confused and shocked, the window at the end of her hallway exploded. Her drapes flew inward, torn off their rod, and shards of glass rained down on the floor.

Somehow Heath had known her window was going to shatter, and he'd pulled Julian to safety. Now he spun toward her. He crossed to her so swiftly, she didn't see him move. "Get back into your bedroom," he commanded, "And lock your damn door."

"Why?" She didn't just take orders—

Some sort of black liquid was pouring in the window. Then the fluid split apart and she could see what it was. Bats. Hundreds of them. Their wings thundered as they whipped in through the broken window and raced down the hallway toward her and Heath.

What was happening? She had to get Sarah out of the house—

But Heath's hands clamped down on her shoulders and she couldn't run. "Go into your room. Sarah will be safe in hers. I can fight them off."

"Good heavens, how?"

He pushed her back and stepped toward the flapping mass of bats. They circled him. "They want *me*," he shouted to her over the buzzing sound of their wings beating. "I've been summoned. You will be safe. I have to go. I have to make sure the council doesn't know what you are—"

Then the small black bodies whirled faster around Heath, until she could no longer see him. The bats suddenly turned and streamed out of the broken window. And Heath was gone, too.

She ran toward the window, but firm hands caught her shoulders and pulled her back. She stared up into the silvery eyes of the blond man called Julian. "Glass, Miss Dare. You would cut your feet."

She looked down at the shards that could have sliced her

soles to ribbons. But she didn't care about that. "What happened to Heath? Where did he go?"

"The bats took him. He's been summoned by the vampire council."

"Vampire council?" she repeated, her voice squeaking in disbelief. "A council of vampires sent hundreds of bats to . . . to fetch him?"

Julian nodded. "Of course. That's how they do it."

But she could see fear in Julian's face. "What's wrong? Is he in danger?"

"He could be. The council wants to destroy him because of his curse."

Her wits were whirling. Curse? The curse of being a vampire? "Destroy him?" she echoed weakly. "He is . . . an immortal vampire."

"We can be destroyed," Julian said.

She felt sick. What would Sarah do if he didn't return? She needed more of his blood.

Another fear, one Vivienne did not want to face, burned in her heart. She didn't want to think of Heath in danger. She didn't want to think he might be *destroyed*.

She knew this sensation. The way her stomach plummeted. The hard, sharp pain about her heart. She was beginning to care about Heath.

She knew nothing about him. Other than the mad fact that he was a vampire, and she was a demoness. Somehow, amidst all this madness and horror, she was opening her heart, when she had promised she would never be like her mother and ruin Sarah's life by chasing after a man's love. She had vowed she would love no one but her daughter.

"We must rescue him."

Julian shook his head. "Impossible. No one can break out of the vampire council's mansion. We just have to wait—and see if he survives."

* * *

Propelled by an army of bats, Heath fell into the foyer of the quiet mansion at No. 10 Curzon Street. His knees cracked against the marble floor. His lungs heaved for breath. The bats had forced him to shape shift into his winged form to fly, then had herded him here with bites and scratches.

There was no doubt he was in trouble.

When had he not been in trouble with the blasted council? What frightened him more was that Vivienne and her daughter were now unprotected, unless he could trust Julian to take care of them.

The door closed smoothly behind him, and Hopkins, Lord Adder's correct butler, stepped forward. Nothing fazed Hopkins. Not even the sudden appearance of a naked earl in the middle of the foyer. The butler held out a robe of black silk. "The council awaits, my lord. If you will be so good as to follow me."

Heath barked a laugh. "As if I have a choice, Hopkins." Hopkins had served Adder—and remained mortal—for fifteen years. "Why have you not run screaming years ago, Hopkins?" he asked, more to torment the staid man than for any expectation of an answer.

"My position is very satisfactory, my lord." The butler's shoes echoed in the enormous foyer as he began to lead the way. "I am most humbled by your condescension of an inquiry."

Heath shrugged on the robe and followed. Adder was not a peer of the realm, but had fashioned himself as a "lord" in the vampire world. All six members of the council had taken the title. At a double door decorated with gilt, Hopkins stopped abruptly. "In here, my lord."

Heath lifted a brow. "Not the usual council chamber?"

"Not tonight, my lord." The butler retreated into shadow,

but Heath could see fear on the man's face. He'd never seen any emotion crack the blank surface of Hopkins's face.

Inside, Heath rolled his eyes at the sight facing him. A star had been drawn in blood upon the floor; a pentagram made up its core. A large gold bowl sat in the middle of the pentagram. It held silvery water, flat as a mirror.

"What do you want? To slap me on my arse for not finding you a villainess yet?"

He never walked in here without insolence on his lips. It wasn't that he hated these men for the fact they planned to destroy him. That would be one of the mercies of his life. He hated them because they intended to kill his brother.

The vampire council sat in large, thronelike chairs arranged in a semicircle around the pentagram. He sauntered toward them. He might look unimpressed by them, but he was wary inside.

"Lord Blackmoor."

Adder was the one to address him. He considered himself to be their leader. All six vampires wore black cloaks, with hoods over the heads shrouding their faces. Adder pushed back his hood to reveal his harsh features—the sharp cheekbones, a blade of a nose, large chin. Black eyes that didn't reflect light like other vampires' eyes but sucked it in. His coal-black hair reflected the candlelight; it was slicked back with pomade.

Adder's voice was a cold slice through the stillness of the room. "You have found her. Last night, we convinced Julian to do his duty to us."

"Convinced?" Heath lifted a brow.

"All right. Tortured. Julian informed us that you have found a courtesan who is also a succubus, who is the woman who drained the souls of the five peers. But you have not brought her to us."

"I have no evidence yet that she is responsible for those men's deaths."

"She had sexual intercourse with them, and she is a succubus."

"This is England, gents." Heath tried to control his anger. No matter what, Vivienne *was* innocent. She hadn't even known what she was. "We don't condemn people without a trial and evidence. I repeat—slowly, so you won't miss it this time—I have no proof. Yes, she took the men as lovers. But I know for a fact she was not with Lord Cavendish when he died. Normally when a succubus kills a man, it is because she has completely drained him during sex. My theory is the succubus is innocent and someone else is the killer."

Adder's hands tightened on the curved arms of his throne. "You know nothing. It is not your place to make theories. The woman is a tool for a stronger power. Your duty is to bring her to us."

Stronger power? Hell, could it be Nikolai? "Not to have her killed without a chance to defend herself."

"We do not intend to kill her. We intend to find out the truth. We must find out what entity controls her."

"She doesn't know. She can't tell you anything."

Adder surged from his chair. "Of course she knows," he spat. "But you have not forced her to reveal anything. You were too busy having intimate relations with her yourself." He lifted a wand from the arm of his chair and waved it.

The water in the gold bowl rippled, like the water in the Dartmoor pool had done. Then scenes of his night of lovemaking with Vivienne flashed upon its surface.

Damn these men. They'd had no right to watch something so intimate.

But Heath couldn't stop looking at Vivienne. In the silver water, he watched her move beneath him, thrusting up along his throbbing erection, her breasts squashed against his chest. He saw her long, naked legs wrap around his waist. He saw her lift to him and arch in her climax.

God, she was exquisitely beautiful.

And of course he got a ruddy erection in front of the council. Fortunately he had the robe on. He heard the mutterings from the council. He heard chairs creak as the vampires responded to the sight of a nude, beautiful, unfettered Vivienne.

That was it. He was going to dump out their bowl of magic water and stop the voyeurism.

But before he could take a step, she moaned huskily in the image, and her eyes opened wide. She was looking at him, but he was climaxing and his eyes were shut. Her eyes shone for him.

She looked dazzled by him.

Stalking to an unlit candelabra, Heath yanked out one of the candles. He threw it into the pool. The splash and ensuing ripples destroyed the surface, and the erotic image disappeared.

He glowered at Adder, who must have arranged for the spying pool. "You had no right to watch her like that."

Adder gave a mocking smile. "If you had obeyed, we would not have to."

Heath could guess what was to follow. The damn council would use someone else to capture her. . . .

Christ. Now he saw exactly why he was here. They had used the bats to get him away from Vivienne and had sent someone else to take her. Possibly Julian.

Which meant he had to get the hell out of here and back to Vivienne.

He closed his eyes and shape shifted. It was like catching fire from the inside out. His body stretched, twisted, and shrank, all in the space of a heartbeat. His scream roared out to the council. Then it was done. He stretched out his wings. Large wings, for he became a flying creature like a big bat.

He beat them fiercely and lifted to the ceiling. The curved panes of glass of the skylight beckoned; he could see stars beyond. He headed straight for the glass at full speed and exploded through it. Shards ripped into his body. His blood began to flow.

No other vampire should have been able to break through the glass. It was one of the advantages to having as his sire one of the oldest and most powerful of the undead.

Heath heard the cries of fury below him, but he tipped his wings on a current of air blowing off the Thames and swooped toward Vivienne's home.

7

"Drink this."

The harsh, cold command broke through Vivienne's grogginess. She forced her eyelids to open. Faint light illuminated a beautiful face. A woman, a stranger with pale blond hair and black eyes, leaned close to her. The woman grasped her chin, shoved her head back with cruel force, and roughly pried her mouth open.

Vivienne struggled, but the woman's grip was too strong. She tried to lift her hands, to shove the vile drink away, but her arms would only move an inch, and chains rattled, mocking her. Her limbs had been spread out and secured to a narrow cot. A velvet blanket lay over her body, but beneath the cover she was nude.

"No," she croaked, but the fingers relentlessly held her mouth open and fluid splashed on her tongue. She desperately tried to spit it out. But she couldn't. It was too thick, and it slithered down.

She shuddered. The taste was horrible, and it made her throat burn.

Where was Sarah? Was Sarah safe?

Desperately, she tried to ask about her daughter. But she could only manage to gasp, "Sar—" before her voice failed. She'd screamed and yelled for so long now she couldn't even whisper through her dry throat.

How long had she been here, held captive? Hours? Or days? Everything was a jumbled mess in her head.

There had been a man in a hooded black cape. He had been inside her *house*. She'd tried to run from him, but suddenly he had appeared in front of her. And within the flapping circle of his hood he'd had no face. There was just a black void where his face should have been. Then he'd grabbed her arms.

She had screamed in panic. All her noise had finally dragged Sarah from a deep sleep. Julian had been fighting the remaining bats to protect her, but a group of cloaked men had burst into her house. Three had swarmed Julian, hitting him. Julian had collapsed; his body had suddenly stopped moving. His silvery eyes had stared blankly up.

She'd struggled wildly, screamed at Sarah to run. But it had been too late. The faceless men had caught them, brought them here, threw them in a dungeon. . . .

She couldn't stand this. She should be there for Sarah, to protect her. She wanted to hold her daughter.

And Heath. Heath must be dead, too, just like Julian.

Tears leaked. The thought of Heath gone made her heart clench, made her feel empty inside. But it was wrong. *Sarah* had to be the only person she cared about. . . .

The burning began seconds later. It flared up in her tummy, then raced down to her quim. Vivienne pulled against the metal cuffs but she couldn't break free. What was happening to her? Sweat prickled her skin beneath the velvet cover. Her skin began to tingle. To feel aware. She took deep breaths. Tension coiled low in her belly. Her cunny began to feel hot and it throbbed, like a second heartbeat. She writhed on the bed. Her quim seemed to explode, raging into fiery, intense sexual desire.

She knew what would quench the need. A man's thick erection, sliding in and out of her. Thrusting deep and hard and slow, just the way Heath made love . . .

God, what was she thinking? She had to get free. But she couldn't reach the shackles on her wrists and ankles. She could barely move. And now she couldn't think. . . .

Of anything except making love to Heath. She closed her eyes, moaning breathlessly. He looked so gorgeous when he was on top of her. When he was driving in hard, kissing her womb with his cock, then pulling back.

She'd loved the way he'd panted when he thrust inside her. Loved everything about his fucking. The thickness of his cock. The rough, raw sound of his grunts. The droplets of his sweat falling to her breasts . . .

"Interesting. That potion should not have taken effect for half an hour. Yet, on you, it has done so already."

Blearily, Vivienne tried to focus on the voice. She tried to stop thinking of Heath on top of her, Heath *coming* in her. But it was so hard to think of anything else. . . .

Dear heaven, there was a man standing over her, and all she could think of was sex—sex with beautiful Heath. But this man . . . she could smell the evil in him. He was danger.

She twisted around on the cot, trying to find him. . . .

There. He paced around her slowly, his hand on his chin. Then he smiled down at her. His black hair was slick against his head, gleaming in the faint candlelight. He possessed a large, beaklike nose. Dark pools for eyes. His lips curled up again, into a hard, cruel leer.

The uncontrollable desire in her cooled at once. Fear took its place.

"Now, Miss Dare, we must release you and take you to the

altar room. You are very beautiful. I anticipate this will be the most arousing sexual experience of my existence."

His evil, gloating gaze felt like a thousand crawling, slithering things on her skin. "No!" Pain shot through her throat as she yelled, but her fear and loathing gave her strength. She would *not* let him do this. She would not let him touch her.

Not after Heath had touched her so beautifully. Not after he'd shown her what it was like to be caressed by a true gentleman: a man who could care, who had compassion, who had saved both her and Sarah.

She would fight. Kick, scream, bite, scratch. She would never let this man defile her.

Even if she died.

Was he too late?

Heath soared over the outskirts of Mayfair, above the houses, the crush of carriages on the streets, the glittering lights of the demimonde's parties.

He wasn't strong enough to face the worst. To find Vivienne . . . dead. And Sarah . . . Hell, he could not face being too late to save an innocent child. Not again. He could barely remember his daughter's face. *Meredith.*

He'd forced himself to forget her at first. It was his punishment. He'd been so angry at what he'd done. He told himself he had no right to console himself with memories of her smiles and laughter.

He couldn't face failing a young girl and a beautiful, courageous woman again.

Somehow, just by making love to him once, Vivienne had made his heart ache again. Her allure had thrown him right back into the terror of love.

Heath swooped to her house and soared through the broken window. The pain of his shape shift screamed through him, then he stood naked in the moonlight, in her hallway. "Vivienne?" he shouted. His voice echoed through still darkness.

He didn't sense anyone here. He sensed the slow breathing of her servants; the council must have taken control of their minds, throwing them into a deep sleep. And he didn't sense Julian anywhere.

He reached Vivienne's bedroom before his next heartbeat. Her sheets straggled across the floor. Her wardrobe had fallen. Her counterpane was in shreds and feathers from her mattress fluttered everywhere. The bats had ripped everything apart.

Sarah.

He rushed to the girl's room, threw open the door. The bedroom was in shambles, too. Lace-edged bedcovers were pulled from the bed, the furniture tossed on its sides.

All Heath could hear was the loud, anguished thunder of his heart.

And he could smell blood in the air. Now his heart slammed in his chest. He spied small splatters of blood on the floor. It had to be Sarah's. It meant she'd been cut, but not badly.

Bending close to the spots, he breathed in the unique scent of them. Giving his blood to Sarah had bonded him, like a parent to a child. Already he could begin to feel Sarah's presence in his thoughts. He could see her. She was balled up on a cold floor. Her fear became a weight on his heart, an acrid burn on his tongue. She was surrounded by darkness, but he could see into it. He knew where she was: in one of the cells beneath the vampire council's mansion.

If Sarah was there, Vivienne must be. He had to rescue them both before they were hurt. Or worse.

Torches flickered outside the grand steps to the council's building. Stone gargoyles snarled along the roof edge. The dozens of paned windows above looked dark, soulless, empty, but Heath suspected the six vampires were within, along with a hundred servants. Breaking in to get to Vivienne would prove interesting.

Vivienne's natural perfume was erotically spicy—cinnamon, jasmine, the mysterious scents of the East. Sarah smelled like daisies. He could detect both scents in the house.

Flapping his large wings, he hovered over the council's mansion. Vampire servants would be guarding the windows on the inside. The doors were locked, barricaded. The skylight he'd broken had already been repaired, and the council had reinforced it on the inside with metal bands.

He needed to find a weakness. He retreated, then circled again. His wings rippled as he soared around the large, Georgian house. He stayed far away so he wouldn't awaken the instincts of the vampires inside, making them recognize a threat.

What in blazes are you planning to do, Heath? She's inside there, but they'll detect you before you get close.

Julian's voice sliced into his thoughts. Heath spun on a current of air and saw the younger vampire in his winged form. He swooped at Julian, his fangs bared, forcing the younger vampire into a dangerous descent to evade him. *Fly away, Julian, before I rip you apart. You led them to Vivienne. You let them take her and Sarah.*

Julian retreated. *I didn't. They almost destroyed me trying to get to the women. I barely survived.*

You work for the council. I saw the spots of Sarah's blood on her floor, which means she was hurt—

I'm going to help you, Blackmoor, whether you want it or not.

Julian suddenly wheeled in the air and flew toward the house. His, lithe, black shape passed the windows, turned, then swooped again. A window flew up and shrieking bats raced out. They dove after Julian, who spun in the air to evade them. Julian had lured the guard bats away. Heath swooped to the roof and flew straight down the chimney.

Streams of smoke flowed up, choking him, and soot fell on him. He carved out of the hearth at full speed, shooting over a fire. Flames licked at his belly, but he made it out unscathed. He landed and transformed in the hot, deserted kitchen.

He knew Julian could fly faster than the bats and escape them. Julian must want to make amends for betraying Vivienne and Sarah.

He smelled daisies. A faint trace wafted through the basement. He could breathe it through the stone walls, and he took off in a preternatural sprint.

He tore through narrow hallways. Down a winding set of stairs. He ran so swiftly past the mortal servants who toiled down here that they couldn't see him. He had to knock out two beefy men at the mouth of a pitch-black hallway, the corridor to the cells. Both muscle-bound vampires dropped with a thud. Cautiously Heath stepped into the entrance. The corridor was the width of his shoulders and arched, formed of brick. At its end, he found a wall of inch-thick iron bars.

Those only slowed him down for a couple of minutes. After tearing them apart, he stepped through the twisted wreckage. He now stood in a large, empty circular space. And paused.

Then he ducked.

An ax blade slammed into the brick above his head, sending dust raining down on him. With lightning speed, Heath grasped the handle of the ax and tore it out of the hands of the vampire who had tried to behead him.

A kick sent his attacker sprawling on the ground and gave Heath a second to look over his foe. The vampire was seven feet tall, with a body the size of an ox. He wore a monk's brown robe and his fallen legs looked like felled trees.

Heath somersaulted in the air, gripping the ax handle tightly, and he flew over the vampire. His bare feet slammed onto sharp flagstones just as the guard launched to his feet. Any beast with sense should run, once he'd lost his weapon. But this vampire had to know the price of failing the council. Boiling in oil. Burning at the stake. Being drawn and quartered by the bats. Nothing merciful for the council.

The vampire roared, fangs bared. Heath held up the ax. "Unwise," he pointed out. "Don't move."

But the beast did. And Heath didn't have time to waste in a fight. . . .

The vampire pulled out a silver dagger and plunged it toward Heath's heart. Heath blocked the blow with the hand of the ax. He couldn't bring himself to slice off the vampire's head.

The vampire pulled weapon after weapon from his robes. Two more daggers. A throwing star. Heath disarmed him with blows from the wooden handle. But he was tiring. And the other vampire was strong.

The vampire launched forward with two small knives. Heath lifted the ax; the vampire slammed directly into it, burying the blade into his chest. A wound like that should only slow such a huge vampire, but Heath watched as the guard slithered to his knees and fell face down. The prone body suddenly shuddered, jerked, then exploded into dust.

So it was an enchanted ax.

All that remained of the guard was his robe. Heath fished the ring of cell keys out of a pocket.

Seven hallways lead from the circular entry, but he could smell daisies from the middle one.

Sarah was huddled in the far corner, a dark blanket wrapped around her. One blond curl stuck above the gray wool and one toe peeked out at the bottom. He could see the torn hem of her now filthy nightgown.

Damn the council. He would rip Adder apart when he found him.

"Sarah?" He inserted three keys before finding the right one. The iron door swung open without a sound. With a squeak of terror, the poor girl huddled the blanket closer.

"It's all right, love. I'm here to take you home."

The blanket shifted. In the dark, he could see Sarah's face pressed against a small opening, one large blue-green eye blinking. "M-my lord?" she whispered.

It speared him. She sounded so much like Meredith. . . . He shook his head. This wasn't his daughter—and he was about to save Sarah, not helplessly watch her die. "Yes, it's Blackmoor," he answered softly. "Can you stand up?"

A sniffle came. "I can't. My legs won't move. They—they're numb."

He couldn't scent blood but he asked, "Are you injured? Did they hurt you?"

"N—no."

"Did they hurt your mother?"

"No, but cloaked men took her away. For a ceremony, they said."

A ceremony. He got on his knees in front of Sarah and pushed the blanket back from her. Too late, he remembered he'd left his clothes behind when he changed shape.

Sarah's eyes went wide at the sight of his bare chest. She gave a horrified squeak and scuttled backward. Loathing rushed through Heath's heart. Sarah was afraid of him. Which must mean some of Vivi's protectors had given the girl reason to be afraid. Had Vivienne quit her life as a courtesan to protect Sarah, only to be forced to seduce men for that damn medicine?

"I won't hurt you. I had to shed my clothes to come and get you. Watch." His muscles jerked and twisted, his bones expanded, his wings grew out on his back. He changed form, lightly moving his wings to hover. Then he changed back.

Sarah's eyes were wide with fascination now, not fear. "He said you could do that."

"Who, Angel?"

She gave a wavering smile. "Julian. He showed me that, too. When I was afraid. He told me he would make sure no one hurt me. But then these men appeared and they began to hit him. I tried to stop them, but then they hit me. I must have . . . passed out, for I don't remember anything else until I woke up in a cart. Mama and I were being brought here."

She tried to lift her hand to him, but it dropped listlessly.

He needed to give her his blood. He sliced his wrist with one fang. Sarah immediately shuffled toward him, drawn by the scent of his blood. He gathered her into his arms. She weighed so little, and she flopped against him. He pressed his wrist to her lips. "Drink this while we fetch your mother."

Sarah drank a little, then pulled away from his wrist. "Do you think the cloaked men . . . hurt her?" she whispered.

Where would she be? The council chambers or a bedroom?

Heath crept up the servants' stairs, clutching Sarah against his chest. After she'd taken his blood, she'd grown stronger. Her arms were firmly wrapped around his neck. Her heart raced fearfully.

"The men looked like monsters. They had black cloaks and . . . and no faces. They told her they would hurt me if she didn't obey them."

The men of the council. What did they want from Vivienne? And of course the bastards would use her innocent daughter as leverage.

Heath knew Vivienne's smell. But they hadn't become bonded by blood so he could not connect to her thoughts. He had to stumble around as blind as a mortal man.

Torches flickered along the walls of the council room, but it was empty. The whole blasted building appeared to be empty. All one hundred rooms. He should have encountered someone—a servant at least. Either a mortal one or a vampire. So what in blazes was going on? He prayed it didn't mean they were all watching Adder do dastardly things to Vivienne.

Footsteps sounded in the corridor. Someone running. Heath put Sarah on the ground. Her legs swayed, and he caught her.

"I don't know what's wrong," she whimpered. "Why does my body feel so weak again?"

"I think you've been drugged. My blood is battling with its effects."

"Drugged?" Her eyes opened into large, blue-green circles. "They forced me to take a drink."

He pulled Sarah into the room beside them and closed the door so only a crack remained. The footsteps stopped. It was a vampire: Heath smelled the alluring scent the Nosferatu used to tempt mortals. Then he smelled French cologne.

Hades. He stalked forward to the door, opened it, and dragged a naked Julian inside. Small scratch marks covered Julian's muscular, bronzed skin. The cuts were slowly vanishing. "You escaped."

Julian scowled down at his wounds. "I wanted to help. Self-sacrifice wasn't my plan, though."

"Goodness." The bubbly little whisper came from Sarah. She was smiling now and hiccuping, like a lady who'd had too much ratafia. Her gaze raked over Julian from his blond hair to his naked feet.

Julian's eyes widened. "What did you do to her? She looks . . . drunk."

"I didn't do anything. The damn council did. They drugged her and locked her in a cell. I let her drink some of my blood. Its effects, combined with the drug, have done this to her. Can I trust you to carry her? I need you to stay with me and bring Sarah, but I need to get to Miss Dare."

Julian nodded. "When the council attacked us at Miss Dare's house, I overheard two of them talking about some kind of ceremony—they needed Miss Dare for it."

A black magic ritual, Heath guessed. "I'm afraid whatever they want to do involves a bed," he said softly.

"Ow!" Sarah cried.

Heath smelled blood and his fangs exploded as he swung around. Sarah had dropped to one knee, cradling her bare right foot. She winced and looked white as a sheet. "I cut it."

Heath bent to look. She'd stepped on a small stone, a shiny, sharp-edged black one. "Here." He lifted her foot and gently kissed the wound. The touch of his mouth healed it.

"Take care of her, Julian." His voice was raw. He remembered kissing his daughter's fingers when she'd cut them. He would whisper, *Now all the pain is gone, because I've taken it away. I've made it better.*

Sarah giggled softly as the lad scooped her up. But as soon as Julian settled her against his body, his cock stood up. Heath stalked over and clasped his shoulder. "Don't even think about a seduction." But when he looked down at Sarah, who suddenly appeared as seductive and sensual as her mother, Heath realized she was older than he'd thought. At least eighteen.

Julian shook his head. In a low voice, he said, "Blackmoor, every time anything touches my skin—even a breeze—I get erect. I thought it was part of being a vampire."

Especially one who'd changed at two-and-twenty. "Just . . . keep her safe."

Heath led the way down the corridor, with Julian behind him carrying Sarah, searching for the next set of back stairs. The council kept a room for "sacred" rituals, one with a stone altar in the middle of it, where sacrifices took place. A gallery ran around it for spectators to watch the gory ceremonies. It would be his best way in.

He refused to listen to the nagging voice in his head that warned him he was already too late.

To Heath's surprise, the gallery was empty. It was a mezzanine that encircled the room and overlooked the stone altar.

Below, the council members stood in two lines on either side of the large dais. Dozens of vampires stood and watched.

But it was what he saw on the altar that twisted Heath's heart.

Vivienne lay on the raised dais, nude. Her arms were bound together at her wrists, her ankles tied to metal rings set on the stone. Limned by the light of dozens of candles, her hair spilled around her head like waves of flame. Heath could feel her fear. And something else that amazed him: her fury.

God, this woman astounded him. His wife's quiet strength had always humbled him. Vivienne was an entirely different woman, and she possessed as much, if not more, courage and strength.

Which meant he wasn't worthy of her.

Good thing he knew he couldn't have her.

Now, he had to get her free—by defeating the six powerful vampires of the council, their minions, and their attack bats.

There was paint on Vivienne's body. Designs had been drawn on her skin. Painted flowers adorned her breasts. Curling vines traveled down her smooth, curved belly. Numbers were painted on her arms and legs.

One of the members of the vampire council, his face hidden by his hood, stepped forward. "Lord Adder, it is time to give the demonstration you promised us."

Adder waved a hand with smug arrogance. "Patience. All must be done as described in the great book." He snapped his fingers and a footman, dressed in gold and black livery, brought a chalice to him. The vampire leader took the silver cup and drank deeply.

The footman retrieved it and scurried away.

Adder ripped off his cloak, revealing a powerful, naked body. The other vampires began chanting.

Damn it to hell. How did he free Vivienne? If his attempt was unsuccessful, he would be destroyed—and Vivienne would be left to Adder's cruelty.

8

Vivienne fought in vain against the ropes binding her ankles. The smooth, stone altar was covered in velvet, soft and cushioning beneath her, but she was tied up, like a sacrifice in a horrid novel.

She felt furious at her nakedness, so angry she could almost forget to be afraid.

Candles flickered as the vampire who called himself Adder dropped his cloak, exposing his nakedness. He had exactly the sort of male body she hated. One that spoke of power, dominance, the ability to inflict pain. Thick muscles, an oxlike chest, and big shoulders.

A whimper escaped her. Instinct warned her he did not intend to let her go.

"You are the one," he said softly. "You were made to be the ultimate weapon against men." He leered at her, then his eyes gleamed with zeal and horrible arousal. "What I take from you will make me as powerful as a god."

She wanted to vomit.

She wasn't a weapon. How could she be? She was strapped to a stone table and powerless.

But that's what the woman had told her, the woman who had painted all the designs on her while four men had held her down. That she was the most powerful of her kind. That her voluptuous body had been made to tempt men and lure them to their deaths. That she'd been made like this—curvaceous and pretty—to be evil.

Adder grinned as he approached. She couldn't bear to look down at his thick erection, red-tipped, a true beast. He moved with pride, obviously impressed with the clublike thing between his thighs.

She couldn't let this monster win.

She could buck and try to fight. Bite him. But she knew in her soul that she wasn't going to escape.

I'm so sorry, Sarah. She'd seen what was on the pedestal beside the one that held the cup. A dagger, with shining blade and silver handle. She was going to die tied up and naked, because she was some kind of monster. . . .

Think, Vivienne. It didn't matter what she was. She was all Sarah had.

The men in the room began chanting. It was a horrible, mournful sound. Adder grinned evilly, then bent and kissed the toes of her right foot. She tried to jerk away. But she couldn't, and he moved to her left foot and suckled. His gentle touch was a lie. She could see the gloating anticipation in his silvery eyes. He held his cock within his right fist, slowly working his hand up and down the thick shaft. He murmured words, soft words that flowed in her head and took control of her.

Then she knew the truth of this nightmare. The drink she'd been given. The incantation Adder was speaking. The words fired up the horrible, uncontrollable lust the drink had caused.

"Don't touch me." She had to force the words out. "I'll kill you just as I've killed many, many other men." It was an empty threat. If she had actually killed men, she had no idea how she'd done it.

Adder held up one of his enormous hands. She'd seen bears in a menagerie, and his hands were bigger than those beasts' paws. The chanting stopped. His thick lips curved into an ugly smile. "Those were mortal men. You let Lord Blackmoor pound himself into you, and it didn't touch him at all. It won't hurt me, for I am undead."

He knew. Knew she had been Heath's lover. But how could he know? Had Heath been tortured to tell? Or was it worse—had he betrayed her? Had he not been "captured" after all? Maybe he hadn't been destroyed. Perhaps he didn't give a fig for her or Sarah because he still believed she had hurt his brother—

"I wouldn't do that if I were you, Adder." Cool, deep, Heath's voice cut through the silence in the room.

Standing at the foot of the altar, the naked council leader spun around. Heath stepped out of the shadows, bathed in gold from the torches. Equally naked. But utterly, devastatingly beautiful as he moved.

The rush of relief, of hope, left her dizzy. He wasn't destroyed. He hadn't betrayed her. Instead, he'd come back to rescue her. Again, when no other man had ever rescued her.

Her heart stuttered. Soared. Then plunged in fear again. Obviously he carried no weapons. All he had were his body and his strength. But armed men surrounded him, servants of the vampire council. He would be killed. In front of her. For her. And she could do nothing.

Adder turned, obviously aroused by the chance to hurt Heath, for he was even more erect. "Seize him," he roared. And of course, all the servants pulled out blades. Six rushed toward Heath.

Heath lifted his hands as though preparing to attack. The men flew back as though knocked over by an invisible wave.

She gaped at him . . . and saw the stunned shock on his face as he stared at his hands. More servants charged, but he lifted his hands again and they flew back, too.

Adder jumped off the stairs, and she knew exactly where the fiend was running.

"Heath!" Her words sounded like a mere whisper to her, but his gaze locked on her. "There's a knife. On the pedestal."

Adder leaped through the air to the pedestal. He snatched up the blade, but at the exact instant he started to run toward her, Heath held up his palms again and Adder screamed and flew back. His back slammed into the wall. The knife clattered to the floor. Then, as if controlled by magic, the knife rose, sailed through the air, and landed safely in Heath's outstretched hands.

In a heartbeat, Heath was at her side. He sliced the ropes that bound her arms. His hands brushed against her bare wrists and set her aflame.

"H—how did you do that?" She could barely hear her voice, but Heath gently lifted her, helping her sit up.

"I have no idea. I've never done it before." He flashed a broad grin. It was filled with wickedness, exactly like the delicious smile he'd worn when he'd watched her come. . . .

"Sarah?" she whispered.

"I've already got her out of the cell, Miss Dare. She is safe with Julian. Let's use this astounding new skill of mine to get us out of here."

He sliced through the ropes at her ankles in seconds. Blearily she saw the room spin around her as he lifted her into his arms. The vampires were picking themselves up off the floor. But Heath cradled her with one strong arm and used his power to send the vampires tumbling like skittles again. The tall, terrifying vampires tried to stagger forward, but Heath sent them back with another blast.

Then the room seemed to rush at her at top speed and everything blurred around her. Heath was racing so fast she couldn't see. And when he stopped, she almost fell out of his arms. He set her on her feet. And Sarah was standing right in front of her.

Tears fell to Vivienne's cheeks and rolled down. She ran to her daughter and buried her face in Sarah's tangled curls.

She owed Heath so very, very much. How could she ever repay him? Dear heaven, she didn't care that he was a vampire. He was the most wonderful man she'd ever known.

Heath had no idea what had happened. Where this power had come from, or how he'd controlled it. The first time he'd put up his hand, he'd willed the servants to go back, and suddenly they'd been flying through the air.

He didn't have time for speculation. They were in a parlor, one ornately decorated in an Eastern style. He hated to break up the embrace between Vivienne and her daughter, but he had no choice. "We have to hurry, ladies. We've got to get out of here."

Sarah pulled away from her mother. And her blanket, which she'd clutched around her, fell to the ground. Her night rail, torn and dirty, hung on her slim body. She shivered. She stooped. "Mama, you should have the blanket."

But Vivienne, still naked, swept it up and wrapped it around Sarah. Heath swallowed hard. He could barely tear his gaze from Vivienne as she moved. He'd never seen a more enticing woman. Her large breasts swayed, her belly had a beautiful, lush curve, and her derriere—

He was supposed to be saving them. Not admiring the generous globes of Miss Dare's rump.

"Hold on to it, Sarah," she whispered. "You've nothing but your nightgown, and that's torn into shreds. You'll be cold when we get out. And you need to cover yourself. I don't want anyone to see you so exposed."

"Mama, we were kidnapped by vampires and rescued by men who weren't wearing any clothing and look just like Grecian statues. I don't think I need to worry about propriety."

Vivienne flushed. She looked almost more disconcerted by her daughter's observation than she had about being tied to an altar. Wearing a motherly frown, she crossed her arms over her bosom. "You are not going out there without covering."

Heath had rarely seen a mother actually carry out mothering before. His own had ignored him. His wife had been a wonderful mother, but he'd spent all his time traveling, so he had hardly ever seen the beauty of a mother's love.

Vivienne's hands had moved with capable firmness as she wrapped Sarah tighter in the rough brown wool. She cuddled her daughter close. It amazed him how Vivienne's entire focus was on her daughter after such a hellish ordeal. Sarah had also been through hell, but he could see how Vivienne's love might just help her to survive it. It brought out a stubborn streak in Sarah, but he saw the way Sarah's face softened in her mother's embrace.

He moved with lightning speed to an ottoman and grabbed a silk throw, one edged with long tassels. This one he wrapped around Vivienne's shoulders. "For you, Miss Dare."

Then he went to the window and shoved it open. Footsteps thundered down the corridor. Julian had jammed a chair beneath the doorknob, but that wouldn't slow vampires down.

"Come, Miss Dare. You first." He held out his hand, helped her leap out the window into the bushes outside. She gave a soft cry of protest as she landed amidst the branches, then fought through them. Sarah stood behind him waiting her turn, but he sent Julian out next, then lowered Sarah into Julian's arms.

Julian treated Miss Dare's daughter with delicate care.

Heath jumped out after. And Vivienne, holding the shawl around her, stalked to him.

"How are we going to get away?" she whispered fiercely. "You men are naked, I'm wearing nothing but a scrap of silk shawl, and Sarah's nightgown is in tatters. We look like we've escaped from Bedlam. I have no money to even get us a hackney."

"Calm yourself, Vivi. I'll get us to safety."

"No, Heath, I can't just calm myself. What is your plan? I can't just risk Sarah's life on . . . on blind faith."

She couldn't trust him. He'd saved her life, but it was as though she could see inside him. As though she knew how he had failed his wife and daughter so many years ago.

"We have to get away as swiftly as possible," he answered tersely. "Julian and I will shape shift, and you and Sarah will have to ride us."

"Ride you?" Three voices—a soft girl's, a throaty woman's, and a stunned vampire's—all shouted it at him.

"It can be done, Julian. We can change into a bigger creature. It will drain our strength quickly, but we'll have enough to reach a sanctuary. Then we'll need to feed. And do it copiously." He wasn't certain if the normal substitute—the blood of livestock—would suffice. He was willing to suffer. But Julian . . .

Julian had never looked more stunned. "Heath, where in hell can we find a sanctuary? We can't go on hallowed ground. No vampire will defy the council—"

"There's one who will. Stop asking questions and transform."

Heath shifted as soon as he finished his command to Julian. His bones rippled, his joints twisted, his rib cage seemed to snap and open wide. Wings erupted. Though his body barely changed in form, his skin darkened to a deep, silvery gray. Vivienne gaped at him as though she was seeing a monster.

After what she had seen, her horror speared him.

The truth was, he was a monster. With his curse, he could destroy all humanity if he turned into a demon. And he would become a demon if he sought the one thing he could never have. Love.

Julian was showing off to Sarah. He flapped his wings and flew in a loop, landing at her feet. Heath expected her to be terrified. Instead she whispered, "I trust you not to drop me."

Julian grinned. He dropped to one knee. "Your chariot awaits, my lady."

She giggled shyly, then climbed onto his back. Her legs slid around his waist, her arms wrapped around his neck. Then she gasped as Julian took off and soared into the air. Heath also dropped onto one knee before Vivienne. It sent him back to the moment he had proposed to Ariadne, it made him remember how arrogant he'd been then. *Of course she would say yes. How could she not?* He'd been so cocksure.

"Trust me, Vivienne," he said huskily.

"This is madness. How can you fly with me?"

He moved his wings. "Welcome to the world of madness, love. Trust me to be your guide through it."

9

Vivienne could hardly believe she was flying over the streets of London, her body lying along Heath's back, her legs wrapped tight around his waist. Her breasts were crushed against strong muscles. She'd wrapped the shawl around her like a gown, but through the silk he was warm and solid beneath her, and the ends of his wings tickled her bare skin as they beat through the air.

She circled his powerful neck with her arms and looked toward her daughter.

Julian flew at Heath's side, with Sarah on his back. Her daughter looked like a true faery with her blond curls flowing behind her dancing on the wind and her thin, white shift fluttering around her. But it was the look of delight on Sarah's face that stunned Vivienne.

Sarah had not looked so happy for years.

This, despite the fact they were fleeing for their lives and her poor daughter had been locked up in a cell. Shock spiraled through Vivienne. She'd tried to give Sarah everything, all the things she herself never had. But something had always haunted Sarah.

She had never seen Sarah look as strong as she did now.

"Where are we going?" Vivienne cried against the rush of the wind.

"A sanctuary," Heath shouted back. They were soaring high, for Heath had claimed this would keep the vampire council's legions of bats from pursuing. A veritable army of the winged creatures had streamed out of the council's building and had followed them, but Heath had been right. When they'd flown through thick clouds, the bats had dropped back, letting them escape.

They were safe—at least for now.

"Hold on," Heath called to her.

As if she wouldn't! Julian went first, plunging downward, and her heart leaped in fear for Sarah. But Sarah gave an excited squeal. Heath followed, and they rushed down through clouds again. Strange how the clouds almost looked like land from above, but they were nothing but vapor when they flew through them. When they emerged, the city was spread out beneath them.

A snaking ribbon of sparkling black cut between the lighted buildings. It was the Thames, and they followed it. They flew away from the city toward the larger estates that dotted the river. Enormous houses appeared to be slumbering in the night, and generous lawns stretched down to the water. Then Heath began to dive downward again, more sharply. Vivienne tightened her hold around his neck. Thin streams of moonlight cut through the clouds as they swooped toward the ground. The silvery light illuminated a house ahead of them—a sprawling, elegant mansion of light stucco, topped with large, slate roofs.

"Is this one of your houses?" she gasped, by Heath's ear.

"No. It belongs to an ancient vampire. It is a sanctuary for vampires hunted by the council. And also a place where the undead can go to indulge every carnal pleasure they desire."

"I don't think I will desire anything carnal ever again," she whispered. But the drink she had been given was making her heart pound again, and heat swept through her body. She fought the urge to squirm on top of Heath. Her quim was pressed right against his rock-hard derriere.

It was as though even the slightest thought of carnal things had triggered lust again. And that made her *think*. Fear sliced into her. "Will Sarah be safe here, in such a place?"

She will be. I will ensure it.

Vivienne gasped in shock. She'd heard his words in her *head*. As though she could read his mind. "How—?"

When you and I made love it created a special bond between us, Vivi. Before that, I could not see into your thoughts. I still cannot, but we can communicate this way. You can send your thoughts to me, just as you would speak to me.

This should be impossible. But again, the incredible was happening. *How do I do it? Can you hear this?*

Yes, Vivienne, love, I can. He half-turned his head to face her. His lips curved in a smile.

But she couldn't smile back. Her heart was too heavy with fear. *I'm afraid Sarah won't be safe here. How can she be, in a house where men indulge carnal desires? How can you ensure it? Sarah is beautiful—I don't want her to become prey. I'm terrified she will be raped. That would destroy her soul. Heath, I can't let that happen—*

She broke off her thoughts as Heath landed on the ground. He gently put her down. Moonlight flashed along his eyes as he gazed intently at her face. *Did that happen to you?*

Despite the silver glow in his eyes, she saw pain there for her. It stunned her. She had clutched the silk wrap that was wound around her body, holding it to her as tightly as she could. No man had ever looked at her as though he cared.

"I was never raped. My mother protected me until I was sixteen. After that, after she died, I made certain . . . I made certain I chose my protectors."

Heath captured her hand and lifted it to his lips, the way a gentleman did to a woman he admired. And his silver-green eyes spoke of such concern for her, she had to lower her eyelids. She shivered even though it was a warm night and she was bundled in silk. It was his look; she couldn't cope with that look.

She drew her hand back, holding her silky cover tightly. "All those things that had once scared me when I was young in the stews—the strength of men, their anger, my mother's drinking—all those things seem so meaningless compared to the fears I now have. Now I know I'm a succubus and a group of demented vampires wants to kill me and Sarah."

"Vivi—" But Heath broke off as Julian dropped toward the lawn. He landed with Sarah, who slid off his back. Sarah's blanket fell to the ground, revealing her slender form, covered only by her thin, tattered nightgown. But Sarah didn't seem to notice. Her cheeks glowed pink. "Mother, that was the most wonderful thing! It was so horrible to be taken prisoner, but to fly about London—oh my goodness, it was so exciting!"

Vivienne wanted to fret—Sarah could have been killed—but she also didn't want to snap at Sarah, when the girl had endured such an ordeal. . . .

Heath caught hold of her wrist. *It's better to let her be happy, Vivi.* It was his voice in her head. *Let's not frighten her.*

She is my *daughter*, she thought angrily. Sarah was all that mattered to her now. Sarah was her life. And she wasn't going to scare her daughter, she was trying to take care of her. She pulled her arm free of Heath's hand.

He let her go. And she hugged Sarah tight. It was so good that Sarah was not terrified, but she wanted to ensure her daughter remained . . . cautious, wary, sensible . . . ? She wasn't quite sure.

Julian draped the throw around Sarah's slim shoulders. His body began to ripple. His muscles twisted and jerked as though they could fly off his body.

"Oh goodness," Sarah gasped. Sarah reached out toward Julian and Vivienne pulled her daughter back.

He let out a roar and another harsh cry came from behind her. Vivienne spun around to see Heath's body writhe, his muscles pop, his jaw shudder from side to side. He looked like his body could blow apart. He looked in agony. Terror for him froze her.

She knew what was happening. They were both transforming as they had before. She knew they would survive it, but it was terrifying to watch. Slowly, their wings collapsed inward and shrank. Heath's skin lightened, as though sunlight was pouring over him, but it was a change from the inside out.

Sarah gripped her hand tightly.

Vivienne glanced from Heath's transformation to her daughter's face. Sarah was watching Julian, obviously afraid for him.

And that frightened Vivienne.

"Christ," Julian muttered. He looked like a normal, naked human male again. He shook his body all over, like a dog throwing off water. She looked to Heath. He was doing the same, stretching his long lines of muscle.

Then, to Vivienne's shock, Julian offered his arm to Sarah like a gentleman escorting a lady. "No," Vivienne said firmly. "I will take her. You are naked and a vampire, and Sarah has on nothing more than a tattered nightgown."

"Mother. I won't look."

Julian looked sheepish, and he swept up the blanket and wrapped it around his hips like a towel. Sarah whispered, "Thank you." And she left her mother to move to his side.

Vivienne swallowed hard. She had gotten so accustomed to seeing Sarah as frail. She'd forgotten her daughter could be strong, stubborn, and determined.

But Sarah was also vulnerable. Vivienne had not given Sarah the same warnings she had learned, when she had grown up in the stews. She hadn't wanted to tarnish Sarah's naïveté. Now she had to ensure Sarah did not lose her heart to a vampire.

For heaven's sake, what was she thinking? There were far more immediate worries. Heath came to her side, utterly naked, to escort her.

She frowned at him, her brow lifted. "You said this is a sanctuary for vampires, but this looks like an estate. I have been to houses here. They belong to earls, dukes. How did a vampire acquire this? Or, like you, is he a vampire peer?"

"We should get inside first."

She noted he had not answered either of her questions, but she let him lead her. They hurried through the darkness to the house. Sound spilled out into the moonlit garden, though all the windows were dark. But when she and Heath followed Sarah and Julian to the flagstone terrace, she came to a halt.

She couldn't just trust him blindly. She just could not do that with any man. "Did the vampire kill someone to get this?" Without answers, she did not want to step foot into this pitch-black, yet obviously occupied house.

"It doesn't matter, Vivienne. It's a sanctuary for you and Sarah. That is all you need to know."

"It's not enough," she cried. "I—"

The glass-paned doors flew open. Two black-clad men stormed out. They carried crossbows. One clicked his boot heels together and gave a sharp bow. "My lord Blackmoor. We did not know you were to return."

"Neither did I," Heath answered casually, as though he was not standing naked with a woman wearing nothing but a silk shawl. "I take it His Grace is within?"

"Of course. Follow me. I will lead you to him."

His Grace. There was a *duke* who was also a vampire? Why would Heath not answer her questions?

But Sarah was happily walking with Julian into the house. And Vivienne's blood ran cold. In stories, vampires were supposed to be able to attract humans. If Sarah hadn't inherited any sort of demon blood from her . . . didn't that make her vulnerable to Julian's vampire skills?

The two men procured four black silk robes. Julian helped Sarah into one. Vivienne pulled hers on with a sigh of relief. It was sumptuous and warm, and finally both she and Sarah were respectably covered. The men bade them follow and led them through the house.

Heath, she noticed, was watching Julian, too.

Within moments, they were passing through a large ballroom. A trio of violinists played, but the guests were not dancing. Beautiful men and women, attired in the most astonishing clothing, lounged on plush chaises of velvet. The women wore only tightly laced corsets and stockings with satin garters of scarlet. Red lace adorned their bodies; some wore satin ribbons around their necks. They drank champagne from gold flutes. Vivienne spied nothing more scandalous than couples enjoying kisses, but she panicked. They were dressed so suggestively, there was a sense of the erotic even about the low, murmured conversations. Breasts were on display everywhere. One handsome man began to remove his shirt. *Sarah*. Sarah should not see this.

Heath made a motion to Julian with his hand. Vivienne jerked around. At Heath's instruction, Julian had covered Sarah's eyes with his hand. And her naive daughter was protesting. "Really," Sarah complained, "I am not a child."

No, but I still want you to be innocent, Vivienne thought desperately. "This is impossible. I cannot let Sarah stay here."

Heath leaned close to her. His voice was soft and seductive.

"I would not have brought her to a place that's not safe. Dimitri keeps an apartment in the house for vampires who need sanctuary. Those rooms are off limits to his other guests, and no vampire would dream of defying one of Dimitri's rules. I promise you Sarah can stay there in complete safety."

She supposed she should be thankful he hadn't pointed out she had nowhere else to go. It was the truth, wasn't it? Her house wasn't safe. The town house she had almost sold her soul to purchase: could they ever return to it?

But that way led to madness, so she concentrated on the present. "Dimitri?"

"A very old vampire."

Why did he give her answers that told her precisely nothing? "I will stay with Sarah—" But she stopped as Heath shook his head.

He bent close. She felt his warm breath ripple over the rim of her ear. It sent shivers tumbling down her spine, ignited desire in her belly. And then—oh heavens—then the throbbing, the aching began.

"I will be bringing you downstairs," he murmured. "You'll need pleasure tonight, Vivienne."

Awareness and warmth fled. Fear left her cold. Even when he murmured to her, "I will be at your side. I will take care of you. But I can't make love to you."

What on earth was he saying? "Why not? Don't you—want me?"

"You have no idea how much I do. But I promise I will look after you—"

"Don't. I don't need anything." But it wasn't true. Her heart was hammering. "They gave me something to drink, Heath. I don't know what it was, but it . . ." She lowered her voice to such a soft whisper, she wasn't sure he would hear. "It makes me desire."

He groaned. "Adder must have given you a potent aphrodisiac."

The servant stopped at a door. Rapped. "Lord Blackmoor has arrived, Your Grace."

A woman's moan floated out into the corridor. A masculine voice, an impatient and terse baritone, followed. "Blackmoor? Has he come crawling back? Or is he stalking arrogantly back into my house, still cocksure of himself?"

The servant remained astonishingly impassive. "He is accompanied by guests. He arrived quite naked, Your Grace. The ladies accompanying him were also inadequately dressed. It is obvious they are in need of your help."

"Ladies? He brought ladies? Intriguing," came the deep voice from behind the door. "Blackmoor must be in trouble. Send them all in."

Vivienne tucked the sheets around Sarah's slumbering form. Sarah was curled up, her arms wrapped around the soft, white pillow. The bed was enormous, dripping with silk tassels and lace.

For the moment, they were safe. Dimitri, the mysterious vampire everyone referred to as "Your Grace," even though he denied being a duke, had allowed her and Sarah to stay in this ostentatious apartment. For as long as they required.

Dimitri had proved to be a handsome giant of a man, six and a half feet tall. He possessed dark, chocolate-brown hair, a long, autocratic nose, and jet-black eyes. He looked a bit like the leader of the vampire council, Adder, but his face, even with his strong features, had looked more gentle. He had done nothing but smile at her and Sarah.

They had been taken into a parlor attached to Dimitri's bedchamber, passing a woman who lay on a chaise, sipping tea, and awaiting her "lord" to finish his business. Handsome Dimitri had worn fashions from the previous century: a silk coat of pale green with six inches of lace at his cuffs.

With a clap of his hands, he'd sent an army of servants in search of clothing and food. Vivienne now wore one of the dresses provided, a scarlet silk masterpiece. It flowed over her body as though made for her. Underneath frothing skirts she could see her heavenly soft silk slippers, which were embroidered with exotic gold-colored diamonds.

The slippers alone must be worth thousands of pounds.

But she had watched the two men, Heath and Dimitri, just before maids had arrived to sweep her and Sarah upstairs to bathe, dress, and settle into the splendid rooms. Heath had looked haunted, Dimitri furious.

What was between the two men?

"Mmmm," Sarah murmured in her sleep. Vivienne was afraid of waking her. She moved from the bed to the window, where drapes of black covered the glass.

Her hair was clean and fell down her back in loose ringlets. All the paint put on her by the vampire's servants was gone. She was safe, but she felt restless. What was going to happen to her and Sarah? Where could they go to be truly safe? Regardless of Dimitri's verbal generosity, she didn't believe he intended to let them stay forever.

She didn't want to. She yearned to go home. But how was she going to keep Sarah safe from the council of vampires—from their weapons, their bats, their utter madness?

Vivienne paced, fanning herself nervously with her hand.

Only days ago, before meeting Heath, she didn't believe vampires existed. And now, she was living amongst some of them and hiding from others.

Could she and Sarah run away? Make a home somewhere where they would be safe and not attacked again? But what of Sarah's illness? Sarah was strong and healthy now because of

Heath. She could not take her daughter away from Heath, because Sarah would get sick again. . . .

She stopped. Cold had swept over her suddenly and she had to rub her arms. It had been like this for the last hour. She would get hot enough to burst into flame. She would be sweating and fanning herself desperately. Then, seconds later, her temperature would plunge to iciness.

And now the pain began. It started throbbing in her womb. It would spread soon, just as it had done before. On the night she had made love with Heath.

Someone knocked on her door. "Vivienne, love. Will you come with me? Julian and two servants will watch Sarah."

It was Heath. He must have come to take her downstairs, to the rooms where vampires indulged all their carnal desires. She hurried to the door and opened it. "I don't want to leave her. I can endure the pain."

Vivienne saw Heath's seductive mouth flatten into a firm line. "You can't, love. They gave you a potion to heighten your lust. The pain will be far, far worse tonight."

Heath leaned on the doorframe and drank in the sight of Vivienne in a scandalous scarlet dress. The neckline was a low scoop, cupping her breasts and lifting them into generous mounds. Her gown clung so tightly to her, it looked more like a deep blush than that she was dressed. He wanted to plant his boot in Dimitri's arse. She looked like she'd been made to be ravished, and Dimitri knew Heath couldn't make love to Vivi again. This was obviously Dimitri's idea of a joke.

And now he got to watch the other vampires in the house desire Vivi, seduce her, pleasure her. He would have to convince her to willingly go to another man. To let another man save her life.

He'd been cursed because he deserved it. Shouldn't he be enjoying the pain?

She and Sarah were safe here. This time, he hadn't failed two innocents who depended on him. But he wanted to make love to Vivienne. He wanted to savor her, pour out his longing for her, work out his terror over the danger to her. But he couldn't.

Ruefully, he smiled down at her. "You're going to need to have a night of wild, wanton sex. It's the only thing that will undo the effects of that potion."

Vivienne bit her lush lower lip. "Oh dear," she whispered. She sagged against the door, and put her hand to her forehead.

He slid his hand there, too. She was on fire.

"I'm afraid to leave Sarah."

He moved his hand. Just touching her had him hard and throbbing with need. "She'll be safe. The council can't infiltrate this place. No one who is a guest here would risk angering Dimitri by approaching her. And no one here would try to seduce an unwilling woman."

"Why not?"

"Because there are dozens of willing ones. And because Dimitri and I would rip him apart." He sighed. "Now, I need to thoroughly rescue you. Very soon, you will be in desperate need of sex—and lots of it."

"And you won't do it again," she said. She spoke flatly. It was that emotionless voice women used that truly condemned a man.

He felt damned, more than he ever had. "Hades, if I could, I would lock you into your bedchamber and spend the night making love to you. But I can't because I'm cursed."

She touched his chest. Christ, her fingers felt like fire against him.

"You mean, you are cursed with being a vampire?"

"No, my curse is something different. It's a magical thing, placed on me by my sire when I was turned—"

"Turned?"

"It's a term we vampires use for the moment when another vampires bites us, then feeds us his blood to make us one of them. My sire, the vampire who made me, used an ancient spell to curse me. If I make love to any woman twice, I transform from a vampire into a demon."

"How?"

"I don't know how it works exactly."

"But what sort of demon? I mean—"

"You mean, aren't I one already?" He groaned. "No, love, because I control my own urges. The kind of demon I would turn into is a violent monster. I would have the power to rip England apart, to completely destroy it. I was told I would have enough power to bring about the end the world."

Her blue eyes were wide with fear. Her tempting breasts rose and fell. She stepped out into the corridor, closed the door to her daughter's room behind her. "But you don't know. You've never turned into a demon before."

Vivienne was dangerous. She seemed to see into his thoughts, seemed to find the darkest things in his heart. He wanted to believe he could make love to her and get away with it.

"I have," he said softly. "When I was turned and cursed, I was given a demonstration of what my transformation would be like. My sire had a sorcerer enslaved to him. He instructed this old man to give me a taste of what I would become if I was foolish enough to disobey the curse. With magic, he transformed me into a demon, then changed me back. I was a demon for a half a minute, and in that short time, I did several unspeakable things. So no, I've never dared take the risk."

Now the magnificent décolleté on display to him was blushing pink. If he bent and kissed her lips, kissed that deep valley between her breasts, then lifted her skirts and tongued her cunny, where would she be hottest?

"So you truly have never made love to any woman twice?" Vivi asked.

"Since I became a vampire. The curse was payment for my wife's death. Intended to ensure I never knew what it was to love again. Or if I did fall in love, I got to suffer without being able to make love." Heath shut his eyes, but even that didn't spare him from temptation. She smelled of rose soap from her bath. "But right now I am thinking about what it would be like to make love to you again."

Vivienne wanted to deny the ache growing in her. But she couldn't. "Well, then, we have a problem. Because you say I need to make love."

Heath's fist banged against the plaster beside the door. Suddenly his teeth grew before her eyes, turning into long fangs. But the sight of him didn't frighten her. "I know," he growled. "Hades, how I know that. And tonight, I will have the honor of watching you be very well pleasured. Come, Vivi."

Vivi. She suddenly realized he had called her that a few times. Along with "Flower." No one had called her by an affectionate nickname for ages. Not since her mother had called her Vivi, when she'd been little. In happier times. In Heath's deep, seductive voice, the name sounded more . . . naughty.

He tried to coerce her to walk with him, but she resisted, digging in the heels of her borrowed slippers. "Exactly what do you think you are going to be watching?"

Then all he said were those two infuriating words. "Trust me."

They asked for so much. "No. You must tell me what you think I am going to do."

"Dimitri has told me there are four very experienced vampires who desire you. I don't want to share you, but you need what I can't give."

Four very experienced . . . vampires? Goodness, he couldn't mean she was supposed to make love to—to all of them at once, like Molly in the brothel? "Heath, no. I know you brought me here, but I don't want any other man but you."

"This is just erotic fun, Vivi. It's not an expression of love but a chance for some play. And I intend to take part—at least to watch. I would not miss seeing you experience sexual play for the world."

Oh, she felt terribly unsure. Uncomfortable. "But aren't you going to be . . . upset? Men are very possessive, I've learned."

"This is part of the vampire world. Vampires do take mates, which is a deep joining of the heart. The games here don't cause jealousy, because the mates know how strong their bond is. I could easily lose my heart to you, Vivienne, even though I know I shouldn't. I recognize this is just a carnal game. Dimitri's orgy will be beginning now, before dawn comes. Indulge me: spread your wings and play."

She had been a courtesan. And as insane as it seemed, she had to make love or she would die. She could do it, couldn't she? It was what she'd done when she was a paid lover to men who were powerful, but whom she simply didn't desire. She could close off her mind.

But she looked at Heath. His silvery-green eyes flashed, as though a fire burned within them. Sensual lines bracketed his mouth, and the way they deepened when he spoke or smiled made her knees weak. It was more than just green eyes, thick auburn waves, and the body of a Greek god that made her desire him. This was the man who had rescued Sarah, who had rescued her. She wanted *him*.

She couldn't do this. She did not want any other man than Heath. Not even because her life depended on it.

And his words rang in her head. *I could easily lose my heart to you.*

Could he possibly be wrong about the curse?

10

Heath had been right. Everything changed.

At first, Vivienne thought he was wrong. There was no orgy. She'd expected to see people having sex in the open everywhere. All those women in scanty corsets and all those half-naked men rolling around in the corridors, in bedrooms, on the stairs, in every possible location and position.

At first there wasn't *anything* like that to see. She walked at Heath's side, following the labyrinth of hallways and corridors on the main floor.

"It's very intriguing to watch the expressions on your face, Vivi."

She jerked around to him. "What expressions?"

"I never saw a woman in the midst of an orgy look so serious. Or so disappointed. What are you thinking?"

She bit her lip. Dimtri's "gathering," as she'd heard the maid refer to it, seemed like scandalous house parties she had attended. At those, the guests moved from bed to bed indiscriminately, but on the surface the event appeared as refined and ordinary as a staid duchess might hold.

"Are you all right?" Heath asked. "You must be exhausted."

"I suppose I should be. But my blood is . . . right now it feels on fire." Her nerves were running riot. She was plunging into iciness, then turned scorching hot.

A clock somewhere in Lord Dimitri's house struck three.

"Now it begins," Heath said.

"What does?"

The door to a drawing room suddenly flew open. She peeked in and saw the shadowy room contained perhaps a dozen men and women. Before her eyes, the people in the room threw aside any pretense of control. They all began to grope and kiss each other on a sofa in the center of the room. This was like the orgies she'd heard about, but it was happening right in front of her.

People spilled out of rooms into the hallway. The scenes around her became utterly bawdy. Couples, threesomes, foursomes were making love anywhere they chose. And no one appeared the least bit shocked.

Heath took her into the main salon. As they reached the threshold, Vivienne saw two vampires lock gazes. The male was astonishingly tall and muscular, with golden hair tied back in a queue. The woman was a beautiful, angelic-looking blonde. Then, without even exchanging a word, the couple began to have sex up against the wall. They moved in perfect unison. They climaxed together almost instantly, without saying a thing. Their only communication had been moans and sighs, and the woman's ecstatic screams.

And it was obvious the woman had truly felt her pleasure.

Then, as the woman drew in slow breaths, the man chuckled. And finally spoke. "Privacy now, my dear?" he asked. "If you would like me to put my tongue in your derriere, I would be happy to escort you to my bed."

Good heavens, they were obviously strangers. And yet he had proposed such a shocking thing, such an intimate thing, without blinking. The woman had simply nodded. Hand in hand, they left.

His tongue inside her rear? The thought left Vivienne's knees shaking. And hot—so hot, the valley between her breasts was damp. Goodness. What would it feel like—to have Heath do that? Had he ever done that. . . . ?

Heath was watching her, a knowing smile on his beautiful mouth. "You're shocked by this."

She lifted a jaded brow. "Truly, I don't believe your story about this place either. How do all these people simply have sex for the pleasure of it?"

"Just believe in it. It happens to be true."

She could smell alluring scents in the air, the tang of male seed, the ripeness of feminine juices. All the men here were muscular, beautifully hewn, and many were completely nude. The women were either abundantly curvy, or sleek and smoothly lovely.

"All vampires are beautiful," he murmured teasingly.

But it was true. They were. And Heath, she saw, was the most gorgeous of all the men. There was an allure to this. She couldn't deny it.

What would it be like to have sex simply for fun? Not because she was the property of a man, courtesan to his protector. Sex had been survival. As a courtesan, she could never simply give in to lust. Anyway, she'd never really felt desire.

What would it be like just to be wanton?

It was so tempting. . . .

No. She was just doing this to ease the pain. She was not going to be foolish, like her mother had been, and become addicted to desire and sex.

This was what was truly dangerous about Heath. Not his fangs. Or the fact he must drink blood, though she'd never actually seen him do that.

His true danger was how he tempted her to forget all the careful, cautious lessons she'd learned.

Heath wanted this to be more than sexual gymnastics that saved Vivi. He couldn't give her much, but he wanted to give her two gifts. He wanted to ensure Sarah defeated her illness. And he wanted Vivienne to lose her fear of sex, to learn to accept pleasure and delight in it.

It was all he could give her.

Though, hell, he couldn't even find his own brother. And he hadn't been able to save his wife and daughter. He must be an arrogant madman to think he could rescue anyone else.

Cloth suddenly flew over his eyes. A pert feminine giggle followed. "Lord Heath! It has been so very long since you were here. Dimitri has told me I still cannot have you tonight, even though you are here. Tell me it isn't true!"

He knew the voice, as he caught hold of the silk scarf and drew it away. He saw Vivienne's pursed lips and highly arched brows. She was surveying the giggling blonde vampiress with an iciness he could feel.

"Good evening, Sadie." He gave a formal bow. "It is true. I can only have a lover once."

"Isn't that convenient for you, Lord Heath, since you are known to have such a wandering eye?"

Convenient. Years ago, before he'd married, he'd been like any earl. He had liked his sexual pleasures easy, bountiful, and varied. Every vice and delight had been available to him due to his title, his money. Then he'd found Ariadne. And he had been faithful. His reputation had endured, but it felt like it belonged to another man, not him.

Sadie leered at Vivienne. "Lord Dimitri told me it was ess—well, *important*—for me to seduce your lady here, Lord Heath."

Vivienne blinked. She glowed like a ruby in her scarlet dress. "Seduce me? What on earth do you mean?"

"Sapphic pleasures," Heath pointed out to her in a low voice. And he saw her chin jerk with shock. "You've never done that before? Made love to another woman?"

"Of course not." She spoke low, another flush blooming in her cheeks.

"Didn't one of your protectors offer you the earth for it?"

"H—How would you know about that?"

"I know how the male mind works."

"I refused. Whenever I saw two women together with a man, it had nothing to do with making love." Her brow lifted in her cool, jaded way. "All the women did was argue, fight, and pull each other's hair, competing over the man."

Sadie watched them both, her large blue eyes slanting from one to the other.

"You see, Sadie," he said. "You will have your work cut out for you. Miss Dare will resist your seduction."

Sadie frowned. "Lord Dimitri said I must do it, though, or your lady will suffer greatly. He said if she doesn't make love, she will die."

Vivienne was trembling. "But surely he meant make love to a gentleman—though I do not want any other man than Heath."

Hell. He didn't deserve such loyalty. Or such . . . desire or whatever it was that made her so steadfastly determined not to enjoy herself with anyone else. And she needed to make love to another man eventually, or the pain wouldn't stop. Still he said softly, "Why not try an adventure, love? If you don't want another man, why not delight in the beauty in other women?"

"I—I don't know."

"Lord Dimitri insists the pleasure will help you," Sadie said.

Hell, what did Dimitri know? But Vivi bristled. She squared

her shoulders, tipped up her chin, and faced Sadie. "But why would you want to do such a thing? We are strangers."

The girl gave a wicked smile. "But some of my most erotic fun has been with strangers."

"Vivi, if it's going to ease your pain, you should do it."

Vivi speared him with a withering look. "You really want to see this, don't you, Lord Blackmoor?"

Heaven. Hell. Both of them were being displayed before him. Heath's hand tightened around his brandy glass.

"What is your fantasy, Lord Heath?" Sadie now wore only a corset. Below its lace-trimmed edge, he could see the trimmed thatch of gold pubic curls, the abundant curve of her hips. She had led him to a well-stuffed wing chair that stood at the edge of a quiet, deserted, dark room.

Vivienne had only just been led into the room. He could see her blinking. She couldn't see in the dark. But before he could ask for candles to be lit, Sadie's voice dropped to a sultry purr. "Do you wish to be a sultan, enjoying the secret play within the harem? Or perhaps you have slipped into an academy for schoolgirls and you are witness to their explorations in their dormitory beds? Or would a nunnery be your fantasy?"

"Good heavens." Vivienne's sardonic tone sliced through the dark. "Men are so . . . silly. What *is* your fantasy, Heath? I would be so interested to know."

And he understood. Vivienne had protected herself by thinking of men as silly, creatures driven by their lust. But he'd also heard the quiver in her voice. She knew he was not quite so simple.

"Light candles, Sadie," he requested softly. It bought him a few moments as she did his bidding. He needed to think of a fantasy to surprise Vivi. Something unusual—though the thought of the harem and Vivienne wearing nothing but silken veils had his cock pulsing.

Veils . . . "Perhaps a wedding," he suggested teasingly. "Where the blushing bride is seduced by her attendants?"

"We've never done that before." Sadie lit the last taper, and the candles brought a golden glow into the room. She looked like a china shepherdess with her yellow ringlets, large blue eyes, full bosom, and tiny waist. She turned to the back of the room, where an area was enclosed with black curtains. "Come out *now*, Jasmine and Zoe. Hurry up."

Two other vampiresses moved elegantly out from behind the drapes. They were now nude. Jasmine had long, straight black hair, and exotic, almond-shaped green eyes. She possessed a lean, sleek figure, with small pert breasts, and long legs. The third, Zoe, was a fiery redhead. Zoe cocked her head. "I've seen Molly boys have a false wedding, even wearing white gowns."

Molly boys were men who sexually desired other men.

"No." That was Vivienne. "I don't want to play a bride, blushing or otherwise."

Heath stroked his chin, making a pretense of considering. "I've always fantasized about what upstairs maids do when they aren't at work."

"Service the gentlemen of the house," Vivienne suggested dryly. But she was shivering and rubbing her arms, even in her heavy silk gown.

He remembered the dream they'd shared of Hyde Park. That was the woman he wanted to unearth: the saucy, joyous temptress who liked to play. He knew she was truly inside Vivi. If he could get to that woman, he believed he could open Vivi's heart. . . .

Hell, that wasn't his plan. With his curse, he wasn't supposed to be messing around with anyone's heart.

"Ooh, I can think of some rather delicious things to do with feather dusters," Sadie mused.

"I think we should just begin," Heath said. "Watching Vivienne explore pleasure; I don't need any more fantasy than that."

He heard her breath catch—before she swallowed hard.

Sadie smiled. The vampiress could sense Vivienne's uncertainty. She readily slipped into the role of mistress of the play. She pointed to Zoe and Jasmine in turn. "You two must show Lord Heath's love what it is like to pleasure another woman. Give her a performance while I help her undress. I must admit, she looks so lush and lovely, I am looking forward to stripping her bare."

Heath smelled the tang of blood.

He looked down. His clenched fist had snapped a large sliver from his empty glass. He suckled his finger and healed the wound—before three vampiresses offered to do it for him.

Vivienne was not prepared to be dragged to a stool, or to have Sadie firmly push her down upon it. The blonde vampire worked swiftly. Vivienne's gown sagged open in moments. Sadie peeled down the bodice. "You are most generously endowed. No wonder Lord Heath is besotted with you."

Besotted. "He isn't, Sadie," she corrected.

Behind her, Sadie tugged at her corset laces. "Lord Dimitri said you were a succubus. What is that like? Is it fun to seduce men in their dreams?"

"No," she said at once. But the dream she'd shared with Heath about Hyde Park; that had been rather . . . fun.

"His Grace told me you just learned you are a demoness. He said you are frightened by it. You should not be."

Vivienne twisted on the stool to look at Sadie, who was plucking the ties at the very bottom of her corset. This brought her eyes almost right up to Sadie's bare, erect nipples. She was quite embarrassed to see Sadie's naked breasts, though they were lovely—so round and full. She was still blushing from looking at the other naked women, Jasmine and Zoe.

This was her first chance to speak to someone who might understand other than Heath. She could not let a bit of shame deter her. "Sadie, weren't you frightened when you became a vampire?"

"Of course. But I was alone. I did not have a gentleman like Lord Heath to help me."

Sympathy tugged at Vivienne. She touched Sadie's arm. "Alone? What happened?"

"We won't talk about serious things now. That's for later. Now, we do this." And Sadie grasped her by the shoulders and turned her on the stool.

Zoe and Jasmine were sitting together on a long chaise, kissing. Then Zoe playfully spanked Jasmine's sleek, slim derriere.

Vivienne was struck mute. Then she glanced to Heath. Oh dear God.

He was sprawled in his chair. The empty brandy balloon dangled from his long fingers. His legs were spread, which showcased how long and muscled they were. How beautiful they looked in his gleaming black boots. A thick bulge was obvious at the juncture between his parted thighs.

The giggling women and their kisses aroused him. And she couldn't stop looking at him. She *liked* watching him watch the women kiss.

She wanted to jump on him, tear his trousers open, and take him deep inside her aching cunny.

"Oh no," Sadie said beside her. "You mustn't make love to Lord Heath. You've done it once. Unfortunately that's all you get. But you can have this."

A plump breast bumped her cheek.

Sadie looked so hopeful. In Sadie's shining blue eyes and her breathless anticipation, Vivienne saw the young woman behind the vampire. "You could kiss my nipple, Miss Vivi."

That must be what Heath had called her to Sadie.

She couldn't.

But Sadie's nipples were so different from hers. Petite and very pale pink. Rather sweet, and quite small for such large, round breasts.

Did she dare?

Heath was watching her. There was a look in his eyes. . . .

He didn't think she would do it. And his eyes slid back to Zoe and Jasmine. Goodness, the girls were now kissing each other's breasts. And their hands . . . Zoe's fingers were playing in Jasmine's dark nether curls, and in return, two long fingers were disappearing inside her quim. Sucking sounds of the thrusting fingers filled the room, along with the rich scent of feminine arousal.

Heath was roughly scrubbing his jaw. He'd put down the glass beside him and his hand was creeping toward his straining trousers.

Suddenly, Vivienne wanted to be the one to excite him. Her natural competitive nature rose.

With a soft moan, for courage perhaps, she kissed the generous mound of Sadie's right breast. It was a swift peck of her puckered lips to dewy skin, which tasted of vanilla and of the sweetness of feminine sweat.

"Yes," Heath growled from across the room.

"Ooh, yes," Sadie echoed.

Both their reactions inspired Vivienne. She let her tongue rove over all that lovely ivory skin, because it gave Heath a more enticing view. And his loud groan was a victory. She let her tongue coast down, savoring Sadie's abundant softness, then flicked over the plump pink nipple.

"Ooh, I do like that," Sadie whispered. "And if you want to suckle, you can—"

"Be hard and rough?" Vivienne answered softly. At Sadie's nod, she smiled, remembering how she'd tried to tempt Heath with that very same promise.

It was strange to take Sadie's nipple into her mouth. She did feel pleasure, of a sort, when a man took her nipple in his mouth. Heath had given her much pleasure that way. But she didn't know quite how to do it to make it nice for Sadie.

So she explored. She sucked hard. Then she flicked her tongue over the nipple. She was really copying what men did to her. Which was rather funny. As a woman, she should know. But she truly didn't . . .

"Suck hard. I do like that," Sadie breathed.

Vivienne glanced to the side. Zoe and Jasmine were lying on the chaise. They thrust their hands—their whole hands—in and out of each other's quims, moaning and squirming on the silk cushions.

As Vivienne stared, amazed at how vigorously they were thrusting, Sadie pulled her breast free. And next thing she knew, Sadie was on her knees before her. Vivienne's dress was still on, but in disarray, her corset loose and falling forward. Sadie flashed a smile, then pushed her legs apart. Her heart pounded; her cunny was aching, and she didn't resist.

She watched, breathless with desire—and shock—as Sadie's tongue slid out and licked her wet, glistening nether lips. "Oh," she gasped. "You mustn't."

But Zoe and Jasmine were doing this, too. They were arranged so Jasmine was on the bottom with Zoe's quim poised over Jasmine's mouth. Zoe's head was between Jasmine's thighs.

It was stunning. As Sadie licked and sucked her quim, she could watch the other two women doing the same things. Each time one of them—or both—wailed in intense pleasure, Vivienne joined them. She rocked on the stool, rocked rhythmically as Sadie skillfully sucked her clit.

"Put your fingers up my bum," Zoe commanded Jasmine. And the other woman did, sliding three fingers between Zoe's generous cheeks.

Vivienne almost screamed as a jolt of agony went through

her. It was . . . delicious to watch. And Zoe . . . heavens, she slid her fingers into Jasmine's quim, and into her derriere, and she sucked the dark-haired beauty's clit. Suddenly Jasmine bucked her hips up wildly. And Zoe came, too, pressing her pussy against Jasmine's questing mouth. The scent of their flowing juices filled the air.

Vivienne glanced wildly over at Heath. He looked in such agony. His hand was cupping the huge ridge in his trousers. His chest rose and fell with his breaths. He looked to her and she heard his hoarse voice in her head. *I want to see you come, too, Angel.*

His command unleashed her orgasm. Her bottom bounced on the hard stool, and Sadie gripped her thighs. Relentlessly Sadie suckled her clit as the pleasure claimed her. Dizziness washed over her. She feared she would faint. . . .

Then she was falling, but Sadie swiftly stood and hugged her. "Oh, Miss Vivi," she whispered. "That was wonderful."

Zoe clambered off the couch. Sweat glinted on her breasts and a pink flush touched her skin. "Tongues are all well and fine, but I've been staring so long at the bulge in Lord Heath's pants. I want something big and long inside."

But Heath shook his head. "No, love."

Sadie sashayed forward. "I may have a suggestion, my lord."

And to Vivienne's shock, the lovely blonde spread her legs and began fingering her cunny, right in front of Heath's eyes. Zoe gave a fierce laugh and dropped to her knees behind Sadie, kissing the curvaceous cheeks. She licked Sadie's rump all over, while the blonde vigorously stimulated herself.

Then Zoe slid her fingers inside Sadie's bottom. And Sadie climaxed with a lusty, delighted shriek.

Poor Heath. Panting heavily, Sadie winked at him. "Why don't you try that, my lord."

Vivienne held her breath.

He opened his trousers.

Flushed, exhausted, Vivienne watched as he released his cock. She'd seen it several times—it was so remarkably long and thick.

The other girls lay on their bellies on the carpet in a circle around him. "Finally, my lord," cried Jasmine.

"How did you resist for so long?" Zoe asked, giggling.

Mesmerized, Vivienne watched him pleasure himself. His hand moved slowly, stroking from hilt to tip. Then he gripped his ballocks and moved his hand faster. Impossibly fast, up and down his shaft.

He was going to come. And the other women moved toward him on their hands and knees. He watched them, and his silvery-green eyes seemed to take fire. Hard and fast, his hand pumped. The women, for some reason, were jostling each other. Trying to push each other out of the way.

Sadie managed to work between the other two. She held her damp breasts up in offer. "Here, my lord. Splatter these."

Vivienne's eyes widened. But she wanted to see it happen. . . .

"God," Heath shouted. His upper body curled over, his legs shot out straight. His hand gripped his ballocks hard, his shaft even harder. And a burst of white exploded from his cock. It sailed in an arc and fell all over Sadie's magnificent breasts.

Zoe and Jasmine laughed. "Lucky girl," they gasped together. Then they blew kisses to Heath, waggled their bottoms, and disappeared behind the drapes. Sadie stood and brushed back her damp curls. Heath smiled and Sadie glowed in delight.

Vivienne should feel jealous. But she couldn't, and she didn't quite know why.

He slowly rose from the chair. And it was to her side he came. He grinned down at her, gasping for breath. "God, Vivi. It was the look on your face. The lusty anticipation of seeing me come. It pushed me over the brink."

She blinked. She had done it? She had made him explode? Not Sadie's breasts and her eagerness to have his come glistening on her generous tits? Not the fact three lovely nude women had been fighting for the honor?

It was you, he said in her thoughts. *You make me climax like that. Like my heart exploded and shot out of me when I came.*

Sadie bustled forward. "Let me fix your gown, Miss Vivienne." After the sex, Vivienne had no idea what to say. She knew she was blushing.

Sadie swiftly re-tied her corset. "You must think of me as your friend. We've been intimate together, so of course I am now your friend."

Vivienne felt a tug. She hadn't had a friend for years and years. As a courtesan, she'd been suspicious of friendship. She'd had to pull her way to the top of her world.

Old uncertainties rose. The feeling she didn't need a friend, she had to fight to survive . . . And she understood suddenly. She was afraid to let anyone in. "Thank you," she whispered. "I am delighted to have you as my friend."

Sadie fixed her gown. "There. A bit crumpled, but you look lovely." Impetuously Sadie hugged her. It was strange to think she had a friend. Yet it was nice, too.

She was not prepared for what happened between her and Heath when the other women left.

He crooked his fingers, a strange, unreadable look on his face, and she approached. Sweat was cooling on her body beneath the silk of her dress. But she no longer went from scorching hot to freezing cold in a heartbeat. The pain was gone.

"It worked," she whispered. "But how?"

"Possibly because I came for you. Only for you." He lifted her onto his lap. His trousers and her petticoats were a barrier between her quim and his now slumbering cock. She wished she could will away all the fabric. . . .

He pinched her left nipple, rolling it, tugging it. His other hand delved down into her damp pubic curls. Masculine fingers parted her lips and stroked her clit. She wanted this. Just a little bit more pleasure with him.

The orgasm claimed her at once. She wailed in pure delight.

A little bit of pleasure? What was she thinking? It was extraordinary. And all he had done was touch her.

Flushed, gasping, she met his smile. She knew she was staring in wide-eyed wonder. "I didn't think it was possible to climax again."

His lips lifted in a wicked grin. "Good?"

"It was beyond good." She glanced down. He was hard again, straining against his form-fitting trousers. "But what of you? You're aroused again." She knew of one thing men always did—complain about the pain when they were lusty and unsatisfied. "You must hurt."

"Nothing I can't endure. And I intend to put myself out of my misery with my right hand again. While thinking of you, love, and remembering how beautiful you look when you come."

She blushed. She had never felt like this after making love.

Normally she felt . . . sad. She didn't know why. Tonight she didn't feel regret, just a deeper yearning for Heath.

And that was foolish. He was an even more impossible dream than her silly, childhood fantasies that a titled man would truly fall in love with her and want to make her more than his courtesan.

"Come, Angel. You've been up all night," Heath murmured. "Time to take you back to your bed, so you can sleep."

The horror of the vampire council had only been a few hours ago, but it felt like days. Still . . . "I don't think I can sleep, Heath. What are Sarah and I going to do—?"

"You and Sarah are going to stay safe. I will take care of things."

"No." She slid off his lap. "I have taken care of myself for my whole life. I want your help, of course, but this is my battle. I cannot just hide and pray you take care of me."

Heath didn't say a word. And she was too tired to argue.

"I must check on Sarah before I go to bed.

He led her back to her room. Though his arm was around her, she felt cold—in her heart. She had wanted to give Sarah so much more than she'd had. She had worked and struggled to provide a fortune for Sarah's sake.

"Penny for your thoughts," Heath said gently.

Suddenly she did something she'd never done before. She confided. She told him of all her hopes for Sarah. "I wanted her to have money so she could be free."

"She will be, Flower. I promise it."

"But what if she is like me? What can she do then?"

"Anything she wants," he said firmly. "She could travel the world. Or buy a lovely house in England. Hades, she could build her own theater and be the most praised actress England has ever known. Money is power."

Vivienne shook her head. "It isn't true. *Position* is power. I always worried that Sarah could never elevate her position because she is a courtesan's daughter. Yet in truth, she is a demon's daughter."

But Heath didn't pander to her fears. "You dreamed of her becoming a countess or a duchess?"

She blushed. "It sounds foolish when you say it that way. I simply wish she could be whatever she wishes."

"She can, Vivi."

They had reached Sarah's door. Heath was a most unusual gentleman. She'd never had a man care to hear about her worries and fears. This was friendship, too. She'd never had friendship and passion with a man before—

A scream echoed from Sarah's room. "Help me!" Sarah's voice was shrill, terrified. "Mama, where are you? Help!"

Vivienne shoved the door open, but it was Heath who rushed in first. Sarah was sitting up in the bed, flailing her arms wildly. Julian, now dressed in a black robe, was trying to stop her. "Sarah, let me help you," he said desperately. "It's just a bad dream, love."

Heath pushed past Julian. "It might be more than a dream." He bit into his wrist and drew blood as Vivienne raced over to the side of the bed. Sarah slapped wildly at him.

"Sarah, I'm here. It's Mama. I'm here for you."

But Sarah didn't stop fighting. Heath cupped Sarah's head and held her to his wrist.

"Don't do that!" Vivienne cried. "You're hurting her."

But he held her daughter firmly and pressed his bleeding wrist to her mouth. Sarah whimpered, but as she tasted Heath's blood, she quieted.

What had happened? And what use was she? Her daughter hadn't been soothed by her voice. Vivienne stood, feeling utterly helpless, with her hands fisted at her sides.

In the past, when Sarah woke from a bad dream, Vivienne would put her arms around her daughter. And all would be well.

She touched Heath's shoulder. "What did you mean 'more than a dream'?" Terror trembled in her words.

"I saw into her thoughts for a moment, then they were shuttered to me. Just as yours always are, Vivi. I saw a vampire. And he was imploring Sarah to open her heart to him. To join him."

She glared toward Julian.

"Not Julian," Heath said.

"Then who?"

"At this point, I don't know. I saw him from the back."

"Can you see more?" Something wet touched Vivienne's cheek. A tear. "How can I keep her safe if these damn vampires can get into her mind?"

"We can stop them from doing it. Don't worry." He eased

his wrist from Sarah's mouth. He bent to her, murmured some words in a gentle voice, then lowered Sarah back into her bed, and drew up the covers.

"What was that? Magic?"

"No." He looked to her, and she saw pain in his eyes. "A lullabye."

Vivienne heard her sharp breath of astonishment. And felt a deep tug in her heart, as deep as the one she had felt when she had given birth to Sarah and held her for the first time.

11

Heath carried Vivienne to her bed. Dropping to one knee, he laid her on the crisp sheets. "Don't worry. Sarah will be safe until tomorrow. She'll sleep soundly, now that she's taken my blood. That will keep her mind calm and relaxed. She won't have another nightmare."

The truth was, it wasn't frightening dreams he worried about. And his blood would hopefully protect Sarah's thoughts so another vampire couldn't enter them.

"All right," Vivi whispered.

He watched her stretch out her long, bare legs, with her shapely calves and creamy, silk-smooth thighs. He undid her robe, helped her pull her borrowed nightdress over her head. At every moment, he was growling to himself, *control, control, control.*

He drew up her covers, but he didn't kiss her good night, as much as he yearned to. There was no point in pretending he could have more intimacy with her. Then he snuffed the candles with his fingers and closed the door.

It was close to dawn. The windows were covered with thick,

black drapes, but Heath's body could sense approaching daylight. A clock struck the half hour. Half past four.

He prowled to Dimitri's rooms.

The elder vampire's private apartments were massive, gobbling up the east wing of the mansion. Heath lifted his fist to knock, but Dimitri called out, "Blackmoor. Come in."

Dimitri was naked, sprawled in a leather club chair, drinking brandy—blood-laced brandy. His host motioned to the decanter, flashing a grin. "Have a drink. This stuff is exquisite. The blood of young female virgins makes it delectable."

He searched Dimitri's expression for a sign he was joking. And Heath knew he had no choice. Sexual frustration over Vivi had brought his other appetite to ravenous life. If he didn't slake it, he knew what would happen. His base vampiric instincts would take control. Control would shatter, and he would go out and feed on a mortal's blood.

He poured. The red-amber liquid sloshed into a tumbler. He threw the contents down, the virgin's blood wasted on his tongue. It didn't sit there long enough for him to taste anything.

"I came to find out if you knew why my sire, Nikolai, is in London."

Dimitri drained his drink, lazily scratched his balls. "Nikolai is here? The last I'd heard, he had been destroyed in the Carpathians by a determined vampire slayer."

That surprised Heath. "You have evidence of his destruction?"

All he had as proof that Nikolai was in London was the seal. It might not even belong to his sire. Or if it did, it could have been stolen from his sire's Carpathian castle.

"Rumors only." Dimitri reached for the decanter and refilled his glass. "But you appear to confidently believe he is in London—"

"No. I'm not confident. I haven't seen him. But I believe he is involved with an apothecary, an establishment off Newark Street, behind the London Hospital. It is where Vivienne was getting the medicine for her daughter, the stuff she had to pay for with seduction."

"So you believe Nikolai wanted Vivienne to take the souls of those men." Keen dark eyes flashed as Dimitri mulled it over. "For what purpose?"

"I have no bloody idea." Which was the truth. He couldn't understand why his sire, who had been a vampire since the fourteenth century, would want to murder English peers with the help of a succubus. Quickly he explained how he had accompanied Vivi there. "The mysterious Mrs. Holt told Vivienne I was the man she was supposed to seduce next."

"And Mrs. Holt knew you were not a mortal earl?"

"Yes." Heath paced. "I wonder if Nikolai brought Vivienne and me together." It sounded like madness, but he knew Nikolai was capable of the most impossible magic. Had Nikolai used Vivienne's desperate quest to get her medicine that night to bring her into contact with him? Had Nikolai captured—or destroyed—Raine to send Heath on his search?

"If Vivienne had seduced me into her bed twice," he said slowly, "she could have unleashed my curse."

"You think he wants you to transform into a demon?"

"Yes, because as a demon, I would be a weapon for him. I escaped him in the Carpathians, and I had believed, when I did, that he couldn't follow me. He carried his own curse. He couldn't go more than one hundred yards from his castle without exploding into dust."

"So how can he be in London?"

"I don't know. He was trying to defeat that curse when I first met him. He's had ten more years to work on it. I wonder if he now wants me to transform, so he can release me onto the world. If I transform into the demon he's cursed me to be, I could destroy all mankind. The curse that kept him 'chained' to his castle for five hundred years was placed by a mortal woman who knew witchcraft."

"And you think he wants revenge." Dimitri swirled his brandy. Crimson tendrils of blood floated in it. "I've never understood the fascination with destroying the world. These ancient vampires should learn to appreciate a good orgy." Dimitri drank, but his glittering eyes were watchful over the rim of his glass. "And what of your brother? Madams from the vampire brothels have told me you are searching for him. But when he is found, the council intends to destroy him. I assume you aren't hunting him to hand him over to Adder and the rest of the council."

"Hell, no."

"You know, you never should have agreed to work for them."

Agreed. Heath laughed bitterly. "I never agreed. It wasn't a choice, Dimitri. Ever since I escaped Nikolai and returned to England, the council has kept me in line by threatening to kill my brother. First when he was an innocent mortal, and now that he is a vampire."

Dimitri observed him in irritating silence. Finally he said, "You are a man with no way out. I do know someone who could help you, Heath. A gentleman who returned to England a fortnight ago from the Carpathians."

"Who, Dimitri?"

"Guidon, the historian of vampires. If there is anyone who will know what happened to your sire, it will be Guidon."

Heath had to accept that was true. He had not seen Guidon since he had been locked up in Nikolai's dungeon. Every night, the historian would shuffle down the narrow, steep stone staircase, his book in his hands, his ink and quill balanced on top. Guidon would sit on a stool outside Heath's cell and ask question upon question. *Where were you born? Who was your mother? Why did you come to the Carpathians? What are the names of the women you have bedded? Have you fathered children?* At first, Heath had doggedly refused to answer. Then the torture began. He had been whipped, burned, bitten. Throughout all the excruciating things Nikolai's lackeys had done to Heath, Guidon's questions had droned on and on.

"Dimitri, I want the truth. Have you seen my brother?"

"No. But I assume you haven't looked in every whorehouse in England."

He needed answers. He needed to find out if Nikolai was manipulating Vivienne.

"All right, Dimitri. Where is Guidon? And what is your price for the answer?"

He had an hour, or possibly less, before dawn.

Heath jumped out of the carriage on Charing Cross Road. As soon as his bootsoles struck the cobbles, the cloaked driver flicked his whip. The carriage creaked on its wheels as it made a tight turn in the middle of the deserted street. Then it rattled back the way it had come. Dimitri's coachman was also a vampire. Heath was taking a mad risk by coming out close to daylight; he wasn't going to inflict the same risk on the coachman.

He could have flown faster than travel by carriage, but he had no way to carry clothes or weapons when he shape shifted.

He was likely in trouble.

Small bookshops lined Charing Cross Road, but at this time they were shuttered. He reached the one he wanted, its name on the sign swinging above the door.

He expected the door would be locked but it swung open to reveal a dark room lined with shelves and filled with books. No one stood behind the door. But he sensed a presence in the building. A vampire.

Paper rustled. In the back of the shop, someone turned a page. "I am back here," a voice croaked. Something loud slammed. "Come forth, so I can see you."

Heath complied. At the rear right-hand corner of the store, an old man bent over a desk. There was no doubt it was Guidon. No other vampire was tiny and deformed, with a curved spine and tufts of yellowish-gray hair. Heath had spent months staring blearily at the little gnomelike body through the bars of his dungeon cell. The historian peered upward as Heath approached, revealing clear blue-silver eyes. "You," he spat. "One of the vampire lords. What have you come about? Your lot let my library be destroyed. All the books—all those treasured *words*—are gone."

"I am not one of the vampire lords. And I believe it was vampire slayers from the Royal Society who found the library hidden in tunnels under London."

Filled with red-faced fury, the little gnome stood on his chair. "And that was due to the arrogance and stupidity of the vampire lords. So obsessed with their power, so fixated with proving their superiority to the vampire queens. Such blasted idiots." He sat again, muttering. "Women are always stronger than men. They bear the children. The human race could survive with only one man, but it needs many more women."

Heath sighed. He didn't want to discuss vampire society. "Guidon, I've come to you, cap in hand, for information." He knew to play to the little man's vanity. "I—"

"I know who you are," Guidon interrupted. "I know every immortal creature in this blasted city. You are Blackmoor. I used to question you while you were rotting in that prison of Nikolai, the great warrior lord." The last words came out with sarcasm. "You were a highly resistant subject. Why should I help you now?"

Of course his past was rearing up to bite him in the arse. "There are two beautiful women in desperate need, and your information could save them."

The blue eyes blinked, apparently unmoved.

"All right," Heath said. "How did you open the door? I had no idea you could do magic."

Thin, parched-white lips split into a grin. "Good trick, isn't it? Looks like magic, but it's simple mechanics." Guidon held up the end of a black cord. "This and a few pulleys. Then it appears to dim-witted mortals and some less than brilliant vampires that I can open the door with the power of my thoughts." He cackled. "And I suppose I have."

"You fooled me. I never thought to search for a practical explanation."

"So what do these women want? I haven't got many kinds of books that would interest you, Blackmoor. Not too many picture books of erotica in here." The old man cackled again, then he looked disheartened. "I don't have many books left at all."

"I don't need a book, I need information. And I'm willing to pay well for it."

"And what could I do with your money? I'm going to spend eternity rewriting all those stolen books from memory. You may ask me one question."

There were so many things he needed to know. About his sire. About Vivienne, the medicine, and what someone wanted from her. And Raine. "I need more than that."

"Make it worth my while."

"You said you didn't want money. What else can I give you?"

"How about your firstborn child."

Heath reeled back. "She—she's dead."

Guidon opened his book again. "That is a pity. You have my sympathies; there is no greater pain than losing a child. Perhaps your next child, then."

But there was no danger of that happening. "There will not be a next child."

"Never be too certain of that."

Heath slammed his fist on the table. "Give me some kind of realistic price, and I will pay it."

But Guidon pushed his chair back and leaped off it. The tiny man scuttled out from around the desk, muttering, "Heathcliff George Stephen Winthrope, Seventh Earl of Blackmoor. First son of Amelia and Harold Winthrope. Followed by a second son, Raine William Harold. I keep geneologies. Two sets. One from each vampire's mortal life, and the other tracing the vampire lineage."

Heath waved it aside in impatience. "I don't care about geneol—" He broke off. Was this intended as a hint? Guidon's questions had always been direct. His conversations were not. "What of a succubus named Vivienne Dare? Do you have her geneology?"

The blue eyes went wide and panic flared on the gnomelike face. "Dare. Succubus." Guidon scurried to a stack of books with a sideways gait like a crab. Books tumbled from the shelves. He sent one spinning to the desk, where it landed and flew open.

Heath looked onto the page. It was a list of women's names. And dates. The last on the list was Vivien Rose Crumley. "It is there, isn't it?" Guidon crowed. "Dare . . . That's not her name. Not her name at all. Took her mother's name, Crumley." Guidon raced back to the desk, and drew a gnarled finger over the entry. "Father's name . . . It is not here. I do not understand. It should be here."

"You don't remember it?"

The old librarian groaned in pure agony and paced in a circle, his hands clamped to his temples. "I cannot. But this is impossible! I committed every word in the vampire books to memory. But this—this I do not remember."

"I can find out, I can give you that name, if you let me ask more than one question."

Longing warred with Guidon's natural churlishness. "All right, Blackmoor. It is agreed. Ask your questions."

"My brother, Raine Winthrope. He vanished two weeks ago. Do you know where he is?"

"Yes."

That stunned him. He hadn't expected this—such a simple solution. "Where?"

"With Nikolai, of course. With the vampire who turned you, Lord Blackmoor."

Heath couldn't hunt his sire now. He emerged from the shop to a sky that glowed with the soft pink of dawn. Pulling his beaver hat low, Heath hunched over. His black cloak surrounded him, covering his skin. It absorbed the sun's warmth. But he would feel the impact of dawn.

His fingers were going numb, as were his feet. He clumsily stumbled against the store's front wall like a drunken man. His body felt it was collapsing; it was growing heavy, as though his bones could no longer support him.

He wasn't going to make it.

He could transform and try to fly, which would take him to Dimitri's faster. But he ran the risk of being caught in direct sunlight.

He had to stay as he was. In human form. He couldn't reach Dimitri's. If he tried, he risked death. Risked not making it back to Vivienne.

He had to find a dark place in which to hide until nightfall. Sinking farther into the gloom cast by the tall, narrow buildings, he scanned the street. He had traveled several blocks from the bookstore. Across from him stood a dilapidated structure. The sheer size of the building suggested it was a warehouse, and grime-covered, broken windows held special appeal. It looked deserted. Also dirty, stinking, and uncomfortable, but it would be the perfect place for a vampire looking for sleep.

Something snorted to the right of him.

A dog? Dogs normally retreated and ran from a vampire.

A whiff of sulfur rolled down the sidewalk to him. Hades, he knew the smell. He hadn't noticed it until now, which meant daylight was weakening him faster than he expected.

His every muscle tensed, but his head was dizzy and searing pain was moving over his skin like patches of daylight.

A large black shape launched out of the narrow alley in front of him. Heath jumped back, and the enormous wing, tipped with sharp, bonelike claws, scraped the sidewalk where he'd stood. The body emerged from the narrow, dark opening between two brick walls. The creature looked like a gargoyle—a man's basic form, an ugly face with a long muzzle, claws at fingers and toes, wings with a twenty-foot span.

It was a demon, one of the most simplistic types. It understood only its mission to kill, and it craved a vampire's blood.

The gargoyle roared, and Heath jumped back again. Teeth snapped together in front of his face.

Weak as he was, the last thing he needed was a battle. The teeth surged forward again and he slammed his fist into the side of the demon's face. The blow should have knocked the creature unconscious but only glanced off its face.

Dawn had drained him too much.

The demon made a huffing noise. The bloody beast was laughing at him. Heath scanned the sidewalk surrounding him for a weapon. A pile of wooden crates stood by a boarded-up door. He spotted a metal post for holding horses' reins.

The winged demon lunged again. Its claws reflected daylight. The streaming light didn't bother the creature, but Heath collapsed against the wall. His legs no longer wanted to stay upright.

Claws swooped for him, and Heath threw his body to the side, grabbed a crate, and jammed it upward as the beast's hand came down. Wood splintered. The hand lifted with the crate hanging off it. Enraged, the creature slammed the box against the brick wall. It exploded into shards.

Heath jumped to the metal post. Tried to rip it out of the ground. But what would have been easy at midnight didn't happen now. The post resisted him.

He threw another crate at the beast, and this one shattered against the demon's black, scaly chest. Again it laughed as the splintered box dropped to its feet.

He couldn't defeat it.

Hating the show of cowardice, he turned on his heel. It was his plan to run for another building, in hopes he could find a weapon, but his legs wobbled and failed.

He heard the sound of a wing rising through air behind him, and he dove. But he was too late. Pain raked down his back as the claws dug in. His cloak tore, his shirt parted. The smell of his blood flooded his senses, and agony screamed from his bleeding back.

The cobbles came up fast, slamming into his knees.

The creature appeared to be amusing itself by watching him try to scramble to his feet.

He was going to be destroyed here. Torn to pieces as he grew too weak to heal.

He would never see Vivienne again. Agonizing loss speared him. He didn't want to lose her. Weeks ago, he would have welcomed his destruction. He would no longer be a curse that could go off and destroy mankind. Now he was clawing his way along the sidewalk, fighting for his life. All because he couldn't bear to lose Vivienne.

Vivienne blinked. The room was pitch dark. Heavens, what was the time? There was no sound. No popping of the fire in the grate, no clatter of the maids and their coal buckets or ewers.

She was alone in the bed.

She slid out of bed, groped her way through blackness toward the drapes, and walked right into their enveloping softness. Desperately she tugged at them. She needed light.

The heavy velvet slid aside and sunlight spilled into her room. Her bedchamber overlooked a modest garden. Green leaves shimmered in the sunlight, and here and there she spotted spring flowers in bloom. It was lovely.

But why was the house so still?

Apparently, even the servants were vampires, or they were forced to sleep in the daytime to be available for their master all night. She pulled on her robe and hurried to Sarah's room.

Sarah was sleeping, a bundle beneath a thick counterpane. Then Vivienne froze. Julian was seated in the corner. He slowly got to his feet and bowed to her. "I was watching over her. To ensure she was safe. The other vampires should be asleep now."

She bit her lip, then decided to trust him. "Thank you, Julian."

He yawned and slowly retreated, closing the door. Vivienne kissed Sarah's curls.

She trusted Heath. But she also knew she could not simply accept that a man would keep them safe. She had to think, and plan, and act.

She must talk to Lord Dimitri. He was obviously a vampire of importance. What could he tell her about succubi? She would have to wait until dusk to find out.

There was no point in trying to leave the house. She had nowhere to go. But just because she was trapped didn't mean she could not try to answer questions herself.

She left her room and padded down the hallway, then the stairs, as silently as she could. Last night, she had seen a room filled with books; it had to be the library. But when she reached it, the doorknob rattled in her hand and wouldn't turn. The library was locked? A hairpin slid easily into the lock, but wouldn't turn it—

"Ah, Miss Dare, you are awake. I thought the daylight would rouse you."

Vivienne almost jumped out of her skin. Even before she spun around, she recognized the autocratic baritone. "Lord Dimitri. But—but how can you be awake?"

"I do not need sleep, little one. What is it you wanted from my library? I have the keys. It would be much quicker than you attempting to thwart my locks."

Did danger lurk behind his silky smooth voice? Some men stoked their rage with their very calm. She wished Heath was with her; she would feel safe with him. Wishing for a man at her side was something she had never done.

The door swung open. "Now, Miss Dare, what do you want?"

His library was even larger than Heath's. And as Heath had done, Dimitri lit candles so she could see. The walls soared two stories tall, and each shelf was crammed with books. "I want to know what I am. I want to know why someone is hurting Sarah to force me to seduce men."

"You won't find answers to those questions in books, love. But I could help you. For a price." White teeth flashed confidently, the smile of a gentleman who knew how handsome he was.

"I won't sleep with you."

"Most women are not unwilling."

"I am not most women." Yet, he hadn't said "all" women, she noticed.

His black eyes glittered with amusement. "You enjoyed yourself last night. And I could make it very, very good for you. Miss Dare, I could make you climax so hard, you would not stop screaming until dusk."

If Heath had said those words, she would have melted. But, of course, Heath was never going to say them to her now.

Her heart gave a foolish pang.

Dimitri cocked his handsome head. As though he'd heard the sharp little tug in her heart. "But I suspect you don't want me to fuck you most deliciously because you love Heath."

"I don't!" A fierce blush flew at once to her cheeks.

"He cannot love you in return—"

"I know that. I am *not* in love. Love is a fantasy for very foolish women. And I assure you, I have far more sense than that. But I am not willing to trade my body for your answers. I've decided if I go to a man's bed, it's because I *want* him."

"I admire you, Miss Dare. There are very few women who would wound me so harshly."

That worried her, until she saw his lips quirk into a smile again.

"It isn't just because of his curse that Heath can't love you, Vivienne." Dimitri walked to her and his hand cupped her cheek.

She was going to move away, but stopped. "Then why not? Are you saying he can't because of what *I* am?"

"Hades. If anything, he will love you *more* because of who you are. You are courageous, loyal, strong, devoted, sensual. But Heath cannot love you because a man needs a whole heart to give it to a woman. And Blackmoor's heart was fractured long ago. Only he can mend it, and he won't allow himself to do that."

"But why wouldn't he?" If he was going to live forever, wouldn't he want to let his heart heal?

"Because he killed his wife. And his daughter."

She could not believe it. But she remembered Heath's words. *The curse was payment for my wife's death*. "What happened to them?" She pushed Dimitri's hand away. "How did he kill them?"

"That is something he will have to tell you, but in his heart, he carries the weight of guilt, regret, and loss. Why would you think he didn't try to break his curse? He didn't want to. He wants the punishment. He wants to ensure that if he falls in love again, he can never have the woman he yearns for. You are his hair-shirt, love, and he's happy with that."

Dimitri turned away and sauntered toward the shelves.

"That's madness," she said to his back. "I do not believe Heath is a murderer."

"No, he isn't a murderer. But Heath was a husband and a father. What if he failed to protect his family? You have only known him for how long—three days? But I believe you could tell me exactly how Heath would feel if he caused an accident that stole his family from him."

She could.

"You want to know what you are." His voice was so soft and gentle, it wrapped around her like an embrace. "You must be very confused and frightened. I want to ease your fears, Vivienne."

His voice seemed to draw her closer. Capture her. She crossed her arms over her chest. "All I—I know is what Heath has shown me." She hadn't wanted her voice to sound so shaky and afraid. "I do not understand how I could be a demon and not know it. I never meant to . . . to hurt anyone."

"Heath is wrong about you."

"You mean I'm not a succubus?" She felt a swift jolt of relief.

But Dimitri's eyes seemed to grow larger. He looked like he wanted to devour her whole. She stepped back.

"No, you have nothing to fear. I wouldn't betray Heath in such a pedestrian way. But you, my dear, are not a normal succubus."

"A *normal* succubus. What in heaven's name does that mean?"

"Who was your father, Vivienne?"

"Why should that matter? I don't know. My mother never told me. I assumed she didn't know. I should think I am the child of some rough London stevedore or butcher who forced himself on my mother in the stews. Now tell me what you meant!"

Dimitri retreated, sat on the arm of a leather chair. "If your mother was mortal, you could only be a succubus if your father was a demon. If you want to know exactly what you are, you have to find your father."

"That's impossible! I don't know his name. I have no idea where he lived, or where he came from. How would I find him?"

"There is a vampire who could help you. He is the historian of our kind. Guidon has recorded the parentage, the ancestry, the life history of every demon who walks the earth today."

"I have no idea who he is. How could he know anything about me?"

"I promise you, Miss Dare, he will know everything about you. Heath went to see him before dawn this morning."

"Heath? Why did he go to this vampire historian? Was it—about his brother?" That must be it. It was the reason he would take such a risk.

Dimitri studied her with a grim expression. "Heath has not returned. The coachman and carriage did. He took Heath safely to his destination. But Heath has not come back."

Icy dread rippled through her heart. "It is daylight now! He can't be outside." Then real fear took root, as Dimitri merely sat in silence. "You believe he was killed, don't you?"

"For vampires, the word is destroyed."

She had her answer. Nausea gripped her. "Why would you let him go?"

In an instant Dimitri appeared at her side. "I did not let him. He chose to go. Even knowing how little time he had left." His eyes seemed to bore into hers and she flinched. "Do you not understand, Miss Dare? Heath went on this foolish quest to find out how to help you. And he may not be dead. If he found refuge in the dark, he should be able to survive for today."

Should. But there were no promises. She had nothing to cling to, except hope.

Was Heath alive? She prayed, prayed, prayed he was. But he could be injured and in danger. She was the only person here who could go out into the sunshine and find him.

12

The door swung open silently, revealing a dingy store packed with books. The smell of musty paper was overpowering. But Vivienne breathed in another scent as she entered the shop. A trace of sandalwood.

Did it mean Heath had been here?

The door closed softly behind her.

"Hello?" she spoke tentatively. The door had opened for her, and whoever had managed to command the door to do his bidding now knew she was here.

Prickles danced on the nape of her neck as she glanced around. Then, in a small shaft of sunlight that had braved the dirt-covered window, Vivienne spied a length of black thread. It ran along the wall, supported by metal eyelets. The string was connected to a contraption attached at the lower door hinge.

"So the door didn't open by magic," she murmured.

Footsteps shuffled. Instinctively she moved back, reaching for the knob of the door.

"Wait," croaked a raspy voice. "Don't go. I've never had

anyone as lovely as you in here. Nor as clever. No one before you has seen my little trick before it was explained."

She paused. A small man peeked out from the shelves. He stood only four feet tall. Thin strands of gray hair hung around his ears. Deep wrinkles lined his face. If Drury Lane wished an actor to play a troll, they should speak to this particular man. Yet there was something sweet in his smile, as ugly as he was. And he was looking at her with awe. He leaped up and down in obvious, and very troll-like, excitement. "Tea!" he cried. "I must make tea. Come, come, my dear. Then we shall speak of what it is you want to know."

"I don't have time for tea," she began, but the man—who must be Guidon—disappeared into the back of the shop.

He could feel the light warming the floor. It hadn't reached him yet. Heath tried to move—tried to roll, flop, crawl, even slither. Anything to get into darkness and escape the shafts of deadly gold light, which slanted more and more through a broken window as the sun slowly arced through the sky.

Nothing worked. His brain sent the signal to his limbs to move, but his body didn't respond.

He lay on his stomach. His cloak lay over his back, arms, and legs, but there were jagged tears in it from the demon's claws.

The demon was now a pile of dust, sitting in the middle of the floor of this empty room, in this abandoned warehouse.

The gargoyle-demon had followed him as he'd lurched across the street and stumbled to the boarded-up front window of the warehouse. Heath had ducked at the last minute and the demon's powerful wing had smashed a hole through one of the wooden boards. It was enough for Heath to fall in through the window.

After that, the beast batted him around like a toy. A gouge into his skin here, a rip of his flesh there. The thing assumed he would be dead eventually, and wanted to draw out the pleasure of killing him. He'd managed to stagger into this big room, at the back of the building, still in darkness. He saw a hook and chain dangling over his head, obviously used for lifting boxes. The chain was slung over a pulley and ran down the wall where it was secured to another hook, and a pile of chain was coiled at the bottom. He dove for the hook on the wall.

Fortunately the demon wasn't particularly bright. It followed him. He'd watched it lumber into position beneath the iron hook. Then he'd dredged up one last burst of strength and ripped the chain off the hook. The beast had looked up, only to have its skull crushed.

Ironic to think he'd managed to defeat a huge demon, but would burn in a shaft of daylight. In maybe an hour, light would land right on him.

So he did what any man would do in the circumstances. He entertained himself with a good sexual fantasy.

"Was there a gentleman here earlier today? A tall man with auburn hair?"

Guidon had lit a small stove and now waited for his kettle to boil, dancing from foot to foot as though he had a fire beneath him. Vivienne felt ready to lose her mind.

Finally he seemed to hear her question. "Is it Lord Blackmoor of whom you speak? I recognized him at once, of course. That is why all the records are kept with me. I've remembered each and every one—every vampire who has walked the face of the earth for thousands of years. And every book ever written by vampires is in here, too." He tapped the side of his head. "The vampire slayers took all my books, and I have had to write everything again. Millions and millions of words."

Vampire *slayers*? She quivered with fear. "Where did Lord Blackmoor go?"

"I do not know, madam. He left my shop. It was close to

daylight. I assumed he had to return to his coffin as swiftly as he could."

"But he didn't get home."

"Then he found shelter."

"But what if he didn't?" This was hopeless. She spun and ran back toward the door. But suddenly the little man was in front of her. He laid a gnarled hand on her sleeve.

"Wait . . . Miss Dare, is it not? Lord Blackmoor was asking about you—" A whistle came then; that had to be a kettle on a stove. "Tea is ready."

"I have to find Lord Blackmoor *now*."

But Guidon shook his head. "If he did not find shelter, then it is too late. There is no point in you running out there without a fortifying cup of tea. Come and sit down."

She hesitated. She almost expected the little man to try dragging her. But he watched her, cocked his head to the side. "Does it feel like you have lost him?"

"W—what do you mean?"

"Look inside you, Miss Dare, inside your heart. Do you believe you have lost him?"

She had no idea what he meant. She refused to believe Heath was gone. But that was her heart speaking, and it did not prove anything. "No."

The gnomelike vampire nodded. He grasped a chair with a velvet-covered seat and hurried back with it. "This is for you, Miss Dare."

Tea came in a heartbeat. He had barely left her before he returned, holding a chipped cup by the saucer beneath it. She took it from her host and took a swift sip. Then she moved to put it on the desk. She must go . . .

She swallowed. The flavor was unusual, and it warmed her inside. Then she heard breathing. Slow, steady breathing. She turned swiftly in the chair. But there was no one behind her.

"A connection between you and Lord Blackmoor. Interesting." Guidon had perched on a stool at the desk. He opened a book. Dipped a quill in ink. "Your entry," he said with a frown, "is not complete."

Entry? "Are you telling me I heard Lord Blackmoor's breathing?"

"Is that what you heard? I knew it was something. But then, you only had a sip of the tea."

She stared down into the cup. Could the tea have really let her hear Heath? Perhaps Guidon was lying to her, tricking her. Even poisoning her.

"I would never do any such thing." His small hands had gone to his hips, and he was pouting at her.

He had read her mind. "I—I'm sorry. It's just that . . . so much has happened. Heath can't be out in daylight—"

"Of course not. And you are worried about him. Like a wife." Guidon nodded. He turned the book so she could see it. "See, I have begun an entry on you."

Her real name looked up at her from the page. Her date of birth. Her mother's name. Details of her life. "How could you know this?"

"When any new being is created—or born—I know of it." He motioned around him. "The problem with Lord Blackmoor: he clings to his mortal foibles. He is fearful of emotion. He seeks to avoid pain by avoiding love, but that denies him happiness." The little man looked at her slyly. "I would not be reluctant to love a woman such as you, Miss Dare."

"But Lord Blackmoor has been cursed—"

"Curses can be broken." Guidon waved his curved hand impatiently.

She blinked. "Do you mean *Heath's* curse can be broken?"

At first she thought the gnarled old man would not answer. He had turned his attention to the book that he had put in front of him. He flipped another page in it, ran a blackened finger over the script. Then he looked up. "Of course it can be."

"How?"

"He has accepted the terms of the curse. He does not fight it. Once he no longer accepts it, then he will be free."

"It cannot be that simple. And I'm certain he has wanted to make love more than once—" She broke off, blushing.

"Apparently not enough. He found ways to get what he wants, yet accommodate the curse."

"You cannot be suggesting we just . . . try to break it." If Heath were even still alive—or at least, not destroyed. "What happens if that doesn't work?"

Guidon tapped his quill to his lips. "He would have to make a choice. His existence or his death. But to live as he is, with his heart closed off, pining for the one thing he will never let himself have, what sort of existence is that?" The vampire peered at her. "You have finished your tea. You may now hunt for Lord Blackmoor. But first, I need to know one thing about you. It is something I do not know, which is annoying—for I am supposed to know everything." He stared intently at her. "I need your father's name."

"I do not know it."

"Of course you do. I cannot let you leave until you tell me."

Vivienne felt dizzy. She grasped the back of the chair. She tried to stand. The room turned black, then it was filled with a harsh, white light. No . . . she was having a kind of vision. In front of her eyes, she could see a stark room. Sunlight poured in high windows. A man's body lay in the shadows. . . .

"Heath!" she gasped. She pushed off the chair and stood. "I must go. I've—I've seen him. He is in a room. Not moving. And there is light pouring in through the window." Heath had obviously been unconscious. Which meant he could not escape the light.

"No, Miss Dare. You have not answered my question. You cannot go."

* * *

Heath wasn't a complicated man when it came to his carnal tastes. So his fantasy began simply enough. . . .

He was in the stables, surrounded by the scent of hay. Vivienne walked in. She wore a snug, velvet riding habit. But she opened her jacket and removed it, revealing voluptuous naked breasts, lifted up by the edge of a lace-trimmed scarlet corset.

In his fantasy, Vivienne stood in sunlight—in the shafts that strayed through the barn windows. Golden light played over her bare shoulders. And danced across her graceful neck. As for her breasts, they wobbled and bounced and the sparkling light struck her nipples so it looked like tiny diamonds hung there.

In her hand, she held a riding crop and she tapped it firmly against her open palm. He swallowed hard in anticipation as black leather smacked smooth, bare skin.

There was no escape. Not when he lay spread-eagled upon a pile of hay, with cords wrapped around his wrists, securing him to wooden posts. The same cords bit into his ankles and held his legs wide apart. He'd tried tugging his legs free but her knots were far too cleverly tied, too strong. He was her prisoner. At her mercy.

He shifted a little on the warehouse floor. But he still couldn't move. His cock was growing long and hard at his fantasy, trapped between his stomach and the floor. The thing was damn sensitive. He let out a low moan.

Vivienne in charge . . . He liked the idea of it. He wanted her to feel strong. Confident. Courageous. He wanted to see her sashay with wicked intent toward him, her breasts swaying with her every movement.

He wanted her aroused by the display he made, tied up buck naked in the stables, with his cock standing to attention.

Anticipation should have him savoring her slow walk toward him. She would stroke her crop along the length of his rigid prick. He would let her play, tapping him here and there with her weapon. And wait with bated breath and shaking limbs as she lightly spanked his ballocks.

And perhaps, just to tease him, she would make her breasts bounce with judicious slaps of the crop. . . .

Heath was too impatient. Too aroused. He skipped right to the part where she straddled him and surrounded every inch of his throbbing erection with the silken grip of her cunny. She rode him like a wild thing and spanked his arse between his legs with her every bounce.

He'd never let any woman tie him up. He'd never let any woman control him.

Perhaps why this was his last fantasy . . .

Vivienne ran out of the shop into the thin, meager sunlight. The light fought its way through the soot-filled clouds that hung around the East End. It fell upon the crowds now jostling along the sidewalk of Charing Cross Road.

She had been in the bookstore only a quarter of an hour. It felt like eternity.

How was she going to find Heath? She kept seeing the same vision over and over. A large empty space. Light spilling through high, narrow windows. Heath's body lying on the floor. He was lying on his stomach and a torn black cloak was draped over him.

In the last vision he'd been groaning intensely. She must be running out of time.

She stood on the sidewalk and turned in a circle. Which building was it? Bookshops lined this section of the street.

Heath had spoken of a connection. He had projected his thoughts into her head. Could she do that now? She had to try. *Heath, if you can hear me, tell me where you are!*

Vivienne?

Her heart stuttered. *Heath, is it you? Where are you? I saw you lying on a floor. I can help you—*

I'm in a warehouse. Go down Charing Cross Road. It's a large brick building. There should be a broken window in the front. . . .

His voice died away. She tried to speak to him through her thoughts again, but got no answer. Dragging up her hems, she began to run.

What would he do to her now? So far he'd broken free of her bonds, then he'd swiftly tied her up on the piles of hay. In his fantasy, he was now licking her everywhere. On her taut nipples. Her sweet, juicy quim. Her puckered anus. And the soles of her feet.

He spanked her nipples lightly with the crop, and she moaned in pure, agonized delight. Her nipples were big and hard and flushed scarlet.

Lightly, he tapped the crop on her cunny, gently tapping her clit. She gasped and squirmed, aroused and slick.

But this was his last fantasy, and as much as he wanted to bury his cock in her quim, he had another plan in mind.

He had tied her wrists together, then ran a length of rope to bind her to the post. He helped her roll over, and gently lifted her, so she was positioned on her hands and knees. The ropes at her ankles kept her legs splayed apart. Her wrists were still tied in front of her.

She enjoyed playing prisoner. The explosive way she had come over and over as he tied her up had told him that. He licked his fingers, then massaged the fluid into the valley between her cheeks. Her generous derriere was displayed to him.

"Oh yes," she whispered in his fantasy, "thrust your cock in my bottom. I want it so deep."

She was giving him permission to slide his throbbing erection into her tight, hot derriere. He didn't need any more encouragement. . . .

Heath groaned in pain. He was trapped on the floor, too

weak to even jerk off, tormenting himself with fantasies that wouldn't come true. His trapped cock was as rigid and heavy as a doorknocker. But he had to keep inventing new positions and ideas. He had an eternity of lovemaking to fantasize in the next few minutes.

Footsteps thundered over the plank floor. "Heath!"

For a moment he cursed his weakened mind for playing tricks on him. For conjuring Vivienne's beautiful voice with such accuracy it sounded real.

Then he knew. This was reality. It was Vivienne's voice. Her soft scent flooded the room. She dropped to her knees at his side. The sunlight was touching his cape, and beneath it, his skin was starting to sizzle.

"Oh dear heaven. What should I do?"

He was too weak to speak. Then he managed to croak, "Out of the light."

He would have thought she couldn't move him. But she hurried to his feet, caught hold of one ankle with both hands, and pulled him. He slid along the floor. It hurt, but he didn't care. She managed to pull him to a corner. Then she gasped.

A black object lay on the floor. His cape. It must have pulled off when she moved him. It meant she could see how badly he had been torn up by the demon.

It was a gargoyle-type demon. Part man, but with claws and powerful wings. Daylight made me weak but I managed to kill it.

"You killed it. Thank heaven. But why haven't you healed?"

Special demon, summoned by the council. Vampires can't heal its wounds.

"What are we going to do?"

"Nothing to be done," he croaked.

"I don't believe that. I can't. I won't. Guidon told me to look in my heart. And now when I do, I know I am not going to lose you."

Her words were like a blade through his weakened body. Tough, jaded Vivienne had looked in her heart and wanted to keep him.

She stroked his cheek. The skin there had blistered with the light, but her touch soothed.

"There must be some way," she said softly. And he heard the powerful emotion of hope in her voice. "Couldn't you take blood and heal the way Sarah does?"

Take blood. She was so brilliant, his Vivienne. "Could try your blood," he rasped. "Not vampire blood. Could work . . . "

But she shuddered and he whispered, "You . . . don't have to, Vivi—"

"No, if it would save you, you can have every last drop of my blood." She tugged up her sleeve, baring her wrist, and she pressed it to his lips. The silkiness of her skin, the rush of her blood beneath her fragile skin, the scent of her brought his fangs exploding out into his mouth.

He didn't have the strength to bite.

But Vivi scraped her wrist along his teeth. The sharp points sliced her skin. Blood dribbled and touched his lips, his tongue. The taste flooded him. God, yes . . .

He could move his hand. Slowly he caught hold of her wrist and held it to his mouth. As her blood washed over his fangs and flowed into him, he knew a rush of pleasure like never before. She had to care deeply about him to do this. And she tasted so damn good.

His muscles contracted suddenly and the pleasure burst. A climax hit him hard.

Vivienne heard him moan. Really, Heath's moans were the most erotic sound. So deep, husky, and seductive. She had never imagined how good it would feel to share her blood with him.

She felt so languorous and sensual. Heath was lying on the

floor, and she joined him there, curled up against him. She could feel warmth flooding through his body.

His hips jerked suddenly. He groaned, deep and harsh. Heavens, he had come from drinking her blood.

And she felt on the brink of a climax herself. Ready to explode. As though, with just the flick of a trigger—

He sucked a bit harder at her wrist. He pinched her nipple through her dress. Then he shoved up her skirts, and his fingers plunged deeply into her sopping wet quim.

Her orgasm burst, like the sun rising over the horizon and flooding the sky with light. Suddenly she was glowing inside. Hot and shimmering. She gasped his name. The climax flooded her with a deep, heart-wrenching pleasure. She fell against him, and their hearts thundered, side by side.

Heath pushed off the floor, trying to stand. His legs wobbled and Vivi helped him. She wrapped her arms around his waist and held his hand. Hades, he had not even let his wife treat him like this. He never revealed any weakness or vulnerability.

"I'm all right," he murmured. He didn't want her to hurt herself trying to bear his weight. "My strength is coming back." The wild erotic fantasies he'd spun about her tormented him. He wanted to live out every last one with her, right now. *You can't, idiot. Remember that.*

"What are we going to do? We cannot get back to Dimitri's during daylight, can we?"

"Flower, it's not safe for you to stay with me. Go back to Dimitri's and wait there. With Sarah."

"I left a note for Sarah. I want to get you back safely." She frowned. "Dimitri was awake during the day. And so was that vampire librarian, Guidon. How can they survive in the day?"

A hard smile touched his lips. "Because nightmares do not exist only at night."

"What does that mean? I raced here to save you and I want more than answers that tell me nothing."

He jerked back. Vivienne was entirely different than his wife Ariadne, who had never confronted him. "You are right, love. I owe you more than that. It's a very long explanation."

She sighed. "Apparently we have a lot of time."

Dust from the warehouse floor had streaked Vivienne's deep green pelisse where she'd lain beside him. Her hair was falling down her back in a disheveled mass. He owed her everything. That was the truth, wasn't it? She'd saved his sorry arse. Not just by appearing here and giving him her blood.

She'd saved his life by giving him something to live for.

"I've been a vampire for a decade, but there is a lot I don't know. My sire didn't tell me anything about how life as a vampire works. When I first returned to England, Dimitri found me before I ended up staked by vampire slayers and brought me to his house. He explained the hierarchy of vampire society."

"There really are vampire *slayers*? People who kill vampires?"

"Yes, love. There is a Royal Society devoted to it."

She shivered. "So how does the vampire world work? Does the council act like its parliament?"

"The council is not at the top of our society, though they like to pretend they are. They try to dominate and control other vampires. There are six of them, and they have taught themselves magic and dark arts. Dimitri, however, is a truly powerful vampire, one of the most ancient ones. Dimitri and Guidon are two of the six oldest vampires who were made by the mating of an angel and a demon."

"So those six vampires must be the strongest?"

"No. They are just the oldest. Vampires have evolved."

"Evolved?" She looked up sharply.

"All creatures do. I know that is considered sacrilegious by

English naturalists but it is the truth. It is what I discovered when I was human, and I traveled the world. It is how vampires have existed for so long. When one vampire makes another, that new vampire is not exactly the same. If you and I had a child, for example, our baby would have parts of us both, yet be an entirely new person."

Her breath caught at what he said. He'd used it as an explanation, but now the thought of it hit him cold. A child . . . with Vivienne.

No. He'd had a child. It could never happen again. And it wouldn't because he wouldn't make love to Vivi again.

"The rulers of vampire society are actually the vampire queens. That's why the council was started. Some male vampires chaffed at being ruled by women."

"Of course. Men like to control women," she said.

"No one controls the queens. They are far too powerful."

"But they let the council continue?"

"I suspect they let it continue because it serves a purpose for them. The queens can manipulate the council members against each other to get what they want."

"It is rather like negotiating English society," she said thoughtfully. "Matrons have their powers, lords have others. And all are in a constant battle to get what they want." Before his eyes, she sobered. "Is this my world now, the vampire world? But I'm not a vampire. And not mortal. Do I belong anywhere?"

With me. He yearned to say it. But it wasn't true.

His back began to grow hot. Had a shaft of sunlight penetrated here into the deep shadow?

"Oh my goodness, your back is bleeding again. I don't understand . . ." Her hand moved gently over him, but he flinched. His back felt like it was on fire.

"You need more blood, Heath."

Her sweet wrist was at his mouth in an instant. He plunged

in his fangs, heard her little cry of pain, then she relaxed against him. He drank. But the pain didn't ease, his wounds didn't heal.

He wanted more of her blood. More of its taste.

"Heath?" She tried to pull her wrist back.

No, he couldn't let her go.

"Heath, stop!" She pushed at his jaw, but he wouldn't break free. She tried to pry his mouth away, but he clamped harder. *She was his. He would never let her go. And he would drink every last drop—*

She slapped at him, but she had no strength. Realization flooded him. He was *killing* her. But he couldn't stop. Instinct told him to shove his fangs deeper into her flesh and take all her blood. His fangs wouldn't release.

Panicked, he jabbed his finger into his eye, and the sharp jolt of pain broke the hold. Limply, she fell to the floor, but he moved swiftly and caught her in his arms.

Heath held her, stunned. Horrified. His arrogance had taken his wife's life, and now he had done something even worse. He had almost killed Vivienne, after she had saved him.

She was so weak now. He licked her wrist, afraid to, but he had to seal the wound.

The taste of her blood didn't take control of him this time and one swift flick of his tongue stopped the flow of her blood. But she was white faced and her lips were a purplish blue. She was dangerously weak.

They couldn't stay here. She could not lie on a dusty, damp warehouse floor until dusk. She needed to get water and food, she needed to lie in a proper bed and regain her strength.

He could put her in a hackney and send her back to Dimitri.

No, he couldn't, not when she was unconscious. She could get robbed or raped. He had to take her, but it would be too far to travel to Dimitri's mansion on the river. He could tend to Vivi at his Mayfair town house. His torn-up cloak would protect him from sunlight.

It wasn't that he was worried about saving his godforsaken butt. He had a duty to stay alive to heal Vivi, then to continue to heal Sarah.

Assuming, after what he had just done to Vivienne, she ever let him try to help Sarah again.

13

Her blood was draining away. Her head swam. Panic roared up. She hit him, clawed at him, screamed at him, but nothing was working. She was dying, and he didn't care. He wasn't going to stop. All he wanted—all he'd ever wanted—was her blood. . . .

Vivienne jerked up in the bed. Sheets tumbled off her chest, and she discovered she was wearing her green gown. It was streaked with dirt and dust. She was still wearing her shoes, as though someone had put her to bed in haste. Somewhere, a clock gave three low, petulant bongs and sunlight peeked around closed drapes. Where was she?

Then she noticed small red marks on her wrist. Her dream hadn't been a dream. It had really happened.

She brushed her tangled hair back, trying to remember everything. She remembered following Heath's voice in her head. She had found him in a warehouse, in a room rapidly filling with light. Then she'd offered her blood to save him and he wouldn't stop drinking. She'd fought him, but he was far too strong. He had almost *killed* her. The one man she'd thought she could trust.

The thought made her feel instantly nauseous. It made her heart ache.

But he was a vampire. As much as she'd tried to ignore that truth, it was there. He had tasted her blood and lost control with her. . . . Vivienne got out of bed. *Think of the practical right now.* Blinking away useless tears, she set about determining where she was. This was not her room at Dimitri's house. If she were a captive of the vampire council, she would be in a cell. That left Heath's place—she must be at his house.

Unlike Dimitri's house, this one was not deserted in daytime. Vivienne went out into the corridor. A maid with a feather duster was hurrying down the hallway. "Wait," Vivienne called.

The girl turned. Her brown eyes were wide and she bobbed a curtsy. "Oh mum, I didn't know you were awake. Did you wish for—?"

"Lord Blackmoor. Do you know where he is?"

"The library, I think, mum."

And that was where she found him. His cravat was ripped open and he still wore his torn and blood-soaked clothes. He stared hollowly down at his mud-spattered boots.

"Vivi? Are you all right?"

The pain in his silvery-green eyes stunned her. She'd never had a man look prepared to cut his heart out for her. She couldn't find words—so she nodded.

In a blur, he leaped up from the chair and crossed the room. He dropped to his knees before her. "Vivi, I'm sorry." His throaty voice spoke of agony. "I don't know what happened."

"You're a vampire. You drink blood. I know it wasn't your fault."

He kissed her belly through her dress, gazing up at her. He looked so fearful, so vulnerable. "That's never happened before. I've never lost control before."

"It's proof," she answered hollowly. "Proof we are not supposed to be together. I tempt you and you tempt me. And it is madness for both of us."

He lowered his head. Then leaned forward and planted a kiss on her quim, through her skirts. "Heath," she gasped.

"I promise it will never happen again. And for now, love, we need to be together. I need to look after you and Sarah."

She rested her hands on his wide shoulders. Her instincts screamed *He is a vampire—it had to end this way. Badly, and with you as a victim if you don't run.* Caution and fear had kept her alive in the past.

But she lowered herself so she was on her knees on the rug in front of him. He had only a moment to look startled before she kissed him. A lush, open-mouthed kiss, where she slanted her lips lovingly over his, and tangled her tongue with his. She gave him a long, hot, sensual kiss that promised trust.

He rose to his feet, took her hand, and helped her up. And she saw hope in his eyes.

Then she saw a pile of books opened on the long table that ran down the center of the library. One was open to an etching. Frowning, she picked it up to study it. The picture depicted a man's body, but with a gargoyle's ugly face, long fangs, and huge wings that were tipped with long, white talons. Claws curved on the beast's hands and feet. "*This* is what attacked you?"

"Yes." A smile actually lifted his lips.

She put her hand to her mouth to stop the quaking that threatened to turn her to jelly. "How did you defeat *that*?"

He came to her side, and wrapped his arm around her waist, drawing her to rest against his chest. "With you, love."

"I wasn't even there."

"You gave me the determination to win. To destroy him, I lured him to stand under a heavy iron hook and chain and dropped it onto his head."

"Heavens. Did you truly go to Guidon to find out about me?" The vampire historian had allowed her to leave his bookstore only because she had promised to return and tell him who her father was.

"I had many questions to ask him, but yes, I wanted to find out about you."

"Why?"

"Why?" His brows drew together. "What a question, Vivi. Why do you think? Your entire existence has changed in days. You're afraid, and the council is hunting you. How can I protect you if I don't know where to start?"

A sharp knock sounded at the door. It creaked open, and a slender man minced into the library. He wore crisp white shirt sleeves, a waistcoat of bottle green, and black trousers. His dark hair fell in tousled curls. He looked like a slimmer Byron.

"My valet," Heath said. "Hensworth."

The man clapped his hands. Maids hurried in, carrying towels, bowls of water, a silver tray with metal implements upon it.

"There's no point in trying to stitch the wounds," Heath growled. "I told you that."

His back? Suddenly his voice flowed into her thoughts. *They opened up again a short while ago. The bleeding is only a trickle but—but they won't heal.*

"My lord, I cannot leave you to bleed all day." Hensworth snapped his fingers and the tray of sharp instruments was presented in front of him. "Damnation," the valet muttered. "There is no thread. I believe what I need is in the naturalist room—"

"Leave it there," Heath said sharply. "I don't need it."

"The naturalist room?" Vivienne echoed.

"No one is to go in there," Heath's tone was cold and fierce. "Leave the room locked—"

"Nonsense." She swept forward to the two men. "The wounds need to be tended." She did not know how much his servant knew. She had to be careful. "We will get the thread, clean and stitch you."

"Vivi—"

"It will be done. I am not going to let you bleed to death, when we can try to stop it." She waved at the small, dapper valet. "Do you have the keys to the room? Take me there." Vivienne turned to Heath. She could not stand by and do nothing. "Give me this. Let me try."

Heath slid his hand into hers. "All right, Flower."

Brow raised, his valet turned on an imperious heel and led the way. Heath suspected he would regret this as Vivi tightened her grip on his hand, and she led him to the room he had not been inside since Ariadne and Meredith had died.

Hensworth drew out an ornate key and opened the door. The room looked almost exactly as he had left it ten years before. Ash still stood in the grate, all that remained of the book he had been working on a decade ago. He'd burned it page by page.

Cobwebs dangled from the walls and ceiling, and draped the desk. Books littered the floor. He had dragged every copy of the books he had written from the library and had thrown them in here. He'd intended to tear each one apart and feed it to the flames.

Vivi turned slowly, taking in the scene of devastation. "What happened in here?"

"I did." He pointed to one of the shelves. Stuffed birds stood on it in a row. "If you need instruments, the case will be there." He hadn't touched the scalpels for more than ten years.

But he'd always treated them with meticulous care. They would be sitting in their velvet-lined dockets, all razor sharp and clean. "There should be thread in there, too."

Vivi crouched by a pile of torn books and shredded paper. She picked up a volume, cradled it gently. "You are the author of this book." Puzzlement touched her blue eyes.

"They are all mine. I wrote six books about the flora and fauna I found in my travels around the world. I'd traveled for over ten years."

"Why did you destroy your work?"

"Because it was all that mattered to me." He stalked to a stack of books on the desk. He had to show her what he had been. An arrogant, driven fool who pushed his family away, who hurt them callously. Hard to say whether he was more of a monster now or then.

Vivi moved to him, her skirts shushing around her slim legs. She placed her hands on his chest. He winced, expecting her to push him away. Instead she said firmly, "You must sit with your back to me. I have to try to peel this shirt off you, and I don't want to hurt you."

"Don't worry about causing me pain." After all, he deserved it. So he did as she bid: he turned his back to her and straddled a simple wooden chair.

"I should tend to him, Madam," Hensworth said behind him.

"Nonsense," she said swiftly. "But you can obtain a pair of scissors for me."

"I should at least open the curtains, Madam. You cannot work in this stygian gloom."

"No," Heath barked, but Vivi spoke over him. Smoothly, irresistibly, she said, "No, thank you, Hensworth. It will be fine. My eyes have grown accustomed to it."

With care, Vivi cut his shirt away, peeling the fine linen in strips. Water splashed in the basin Hensworth had put down. Heath hissed through his teeth as a wet cloth stroked along his raw flesh.

"Careful washing is the key," Vivi said. "We must ensure there are no fibers from your shirt inside. It is usually the subsequent infection that is more deadly than the wound." She spoke with confidence.

To Heath's surprise, Hensworth did nothing more than make a soft sound of agreement. Normally it was impossible to shut the man up. But how did she know all this?

Something cold probed into one of the wounds, deep and hard. "Christ Jesus," he exploded.

"I'm sorry, Heath. But there was grit in there. It's . . . hard to see."

His teeth ground as she worked. He knew it would make it easier for her if he didn't move. It would be better for him if he didn't shout and startle her. But he also knew why he was trying to stay silent and stoic. It was his pride, the damnable pride that had cost him everything.

"Now, to stitch the wounds closed."

He half-turned. She held a needle high. In the gloom, she squinted at the needle, threaded it swiftly. He closed his eyes, settled his chin on his hands.

Her hand rested firmly on his shoulder. "You will feel a prick, Heath."

His own prick stirred at her touch. Then a sharp jab of pain lanced his skin, followed by a long tug. He felt the thread slide through. Another stitch followed, her fingers deftly pushing the needle through. His hands were fisted tight. Sweat rolled along his forehead. Normally, he didn't respond to pain; he could tolerate a great deal.

"Why did you destroy all your work?" she asked softly. "Tell me. You must still be angry if you have kept this room locked up, and let it get covered with cobwebs and dust."

He had told himself he owed her the truth. Now he had to see it through. "It was because of all this"—he encompassed the room with a sweep of his hand—"and my stupid, arrogant pride that I lost my wife and child." He paused. "That will be all, Hensworth. I believe Miss Dare has everything well in hand."

"Very good, my lord." Then Hensworth was gone.

"What happened to them, Heath?"

Where did he begin? "Ariadne drowned in a carriage accident I caused. Meredith, my nine-year-old daughter, died afterward." He closed his eyes, the memories tumbling thick and fast.

He remembered swimming desperately through murky water toward Meredith. She was floating beneath the surface, her dress swirling around her. He'd scooped her into his arms and carried her to the riverbank. . . .

"I'm sure," Vivienne said softly, "you didn't cause the accident. I know you, Heath. I am sure you tried to stop it."

"The fault was entirely mine," he said harshly. "I was at the reins of the carriage. I was traveling to London at high speed because of my pride. My intention was to reach town before nightfall, so I could attend a meeting of the Royal Geographical Society. A competitor of mine, Lord Crawley, was supposed to present a paper the next day. It was on the same topic as mine, a study of the causes of malaria on the African continent. I was obsessed with the drive to present my work first. I had spent four years on it, and for much of that time, I had been on the coast of Africa, away from my family. My work had kept me away from Ariadne for years, away from Meredith for most of her life. I was a stranger to my own daughter, and too much of a damn fool to recognize how stupid that was. It was my intention, that day, to travel swiftly to London, alone. But Ariadne insisted they would travel with me. I forbade it, yet when I went to the carriage they were both inside, waiting for me. My wife's act of rebellion infuriated me. I believed I didn't have time to argue so I took off at top speed. Angry and late, I was reckless. I was like any English peer: I saw only what I wanted. I definitely didn't see a farm cart trundle out of a field as I was racing over a narrow bridge."

Vivienne was halfway through stitching his wounds. His story had let him ignore the pain, but it had brought pain to her heart.

"I jerked on the reins to slow the horses. Even then I was too damn arrogant to see the danger. I was enraged the delay would cost me precious time. But as the horses reared and the right side of the carriage began to tip, I realized the bridge was collapsing beneath us. Heavy rains had turned the river to a torrent, and it had washed out the old bridge. The posts under us gave way and the carriage went in."

His voice sounded so flat and hollow. She re-threaded her needle with shaking hands.

"I remember the shock of icy cold water. The carriage had fallen in on its side and was sinking toward the murky bottom. But the current was strong. It slammed us into rocks, then the carriage began to splinter apart. I swam for the door, but the current took me. Luckily it pounded me against a rock. I grabbed onto it before I was swept away. I managed to grab the carriage's roof. I kicked in the window glass with my boots, then I reached in and pulled Meredith out. The carriage had air in it, but water rushed in when I smashed the window. I didn't know whether Ariadne was still alive or not."

Vivienne stayed silent. She knew he was reliving his own private hell. She was afraid he would stop if she said anything.

"I kicked through the current with Meredith clamped to my chest. The water tried to pull her away from me but I managed to reach shore and push her up onto the bank. Then I feared the water would suck her back in so I dragged her farther away from the raging river. I pulled off my coat, even though it was soaked, and draped it over her. Then I jumped back in after Ariadne—"

He paused, shuddered. "Before I even dove under, I heard the rending sound, the splintering of wood. The water was pounding the carriage against the rocks, tearing it into kindling. I let the current drag me toward the rocks, but pieces of the carriage were shooting down the river. I thought . . . I thought I saw Ariadne's hand, reaching for me. Like a madman, I swam, letting my body get pummeled against the rocks. I was too late. I stopped fighting the water, let it drag me. I prayed it would take me to where it had pulled Ariadne. But it didn't. Minutes later, my limbs were numb with cold. I managed to drag myself out to get back to Meredith, but I was sick with fear for Ariadne."

Gently, she stroked Heath's shoulders. He hung his head. "I found my daughter surrounded by people. The farmer had stopped his cart and brought help. A coachman, bless him, had brought a fur throw from a carriage. Desperately, I wrapped Meredith into it. I didn't know what to do. I knew she needed warmth and shelter, but I had to keep searching for Ariadne. In the end, I had to let strangers take her so I could keep looking for my wife. By nightfall, men dragged me away from the river. They told me it was hopeless. They took me to an inn, and I found out they had brought Meredith there. She was lying in one of the rooms, and she looked so pale. I sat at her side all night. But close to dawn, she wasn't cold anymore. She was burning hot and shaking. She looked . . . looked like the men I had seen die of malaria. She had a seizure. Then . . . then she was gone. Her breathing stopped."

Heath closed his eyes. "They both lost their lives because of me. My pride. My blind, all-consuming drive to be the best. My refusal to be beaten. I never went back to my country estate. I bought a desolate house on the moors. But even so, memories haunted me at every turn. For years I had ignored my wife and child, and once I'd lost them, every precious memory I had became a torment. I burned the papers that were going to be my next book, and vowed I would never write anything again. Drinking blocked out the pain and began to steal the memories. Finally I fled England. I went to the Continent."

She fought to focus on her stitching. To take great care. There must have been dozens of times she hurt him, but he didn't even flinch. "And you were bitten there, turned into a vampire."

"I knew if I took my own life, I would have no chance of seeing my family again. Ariadne and Meredith are in heaven. I was sure my daughter was looking down upon me, hating me."

There, the last of the wounds was stitched closed. She stroked his back. The beautiful expanse was a patchwork of black thread and raw, red skin. "You tried to save her life, Heath."

He shook his shoulders, as though shaking off her soothing words. Slowly, he got to his feet, and she gasped. She had never seen such agony written upon a man's face. The handsome mouth contorted in a twisted sneer. His eyes burned like fiery embers.

"I went to the Carpathians because I was a selfish man. I ran away from my estates, from grief, from guilt. And when there was nowhere left to run, save Siberia, I tried to run to the bottom of a bottle. I got so stinking drunk, I was lying on the frozen ground, wondering if I stayed there and died if that would be considered suicide and I would go to hell. Next thing I knew, two hunchbacks in brown cloaks found me. They hefted me between them and dragged me to a cart. My head slammed against wood planks and I passed out. When I awoke, I was chained in a dungeon lit by four flaming torches. A man entered the room; I watched him float through the air. His eyes were gleaming red."

"That was Nikolai?"

"Yes. He tore open my shirt, which stank of spilled drink

and vomit, and he touched my heart. Every memory of Ariadne and Meredith flashed through my head. It was the worst agony I'd ever known. I saw every moment, compressed into the space of heartbeats. I saw them die again. But this time, I experienced memories I didn't know I had. The scream of my wife and child as the carriage started to go. My wife's desperate, calming words to Meredith. Even facing death, Ariadne's first thought was for Meredith—for our daughter, not herself." He sighed. "Ariadne was like you. She was so loving, so giving."

Vivienne stared at him. "Your wife sounded like a good woman. I don't believe I compare to her at all—"

He suddenly caught her shoulders. His mouth slanted over hers, hot and loving. When he stopped, he glanced at her hand. She still clutched the needle.

"Where did you learn how to treat wounds, Vivienne?" he asked softly.

"From my mother. She would do it in the stews. She'd learned from her father. He was a doctor in Exeter."

He gazed into her eyes. "How did the daughter of a doctor end up in London's stews?"

After all he had told her, perhaps she owed him some truths. "That doctor married his daughter to a violent man," she said bitterly. "I never understood why he did it. He tended to people and worried about his patients, yet he sentenced his daughter—my mother—to a living hell. Her husband beat her. And he was unfaithful. He enjoyed hurting her. Then he died. There were rumors my mother had poisoned him. So she ran away."

Heath frowned. "But you said you didn't know who your father was."

She wrapped her arms around her chest. "That man was not my father. My mother had become pregnant twice and both times she lost her baby after *he* had beaten her. But he blamed her for the miscarriages, and beat her for that. She became pregnant with me in London, by some unknown man." She didn't want to speak of this anymore. "As soon as it is dusk, can we go to Dimitri's? I'm worried about Sarah."

"She will be safe, but I promise we will go as soon as the sun sets."

After Heath's story, she desperately wished to see Sarah and hold her. How she wished Heath could have another chance. She'd seen how protective he had been of Sarah.

He had changed, even if he did not believe it himself. She was sure of it.

"The night will be coming soon," he said softly. "I need to plan how to make love to you."

Swallowing hard, Vivienne remembered. How could she forget that tonight would be the same as the other nights? She would crave sex, and Heath would have to think of a way to give her what she needed, without being the one to do it.

First he had to leave Vivienne sexually sated. Then he had to find Nikolai.

Standing outside Sarah's bedchamber in Dimitri's house, Heath cocked his head. He heard feminine laughter. A light giggle that belonged to Sarah and a sensual, throaty laugh that must be Vivienne's. He cracked open the door to Sarah's room. Vivienne and her daughter sat on the edge of the large bed. He saw the soft love in Vivi's face for her child, and his heart gave a low, hard tug.

She was like Ariadne. It was a good thing he carried a curse and already knew he couldn't hope to have her.

Silk skirts whispered behind him. He turned to meet Sadie's large blue eyes. "Lord Heath, I thought I would find you here. Lord Dimitri sent me to entertain Vivienne again tonight."

He shook his head. "Thank you, Sadie, but tonight I intend to pleasure Vivi myself."

The long, amber lashes blinked. "Are you quite certain, my lord, it's safe?"

"I know to take care, Sadie." Then he sent his thoughts to Vivi, hoping he didn't startle her. *Vivi, meet me in my bedroom.*

He lifted Sadie's hand to bestow a kiss, then he went to his bedchamber where he stripped off his clothes. A long cheval mirror threw the reflection of his naked body at him. His skin was so pale it almost shimmered in the firelight. Being undead had made his body leaner. Muscle rippled beneath his skin. His back was still unhealed.

Suddenly, Vivi's voice came into his thoughts. *I know what I wish to do tonight, Heath. I want you to tie me up.*

14

"I want to leave this room and find out what scandalous things happen here," Sarah cried, petulantly. "I am eighteen years of age. That's hardly a *child*."

Hiding nerves, worry, and fear, Vivienne lifted an eyebrow in the way known to mothers—the arch that spoke volumes.

Sarah stomped her foot on the floor and folded her arms beneath the bodice of her nightdress. "You do not let me have any adventures."

"No, I do not. That is what mothers are supposed to do. Keep their daughters safe from dangerous adventures."

At Vivienne's side, the pretty vampiress and new friend, Sadie, tried to muffle a giggle.

Sarah flopped down on her bed, bouncing on the mattress beside a small pile of books. Dimitri had sent many books to keep Sarah amused, including *Pride and Prejudice*, the novel that had so pleased the Regent. Sarah lifted a chocolate truffle from a velvet-covered box, flipped open her book, and popped the entire decadent chocolate into her mouth. "Fine then," she mumbled around the candy.

Leaving Sarah to read, Vivienne motioned Sadie to follow her into her bedroom. As soon as she gently closed the door, Sadie flashed a look at the bed and gave Vivienne a wicked smile. "Well, Vivienne, do you wish to—"

Flushing, Vivienne whispered, "Not tonight." And she swiftly posed her problem to Sadie: how to break through Heath's guilt and touch his heart. She remembered how Guidon had told her Heath welcomed the curse. Tonight she'd learned the vampire librarian was right.

Sadie tapped her chin thoughtfully.

"I must show him I trust him," Vivienne whispered.

Sadie had brightened. "Is there anything you could do with him that would show him? It took me a long time to let a man make love to me in my rump. But eventually I knew he would be gentle, and he made me so hot and bothered by stroking me there that I wanted it, too."

Vivienne frowned. She couldn't do that. Then she remembered the shackles in Heath's carriage. And she knew. One way to prove she trusted him was to allow him to tie her up.

Vivienne didn't expect Heath to be wearing such a look of blatant confusion in his silvery-green eyes when he opened the door. Surely he could hear her heartbeat. It hammered so loudly. And it galloped faster when she saw he'd opened a tall wardrobe in the corner of his bedchamber. Ropes hung on hooks within. Whips—heavens, whips—lay across brackets on the door.

He led her in, then cocked his head. "Are you sure you want me to do this?"

"Yes. Do it now." She might lose her nerve if he didn't.

"Why?"

Dear God, why would he ask that? Men were not supposed to. A woman offered an invitation and they hastily acted upon it, lest it went away.

"I want to—" She wildly searched for a reason. His robe was open and she could see his body. All the hard muscle, the beauty of him, the large, heavy erection. Do this and she let him control her. Once her hands were tied, she would be entirely in his power.

But desire now pounded inside her. She knew exactly why she had whispered the idea to Sadie in her bedchamber. "I want to do something with you I've never done with anyone else."

His breath hitched. His eyes glowed, more silvery and reflective than she'd ever seen them. He inclined his head, then prowled to the cupboard. Before her eyes, he took a length of red velvet rope. Crinkles appeared around his eyes, and he smiled wickedly.

She expected him to tell her what he intended to do. Instead, he came to her, took hold of her wrists, and wrapped the rope around them. He wound an intricate figure eight with long trailing ends. Without a word, he pulled on those ends, forcing her to follow him. He looped them around a hook in his ceiling. And she was bound, with her arms extended over her head, secured like this.

This wasn't what she'd expected.

She wished he would speak. It unnerved her.

But this was to be about trust. She had to trust him.

He undid the knot in the belt of her robe. One twitch of his hand and the silken thing slithered off her shoulders and fell to the floor. Underneath, she was naked. Now her breasts, with erect nipples, bounced slightly. She saw them move in the cheval mirror. And she saw . . .

Her backside, too. There were two mirrors in the room. One placed behind her, so when she looked in the mirror in front of her, she could also see her rear. Her naked rear, provocatively displayed. And not six feet from her exposed derriere stood a closet full of whips.

Trust, Vivienne.

He moved so swiftly, she did not know where he was until he appeared before her and kissed her breasts. His mouth worshipped her nipples. Heat spiraled from each taut, happy tip and burst down in her quim. She ached. Throbbed. Needed. "Heath—"

But he opened his hand and a black leather strap fell. He held the end with his fingertips. It seemed too small to be a rope. . . .

Grasping both ends, he gave it a firm snap and brought it to her face. With her hands bound, she couldn't stop him. He slipped the strip of leather between her lips, tied it around the back of her head. He took care not to tug the tendrils of hair falling from her loose coil.

Raw sexual anticipation shot from her sensitive mouth to her quim. But in the next heartbeat, she thought, *Dear heaven, he has gagged me.*

Part of the game, he said gently in her thoughts, and she realized she had sent them to him. *I don't mean you any harm, Vivi. This is play. You can allow yourself all the thrill and excitement of being at my command, yet know I would never hurt you.*

She nodded. The point of the gag, she supposed, was so she couldn't protest.

You can speak in my thoughts whenever you wish. To tell me to stop.

Never would she have dared try this. Never would she expect she would be so excited. She would never have done this with any other man but Heath. Her cunny was hot, slick, truly bubbling with juices. And he had barely touched her yet. So she whispered her thoughts to him. *Don't stop.*

From behind, Heath cradled her breasts. His large, almost glittery pale hands cupped her ivory curves. He tweaked her nipples.

But she couldn't see him in the mirror.

Then he moved away, and she gave a little sob of frustration into the gag. When he returned, he plucked both her nipples at once. Something in his hand was metallic and cold and she jumped. Or as much as a woman could when her arms were stretched above her head and she was balanced on the balls of her feet.

Then something clamped onto her nipples. Sudden pressure shocked her. "Ouch," she gasped, but the gag absorbed it all.

The mirror reflected her raised brows and quivering lip, her vulnerability. And she knew he would free her if she asked him to in his head.

But the pain was easing. He had put clamps on both of her nipples. Small clamps lined with velvet. Chains fell from each and rubies hung from the links. Many massive stones, and they reflected the flames in the grate, flashing red fire around the room.

Heath sank to his knees in front of her and kissed the plane of her bare tummy. Vivienne giggled into the gag. His tongue flicked out, tracing the round indent of her navel. She squirmed. The rubies danced as her breasts swayed.

Then he kissed his way down.

He parted her nether lips and a flood of her juices gushed out. She could tell from his growl he was surprised by how aroused she was. And excited by it. He slid two fingers inside her. She moaned, the gag smothering the throaty sound.

Gently, he stroked between the cheeks of her bottom. Wet from her quim, his finger slid around her tightly closed anus. Slowly, he eased his finger in. Just the tip. But she gasped at the intense sensations.

Two fingers. He had pressed both his index fingers inside her. They were filling her passage, stretching her. Her tight anus resisted. Her muscles tensed and she made a sharp squeak of protest into the gag.

Relax. I wouldn't do anything to hurt you.

She knew that. She had wanted to *show* trust, but it meant nothing unless she could truly follow through. But a little bit of doubt surged up. She knew men did new things, exotic things when they were growing restless. When they were going to leave.

No, Angel, Heath insisted. *I want to explore with you because it delights me to see you discover new pleasure. It thrills me to see your eyes open so wide, to watch you pant with anticipation.*

She froze. *How did you hear what I thought?*

You must have sent it to me. By accident, I assume. Vivi, I'm not doing this because I'm bored or restless. And this is from a man who sailed thousands of miles to find new creatures, new worlds, new sensations. It took me a long time to understand that every moment with someone you care about is the most astonishing adventure of all. Trust me, love. I'm doing this because I want to share pleasure with you.

His tongue flicked lazily over her clit.

She moaned desperately at the burst of sensation. She saw herself in the mirror. His prisoner—tied up, gagged, with things hanging from her nipples that should be torture but were thrilling instead.

No, Vivi. Even with your hands bound, you control me. You have my heart tied up in knots. I'm your prisoner.

Those words would scare her—could *she* say them? Say her heart was held captive? To not just feel it, but admit it.

Pleasure was like a silky wave flowing inside her. But she stared down at Heath as he tasted her and licked her and loved her. Was that why he'd traveled and stayed away from his home? Was he afraid of love? Afraid, like she'd always been, of losing control? Perhaps it hadn't been grief that had closed his heart; perhaps it had been closed before that. But why?

His tongue surged into her quim, sliding against a secret place that made her legs melt beneath her. She was sagging now, the rope was taut, and he lowered on his knees so her exposed cunny was pressed right on his face.

They were both afraid.

But in this, she could take a step toward being fearless.

His fingers thrust in and out, plunging deeper with each stroke; his tongue swirled over her clit, twirling faster and faster. He moved, lifting her feet off the floor. She was suspended on his mouth and the pressure made her head swim. Her eyes were shut tight. She opened them wide. This was the very first time she'd been bound and suspended and she was going to witness every stunning, erotic second of it.

Tension wound up inside her, and she rocked on his mouth, growing closer and closer. The ropes tugged, the metal hook creaked, and she bounced desperately on his face.

Yes, he urged in her head. *Come for me.*

Like a slave to a master, she did his bidding at once. Her climax broke free. Her scream filled her head, but the gag kept it in. She sobbed his name over and over. She tore so hard at the ropes as she came, plaster dust rained down upon them. The hook stayed in place, at least. And he brought himself to climax.

Vivienne floated in the wave of luscious pleasure.

In my thoughts, Vivi, I heard every moan. I heard you cry my name. Heath spoke the words in Vivi's thoughts, then he tugged the ropes free and released her. The red rings around her wrists made him feel guilty. Gently, he massaged them, but she gave a breathless sigh. "You were right," she whispered. "It was an adventure. It was thrilling."

At once, he turned into a protector. He had to take care of her. Quickly, he wrapped her robe around her. Dimitri had sent sherry to his bedchamber; Heath assumed it had been intended for Vivi. He poured her a glass as she sat on the edge of his bed. She looked delighted but a little shocked, and that gave a tug at his heart.

Finally, he sighed. "I have to go now, Vivi. Tonight, I have to try to find my brother. And now that it's dark I can go out safely. You are free . . . I mean, if you need more . . ."

She was watching him with patience as he stumbled over his words. "I understand if you need to bed someone else tonight. That's what I'm trying to say."

She shook her head. "I won't need to. And I don't want to."

She'd told him that before. This time, deep inside, he hoped it was true. He had no right to want her fidelity, but he couldn't stop the words before they spilled out. "I meant what I said. I'm your prisoner."

"And I can see that scares you."

He jerked his head up. No, she could not read his thoughts. He could see that in the pensive look on her lovely face. In her thoughtful frown. She knew what he felt because . . . because she could understand him.

Christ, that terrified him. He left the bed.

"Is it because you still love Ariadne?"

He had been preparing to pull on his shirt. Surprise made him drop it on the floor. "I don't still love Ariadne," he growled. He hated himself for saying it, because he now knew it was true. Had he ever really loved her? Properly, the way a woman should be loved? Immaturity and arrogance had made him an idiot. His position made him look on his wife and daughter as beautiful possessions befitting an earl. Was an arrogant idiot capable of love?

In Vivi, who was so strong, who cared so deeply for Sarah, he could see what love should be.

He grabbed his shirt off the floor roughly. "I don't love her anymore. That's what I feel so damn guilty about. That was the one thing I had the obligation to do—remember Ariadne and Meredith forever. But when I'm with you . . . you are the only person in the world I want to think about. When I was married to Ariadne, I was running away in search of glory and excitement. Every moment with you excites me, Vivienne." He gave a hard, curt laugh. "That's the madness of this. The very fact that I want you so much means I'm betraying Ariadne. I'm a wounded fool, Vivi, and you deserve what I'm not capable of giving."

With that, because he couldn't face the gentle understanding in her eyes, he took his shirt and walked out.

Heath headed to Dimitri's study first. He walked in to find Sadie lying on a chaise, utterly naked, running her tongue suggestively around a bunch of hothouse grapes. She waved cheerfully at him.

"No, my love," Dimitri growled to Sadie. "You must leave. We have matters to discuss not fit for your tender ears."

An odd thought for a vampire, but true. Sadie still possessed naïveté and innocence, at least about certain things. And ancient vampires like Dimitri believed in old hierarchies and paternalistic views. Young vampires were kept ignorant and women were treated as playthings. Except for the powerful queens, of course.

As soon as Sadie had gone, Dimitri brought out a stack of folded news sheets from a drawer in his desk. He tossed them down. "There have been a series of murders in the last fortnight on the streets surrounding your apothecary. My investigators confirm the finds. Eight people have died from slit throats in the last two weeks."

There were always footpads prowling the slums, ready to cut a throat to steal a few coins. But slicing a victim's throat with a knife, at the end of a feeding, was also a method vampires used to disguise their attacks. Heath knew Nikolai would be determined to feed. There would be no moral compunction against taking human blood for Nikolai. That proud, arrogant man would not dream of drinking animal blood instead.

The papers rustled in Heath's hands. "Did you hire lads to

watch the apothecary, as I asked you to do?" On the first night he'd arrived here, he'd spoken privately to Dimitri about this.

Dimitri nodded. "My investigators would visit them and get reports. They are here."

First, Heath scanned the stories in the newspapers. The first murder had happened two weeks ago. A middle-aged woman had been found dead in an alley, and the small alley was about twenty feet from the apothecary. Within minutes, Heath quickly read all the reports. Eight murders had taken place within a two-hundred-yard radius of the apothecary. The Whitechapel denizens were in a panic, the Bow Street Runners mystified.

Then Heath read the reports Dimitri's investigators had transcribed from their visits to the four boys stationed around the apothecary. They hadn't seen anyone go in or out of the building.

Heath frowned. "I'll start my search there. There must be another place nearby Nikolai is hiding."

His carriage halted on Whitechapel High Street. Heath jumped down, instructed his coachman to wait, and eased his way through the crowd of inebriated dandies, rough tradesmen, and bold penny-whores who filled the sidewalk.

No point in taking his gleaming carriage into the rabbit warren of streets. Not when he could be infinitely more lethal than an armed driver. At least, when he chose to be.

The blood and brandy mixture Dimitri had again provided him had defrayed his need to feed. But it was still a struggle. It wasn't just blood his vampire nature required. It was the hunt and the victory over a frightened prey. Night after night, for years, he had fought that need.

He ducked off into an alley and plunged into darkness. He was haunted again—and a haunted man liked to be left alone.

For the first year after he'd lost Ariadne and Meredith, he'd seen their faces everywhere. They weren't ghosts, but his memories were. His memories flitted everywhere and he could never turn away. Now Vivienne was haunting him.

He couldn't have her. What was it with his bloody stupid head—and heart—that it wouldn't understand the word "impossible"?

He took a deep breath. Even on the fetid air that rolled in from the Thames, he could detect the scent of human flesh and sweat, could pinpoint it to the shadowy place where his quarry was hiding. He found the first of his young lookouts crouched in the dark of a doorway, watching the apothecary from across the street. The skinny, stunted lad wore a dirty brown cap and ragged trousers, and eyed him warily even as he pointed out he was the boy's employer. Finally, he pressed a sovereign into the dirty hand to coerce the lad to speak. He supposed he had to admire the boy's determination to make money. "So lad, tell me everything you've seen. Have either a gray-haired crone or a black-haired man come here?"

The boy shook his head so vehemently, his cap fell forward.

"No, my lord. There's been no one come 'ere in the two days I've been sitting 'ere."

Two days stuck on a foul doorstep. Heath gave him two more coins. "What's your name, lad?"

"Harry."

"You've done a good job for me, Harry. Stay another day and I'll pay you a sovereign for it."

He left Harry fairly leaping with glee and checked with the other boys. Each one watched a side of the apothecary. He was generous with his payments to each, and all the boys gave him the same answer. They'd seen no one. He'd looked into their thoughts. Even if Nikolai had manipulated their memories, he would have detected a sense of blankness or confusion at some point. But there was nothing. Just a stretch of boredom, and the occasional break for a piss.

So why hadn't Mrs. Holt come back? Wouldn't she have expected Vivienne to return? On the other hand, she'd recognized him. Had she also guessed he could help Sarah escape her mysterious "illness"?

One question deeply worried him. What did Nikolai want from Vivienne? What was his plan, what was her role?

He'd spent two years with his bloody sire as a prisoner in a castle in the Carpathians. Nikolai lived like a monk, spending his time writing in large, leather-bound books, while Heath had been rotting away in a dungeon. At night his sire prowled for blood in the local villages, hunting with a pack of wolves that ran with him on leashes.

Heath defeated the lock on the apothecary door again and went in. Eight murders had taken place close to this building. If someone had returned—mortal, demon, or vampire—he should smell a trace of their presence. There was nothing but a gut-curling stench coming from the jars of ingredients, and the smell of abandonment and must.

No one had been in here for days. So why would Nikolai kill victims close to this place? Was he watching over it, waiting for Vivienne to return?

Heath crossed over to the grimy window. Fog rolled down the narrow lane, engulfing the street flares. Narrow shop fronts faced him. Candlelight glimmered here and there behind darkened windows.

Where in Hades would Nikolai be living? Would he really choose to live close to here? Nikolai had taken pride in his five-hundred-year existence, his noble bloodlines, his wealth. He had decorated the interior of his castle to look like a Turkish sultan's sumptuous palace—

Heath? Where are you? Are you . . . safe?"

Heath jolted so quickly, he almost sent a pile of jars to the ground. It was Vivi. How had she projected her voice so far?

I'm safe and am at the apothecary. You are supposed to be sleeping.

I did. For a little while. Now I can't sleep. And Dimitri came and told me he believed I could speak like this to you, even though you are so far away.

It was a testament to the power of the connection they were building. That was what Dimitri would say to him when he returned. For a vampire who held orgy after orgy, Dimitri had a lot to say about love.

Vivienne. Heath suddenly realized how dense he had been. She was a connection to his sire. *Vivi*, he called to her with his thoughts, *why did you come to this apothecary? How did you know you could find the medicine you needed here?*

My mother used to go there, when we lived in the stews. She knew the chemist, old Joseph Hartley. He was an honest man. I suppose he was the only chemist I knew, but I just felt . . . right to go there.

His sire had a great deal of power. He could easily influence mortals, lure them, plant ideas in their heads. Could he have drawn Vivienne to this place?

Had Nikolai arranged all this to send a beautiful succubus to Heath, believing he couldn't resist? His sire knew he would yearn for what he could never have. A lover. A wife. Love.

Vivi, when you lived with your mother in the stews, where did you live?

In many places. We had to go from one flashhouse to another, desperately searching for a bed.

Where were you born? Do you know that?

I was . . . Her voice died away. *I was born in a brothel. It was on a small lane off the Strand.*

Close to here. Was there a reason Nikolai had come to the place where Vivi had been born? Then he blinked. He'd heard the shame in her voice. *Vivi, there is no reason to be embarrassed.*

Heath, I was born in a brothel. A prostitute's child. And you are an earl.

Are you trying to say you believe I think I'm better than you? Hell and damnation, Vivi, you are infinitely better than I am. Now, there's something I have to do. From now on, you can't talk to me—don't try to contact me through our thoughts. He feared Nikolai, with his strong powers, would hear. *I'm going to find my sire. I'll be back soon.*

Heath, wait for me there. Dimitri is worried for your safety and that completely terrifies me. Let me come and help you.

No, love, you can't. There were a thousand reasons why not, beginning with her safety. And he could hunt better if he was not restricted. But he knew he had said no because if he searched for his sire with Vivienne at his side, he would want her at his side for . . . hell, forever.

Stay there, Vivienne. I will come home to you. And this is between Nikolai and me.

Then he smelled the presence of another vampire. He raced to the door, stood in the shadows of the door stoop.

One man sauntered down the road. He moved so swiftly, he looked like he was floating. The light touched on his hair, but Heath had already noted it was auburn, like his. And he knew the silver-green eyes, the shape of the face, as well as he did his own.

Raine.

A prostitute came out of the shadow, right in front of his brother. Her hair fell in matted curls of soft blond, the color of butter. Her oversized dress slid off her shoulder. Dirt streaked her neck, but the display of collarbone and small, round breast were surprisingly clean.

He could feel Raine's blood lust.

And surprisingly, he could also feel his brother's internal battle. Raine hungered for blood, but he didn't want to feed.

That startled Heath. When he'd turned Raine, his brother hadn't been squeamish about drinking from mortals.

Raine was watching the girl but not approaching her. But he wasn't drawing away. Heath knew why. Raine was now caught between the compassion and morality of being human and the driving instincts of the vampire.

Agony was etched on his brother's face. It was how Raine had looked when their parents had died. Their mother first; she'd died in childbirth. Their father soon after, felled by a bee sting. Raine had worn this same look—this stricken expression—when he had looked upon their dead father. He had been only seven, young and frightened. Heath had taken care of Raine as best as he could, but an older brother, one suddenly thrust into the role of earl at thirteen, could never replace a father.

"Oh my god," the girl cried suddenly. "What are ye?"

Raine gave a fierce shout of agony, tipped his head back, and his fangs shot out, lengthening to lethal arcs. The girl shrieked. Heath leaped forward out of the shadows and he dragged the girl against him as his brother launched for the girl's neck. Raine stumbled and his hands shot out. His brother's palms slammed into the brick wall so hard, chips flew off.

Heath pushed the girl behind him. "Run," he told her, knowing she would for he had commanded it. She wasn't like Vivi; she wasn't strong enough to resist him. The girl dragged up her hems and ran, sobbing with fear, down the lane.

Raine swirled to face him, his fangs bared, hissing in animal fury. His eyes gleamed red. The glowing irises went suddenly black as his gaze fell on Heath.

And the older brother erupted inside Heath. "Raine, what in the name of Hades are you doing? Where in hell have you been? I was told Nikolai had you. Is it true? Nikolai made me; he's a brutal beast, a sadist, a raving lunatic. You have to bloody well come home." He was shouting at Raine, drowning him with questions and commands, like he had done ever since he became head of their house at thirteen.

Raine took a step back. "That home is yours." He glowered. "I was always second place to you. I was born to be a spare, and you've always treated me as less. Now I'm as strong as you—stronger—with the magic Nikolai has bestowed on me."

This was his fault. He had pushed Raine too much; all he had done was make Raine crave power and position. Damnation, he hated himself at that moment. "What happened?" he asked sadly. "Did you run away willingly to my sire or did Nikolai find you and take you?" As Raine merely snarled at him, Heath grabbed his brother and shook him. "What is Nikolai doing? I think he wants to unleash the demon in me—or in you. Is that true?"

Raine hissed, flashing fangs.

Christ. "We can't let that happen. Use sense. We can't destroy the world. You have to come with me."

"No." Fierce pride blazed in his brother's reflective eyes.

He'd started wrong. Things had changed. Since their parents' death, he'd kept Raine under control by issuing orders. Once Raine had listened to him, up to the age of sixteen, then Raine had rebelled against every one. Another sixteen years had passed and he was still rebelling now.

Hades, what had Nikolai done to Raine? Heath could guess. The same way his sire had used his guilt and regret and despair to create a monster, he was using Raine's youthful pride and competitiveness to turn him into something destructive and vicious. He didn't want to have to do this—fight his brother. "Have you been with Nikolai since you left the moors?"

"Yes," Raine spat. "He came to me there and offered me a way to enjoy my life as a vampire. He wasn't like you, insisting we had to fight the urge to feed."

"There have been eight innocent people murdered around here. Was that you or Nikolai?"

An evil smile touched Raine's face, distorting the recognizable features. "Why did you come to find me? What do you want? To haul me into the vampire council and watch while they tear me apart?"

"Of course not. You're my brother." God, he loved Raine. And he had failed Raine, if his brother believed him capable of betrayal.

But Raine reared back and looked upward. Heath had been focused on his brother and stupidly, dangerously blind to everything else. A dark figure swooped down from a rooftop and landed silently on the cobbles. Suddenly Heath was facing a man with white-blond hair, black eyes, an unlined and angelic face. Nikolai. The vampire who had made him a decade ago, who had chained him in a dungeon. Heath expected to feel a rush of hatred, even a long forgotten sense of fear. But all he felt was the need to grab Nikolai by the throat and force him to reveal what he wanted from Vivienne. . . .

Nikolai lifted his hand, palm out, toward Raine. His brother howled, clamped his hands to his head, sank to his knees. "Raine, patience. I cannot allow you to destroy him." He turned to Heath. "But if you attack me, I will destroy your brother."

Blue light swirled suddenly around Raine. And when it wafted away, there was nothing there. Raine had vanished.

Heath leaped toward Nikolai, but his sire, older and stronger, could move faster. The blond vampire somersaulted over his head. "Not yet, Blackmoor. We will meet again later, though, I promise."

And in a burst of blue light, Nikolai disappeared.

15

Damn his brother for being such a blinking idiot.

And damn himself for pushing his brother right into Nikolai's hands. For being more of a commanding officer than a brother. For not showing Raine how important and valuable he was.

Heath stalked into his bedchamber to undress. He ripped his tailcoat off and threw it across the room, where it hit the wardrobe and slid to the floor. His waistcoat followed, the buttons popping off and clattering to the floor.

Then he scented *her* at the exact instant she sat up in his bed. The thick claret-red comforter slid off Vivi, revealing her lovely ivory skin, her voluptuous curves. Sleepy blue eyes looked him over from head to toe. "Thank heavens you are safe and in one piece."

Anger at his brother, at himself, and white-hot rage at Nikolai still pounded in his head, but desire overwhelmed it. The kind of desire that a man had to act on, or he'd explode bit by bit—starting with his cock.

Dimitri, damn him, had given Vivi a new nightgown. This one was concocted entirely of ivory lace. Two skinny little lace straps lay on her smooth shoulders, then the lace cascaded down to cling tightly to her generous breasts. Her nipples, when they got hard, would poke right through the lace. . . .

He was going to have to explain to Dimitri the concept of avoiding temptation.

"You shouldn't have waited up for me, love." The sight of her, the knowledge he could never have her, turned anger into tormenting agony. But for the first time, his next thought wasn't "and the curse is your own damn fault." For once, he didn't want to punish himself.

"I didn't. I went to sleep." She stretched her arms to the ceiling.

The movement stopped him cold. Her breasts rose and fell, mesmerizing him. He was right: her nipples did peek through the scanty lace.

"You look so frustrated. So angry. You didn't find your brother?"

She was offering him a welcoming embrace. Christ, it floored him.

Longing overcame him. He whisked his shirt over his head and prowled to the bed. She held the sheets open, a saucy, yet sweetly inviting smile on her lips. It was like a dream. A wild, impossible dream in which he was a normal man, one who could marry, who could offer a woman a future.

He yanked off his boots. A vampire had the strength to tear off even the tightest-fitting Hessians. Still wearing his trousers, he slipped in between the sheets.

He didn't want to make another woman wait for him. He didn't want to think of Vivi wasting her time, the way he'd demanded it of Ariadne.

His sheets smelled of her perfume and the lush natural scent of her skin. He couldn't resist wrapping his arm around her and drawing her close to him. Her lips were poised a mere inch from his, soft and ready.

He couldn't do this anymore. He couldn't stand wanting her so much and not having her. He knew he should leave her before he went out of his mind with the torment. But he couldn't go until he had freed Sarah from her illness and ensured Vivi and her daughter were safe.

Then he would have to face spending eternity without her.

"Did you go to the brothel where I was born?" She bit her lip as she asked. "What was it like?"

"I did go." It had been after his confrontation with Raine and Nikolai. He had wanted to see where Vivi had been born. "There's no brothel there anymore, love. The building burned down. Probably years ago." He stroked her cheek, and she stared at him with eyes filled with raw, open pain.

"I wasn't sure what I wanted—for you to go and find out what the place was like, or to never know. Now I will never know. I'm not certain whether I'm happy about that or not."

He wanted her to understand it didn't matter to him where she was born. And a very naughty way of doing it came to mind.

Vivienne gasped as Heath suddenly turned her so she lay on the bed on her stomach. "What are you up to?" she whispered as he moved over her from behind. His legs rested on each side of hers; he braced himself on his powerful arms.

"If I were to tell you what I'm going to do, you wouldn't let me," he murmured by her ear with cheeky arrogance.

Oh no. Suddenly her nightgown slid up. He lifted it higher and higher, until her bottom was bared to him. He gave her cheeks a gentle tap. She'd never allowed any man to spank her, but she liked this. She liked being on this breathless edge, wondering what he would do. The way her bottom quivered when he gave her a light slap . . . It was very arousing.

"Touch yourself," he instructed, hoarsely. "Play with yourself, while I play with you."

Daringly, she lifted her bottom to let her fingers skim down to her quim. She stroked her cunny. Already, she was soaking wet, her nether lips slippery and slick. With her rump in the air, he could see her fingers dallying in the folds, boldly pleasuring her clit.

He growled, grasped the cheeks of her bottom, and spread them apart. "Heath, what are you—?"

Something warm and wet touched her tailbone. Who knew that one spot could make her toes curl in delight? She twisted to see what he was doing, and he licked the base of her spine. He slicked his tongue over her, then ran his tongue daringly, shockingly down the valley of her bottom.

She tensed. Gasped. Moaned. Protested.

But he didn't stop. He licked the tingling, tensed, sensitive entrance to her bottom. He circled the rim, then plunged his tongue inside.

Good heavens, he was doing . . . what those two vampires had spoken of doing on the first night she came here. Now she knew why. It was exotic, forbidden, and utterly exquisite.

He thrust his tongue in her bottom, and it felt so hot inside her. At the exact same instant, she raked her fingers over her clit. Pleasure forked through her. His tongue thrust in and out; she screamed to the heavens, and came.

She fell on the bed, her derriere tingling. Behind her, Heath laughed, then stroked the sole of her left foot with a firm, devilish touch. She almost leaped off the bed. "Don't do that! It tickles—"

Her words died. Heath was up on his knees, his right hand wrapped firmly around his thick shaft, his left harshly massaging his balls. Still breathing hard and floating on the velvety bliss of pleasure, she watched.

He was a typical man, containing his moans. His eyes shut,

his long auburn lashes dusting his cheeks. He looked absolutely adorable when masturbating, and she watched every swift moment of his jerking hands.

He let his head drop back. His mouth opened wide, but he didn't shout. Instead, his hands gripped so hard she feared he'd break either his cock or his balls, then his hips jerked and he came. His white cum jetted out, spilling over his hand.

He groaned. Then he collapsed on the bed beside her, panting hard. "Flower, even when you don't touch me, you slay me."

She had to laugh. Despite her fears for the future, her fear over the danger to her and Sarah, her worries for him, Heath could make her laugh.

He gave her a smug grin. "There. I don't care where you came from. To me, you are beautiful, wonderful, exquisite. Every blessed inch of you. And I proved it, didn't I?"

"Yes," she whispered.

A knock sounded at the door, and a soft voice called, "Mother?"

Vivienne shoved her nightgown down. "Sarah?" she called. "Just a moment, dear, and I'll come to the door."

Heath must have recognized her embarrassment. He swiftly fixed her nightgown—heavens, one of her breasts had fallen out of the bodice, and she hadn't noticed. Then using his preternatural speed, he slid out of the bed, yanked on his shirt, and reached the door.

Sarah blinked at Heath, startled. "Oh, Lord Blackmoor. The maid said you hadn't come back yet." She looked over to the rumpled bed. Vivienne had never felt so embarrassed as now, as her daughter's eyes widened at the sight of her open robe and disheveled hair, and heaven only knew if she were still pink-cheeked from pleasure.

Seeing this, what would Sarah think? Oh, Vivienne knew exactly what her daughter would think.

"Come on then, my dear. Do you wish me to leave while you talk to your mother?"

Sarah smiled. One of her fey, lovely grins. "You don't have to, you know."

"Don't have to what?" Heath asked. He remembered being perplexed by half of the things Meredith had said to him. But how could he have understood her world, when he'd rarely been there to see it?

He admired Vivienne. For devoting so much to Sarah. For caring so deeply for her daughter.

Sarah gave a knowing look to her mother. She crossed her arms in front of her pink silk robe. "I know he is your lover, Mama. I'm not a child anymore."

Vivienne's blush was as dark red as his bedspread.

Sarah suddenly smiled again. She looked like Meredith had when he'd returned from a long voyage and had pulled a wrapped gift from behind his back. He realized he could remember Meredith's face clearly again. The way she looked when she smiled. The quiver of her lip before tears would come. Talking about his family to Vivienne must have brought his memories back.

"Goodness," Sarah said. "You have captured my mother's heart. I thought no gentleman ever would."

If the realization about his memories had astonished him, this slammed into him like a runaway carriage.

"Sarah, are you upset about this?" Vivi asked cautiously. "About . . . Heath and me?"

Heath noticed she did not say anything about whether her heart had been captured.

"Of course not. I'm absolutely delighted. I'm upset because I am tired of being stuck indoors reading books and eating chocolate. What is going to become of us? What are we going to do? I don't want to hide in here forever. I would love to go riding again. Or go shopping. Or eat ices at Gunters. I want to do the things I haven't been able to do for so long."

Heath, I have no idea how to answer her. I've always been able to comfort her. Now I can't.

The intimacy of Vivi's words, the fact she would turn to him, touched his heart. "Sarah, love, this is for your protection," he said. "It won't last forever, I promise you. But I'm the one who is making these draconian rules, to keep you and your mother safe."

"You are? And my mother is listening to you. I was right about how much she cares for you. But I want to stop being a prisoner." Sarah gazed at him with impossible-to-resist blue eyes. "Can't we at least go outside?"

Vivienne saw pain flash in Heath's eyes. He literally flinched as Sarah laid her hand on his forearm and whispered, "Please."

"I'm sorry, Sarah. You can't go out."

"No, we cannot," Vivienne added firmly. "There is too much risk."

Sarah turned to her. "But you went out to save Lord Blackmoor. Nothing happened to you."

"I refuse to let you be put at risk."

Sarah stuck out her lower lip. "You said it won't be forever. But how can it not be? It feels like we've been trapped for eternity!"

Heath sighed. "Sarah, the council controls creatures who could pursue you in the daytime. Your mother should not have risked her life for me. It's a miracle the council didn't attack her."

Vivienne saw Heath give her a disapproving look as he said it, but the sort a husband would give a beloved wife. It startled her. "Dimitri might have some solution so you could at least go out into the garden," he said.

"Lord Dimitri spoke to me while you were gone," Sarah

said. "He had me brought to his parlor. He asked me not to speak of it to you but—"

"Dimitri brought you to his parlor?" Heath asked sharply. "And he didn't want you to tell us. What in blazes did he do?"

Icy shock stole Vivienne's voice. But Heath's barked words made Sarah draw back. Vivienne hurried to her daughter. "Don't shout at her, Heath." But her legs felt wobbly. What had Dimitri done to Sarah? One unwanted touch could devastate Sarah forever. "What did he do?"

"He just talked to me." Sarah's large blue-green eyes filled with uncertainty. "I didn't want to keep it a secret from you."

Vivienne was ready to kill Lord Dimitri. To stake him in the heart, the fiend. "What did he talk about?" She knew what men did. They used suggestive banter, seductive words, to try to put all sorts of erotic ideas into an innocent girl's head.

But Heath grasped her wrist. "Don't worry, Flower. If Dimitri deserves to be staked, I'll do it."

And she knew he would. But she realized she hadn't projected those thoughts to him, yet he'd heard them.

"S—staked? He just asked me about my father," Sarah cried.

"Your *father*?" Vivienne echoed.

"He asked who he was. I had to tell him I didn't know. I was so ashamed . . . because I couldn't tell him."

"Ashamed," Vivienne repeated, her heart shattering. "You shouldn't be ashamed. It is not your fault I was not married when I had you. You are perfect and wonderful and beautiful and you shouldn't feel ashamed!" And suddenly she realized this was what her mother used to do. Even though they lived in squalor, even though her mother, Rose, started drinking and wouldn't defend herself, she had always defended Vivienne.

Heath's hand slid across her low back. As though he was touching her to give her strength and support.

"Who was he?" Sarah cried. "Why would you never tell me?"

Vivienne couldn't answer. She didn't want to lie to Sarah, as her mother must have lied to her. Rose had insisted her father was a gentleman, but since she was a succubus, her father must have been a demon. She shouldn't lie, but she wanted to protect Sarah. . . .

"He must have been one of your protectors," Sarah said. "I know he must have been some peer of the realm. I won't go to him and tell him I know, if that's what you're afraid of."

Guilt slammed into Vivienne. Of course Sarah would believe she was a peer's illegitimate child. "I simply can't tell you, Sarah." She could say she didn't know, but it would sound terrible. It would make her sound like a whore.

"I need to know!" Sarah cried.

She knew it wasn't fair to deny this to Sarah.

Heath suddenly stepped forward. "Shh, Sarah. Perhaps Vivienne—"

"No, Sarah is right. She deserves to know." Vivienne knew what he was thinking. That she didn't know, and he was going to save her from the pain of revealing that and the pain of breaking her daughter's heart.

"It is not right for me to keep this a secret." She clasped Sarah's hands. Never had her heart beat so fast. Not even when she'd feared for her life at the hands of the vampire council. She would make her daughter hate her; that seemed worse than death right now.

Heath's hands slid up over her shoulders. He had moved behind her. He had told her he was a man who had kept away from his family. Yet he was here, supporting her.

She spoke desperately in his thoughts. *Heath, I don't know what to do. Sarah's father was a peer but he . . . coerced me.*

He forced you?

No, not quite.

Tell her. I think your daughter will be strong enough.

He was right. She clasped Sarah's hands and led her to the

edge of the bed, drawing her to sit down. "First, Sarah, you have to understand I was born in a brothel near Whitechapel. And my mother never told me who my father was. I always wanted to know. I always tried to imagine who he was. Someone rich, and titled, and dashing. But I suspect the truth was not what I imagined. Your father was titled. He was a duke, but he was not one of my protectors. The truth is, he pursued me even though I turned him down. He was a very arrogant, very strong man, and as a duke, he was used to getting whatever he wanted. He wanted me, and he . . . took me."

Sarah stared at her, in shock. "He raped you? My father raped you?"

"He didn't use physical force." No, the duke's particular pleasure was not forcing himself on an unwilling woman. He liked to place his victims in a trap from which they could not escape, until they begged him to do whatever he wished, just so they could go free. The duke had stalked her. Then he had hired a dozen investigators to look into her past. She had always pretended to be a gentleman's daughter, born in the country. Her protectors wanted to believe she was a pretty gem with a pretty little past. The duke had found out the truth, and he tormented her with it. She had been seventeen—young and afraid of such a powerful man. Finally she let him fuck her, just so he would get bored with her and not reveal the truth about her birth.

And she gave Sarah the truth, as gently as she could. She tried to make his obsession sound like it could be considered passionate love instead of a lust for power and control.

But Sarah was far too astute. Her face blanched. Pain and anger flashed in her eyes. "But . . . but my father was . . . a monster. He was horrible. And I'm his child."

"His character has nothing to do with you," Heath said softly.

"How can you say that? You are an earl because of your bloodlines! If I am the daughter of such a man—"

"You are the daughter of a strong, courageous woman."

Heath's vehement defense wrapped around Vivienne's heart and squeezed tight.

He grasped Sarah gently by her shoulders. "You were raised by that woman. It is not your birth that makes you who you are. You choose to become what you are. I might be an earl, but I was never a noble man."

"That isn't true, Heath," Vivienne declared. "You are noble."

He ducked his head. "It took becoming a vampire for me to learn how to be noble. It is the events of your life that shape you, Sarah. And the people who truly love you."

Impulsively Sarah stood on her tiptoes and pressed a sweet kiss to Heath's cheek.

Then Sarah suddenly smiled like a little sprite. "Goodness, are your eyes becoming watery, Lord Blackmoor? I did not know vampires could do that."

16

Vivienne unlocked the library door and negotiated her way through the dark to the curtains. Pulling them open, she saw it was raining, but enough light spilled into the room so she could see. Dimitri had given her the key.

She had stormed into Dimitri's room this morning. . . .

"You had no right to speak to Sarah about her father," she had furiously declared.

Her host was dressed as he often was, in nothing more than a silk robe. "I was trying to understand whether Sarah could be a succubus, too. If she had a mortal father, it means she is likely human and mortal."

Vivienne had almost swayed with relief. But she tersely said, "You should have spoken to me, not to her."

"Your daughter is a grown woman, Miss Dare. And this is my house. You have my word I would never harm your daughter, but I cannot promise I will not try to help her understand what is happening to her." He had slanted her an ominous look. "You must tell her what you are."

"I don't even understand what I am."

He had casually tossed her the key to the library. "Then find out, Miss Dare. The last section of bookshelves beside the window contain my books on the succubus."

So here she was, running her fingers along the spines of the leather-bound books. She pulled out one, *Anatomy of the Succubi.* But it proved to be filled only with pictures of naked women—many breasts, cunnies, and derrieres. After an hour, she knew little more than she already did. Many of the books detailed erotic tales of bold women seducing men. Some of the stories were so outlandish—including one about a peer who was seduced in the middle of the House of Lords, for heaven's sake—they had to be fictional.

"Mother? What are you doing in here?"

Vivienne jerked her head up. She had been so busy reading, she hadn't noticed Sarah walk into the library. "Ew." Sarah was flipping through a book. "Why are you reading these ghastly things?"

Her heart constricted, but she knew Dimitri was right. "Sarah, there is something I must tell you. At first, you may not quite believe it. I know I refused to. But it's true."

She couldn't look Sarah in the eyes, but she spilled everything out—everything she now knew about what she was.

And when Vivienne finished Sarah threw the book down to the table. "Mother, that's ridiculous!" She was trembling, staring down at one of the pictures—of a naked fanged woman who was fiercely sucking a man's neck.

"I know I am not like that. But I—" Words failed her. She tried . . . "If I do not engage in . . . in sexual intercourse, I develop intense pain. I come close to death. Sarah, it seems things we once thought existed only in horror stories are real." *And I am one of them.*

Sarah leaped up. "No, this is madness."

"It is why the vampire council wants me."

"Am I a succubus?"

She had no answer except the one Dimtri had given her. Slightly altered. "Lord Dimitri doesn't believe so."

She reached for Sarah but her daughter pulled away. Sarah yanked up her hems, whirled around, and ran like a gazelle out of the library.

Vivienne wanted to follow, but she knew Sarah needed time. She slumped into one of the high-backed chairs. Her shoulders felt heavy, her heart barely wanted to beat. Frightening your daughter was exhausting business.

Sarah probably wasn't a succubus. Vivi closed her eyes, repeating that over and over. . . .

Hot, brilliant sunlight splashed across her closed lids and she opened her eyes. Instead of stacks of books, she saw a stretch of lush green fields, a vivid blue sky, neat hedgerows. She was *outside*, in the country, and perched on a sidesaddle on a dappled gray mare. Skirts of emerald green velvet flowed over her legs, and a peacock feather dangled in front of her face.

She was in a *dream*. At her side, a horse snorted and hooves pawed the ground. She turned, afraid to look at the man who sat astride a horse beside her, the man she must be preparing to seduce in her dreams.

Relief and desire slammed into her at once. Beneath a tall beaver hat, Heath dazzled her with his wide grin. The lazy arrogance in his smile set her on fire. It ignited her desire to do something . . . mad. She had never ridden before, but here, in this fantasy world, she gave the reins a snap and sent her gray mare off at a fierce gallop.

Heath charged in pursuit. Wild, fey exhilaration shot through her as her horse galloped across the grassy meadow. She leaned forward, whipped by the flying mane, but feeling as though she was the one taking up the ground in long strides. This was soaring. *Flying*.

A low green hedge rushed toward her. She took it and flew up into the sky, weightless for a thrilling moment before landing. Before the mad chase continued.

Heath raced after her. His beaver hat tumbled behind him. He caught up on the right side of her, grasped her horse's bridle, and brought both horses to a stop. The animals panted and so did she.

She turned to him, then he caught hold of her chin and forced her to lean to him. He captured her mouth in a kiss. Her heart galloped every bit as fast as she had just raced. Through corset and velvet, her nipples strained.

Heath leaned back and murmured, "I've always wanted to do this. And doing this with you is a fantasy come true."

"What? Kissing? Riding?" Or perhaps he meant being outside in the sunshine . . .

"Fucking you on horseback."

His hands slid to her waist, and she knew the sensation of floating through the air one more time. He planted her in front of him on the saddle with her back to him, between his warm, hard body and the horse's long, elegant neck.

"How?" she gasped, but he pushed her skirts up, revealing leather half boots, filmy stockings, then her bare thighs. Sun warmed her suddenly naked skin. Beneath her, the horse shifted, and she cried out. "This thing is rather huge, you know." She twisted to see him.

Hand on his trousers, he grinned. "Thank you."

"The horse. I meant the horse is enormous, and we're very high off the ground . . ."

His trousers opened, and he withdrew his cock, which was, of course, magnificent, hard, and very huge. "Never fear, love. I'll keep you safe. I promise: once you're on top of my cock, I'm not going to let you fall off."

"You are—incorrigible. Terrible. We can't do this on a horse."

He laughed, eyes glinting in the sunlight. "Flower, you're supposed to be seducing me. You're supposed to be driving me mad with lust. Then you climb onto me and give me so much damn pleasure, I give you my soul when I come. Like this—"

He pushed his shaft down to stroke her with his cock. With his strong arms, he lifted her, lowered her, and she cried out as inch after inch slid inside her bubbling cunny. She lowered until her bottom pressed against his balls, which rested outside his trousers, and her clit brushed the curls at his pubis. He kissed her—a hot, melting kiss—and his horse moved beneath them, dancing lightly on the grass. Together they rose and fell, his cock stroking sensitive places.

"Now, love, we ride."

A light tap of his heels and his horse cantered. He moved with his mount's stride, and impaled on top of his hot, luscious cock, she moved, too. Up, up she went as he did, and when his hips lowered, she was suspended for one breathless moment before sliding down along his rigid shaft.

He held the reins in his right hand, held her waist with his left. And urged his horse to gallop. Each bounce sent his cock thrusting deep inside her. She was sobbing with delight. And they were cantering swiftly now. Her jaunty hat sailed away. Her hair tumbled. And she saw another hedge approaching fast.

Heavens, he was going to take it, with her on top of his cock. She closed her eyes as he squeezed his thighs, tightened the reins, and lifted. She went with him. And as they soared over the hedge, she cried out and came explosively on top of him.

Hooves struck the ground. Sobbing with ecstasy, she held him. And as the horse galloped and she laughed with the thrill of her orgasm and the giddy relief of survival, he came, too.

Heath laughed lustily as he brought his beautiful black

mount to a stop. "You, sex, and sunshine," he murmured. "Someday, Flower, I'm going to have all three. . . ."

Then he was gone. The green grass vanished, the sky went dark, and the dream whirled away from her. She tried to hold on to it. But she jolted back to earth—or at least she woke in her chair. Rain spattered against the tall windows.

Vivienne.

Gruff and low, the eerie masculine voice slipped into her head. It wasn't Heath's, though he could speak in a similar way, raw and hoarse, when he was aroused. She refused to dream of another man. The succubi in Dimitri's books went to many men, a different one each night, stealing little pieces of their souls. But she didn't care what she was. All she wanted was Heath.

Vivienne.

She tried to push up from the chair. Why did she feel awake, but also trapped, pinned to the chair and held in a dark fog? Sound whispered behind her—the brush of boots over the carpet.

But the chair wouldn't let her escape. Desperate panic gripped her. She was not going to seduce another man.

This is not about sex, Vivienne. The man spoke in her thoughts. *I am not a mortal man, not one of your prey. I am your father. I've waited a long time to be able to come to you. My name is Nikolai. Now turn around and look at me, Vivienne.*

Fear tumbled in her tummy. How could she dream of her father when she had no idea what he looked like? But the spell—or whatever it was—that bound her to the straight-backed chair vanished. Suddenly, she surged to her feet. She spun around.

A dark figure stood in the shadows, completely shrouded in darkness. She couldn't see a thing. Not his face, nor his attire. She had the impression he stood very tall, far taller than she did.

She could barely distinguish the edge of a cape, and a tall beaver hat upon his head.

I cannot come closer, my dear. Not close enough so you can see me. I cannot penetrate this house. There are shields around it. You have to come to me, Vivienne. I want to explain to you what you are, what your past was. Follow me now, and then you will be able to see me. I've waited so impatiently for this, my beloved child.

Beloved child. "I'm not your beloved anything," she snapped with pride. "I have no idea who you are. You abandoned us. You didn't care then, and I don't care to know a thing about you now." She knew she shouldn't do this. She must find out what her father was and what had made her. Pushing him away was a foolish thing to do, but it was the pain of so many years of knowing she'd been abandoned.

"I never abandoned you, my dear." His voice flowed, deep and coaxing. "But the rules of my existence are strict. I could not take you with me. I could not let you know what you were; it would have put you at risk from the vampire queens. By leaving you with your mother, by letting your power stay dormant, I kept you safe. I watched you from afar, watched you grow up to be beautiful and strong." His voice was husky and lulling. Filled with aching regret.

"I am a vampire," he said. "And we are not supposed to beget children with mortal women. It is against our code. But now, you have brought your true nature to life. Now I can be with you."

"How could I be a succubus for years, yet didn't know it until now?"

"Come to me, Vivienne, and I will explain everything." He retreated, slowly floating backward toward the window.

Sense told her not to move, but her feet wouldn't obey. They took a hurried step in his direction. Then she ran after him, her hems flapping around her legs. The wall loomed closer, but she could not stop moving. . . .

She suddenly stepped forward into unfathomable blackness.

Strong arms grasped her around the waist. *You can walk right into your dreams and go anywhere you wish. I have waited a long time for the moment you were awakened. But now you will see the power you have.*

She sent a message desperately through thought, as she felt herself rushing through an icy cold void. Perhaps her father would hear it, but she had no choice. *Dimitri. My father has taken me. I don't know where I am going but I will try to tell Heath when he awakens. If I can.*

Vivi, can you still hear me?

Heath ran down Whitechapel High Street, jostling through the crowds of tired workers, drunken men, and tattered prostitutes. The street flares barely cast light into the fog. He had wanted to strangle Dimitri with his bare hands. How could the damn vampire have let Vivienne's father get to her? Yes, the demon had done it through Vivi's dreams, and logically he knew it wasn't Dimitri's fault. But anger sizzled wildly inside him.

Heath? Your thoughts are so faint. It is like you are miles and miles away.

He prayed he wasn't. Her directions had brought him here, to the stews where he had encountered Nikolai last night. His senses tingled with apprehension.

I remember a street name. She whispered it in his thoughts.

Heath paused. That was a street on which one of the murders had taken place. He found the narrow lane and turned down it. The mist made the cobbles shine. Hooves clopped. In the fog, bawdy female voices shouted rude remarks and burst into boisterous laughter.

The building was tall and narrow and a brown brick, she went on.

He stood in front of a structure that matched the description. His nape hairs lifted, like a dog scenting trouble. This had to be—

A brilliant bolt of silver light slammed into him at the exact instant he recognized his sire's white-blond hair and handsome face. What in hell? How had he let Nikolai get so close without scenting him? He knew how. He'd focused all his senses on tracking Vivi.

Another bolt of light hit his chest, and he reeled back. Stars shimmered in front of his eyes, then everything went black.

Heath awoke to see silvery-green eyes, eyes exactly like his own, staring at him. He jerked up and the chaise he was lying on threw up dust as he moved. Faded and torn curtains framed dirty windows. A chandelier sagged from the ceiling. He blinked, recognizing the place as a former brothel, apparently abandoned.

His brother greeted him with a wary stare. Then Heath's heart sank. Raine held a crossbow aimed at his chest.

"Raine, for Christ's sake, whatever Nikolai has promised you—whatever power or wealth—it's a lie." His brother didn't flinch, just stared at him so emotionlessly it terrified Heath. "Let me tell you what he did to me in the Carpathians. . . ."

He had never told Raine. Even after he had been forced to transform his brother into a vampire. Even when he'd explained the curse to Raine. He had never told his brother about Nikolai finding him in the mud, branding him, torturing him, and locking him in a dungeon. Now he told his cold-eyed brother everything.

"Raine," he implored. "He wants to change one of us into a demon, a monster capable of destroying the world. I know that is not what you want. It is not who you are. I remember you as a boy." Christ, why did Raine just stare at him without speaking? "Do you remember sailing boats together in the stream that ran behind the house? Do you remember capturing salamanders? I put mine in our father's bed, but you made yours a pet."

And as he spoke, he remembered how harsh a brother he had been after their parents died. No wonder he had driven his brother away.

Heath, I—I think my father has done something to your brother. He is controlling his mind. You must be careful. You must try to escape. My father has vowed to destroy you. I don't understand why. He says it is to protect me—

He heard Vivi's desperate voice and turned his attention from Raine. He could be destroyed, because Nikolai could use Raine. And Nikolai was Vivienne's father. *Vivi, are you all right—?*

He couldn't finish his thought. Raine punched him in the jaw. Hard enough that his head snapped back. What the hell?

Raine stared at him, blankly, as he doubled his fists and bounced lightly on his feet, the way they both used to do when sparring in Gentleman Jackson's ring in London. A flurry of fists came at Heath, and he tried to dodge each blow. One caught his shoulder, another slammed into his cheek. Driven by a vampire's strength, Raine's blow hit him with the force of a cannonball.

He couldn't hit back. And Vivi was right. Nikolai was controlling Raine's mind. Heath would not beat up his brother. No matter what.

But Raine was backing him into a corner. What happened if he let his brother kill him? Would Nikolai try to use Vivi to invoke Raine's curse?

Another punch connected with his jaw, sending him reeling.

His skin had split on his cheek and blood flowed. His wounds didn't heal. And he felt weak. If Raine kept this up, he could be beaten to death. He was losing his strength.

"Yes, my foolish young vampire, you are losing your strength and it is because of Vivienne." Nikolai strode into the room, his hand gripping Vivi's wrist. Wild fear flashed in her eyes at the sight of Heath. He supposed bruises were blossoming, and blood was running down the right side of his face.

"Stop," she cried. "You are going to kill him."

"No, my dear. His desire for you is killing him. It is weakening him. He is tearing himself apart inside because he wants you so much, yet he cannot have you."

Vivi had been crying; tears had tracked down her cheeks. If Raine would stop hitting him and get the hell out of the way, he would tear Nikolai apart.

His sire was Vivi's father. The truth of this stunned him. Knowing what a vile monster Nikolai was, learning the truth must be killing Vivi. How could her good heart and her capacity for love withstand learning she was the child of a purely evil vampire? He had to get her out of here.

But Nikolai had slid his arm around her shoulders, in a sickening parody of the way a parent would hold a child.

"You are so strong, Vivienne. See your strength in his pain."

"Stop!" she cried. "I don't want to hurt anyone. And stop forcing his brother to hit him. It's cruel and vicious. Heath won't hit back. He loves his brother."

"And that is what makes it so amusing."

"Amusing?" she cried.

Nikolai grasped her chin and stared into her eyes. "You are not what I thought you would be," he mused. "There is much work to be done. I thought you would be hungry for power. Haven't you learned, Vivienne, that you need power or you will be a victim, just as you once were in the slums?"

"Not this kind of power. What you want to do is mad. Vicious. How can you turn either of these men into a demon?"

"And can you look me in the eyes and truthfully tell me you believe I should spare mortal men? By destroying them, I am making them pay for their brutality and cruelty. You should embrace what I am going to do."

"I—I won't," she whispered. "Let Heath go. Let all of us go."

"This is your destiny, Vivienne. You are the first of the most perfect succubi. You are stronger than any female demon there has ever been. Of course I am not just going to let you go."

She pulled away from Nikolai just as Raine hit Heath in the gut. That was enough. Heath grabbed his brother's arm and swung it behind Raine's back, pinning it there. He could taste the coppery tang of his own blood. "Let her go," he growled.

"No, she is mine." Nikolai's black eyes flashed red. "I created her, and now you have fallen in love with her. But you are far stronger than your brother. Much stronger than I expected you to be. But now, let me show you how powerful I could make her, if I wished."

Foreign words flew out of Nikolai's mouth and suddenly Heath was overpowered by Vivi's unique, feminine scent. The lush smell of her skin, the ripe earthy aroma of her cunny. Her scents called to him as though he were a wolf ready to mate. His cock thickened and stood upright. His fangs exploded. Lust hit him like a wave.

No. He had to fight this.

Nikolai snapped his fingers and a frightened-looking man in grubby clothes stepped out of the shadows. "Ye want 'er now? Am I supposed to give 'er to 'im? Like I gave the others to ye?" The man pushed a woman forward. A bedraggled-looking woman who wore a dirty gown and a fussy bonnet. Nikolai grasped the woman's arm.

Heath could smell the mortal woman's blood. His hunger was swamping his head. He shoved Raine aside so hard, his brother sprawled onto the floor. The woman screamed and she tried to run, but she crashed into the locked door. Realizing she was trapped, she pounded on it.

"Look at him." He heard Nikolai triumphantly shout to Vivienne. "You are turning him into that. It is your scent that has brought out the beast in him. You made love to him once, and that has given the curse more power over him."

Dimly, Heath saw Nikolai grasp Vivi's arms and force her to look at him. "He never feeds from mortals. Never. He has denied himself blood for months at a time. But because of you, he will become the very thing he has fought against. A mindless animal. He will act like the demon he is destined to be."

"No, stop it. Please."

Heath could not stop prowling toward the terrified woman. Her blood lured him. His body throbbed with the desire to feed.

"Stop it!" Vivienne screamed.

"That is what you want?" Nikolai asked, and the conscious part of Heath's mind heard the triumph. What in hell was his sire doing?

"Yes. Please, yes," Vivi desperately answered. Her blue eyes were huge with fear. And—hell, and guilt.

Laughing happily, Nikolai pulled a long wooden stake from a pocket in his flowing cloak. "This is the only way to stop him." Heath knew he had to regain control, but the scent of blood was flooding his head. *Think. Think like a damn man, not a beast.*

Nikolai stalked toward him. He couldn't turn away from the terrified woman, even to protect himself. He wanted to take her—

So he did. He scooped her into his arms, like a rescuer, and the motion seemed to snap his senses free for a moment. Long enough that he was in control and ran straight toward Nikolai. He jumped over his stunned sire and ran to Vivienne.

She was swaying on her feet. And she shut her eyes as he came near her. "No," she mumbled. "No. I want to wake up."

Hell, Nikolai had brought her here through a dream, the way succubi went to men in the night. Could he take control? He had to get them out of there. He knew now what Nikolai wanted: to drive that stake through his heart and destroy him, then force Vivienne to make love to Raine and trigger his curse.

Vivi, he shouted into her thoughts. *Take control. Dream that we are outside, that we are at my carriage. We are going to escape.*

The room suddenly swirled around them. Vivi screamed, and the woman in his arms did the same. Surrounded by women's cries, Heath felt himself hurtled forward into darkness. And in the next instant, hard cobbles were beneath his feet, snorting horses stood in front of him. Dimitri's coachman held the door open. He still held the mortal woman. And Vivienne faced him with wide, startled eyes.

"You did it, Flower." He hugged Vivi tight. "You saved us all."

17

Her father was the vampire who had made and cursed Heath.

Heath wrapped his arms around her, but Vivienne pulled away. Shame and horror brewed inside her, making a caustic mix of acid and bile. She slid into the shadows by the carriage wall and pressed her shoulder hard against paneled wood, filled with ruthless anger and despair.

Her father was not just a demon; he was a brutal, unconscionable killer, and she had seen the proof of it with her own eyes. He had planned to drive a stake into Heath's heart. He wanted Heath to bite and kill an innocent woman. They had taken that poor woman to her home, and Heath had soothed her with a handful of sovereigns.

Nikolai had told her he was going to destroy Heath to protect her, because Heath would make love to her and change, then kill her. She didn't believe Nikolai. Her *father* had been delighted by the prospect of killing the man she loved in front of her eyes. Never would she believe he was doing that for her.

How could Heath look at her without thinking of what a

vile monster her father was? Vivienne jumped from the carriage, slipping her hand free as Heath tried to clasp her wrist.

"Vivi, love, wait—"

But she didn't. Stones skittered from beneath her feet as she rushed up the steps, passed the footmen who stood as guards at Dimitri's door, and plunged into the cool darkness.

She stumbled through the house, winding blindly through the corridors. Dimitri's guests halted their conversations and turned to stare at her. One couple even paused in the middle of a fierce session of lovemaking against a wall, stunned, apparently, by the sight of a tearstained woman running as though for her life. She reached her room and slammed the door behind her.

Her father was a monster. What did that make her?

She knew what she was. A horrible, destructive demon, like Nikolai. She would destroy Heath just by making him care about her. Her father had created her for that very reason. In her, he had wanted to create an irresistible evil intended to destroy human men. She was to have been the first of an army of succubi.

Tears dropped to her cheeks. This was the exact same torment Sarah was going through—

"It's all right, love."

She knew it was Heath, and his deep, throaty voice made her throat tighten. His lips slid over the back of her neck. At once she shivered with heat and awareness.

"How can you bear to touch me?" she cried. Guilt dragged at her shoulders, pulled at her as though trying to swallow her up in the depths of hell. "The vampire who ruined your life is my father. He has taken the one thing that you've wanted. The promise of love."

Heath only hugged her tighter. He pulled her back against his wide chest, and rested his chin on top of her head. No one had ever held her like this. No lover. Certainly not her vicious father. No one but Heath.

"It's not entirely his fault, Flower. When I went to the Carpathians and tried to live in a constant drunken stupor, I was looking to destroy my life. Your father merely helped a man find the eternal damnation he wanted. It has nothing to do with you, Vivi. You didn't control what he did. You didn't even know who he was."

Heath undid the fastenings of her gown. His breath teased her ear as he peeled her dress from her, his touch gentle. Not like a hot, lusty lover, but like someone who could love her.

He deserved to love someone, and not the person who could destroy him. "No, you cannot do this."

"Vivi, you are no more like your father than Sarah is like hers."

"But I'm destroying you! My father explained everything to me. I am the reason you aren't healing anymore, why you almost attacked the woman to drink her blood. My very presence is destroying you. Just by making love to you once, I've given the curse more power over you. And it's killing you."

She covered her face with her hands. "My father tried to kill you. And I am so terrified that he will use me to do it."

"Angel . . ." His voice was so soft. "You don't have to be afraid of what you are."

She half-turned and met his silvery gaze through the veil of her fingers. "Yes, I do. I am a demon. It's my fault those men are dead. I didn't mean to do anything—I didn't know—but it doesn't change what happened. Wouldn't the world be better if I was destroyed? But then I think about Sarah; I can't leave her alone."

Heath's hand cupped her chin. His eyes flashed sparks at her, like flecks of gold leaping off a roaring fire. "No. Don't ever say you should be destroyed."

"But it's true. I told my father I would never take a man's

soul again." She flushed. She had shouted it at Nikolai and he had given a sardonic, infuriating laugh in return. "He told me I will become worse. The pain I feel will get stronger. He told me I won't age; I'll stay like this so I can be pretty enough to lure men into making love to me. I don't want to do that! I won't ever do it again." And her father had not told her she was immortal.

But then, she guessed Nikolai intended to destroy her when he was finished using her.

Heath stroked her trembling arms, then cradled her. "You won't have to."

"But don't you see? I've only survived because you have given me pleasure. But that is destroying *you*."

"You are shivering." With brisk efficiency, Heath peeled her gown down to her ankles. She had to step out of it. And before she could blink, he returned with a thick velvet robe from her wardrobe.

He drew it on her, and just as she was about to protest, he slanted his mouth over hers. She tried to pull free because she had no right to kiss him. But his grip on her waist was far too tight. And the kiss turned her shivers into ripples of desire.

I want to prove to you how lovable you are, he whispered in her head.

"You—you can't make love to me."

"No. But I can do this—"

His tongue traced the line of her neck, along the back. His tongue was so warm, so firm, trailing hot and moist over her tingling skin. The tip ran up and down, making her quiver, and ache, and need.

She tried to pull away, but his hands locked tight around her waist. "You have to stop," she whispered. "The more you do this, the more you are turning yourself into a demon. These kisses mean my father is winning."

But he shook his head. "There is no way I could stop touching you now, Vivi." His palms skimmed up along her side, following the now wrinkled silk of her velvet robe. She had to moan at the firm, delicious pressure. "I need this," he murmured, and cupped her breasts.

Her breasts almost seemed to swell and plump at his touch. His palms brushed her soft bosom inside the robe, rubbed over her nipples. Her cunny ached for him.

"Stop," she gasped. She shoved at his broad, heavily muscled chest, trying to push him away. But he didn't budge. "I can't do this. It only proves my father was right. I'm a monster. I just vowed I would never bed a man again, yet here I am, on fire for you. You only have to touch my nipples and I'm burning for you. I can't resist you—"

"Then don't. I know exactly what I'm doing, Vivi. This is about love. You don't believe you should be loved. And I intend to show you how much you are."

He bent his head, held her breasts up, and flicked his tongue over her nipples. Deeply, intensely, he sucked in her right nipple. Pleasure shot through her, leaving her weak in the knees. Then he let her nipple slide out, reddened to a happy scarlet. And it no longer looked like a plump little thimble; it stood up higher, fuller, harder. Her nipples adored him.

And her heart . . .

Love.

Another four-letter word. Very similar to hope, yet even *more* dangerous.

She clutched his shoulders. Pleaded with him through her thoughts. *Stop. Stop. Stop.* But he didn't obey. And she wasn't strong enough to push him away—because he was big, and as immovable as a brick wall. And she wasn't strong enough in her heart.

From nipple to nipple, Heath moved. Licking. Caressing. Suckling hard. She let her head drop back. And sobbed with the sheer agonizing pleasure of it. "It's hopeless. I don't want you to stop."

"I've only started, Vivi."

He dropped to one knee in front of her. He lifted her foot, balancing it on his palm. The position opened her cunny to him, parting her nether lips with a sticky little tug.

Smiling, he arched up and pressed his mouth to her dark gold curls. He kissed her there, between her thighs.

She had to grasp his shoulders or she would have melted to the floor. She blotted everything else out. Fear. Guilt. The future. Instead she shut her eyes tight and *felt*.

His tongue was firm at the tip and could flick her most sensitive places with teasing punishment. When he applied the flat of it in a long sweep over her clit, it rasped in a way that made her very soul quiver. His breath was a swift breeze of heat. He was thawing her. She knew it. He was making her so hot, he was melting the cold fear wrapped around her heart.

She clutched his shoulders and ground against him . . . and surrendered to the pleasure.

Next thing she knew, his mouth was on hers, tasting salty and earthy. He broke the kiss, rested his forehead against hers. Tears lay in her eyelashes. Tears . . . tears that slid out and would not stop.

He scooped her into his arms. "I could make love to you," he rasped.

Pure terror sliced icily into her heart and stopped the tears. "No, you can't. You cannot forget about the curse."

"I could cut my own heart afterward; destroy my body before I became a demon."

"Heath, you can't." She would not allow it. She would not let him make love to her.

"It would be worth it. For one more time with you."

Now she was scared.

He carried her to the bed, and her heartbeat became a roar in her ears. But he shook his head. "Don't worry, love. I won't do anything stupid. Just touch me, Vivi. I need your touch."

He needed her touch, when she was bringing him nothing but destruction.

"I need it to live, Flower. It's as simple as that. My existence isn't worth anything if I don't have your touch. That's how I feel." He got off the bed and took off his clothes. He never stopped looking at her as he did.

He was so beautiful. She'd never savored a man's body as she savored his. But Nikolai had said each act of pleasure between them was making Heath weaker.

"My heart needs your touch, Vivi," he said. "You talked about destroying yourself to protect the world. That's what I should do. And I would, except—"

Dear heaven, was he going to say except for her?

"Except I need to stop Nikolai. I'm sorry—I know he is your father—but I have to stop him. I can't let him unleash either Raine or me on the world."

"There's nothing to be sorry for. He's a monster. I know that. I know what you have to do."

"Your touch," he said softly, "gives me hope. I know that's hopeless—" He gave a wry smile. "But for a little while when I'm pleasuring you, I can forget the future. So please, love. Give me what I crave so much."

Her hand trembled a bit. Her fingers brushed the bare skin of his forearm. She stroked his arm, tracing the lines of his veins. He had such beautiful arms. She got on her knees. Put her mouth to his right bicep, kissed along the hard bulge, and watched him shudder.

"What are you proposing?" she whispered. "Are you going to take me to Dimitri's orgy and watch me again?"

"I don't know." Deep, harsh lines framed his mouth.

She swept her fingers up over the crest of his shoulder, then slid her hands down his chest. Daringly, she tweaked his nipple. She had to swallow the bite of tears. She wished they were both normal. Mortal. She wished she was pinching his nipple for erotic play before he would lay her down and make love to her. . . .

She ran her hands over the ridges of his abdomen. Then, with two hands, she clasped his cock.

But he eased her hands away, his prick moving with a swift upward jolt as she released him. "I know of a way we can have a night of pleasure ourselves. Just the two of us."

"You aren't planning to make love to me and then . . . drive a stake in your heart, are you? I am not going to allow it."

"No, my beautiful one. We're going to share pleasure, but my cock won't touch you."

Vivienne had pulled on a scarlet robe, but Heath prowled naked along the corridor. With his long stride, his relaxed posture, he moved as comfortably as if he wore evening dress. Vivienne knew she would never feel as natural about sexual things, about being naked, as he did.

He reached a door, jiggled the doorknob. Then he whispered some words in a soft voice, and the lock mysteriously clicked and the door swung open.

She blinked. "Was that magic?" She thought of Guidon's door. "Or a trick?"

A sly grin curved his mouth. "Both. I believe this was Guidon's invention for Dimitri, created a century ago. The metal inside responds to the resonance of a voice."

Heath winked, looking rather like a naughty boy. A naked, muscular, beautiful naughty boy. He crooked his finger. "We have to sneak in. Dimitri won't be pleased if he catches us. He saves this room for his female conquests."

Now she was terribly intrigued. She glanced up and down the corridor, but really, for all she knew Dimitri could sense them from the other side of the enormous mansion. Heath pulled her inside and closed the door behind them. The lock clicked again. A golden glow filled the room from a small fire in the grate. Light slanted along the polished doors of six closed wardrobes. It fell upon two chaises of Grecian design, two wing chairs, and a low table that stood in front of the fireplace.

She had expected the room to be lit only by bluish-white moonlight. Instead, several lamps added to the golden glow. Heath flashed another smile that made her legs shake, her quim throb. "I think our host intends to use the room later." He crossed the room toward one of the large wardrobes.

"What is in those?"

"Dimitri's collection of carnal toys." His eyes glinted teasingly.

"You are joking," she said.

"I'm not. Honestly."

"He collects them?" The half-dozen wardrobes were enormous. How many whips and riding crops and shackles could any man need? Giggles hit her then. "Are they . . . used toys?"

"I assume so. Though washed, or repaired, and then given a place of pride in his collection room."

"Repaired. Heavens, how does one break a sex toy?"

His grin sparkled with wickedness. "Vigorous thrusting?"

"I suppose." She giggled as she tried to imagine how. "Would it be possible to break one in half? Perhaps by trying to balance on it before it was completely inside?"

"Balance on it? What naughty things have you done before, Flower?"

She couldn't answer. She had used a dildo for her own pleasure. She would put it inside and lie on her bed, using the mattress to thrust against.

Heath's low laugh seemed to flood through every nerve. Deliciously. She had never done this. Laughed so openly and freely with a man.

Heath opened the set of doors in front of him. He reached up onto a shelf, his buttocks tightening as he did, turning his derriere into two hard, rounded globes. She swallowed hard.

He turned, holding the most enormous carved . . . thing. Long, ivory-white, and gleaming. He held it up. "A phallic toy, carved from an elephant's tusk."

"But it must be two feet long! Surely no one would ever want that inside them."

"I know for a fact this one was used. Dimitri had a woman masturbate with it—on his dining room table while his guests ate dessert."

She clapped her hand to her mouth. "This time you *are* joking. You must be."

"No. The woman in question enjoyed herself."

"Well, *I* am not going to try that. *You* can." Then she flushed. For she knew how men used such toys on themselves. Many men liked to have their anuses pleasured.

Heath leaned against the bedpost, legs crossed at the ankles, his erection straining in front of him. "Would you like to see that?"

"I should call your bluff, Heath, and command you to do it. What if I were to tell you I won't have an orgasm with you tonight unless I see you take all of that massive thing inside your arse—?"

Suddenly he was in front of her, his palms clamped hard on her derriere. He pulled her against him and slanted his mouth over hers.

It was a kiss to launch a wildfire, a fire hot enough to scorch half of England. He yanked open the belt of her robe and the sides parted. The smooth, rounded tip of the ivory phallus he held brushed her tummy. So did the taut, shiny head of his rigid cock. The ivory cock stroked over her, moving lower. His penis stayed put, dabbing sticky fluid against her belly.

Heath nudged the fake cock between her thighs. Rubbed it

back and forth until she quivered, and grew wet and creamy inside.

"Just the tip," he whispered against her lips. "Just the tip to tease you. Watch."

She looked down. And gasped at the sight of his large hand wrapped around the gleaming ivory shaft. She saw it disappear between her legs, between the scarlet silk.

"I wish this was my cock doing this to you."

Heavens, Heath's voice was strained. She looked up at his face. His jaw was tense, and deep lines bracketed his mouth. His lids had turned sleepy with lust, and his thick lashes hid his eyes.

He looked daringly experienced, yet astonishingly innocent and vulnerable.

She wanted him. She didn't care about unleashing demons. Or destroying the world. She burned too much.

"It feels like your cock. As big and long as you are," she whispered. He had rested his head on her shoulder as he slid the shaft in and out from between her thighs. Smooth ivory stroked between her nether lips like a bow coaxing music from a violin.

He brushed the dildo along her throbbing clitoris with each pass. Her toes curled; her legs were swiftly turning to jelly.

"Look down, my love. See how wet you've made it. I wish, love, I could dip myself in you and get drenched."

The ivory was glistening with her juices. She reached down and touched her quim, moistening her fingers. She touched her damp fingers to his balls. "I want to make you wet with me. This way. With my fingers."

She heard his breath catch. And she looked at his face. His thick lashes were lowered over his shimmering eyes. He looked like she felt: so caught up in desire he could barely open his eyes.

"All right, Vivi, my love. Stroke yourself. Then make me wet."

She trembled as she delved her fingers around the dildo he still held there. Goodness, her juices were bubbling out. She was so astonishingly wet. And in an instant, her fingers were slick and sticky. She stroked them along the hot, remarkable length of his prick, loving the velvety feel of him, the rigidity beneath.

"God, yes," he growled. He watched every brush of her fingers. He'd forgotten his duty to ply her with the enormous gewgaw between her legs. But she didn't care. She wanted to please him for a while. Then she could give him a tap and remind him to pleasure her. . . .

His fingers brushed hers out of the way. The dildo fell to the wood floor with a clatter.

He gripped his cock in his tight fist. The veins strained on the back of his hand, on his forearm, and on his shaft. "I can't resist you anymore," he growled. "I want you *now*."

18

"Oh no. No. No." Vivienne danced back from Heath, almost stepping upon the dropped dildo. Would he unleash his demon if he just put his cock inside her?

She had no idea how much he had to do. Just one thrust? Did he have to climax? In the demon world, what was making love considered to be? The attempt or the conclusion?

She couldn't risk anything. If Heath even thought he had unleashed the curse and was going to become a dangerous demon, he would stake himself. She knew him well enough now to know he'd do it without hesitation.

Vivienne placed her hands over her quim, ready to fight him. But he turned, slowly stroking the remarkable length of his thick cock, and he strode to the wardrobe. When he returned, he held two more ivory toys, one in each hand.

She took several quick breaths of relief as she tried to take her next thought in stride. "One for me, one for you?"

He shook his head. "Both for you."

"How?" But she could guess his answer before he said it.

"Trust me," he said. "Now go over to the chaise. Position yourself on all fours upon it. Wait for me."

Heath spoke in a dark, hot, commanding tone. She should have bristled; she'd never let a man order her about. That was the delight of becoming London's most desired courtesan: it allowed her to make rules, set limits, take charge. But this time . . .

This time she wanted to surrender control.

She wanted to surrender everything to Heath. She was ready to claim what she'd always wanted.

A man with whom to share pleasure. A man all her own. A man who did not use gifts to buy her, contracts to control her, arrogance to subdue her.

Heath treated her as his partner. His equal. Not as a toy to be owned, played with, and discarded.

Her palms and knees sunk into the soft padding of the chaise. In this position, her bottom stuck up in the air, high, rounded, and naughtily exposed. Her full breasts hung down and bounced as she moved.

Footsteps sounded, whispering over the Aubusson carpet. "This will be warm." Heath's voice came from behind her. Something hot and wet splashed on her tailbone. At once the fluid ran down between the cheeks of her bottom.

His fingers delved in there, too, from below, and caught the droplets of fluid. Slowly, he massaged the warmth into her snug, closed anus. The puckered, sensitive entrance remembered his touch; it seemed to blossom open for him.

Gently, one of his fingers slid inside her, moistening her with the warm fluid, making her slippery. Readying her—that was what he was doing. Panting, waiting on a knife's edge of arousal, she rocked back against his finger. He slowly thrust it in and out. Then, when his finger was deep inside her and she was gasping against the tingling, lovely sensations, he swirled his finger inside her in a sweep that made her cunny clench.

"If this hurts, tell me. I'll stop."

She braced herself, but he laid his hand on her back. "Relax. Try to enjoy."

She wished she could see. But perhaps it was best if she couldn't. At least the monstrous two-foot-long dildo still lay on the floor. *That* she could not take inside her bum.

Something stroked along her cheeks, then nudged its way between. A smooth tip pressed to her slick, well-greased anus. And the long, slender object pushed inside.

Oh! She clamped her cheeks together instinctively, to stop the invasion. She dared to half-turn. Over the arch of her spine, the spill of her hair, she saw Heath holding a long shaft of ivory, pointed at her bottom, and it disappeared from view between the twin globes of her cheeks. Slowly, he withdrew it.

She moaned. The sight of the tapered shaft in his hand was so enticing, she did want more. But she was too . . . shy to even whisper to him in her thoughts.

Yet he seemed to know. He pushed the large dildo again, and she took a deep breath. Trying to relax. To let more inside. Ooooh yes. It went in, and her tight ring felt a little pop as the carved head slid past.

She thrust back as he thrust forward, taking more in. Deeper and deeper. Inch by stunning inch. The pressure was amazing. The sensation startling, good—deliciously so.

Lightly, he fingered her clit as he gently eased more in, withdrew, then thrust again. "Your muscles are strong," he advised her softly. "You're fighting me. Just relax and breathe."

He thrust deeper and she bowed her head. It felt so good. He gave a low, hoarse chuckle. "It looks so erotic . . . the shaft of ivory framed by your very voluptuous derriere."

It felt erotic. She felt naughty and she waggled her bottom in front of him. Only with Heath would she have dared try this, and her reward was intense pleasure.

She felt so sexually exotic with her ass filled, her bottom all but sticking into his face. Then—shock of all shocks—he put his mouth to the end of the shaft. Using his teeth, he thrust it in and out of her. Her clit throbbed at the sight. Her nipples went hard as she watched and watched and grew more and more aroused.

His fingers slipped between the lips of her quim, and he stroked her slippery clit. Then, as she expected, the second dildo nosed between her cunny lips. As soon as he thrust the toy into her creamy quim, the shaft in her arse tried to come out. But he held it in his teeth, pushing it back in.

Her cries of delight echoed in the room. She was far too shy now for words. She was now completely stuffed. So wonderfully full.

And when he finished pushing both ivory wands deep inside her, he took a length of rope, looped it around the end of the dildo up her bum, and tied the ends of the cords around her thighs. This locked the thick shaft in place. She moaned fiercely. Her clit was throbbing intensely.

Yet for some reason, she didn't want to come yet. She wanted the dizzying sensations to build and build.

The gewgaw in her quim was carved around its base, too, Which allowed Heath to tie a cord there and secure the second rope around her bare thighs. The trailing ends of the cords dangled against her sensitive skin.

She wriggled, but that brought her dangerously close to a climax.

Heath held out his hand. Even without words she knew what he wanted. For her to stand. She did, then she prowled to the mirror. Each step tugged the ivory wands deeper inside her. She could barely take steps. But finally, with her heart hammering toward an explosion, she reached the mirror. She bent over and heard Heath's low growl as her bottom—and the fake cocks—pointed at him. She was so aroused, her knees shook.

She twisted to see what she looked like. Her throat dried as she saw the thick ivory toy sticking out of her rump, the one in her cunny, and the cords that bound her thighs.

Heath must have gone swiftly to the wardrobe and returned. Wearing a look of fierce anticipation, he held more of the carved dildos. She was nervous. But this was about trust, and it astonished her how easily she could now have faith in Heath.

He approached her and held one to her lips. A small one. Breathing hard, she opened her mouth and took it all inside. Let him tie the cord around its base, let him knot the cords together behind her head.

She was trapped, essentially gagged again, but with an ivory shaft to suck and lick.

Then, before her eyes, he did the most scandalous thing. He licked his fingers and wet the head of another curved cock. To see a masculine hand fondling it stole her breath. Her juices dribbled around the false penis filling her cunny. He held the dildo, braced against the back of the chaise, and he sat down hard on it. Her eyes widened as it disappeared up his tight rump in one swift motion.

Her heart hammered. Her chest felt tight.

He picked up a small glass vial and dribbled golden oil upon the tip of another toy, then motioned for her to turn around. She did but watched him walk toward her. It made her knees shake to know he, too, must feel the erotic pressure in his rump.

He lifted her hands so she gripped the frame of the mirror. Her position spread her legs, tightened the cords, and pushed her toys a little deeper inside her.

Oh heavens.

He took the other gewgaw, the one that glistened with oil, and pressed it gently against her rear. She arched up on her toes against the invasion. But he did it slowly. Carefully. Stopping when she tensed. Her rump was open, ready, receptive. And soon she was thrusting back to him. Wanting to be crammed full. To be stretched and pleasured beyond belief.

Her clit felt as though it was going to burst and it had not even been touched. The sensation was unbelievable. Dear heaven, she wasn't going to last.

Then he took her hand and walked her around. He had to hold the toys crammed inside her bottom.

She gazed in the mirror, ready to explode, like a keg of gunpowder anxiously awaiting a sizzling fuse. The other ivory wand was bejeweled at its base. Rubies, diamonds, and emeralds winked at her.

Oh dear heaven, she couldn't stand it. She bent over, pointing her rump at the mirror. She reached behind, clamping her hand around the toys. She thrust back fiercely and thrust them forward. With wild abandon, she masturbated her rear with the two slim cocks. While she sucked fiercely at the one filling her mouth. While she clutched her cunny around the cock buried deep inside.

And she came.

So hard, her legs collapsed and Heath caught her. Her bottom pulsed. Wave after powerful wave rocked her. She sucked madly at the cock in her mouth, and that made her come again.

Heath lifted her while she was still jerking with her orgasm. He cradled her against him and held her bottom, which stretched her, then put his hand against the base of all those ivory wands, making them thrust deep. She burst again.

She wrapped her heels around his hips, her arms around his neck. She gazed up at him, weak with pleasure, realizing he was staring at the cock held in her mouth by rope. His eyes flared with a silver gleam. His mouth was tense and harsh. He kept thrusting that thick bundle up her bottom. She struggled, strained, and managed to bump her heels against the toy in his derriere. He fiercely rubbed his cock against her belly. Sobbing in delight, she came once more.

She couldn't count her climaxes anymore.

He sank to the floor. She collapsed beside him, lying on her back. Which only pushed everything up her bottom again. She bounced beside him, wild with pleasure now. How many times could she come? Another. Then another. Until she was too weak to move. But even just breathing lifted her slightly up and down on the dildos up her arse and made her come.

Her thighs were slick with her juices. Her nipples were scarlet and standing straight up.

Finally she gave one last fierce bounce, just for fun, and the explosion that took her was blinding.

Everything went black.

He'd never seen a woman drive herself to so many orgasms she lost consciousness. Heath grinned down at Vivi as she stirred, blinked her eyes, and focused on him.

"Goodness," she whispered.

"Very good, I think."

"I've never had anything like that before," she whispered.

Pride swelled him—his heart and his cock. He had slid the toys out from her and bundled them in a basin to be washed, along with the one he'd used to stimulate himself. But he hadn't come yet. His cock curved up toward his navel, rigid and so engorged it was almost purple.

Vivi slowly sat up on her haunches. Her full breasts fell in two enticing slopes and her mature nipples had grown long and firm. He savored the sight of her.

Soft firelight flickered over her face, playing along her pursed lips. She watched him, her gaze intensely thoughtful. Her tongue ran over her lower lip as she did. His cock jolted up as he followed the sensual path of her little pink tongue.

"What is it?" He managed to get the words through a tight throat.

"I want to give you pleasure, but I'm afraid of hurting you by doing it."

"Ah, love, you don't have to." He gave her a teasing grin, wrapping his hand around his throbbing shaft. It was thicker than it had ever been in his life—both his mortal life and his undead one. "I am content to tend to it myself."

It was how he'd been surviving his lust. Thrusting into his own palm brought him temporary relief, so he'd done it several times every night. But after he came, when he'd finished jerking with the intense pleasure of his climax, when he'd finished shooting his scalding cum onto his hand, he would fall back onto his bed and think of Vivi. And all he had to do was let a whisper of her tease the edges of his mind, and he was rock hard again.

"My mouth," she whispered. "Can my mouth turn you into a demon?"

Hell. "No, it can't," he lied, surprised at how easily he could. If it did, he'd destroy himself. He couldn't say no to this.

Suddenly her hand was around his shaft, too. Her fingers were far softer, but gripped firmly. "I do not know if I can bring you to climax with my mouth."

Yes, you can. Just listening to you talk *with your mouth is bringing me close.*

"Experienced men are difficult to bring to climax. I've never been able to . . ." She ducked her head shyly. "This is something I'm not very good at."

He understood she was making an admission. She was vulnerable and unsure. "Skill in that area is overrated. Just your hot mouth will drive me wild."

"But you will want to be satisfied. I don't want you to be . . . disappointed."

"Disappointed? Christ, I could never be disappointed with you. Never. And what we should do, Vivi, is return to either my bedroom or yours."

He scooped her up and carried her back to her bedchamber, with his cock wobbling in front of him like a jousting lance. But he suspected Dimitri would interrupt them if he didn't. And he damn well refused to be bothered if Vivi planned to pleasure him with her mouth.

Could having her suck him change him? He didn't know. Soon he was going to find out.

This might be his very last orgasm.

"All right, lie down on my bed," Vivienne commanded. "Now it is your turn to take orders from me."

Of course he laughed, obviously assuming she was teasing. But Heath spread out naked on her bed. And Vivienne lost her breath at how sensual his well-muscled nude body looked on her dainty, embroidered counterpane.

He looked so . . . boyishly hopeful.

She gathered courage, took a deep breath, and leaned down and kissed the purplish-bronze head of his long cock. At her touch, silvery fluid bubbled out of the little opening at the tip. She licked it up. It teased her tongue, surprisingly sweet and sour at the same time. She brushed the little eye along her lips. The touch of taut velvet made them tingle. His flowing juices left them sticky and glistening. Then slowly, watching his silver eyes, she licked her lips.

His powerful chest rose on a deep, sharp breath.

He liked this.

So far, so good.

She kissed the tip again. A playful buss to the velvety head. Then, with lashes lowered, she opened her mouth wide and gobbled him up.

Her lips slid over the steel and softness of his shaft. Her tongue tasted him—salty, sour, earthy. He moaned deeply. Harder than she had ever heard a man moan before. From beneath his thick fringe of lashes, Heath watched her with adorable, lusty, awed eyes.

She ran her tongue around his astonishingly thick shaft, tasting dewy sweat, the tartness of his juices, the sweetness of his skin. Then suckled.

His lean hips made a sudden jolt upward on her bed, and his cock surged deep into her mouth. At first she was stunned, then she saw he was beyond control. His hands fisted, his arms tensed, his eyes shut tight. And he roared at the exact instant a rush of hot fluid burst into her mouth.

Heavens.

She'd thought he would be far too experienced for her to please him so easily. Yet he'd exploded at just the touch of her mouth around him.

Inside, she felt rather smug. Warm. Glowing. Delighted.

Suddenly, he flipped her onto her back. "Your turn," he whispered.

Hours later, Vivienne lay sprawled over Heath's naked body. His left hand rested on her bottom, cupping the plump curve. The quiet intimacy left her breathless.

Or perhaps she was still breathless after the three more orgasms she'd had since returning to her bedchamber.

Her cheek pressed against the silky hair that covered Heath's chest, and she'd never felt safer, more secure, more wonderful in her life. She ran her tongue over her lips and tasted his cum on their swollen contours—tangy, a little sour, and richer than sweet cream. He had grown hard each time he brought her to climax. Then she would suck him, and each time he came just as quickly, just as readily when her mouth closed around him.

It truly had astonished her. She had felt saucy and victorious making him come so much and so hard. She felt . . . strong and invincible. Like she could spread her arms wide and fly like Heath, if she wanted to.

Of course she couldn't. But exhilaration was a heady thing.

He stirred beneath her. "Now, Vivi, I think it is time to bathe you."

She sighed with languorous exhaustion. She didn't want to move. "Bathe?" she repeated groggily.

"Indeed. I will summon some of the maids to tend to you." He lifted her, eased her onto her back, and got out of bed.

Intimacy was done for tonight. Her disappointment must have been plain on her face.

He gave a cool shrug. One that hurt deeply. How could he change so swiftly? Go from a man who wanted to hold her to one who looked like he wanted to run?

"Sorry, love. I have to go," he said. "You should be able to last through the night now."

Go? Then she knew exactly what he planned to do. "You are going to go after my father, aren't you?" She sat up, still a little dizzy from lovemaking. As he got off her bed, she followed, unsteadily after all that pleasure.

"Get back into bed," he commanded.

"No!" she cried. "My father almost killed you." She needed practical clothes to go out with him. A serviceable gown, which would not take too long to fasten.

"You are not coming with me."

Halfway to the large wardrobe, she stopped and jerked around. "I thought you couldn't read my mind."

"It's obvious what you're planning in that lovely head of yours. Why else would you be stalking toward your clothes? You want to come with me to help me." Green eyes flared at her. He crossed his arms over his naked chest. "I'm not going to permit it. You must stay here."

"Why?" She planted her hands on her hips. "Do you not see how dangerous this—?"

At once, he moved to stand in front of her. At over six feet tall, he towered above her. Instinctively, she froze. He looked so aggressive. So unlike Heath.

He grasped her arms. Hard. "What are you doing?"

"I am not going to let you put yourself in danger."

She tried to break free, but he only clutched harder. Enough to make her whimper with pain. He was so strong, and he wanted his own way, and she suddenly realized she didn't know what he would be willing to do to get it. A spike of fear shot through her heart.

"Listen to me, Vivi," he growled. Fury crackled in his eyes, like lightning forking in front of dark emerald trees. He was different from every other man she'd known—except when he wanted his own way. Then he took on the hard, arrogant look she recognized.

"Release me," she hissed. But he didn't.

"You have to understand, Vivi." His voice was low, soft, like a whisper on a sultry night. He was trying to get into her mind and force her that way.

"Your father knows my brother is the same kind of demon I am. For whatever your father is planning, he needs to set the curse free. He'll do it to Raine."

"I know," she cried. "That was why he was willing to kill you. To use your brother instead."

"I have to rescue my brother against his will. Drag him from Nikolai. That's why I need you to stay here. I'm going to have to fight Raine and . . . hell, I can't destroy him, if it comes to that."

"Then you need me to protect you," she declared fiercely. "Now let me go." To her surprise, he did. She whirled and ran to her wardrobe. Unlike most of the cupboards in this house, it actually contained clothing. "It is not your fault your brother turned to Nikolai. If he was willing to be my father's tool, knowing what he will become if the curse is released, that means he is cruel and foolish. I'm not going to let you die because you refuse to raise a hand against your brother."

She yanked open the doors. A row of gowns faced her, along with three items she'd never seen before. Dimitri must have sent them. She pulled out a pair of tan breeches. This was brilliant, far better than a dress. Hastily she stepped into them.

"I'm not just going to let myself get killed," he growled.

"I'm afraid you will," she said. "You think you deserve to pay with your life." There was also a white linen shirt, and she dragged it over her head. As she shoved the tails into the skintight breeches, Heath's brows shot up. Her full breasts strained at the fabric—the shirt had been designed for a slender, young male. The white linen revealed the dark circles of each areola, and her hardened nipples poked the material forward.

"Well, it is not as though I'm trying to disguise the fact I'm female. These clothes are just better for a battle." A dark blue tailcoat hung in the wardrobe. At least that would cover her nipples.

"Breeches and an almost transparent shirt are appropriate fashion for battling powerful vampires who would destroy us both?" He had crossed his arms over his bare chest again, glowering like the devil himself.

Her heart ached. All the lovely pleasure of the night was lost. They were combatants now.

"I will go," she said flatly. "Either with you, or I shall follow you."

He tore his hands through his hair. But she had pulled on tall, black leather boots. "I must tell Sarah that I am going with you," she stated. She wouldn't fight with him anymore. She was going to do exactly as she wished, and he could be damned. He intended to save Raine whether the lad wanted it or not? She would do the same for him. She stalked to the door. "You should stop lallygagging about and get dressed, Heath."

"Good bloody Christ," he shouted.

She shut the door. She had reached Sarah's room when Heath appeared at her side. He had dressed in the few moments it had taken her to reach Sarah's room, then raced at vampiric speed to reach her side.

Sarah's door opened and a surprised maid stood on the threshold. "Oh! Miss Dare. Your lordship. Miss Sarah isn't here. She went to the music room. With Lord Julian."

Heath's brows jerked up in shock. "Julian? Julian is listening to a young lady play music?" His anger vanished. Now he looked highly suspicious—and guilty—as he rubbed his chin.

What did he know about Julian that was making him look as though he'd done something wrong? Vivienne's heart started to pound. "Perhaps he is pretending to like music, as part of his seduction." She spun on her heel. "If that's his plan, he is going to regret it very quickly."

Soft, melodic harp music rippled out through the slightly open door of the music room—a room Vivienne had not been in before. Then the music ceased and she heard a woman's soft voice. "I like kissing you. I've never kissed anyone before."

Vivienne halted. The voice sounded so much like Sarah. But much more . . . sultry.

"I want to be the first man to kiss you," came a gentleman's hoarse, desire-filled answer. "And I want to be the last. I want you to be mine, Sarah. Forever."

Vivienne let out a small scream, but Heath reached the door before she did and threw it open. It banged into the wall with enough force to rock the entire hallway and send plaster flying.

Her heart slammed into her throat. She tried to take in every detail, tried not to panic. Sarah was kissing Julian. Dressed in a deep pink gown that made her skin glow like pearl and her hair shine like the sun, her daughter had her arms wrapped around his neck and her lips pressed hard to his. He had no shirt on.

"Stop!" Vivienne shouted. "Touch her mouth and I'll geld you, vampire or no!"

But again, Heath reacted far faster than she could. He appeared behind Julian, clamped his hand on the young man's shoulder, and dragged him away from Sarah.

Sarah stalked forward. She blushed a brighter pink than her dress. "Mother! How could you?"

Fear and shock and more fear tumbled about inside Vivienne's chest. If she had been a moment later, what would Julian have done? "How could I what?" She sounded like a terrified harridan. "How could I protect you? I am not about to stand by and let you be seduced by a lusty, despicable vampire." And she saw Heath wince.

"He's not *seducing* me. He was kissing me."

"This house is no place for you to be wandering around. There are things going on here that you should not see."

Sarah put her hands on her hips. "For heaven's sake, Mother. I know about sex. That doesn't mean I am going to engage in it."

Sex. The word almost strangled Vivienne's breath from her chest. She blushed more fiercely than her daughter. She hadn't wanted Sarah to even *know* about sex. She'd wanted Sarah to be innocent forever.

"Julian will expect more than a kiss," she said flatly.

"I don't," Julian erupted. He tried to break free of Heath's hold, but he didn't succeed. "I intend to court Miss Dare. As a gentleman should."

"Mother, this is ridiculous. I know what you've been doing. I know you are having an . . . an affair with Lord Blackmoor and I am *happy* for you. All I wanted was one kiss! Julian knew that."

"Sarah," Heath said softly. "Vivi is only trying to protect you."

"And Julian is half dressed. If he only wanted a kiss, why

would he take off his shirt?" Vivienne demanded. Sarah was only eighteen. And naive, for all her bold words. "The point is, Sarah, he is a vampire. And you are not. There can never be any romance between you. And this house is a den of . . . sin."

"Mother." Sarah's laugh rang into the room. "It's not evil. Or bad. It's just sex and pleasure. These people are all happy. That's what I want to know about. Passion . . . and love."

"You can learn all about passion when you are married." She sounded foolishly prim. But she could not help it. "That is what I want for you. What I could never have. A good marriage, a good husband—security, position, happiness."

A terrifyingly wise look came into Sarah's blue-green eyes. "Mother, who am I going to marry? No matter how well behaved I am, I will always be a courtesan's daughter."

Vivienne's heart broke. It simply shattered. Sarah had gone through the agony of learning about her father. And now she'd heard Sarah say the words she'd always feared. Sarah knew her mother had ruined her life before she'd even been born.

Then Heath stalked toward the door. "Julian," he said coldly. "I wish to speak to you."

And Vivienne saw the role Heath had taken on: that of irate father.

19

Heath hauled Julian into a bedchamber down the corridor before he understood what he was doing: behaving with the younger vampire exactly the way he used to with Raine. He released Julian. "Was this just about a kiss with a pretty girl? Or were you planning to seduce her?"

The younger vampire ran both hands through his fair hair. "I wouldn't hurt her. I love Sarah."

Heath sighed. "You can't love her because you can't ask her to love you in return. Vivienne may be a succubus, but as far as we know, Sarah is mortal."

"As far as we know. Christ, Blackmoor, you *don't* know. All we know is that she's sick. That she would probably die if you weren't giving her your blood. I want—" His silver-blue eyes were full of pain. "I want to try giving her my blood. I want the bond to be between Sarah and me. I don't want you involved anymore."

The boy really was in love. But Heath shook his head. "I intend to protect Sarah." He owed it to Vivi to do so, but he also *needed* to protect Sarah. He had done so many things wrong.

He had hurt Ariadne, Meredith, and Raine. Saving Sarah was one thing he could do to balance his accounts.

Julian grasped his shoulder. "Please, Heath. If she gets ill again, I want to save her. I want to be the one. I won't let her die."

Now he understood. "You can't turn her into a vampire."

Folding his arms over his chest, Julian glared defiantly. "To save her life, I'd do it."

"Julian, you have no right to damn her to this life because you want her. And we don't know if it would save her life. We don't know exactly what Sarah is, if she really is mortal or not. Turning her into a vampire could destroy her."

Agony flashed in Julian's blue eyes. "What am I supposed to do, Heath? I love her. I'd do anything for her. How do I find out what Sarah is? Who will know? Who in hell can we trust, Heath? I want to ensure Sarah is safe and healthy and free. But how are we going to do that?"

Sympathy rose in him. "I don't know yet, Julian. But we will find a way." He gave Julian the autocratic look he once used on Raine. "And if you break Sarah's heart—if you misbehave with her—I'll stake yours myself. If you love her, it means no more brothels. You have to be faithful."

"I will be," Julian vowed. "I would never hurt her. But if she's mortal . . ."

"Then your heart will end up broken," Heath said softly. Then he left Julian and found Vivienne as she was leaving Sarah's room.

Ruefully, she faced him. "Sarah absolutely despises me now for telling her she can't have Julian. I was always afraid she would hate me for ruining her life the moment it began. She's right; she'll always suffer for being a courtesan's daughter."

Heath remembered how Sarah's face had been filled with defiance, but he'd also seen her need for her mother's approval displayed in her expressive blue eyes.

Vivi hugged herself and strode away from him. Heath knew what she was doing: running from the pain in her heart. He followed until she reached the end of the corridor, then he caught her arm and drew her into an empty bedroom to talk to her.

He tipped up her chin and stared firmly into her large blue eyes. "Sarah doesn't despise you. If your daughter is shouting at you, rather than being too afraid to speak in case she drives you away, you've done a wonderful job as her mother."

Vivi blinked in astonishment. "You mean your daughter was afraid to speak to you?"

"Yes. I was so arrogant and self centered, I didn't even realize she was afraid that if she displeased me, I would leave. And I always did leave, on my travels around the world. If Sarah is confident enough to shout at you, she loves you and she knows you love her."

He kissed Vivi's startled lips. "In the music room, I didn't see a girl who resented her mother. I saw a young woman who respects her mother. But I think Sarah now wants to blossom into her own."

"I know; she wants love and passion. But with Julian? I saw the worried look on your face. Was it because you fear he'll . . . bite her? Or change her into a vampire?"

"No, it was that I knew what a rake Julian is. But I spoke to him, and I believe he adores Sarah and won't hurt her. A vampire can love, Vivi. He can love very deeply." He shook his head grimly. "Vampires can. A demon like me doesn't dare."

"Heath—"

But he put his finger to his lips. Vivienne could barely see him as he raced to the window silently. He pushed open the thick drapes, letting moonlight spill in. Then he cocked his head, listening intently. With her heart thumping, Vivienne strained to hear.

Then Heath spun around and moved to her so quickly, she didn't see the motion. "Run. With me," he growled, then he lifted her feet off the ground and the door hurtled at them so quickly, she shut her eyes.

"What is it? What's happening?" she cried. Sarah . . . if something was wrong, she had to get to her daughter.

Before Heath could answer, the windows in the bedchamber behind them exploded. Fragments of glass flew past them, glinting like diamonds. She twisted to see. And a black mass, like a thick fluid, poured in the window. The black shape broke apart suddenly, just as it had in her house, and became hundreds of small bats. Their wings flashed through the air, their noise became a deafening squeal.

It's the council. Heath spoke tersely in her thoughts.

Sarah, she cried. *You must take me to Sarah.*

That's exactly where I am going. We must get Sarah and get out of here—

"And go where?" She shrieked aloud. "This was our safe place. This house was supposed to be impossible to be attacked." Then words slipped out, ones she never should have said. "*You* promised."

Heath whirled her down the hallway and into a large moonlit room, where she gaped in astonishment at the scene before her. Long tables filled the room, and a dozen vampires were racing through it. Spread out on the tables were weapons—swords and crossbows and quivers of arrows. One by one, each vampire snatched up a weapon.

Heath pressed her back against a wall. *Stay there. I'll get armed, then take you to Sarah.*

She felt so guilty for what she'd said. But there was no doubt she would be captured and dragged back to the council. She would be assaulted on that altar and killed. Then what would happen to Sarah?

Vomit churned in her throat thinking about it. This wasn't Heath's fault. But she was not going to stand back. She was going to fight for her own life and Sarah's.

Crash!

The window shattered at the end of the long room and the bats flew in. The vampires lifted their weapons, turned toward the advancing bats, and fired. But the black mass of bats swirled around one of the vampires, a man who stood close to the window. They engulfed him and no one dared to fire. But when the bats soared up, dust floated down from the air, and the vampire was gone.

Dimitri stood by the table, a crossbow in his hands. He threw it down, lifted his hands, and barked out an incantation. A brilliant flash of gold light shot from his palms and engulfed the whirling bats. The tiny creatures let out a scream that rippled through the room, then they flapped their wings wildly and retreated through the window.

"They'll return," Heath growled.

Dimitri lowered his hands. He looked to Heath, who had grabbed up a crossbow. "You're correct. They will attack from somewhere else. And you need a different weapon."

Dimitri's black eyes looked more soulless than before. Grim. Resigned. And Vivienne understood. Dimitri didn't believe this battle could be won.

There was one way to save everyone. To save Sarah.

She stalked away from the wall to the two men. "Those creatures want me. They are here to take me. If I go with them, they won't hurt anyone else. They won't hurt Sarah—"

"No!" Both Heath and Dimitri shouted the word at once.

She grasped a crossbow. She'd never used a weapon in her life. But all her years of fighting for survival were worthless if she could not do this now. "If I go outside, won't they follow me? Won't it protect everyone else? If we lure them away from the house, that will keep everyone else safe. Maybe then I could—I could run." *Where? How?*

But Heath moved so he was directly behind her. "It's too

dangerous. You can't outrun them. The house is the safest place. They have to come in here to fight."

Heath was only thinking of protecting *her*. He wasn't thinking of everyone else. If it was true, it meant he had sacrificed the nobility he'd wanted to claim. Over her.

Feminine screams came then, obliterating her argument. *Sarah.* Vivienne ran blindly for the door, but Heath caught up to her. A vampire woman lay on the floor of the hallway writhing in pain while the bats tore at her body.

Vivienne stopped in her tracks, too numb to move. Then something sharp prodded her leg through the breeches. The crossbow. She jerked up the heavy weapon, but Heath stepped in front of her.

He carried a huge sword; he must have taken it from the room at lightning speed, then run to catch her. He swiped it in a ruthless arc just above the fallen woman's body. The bats flapped their wings madly, trying to escape. Some were caught by the blade, cut into pieces.

Nausea crawled up her throat. She moved to the fallen woman, but the victim jerked wildly, then suddenly dissolved into dust.

Vivienne reeled back. Bearing the weight of the crossbow, on legs that had frozen with terror, she would have fallen. But Heath pulled her against his warm body. And they ran.

More bats flew in through the shattered windows. It was like someone had spilled black ink in the air, and it was pouring everywhere. It was like a nightmare. "What are these things?" she managed to gasp to Heath.

"A form of demon. Enslaved by the council, who use them for reconnaissance."

"And to collect succubi?" The words came out bitter and sharp. And two vampires already had been destroyed because of her.

A mass of bats was flying up the hallway toward them. The front ones stopped, flapped their wings, and the tiny bodies started to wriggle and stretch. Then they transformed into black shapes like humans, but with the broad wings of a bat. White claws protruded from the wings.

She froze. One of the creatures jumped into the air and flew at her.

Heath's sword arced cleanly through it. Black fluid spurted out, but Heath had pulled her back with his free hand, and the demon dropped before her eyes.

The second demon flew at them, then the third, and more did. Her heart gave a hiccup of icy fear. There was no way to fight so many of these monsters.

Heath pushed her back. "Stay against the wall." Then he charged forward, with Dimitri on his heels. Their swords cleaved the demons now whirling toward them, but so many bats came in Heath and Dimitri finally had to retreat. Chest heaving, Heath leaned back against the wall beside her.

Stomach churning, she saw inky blood spattered on Heath's face. Dimitri wore the same amount of horrible black spray. He held a six-foot-long broad sword in one hand. And even as he turned to her, he swung it, slicing a new advancing demon in half.

She couldn't just stand here. She fumbled, trying to load an arrow from her quiver. It fell to the floor. She ducked down to retrieve it, but Heath grabbed her arm, pulled her up. *Ignore it,* he shouted in her head. *Just stay back.*

He swung his sword behind him without even looking. Her heart lurched as he beheaded another monster and somehow managed not to hit Dimitri. Then Heath shoved her toward Dimitri. *Take care of her. There must be a leader somewhere in the mass. If I can get to him, I can throw them into confusion.*

"A leader?" she gasped. "You mean one of those creatures is in charge?"

To her horror, Heath plunged into the group of transforming bats, swinging his sword from left to right. He was carving a path through the bats.

She had to get to Sarah. What kind of mother was she that she wouldn't charge through the demons and risk everything? She loaded the crossbow. This arrow stayed in, and she ran forward.

Dimitri grasped her shoulder and jerked her back. He paused to kill another demon, then he turned his eerily dark eyes to her. "If you want to escape the council's army, the only way for you to do it is to seek refuge with your father. He's so powerful, Adder and the others would never dare attack."

That was madness. "But—but my father is our enemy."

"Yes," Dimitri said. "But he needs you. He would not hurt you."

Ahead she saw Heath working his way back to them, cutting his way through the transforming bats. Other vampires had joined them in the fight. She heard screams and cries and harsh sounds echoing through the house. There were battles everywhere.

Two shrieking demons swooped at Heath. Vivienne hefted the crossbow but her arms began to fail as she pulled the trigger. The complex pulleys moved swiftly. The arrow whistled. Her shot went through one of the demon's legs.

It looked down.

In the next instant, its head was gone.

"Your father won't want the council to have you. It's in his best interests to protect you, Miss Dare. We can hold them off long enough for you and Heath to escape—"

"I'm not leaving without my daughter."

"Of course. Take her, too. Go to your father. These demons are tenacious but not intelligent. In the heat of battle it could take them an hour to discover you've gone."

An hour. To reach her father. And he was hardly going to

offer them safety. He wanted to destroy Heath. He wanted to make use of her.

"What will he do to Heath? To Sarah? To me?"

She expected no answer from Dimitri. But he snapped. "You are a very intelligent woman, Miss Dare. You know he will not hurt you; you will have time to outsmart him. But if you stay here, you will be captured and taken back to the council."

"And they will take Sarah, too," she whispered in fear.

"Possibly. Or they will want to break you, force you to plunge you into fear and madness so you lose the will to fight. These demons could be here to take you—and kill your daughter."

Black goo sprayed Heath and he cursed. There was nothing worse than the stinking of the bodily fluids of your opponent. But he had to carve his way through these demons like a sculptor through marble.

Then he saw Vivi turn stark white and sway on her feet. Her legs collapsed beneath her. Dimitri tossed his sword to his left hand to grasp her around the waist.

With a snarl of fury, Heath sliced through five flapping demons with one stroke. He launched to Vivi's side, turning a somersault in the air. "What happened to her?" he snapped at Dimitri.

Vivi grabbed his arm. Color flooded back. "We have to get Sarah out of here. The demons want her."

"How do you know?"

"Dimitri believes it to be so," she cried. "I have to get to Sarah. We have to run."

At Sarah's name, the mass of bats in the hallway paused as though they were listening. Then they all turned and raced up the hallway toward Heath, Vivienne, and Dimitri. She was right. Adder had taught his demon bats the name of their prey and now, recognizing it, they were attacking.

"What the hell do they want with her daughter?" he barked

at Dimitri. He held his sword up, at the ready for the onslaught of the flying beasts.

"They want to hurt the young Miss Dare to break her mother's spirit and make her rage and grieve. They need to heighten Vivienne's emotions. Adder will know he can't make her feel lust. But he can make her hate. That will heighten her power and then he can draw her strength out of her. She's a weapon, Heath. A powerful one."

As he spoke, Dimitri beheaded demons with one swing of his sword after another. Heath worked at his side, doing the same. "If we run, that will put Vivi and Sarah out in the open and at risk from both Nikolai and the council." Heath's eyes narrowed. "What is it you really want, Dimitri?"

A feral grin split Dimitri's swarthy face. "The truth? I'd like to see both Nikolai and the council destroyed. You and Vivienne could defeat them. I'm tired of battles amongst the vampires. If I'm going to live forever, I want to spend my time in orgies, not battles."

He stared at Dimitri. He and Vivienne defeat them? The older vampire was completely serious. But before he could ask how in blazes they could do it, shrieking filled Heath's ears, drowning out all other sound. More demons flew at them. He swung his sword, felling one after another. But even a vampire couldn't slice through thousands of demons. His body was starting to tire.

"Take Vivienne and run," Dimitri shouted. "We'll keep fighting to give you time to escape. I told her to go to her father. Nikolai is the only vampire strong enough to protect her."

It was the truth. It was danger for Vivienne. But whatever her father was plotting, he would protect her, if only because it suited his plan. Heath gave a curt nod. But there were hundreds of demons coming and no way to get through them.

Dimitri shouted to other vampires. "Come here." Then Heath heard Dimitri's voice in his head. *Retreat, then grab Miss*

Dare and run for her daughter. Get them out of the house through the underground passage.

Vivienne reached Sarah's bedchamber with Heath. Of course, he charged in first. Vivienne rushed to his side, her crossbow armed, her finger on the trigger. Then she froze in horror.

Bats filled the room from wall to wall, swooping around the ceiling. Julian stood in front Sarah, who was pressed against the wall beside a wardrobe. The young vampire swung an iron poker desperately, bringing down one small black body after another. Heath swung his sword and killed dozens of the creatures.

"Heath, there are too many," Vivi screamed.

Julian fell, covered by the tiny winged animals. They clawed at his body. His flesh was being ripped open.

Shrieking desperately, Sarah ran out from the wardrobe, desperately trying to reach Julian.

"No, stay back," Vivienne shouted.

And Julian yelled, "For Christ's sake, forget me. Get her out of here."

Heath ran through the bats and they whirled at him, biting and slashing, until blood soaked into his shirt and ran down his face. Vivienne fired one arrow after another, taking care not to hit either man, but her shots were not even frightening the bats.

Heath grabbed Sarah, tossed her over his shoulder, and ran back toward Vivienne and the door. But Sarah beat her fists on Heath's back, kicking wildly. "Julian!" she screeched. "Save Julian."

Suddenly Heath reached Vivi's side, and he put Sarah down. Vivienne grabbed her daughter and tried to pull her out of the room. Julian was covered with bats, just like the vampire woman had been. Vivi was trying to spare Sarah the horrific sight.

Heath tried to drive the bats off Julian with his sword, but then he ran back toward them. His face was stark white. "We have to run."

Nausea roiled in Vivienne's stomach. Dear heaven, not Julian . . .

"No," Sarah screamed, but Heath swept her up again. Vivienne almost lost her balance as he grabbed her wrist and dragged her out the door.

Behind them, they heard Julian's howl of pain.

She had never seen Heath so angry. His boots slammed into the door again and again, until he tore a hole through a two-inch slab of solid oak. Splinters flew everywhere.

She understood his fury, but it scared her. It made her feel small inside.

It brought out every moment she had lived in fear, when she'd thought a man might kill her drunken mother and then turn on her. Instinct told her to back away, but this was Heath, and he needed her to break through to him. "Stop it!" she shouted. "You don't need to do that."

He spun around. Silver flashed in his eyes as he looked from Sarah to her. "You are correct," he said softly. And he opened the door.

She gripped Sarah's arm tightly and helped her daughter walk. Sarah's face was sheet white. Tears poured down Sarah's cheeks, but she made no sound, not even a sob. She stared blankly ahead. It was as though she was in a trance.

Vivienne's heart felt like a cube of ice: small, cold, easily crushed. She had no idea what to do. Did she really want to try to snap through Sarah's shock? Or was this blank state protecting her from the horror she'd just seen? Would Sarah ever survive losing Julian almost right in front of her eyes?

A dark passage stretched before them, and when Sarah wouldn't take another step, Heath swept her up into his arms. "Here, little one. I'll take you."

Vivi, I'm sorry. I killed the leader of the bats, but it didn't stop them. And if I hadn't wasted time on that, I could have saved Julian.

You tried, Heath. And you saved my daughter. I will admire you for eternity for that.

Heath had been wrong when he'd told her a demon like he did not dare to love, Vivienne thought. He might be a vampire, cursed to be a demon, but he was capable of a love that stunned her with its depth and strength.

She had to hold on to Heath's bloodstained shirt to find her way through the inky-black passage. The door he had broken through had been a second one in the dark tunnel. The first had been in the basement of Dimitri's house, and was a barrier of four-inch-thick iron. Heath had bolted that thick, heavy door behind them. The oak door had been locked, and admittedly they'd had no other way through it.

"You—you don't have to go to my father." The words came out breathlessly. Ahead Vivienne could see nothing, but she could tell the cobblestone floor of the tunnel was sloping down. They were descending. *Into the bowels of hell*, she thought, her heart sick.

He walked faster. "I have to ensure you two are safe."

"I will make sure my father doesn't hurt you—" She broke off, breathing hard.

"I'm not afraid of him. I want to confront him. I want you and Sarah to be safe, and free, and to be able to live without fear." He slowed his long strides so she could catch up to him. "I'm not afraid of your father, Vivi. I'm afraid of myself. Your life and Sarah's life depend on me. And I've failed at that before."

"You haven't failed. You saved both of us tonight! Heath, you have to accept how good and strong and noble you are."

But she knew it was for those very reasons he could not

leave the guilt and pain of his wife and daughter's deaths behind.

Suddenly Heath stopped walking. He put Sarah down, then stepped back from her and Vivienne. He clapped his hand to his head and let out a fierce grunt of pain.

Vivienne rushed forward and wrapped her arms around his chest. "What's happening? What's wrong?"

He pushed her away and dropped to his knees. The skin of his face rippled and his body flexed and jerked beneath his clothes. "Are you shape shifting?" she cried.

He shook his head. Then with a howl of sheer agony that made her spine go rigid, he whipped his head back. His fangs shot out. His features seemed to turn to liquid and move around on his face.

"This is what happened before," he gasped. "When Nikolai gave me a taste of what his curse meant, what I would become. I'm transforming into a demon."

20

Vivienne stared in horror as Heath's jaw twisted sharply to the right and then left with such vigorous force, she heard the *crack*. His forehead swelled and receded and she had to clap her hand to her mouth to hold in the scream. The large, solid muscles of his arms, which bulged against his linen shirt, rippled and undulated like live snakes.

He bore it all with his teeth clenched. "Hell, it's happening," he rasped through his tight mouth.

"Why?" Vivienne gasped. "I didn't make love to you again. We didn't do it twice." Sarah was whimpering in fear, but she couldn't go to Sarah and comfort her. She had to race to Heath. She tumbled to her knees in front of him. Mud soaked into her skirts, but she ignored the damp and the terrifying darkness. She caressed his face and felt his cheekbones pulse beneath her hand.

"No." He pulled back, tore away from her. "Don't touch me. It's too dangerous."

"This is my fault. My—my father said that making love to

me *started* the curse," she whispered. "We made it begin to work, even though you didn't make love to me again."

He doubled over, and his spine bulged beneath his skin, stretching it as though the bones would rip through. "I fell in love with you. With everything you've done with me. That was enough."

His words speared her.

"No. No, you cannot be in love with me, Heath. I won't allow it." Not if it was going to destroy him. She had to stop this. Guidon had told her Heath had to fight the terms of the curse. But how did they do it?

A shadow moved beside her and Vivienne gasped in shock, turning swiftly. But it was Sarah. Her face was white and stricken, and she laid her hand upon Heath's undulating back. "Mother, we must do something."

"I know." But what? Yet her daughter's strength humbled her. Sarah had just lost the man she loved, but she'd found the courage to break out of the shock, to come to Heath, to try to save him. Both Vivienne and Heath had to be as strong.

He had to fight the curse. But he believed he should be punished. He believed he should be cursed.

She put her hands on Heath's shoulders. Beneath her palms, muscle and bone moved and popped. It sickened her, but she kept her hands there. "Fight it, Heath. We both love you. We will not let you go. We are your family now."

She heard Sarah gasp. Saw a tear roll down her daughter's cheek. "Yes," Sarah whispered. "We are your family. You saved me, and you saved my mother. I will love you always."

Heath's face contorted into a grimace of sheer agony. "God no," he growled. "I am not going to let this happen." Then softly, so Vivienne could barely hear, he murmured, "You need me—I won't fail you."

The undulations of his spine ceased, his muscles stopped

pulsing beneath his skin. His face was no longer twisting and distorting. His clothes were torn, the seams ripped by the powerful motions of his body, but it appeared to be over. He bowed his head and sucked in sharp breaths.

Vivienne cupped his jaw, tilted his head up so she could see. He reached up and clasped her wrists. "It's stopped," he whispered, his voice hoarse. "Thank you, Vivi." He turned to Sarah, and gave her a smile. "Thank you, Sarah. You have no idea how much it means to me to have won your love."

"I don't care about who my father was," Sarah declared. "I want you to be a part of our family, Lord Blackmoor." Then tears began to flow down Sarah's face again.

Heath cradled Sarah close, held her and whispered, "I love you," until Sarah's sobs stopped. Shakily, he stood. And he held both Vivi's hand and Sarah's and lifted them to their feet, too. "I am honored. Humbled. I promise I will never fail either of you."

He tucked Sarah's arm in his, and he began to move into the foreboding dark of the passage. But Vivienne couldn't move. "Are you certain you are all right?"

His mouth cranked down. "You're afraid of me, aren't you?"

"I'm not afraid of you," she said firmly. "I am afraid *for* you." Had they truly stopped his transformation? Did it mean the curse was broken? Had it been enough to tell him they loved him? He had promised not to fail them. She feared he didn't yet believe their love was unconditional. Or perhaps he was afraid of unconditional love, because he'd had it before. Perhaps their very offer of love was a torment for him.

"Come, Vivi." She could not see him in the dark, but there was no ignoring the deep authority in his command—and the note of fear beneath it. "We have to move."

She knew they did. She had to rush onward and throw herself into the power of her father, a man she feared and hated.

Heath had hoisted Sarah onto his back, the way a man would carry a small child. He held out his hand to Vivienne. She hurried to his side and raced along with him.

Somehow, she had to make Heath see he didn't deserve to be cursed.

Heath knew the secret passage well. Designed as an escape route from the council or from slayers, it sloped downward, then branched in three directions. Two tunnels were false paths, dead ends that led to booby traps. He knew the route they had to take. And as he plunged forward, he knew it was his responsibility to plan beyond this desperate race for safety.

He had a family again. The truth: he was not ready for a family. He could not give either Vivi or Sarah what they truly needed. They had declared their love to a man who had no choice but to destroy himself. All he had done was force them to open their hearts; now they would know heartbreak.

Sarah was so light seated up on his shoulders with her heels bumping against his chest. She'd wrapped her arms around his neck. She trusted him and cared about him. Two things he had thrown away a decade ago, when he'd lost Meredith. Sarah did not know about his past. But Vivi did. How could she say that she loved him, knowing what he had done?

He could destroy Nikolai, which would protect Vivienne from whatever evil plan his sire had concocted. But how did he protect her from the council? How did he give Vivienne what she truly deserved—real freedom?

"There must be another way."

Vivi's soft voice beside him jerked him from his thoughts. "Another way? No, love, this is the only way out. There are three branches to this tunnel; we'll reach the fork soon. But trust me, I know which way to go."

"No, I meant, is there any other way we can hide without going to Nikolai? This is absolute madness. I do not have to do what Dimitri says. I do not have to let anyone dictate to me." In the dark, he saw her brow arch. "Except perhaps you, because I trust you."

"Dimitri's plan is to put you under the protection of a vampire who is more powerful than any man on the council. He knows your father won't hurt you. Dimitri is trying to buy us time, time for me to devise some way to rescue the two of you."

"And it should not be wholly your responsibility, Heath. I am not going to stand by like a ninny and wait to be rescued. Could we not just run and keep running? We could leave England."

"The vampires of the council can fly around the world if they wish." A rank odor rose from the ground and his boots squished in mud. Vivi's slippers made an answering *squelsh*. She wrinkled her nose and gasped, "Ew," making him chuckle. Hades, he adored her.

They had reached the lowest section of the tunnel, where it branched into three more tunnels. Heath clasped Vivienne's hand to lead her forward into the pitch darkness.

He could detect the faint sound of hammering behind them. It had to be the demons, trying to bludgeon their way through the special iron door that secured the tunnels. He prayed—if a vampire could—it didn't mean all the vampires in the house had been destroyed.

Vivi followed him, plunging into the tunnel without question. If he needed any more proof of how much faith she'd given him, he had it.

"If the council could not get into Dimitri's house before," she whispered, "how were they able to do so tonight?"

"Dimitri's defenses are based on ancient magic spells. Someone must have betrayed Dimitri; they must have told the council which spells he uses."

Could it have been Julian? she asked in his thoughts.

I don't believe it was. Julian gave up his life for Sarah. He truly loved her.

Vivi gave a soft sob. "What about Guidon? Would he know ancient spells?"

"It's possible. And if it was Guidon, it's my fault."

"It can't be."

"Guidon returned to London from the Carpathians. No one but Dimitri knew he had done so, or knew about his bookstore. I led the council right to him."

"Or I did. But why would Dimitri leave Guidon without protection?" Vivi asked.

"I don't know." But he agreed with her. Why didn't Dimitri protect Guidon, and thus protect his home?

"J—Julian," Sarah began, above him, but her voice choked on a small sob.

"Sarah, it's all right. Shh. You don't have to talk about it," he soothed.

"I do not need to be soothed and silenced." Suddenly the girl sounded very fierce. "It is hard for me to say his name, but I *can* do it. Julian told me there are vampire queens. They are the most powerful beings of all. He told me the vampire council was created because male vampires could not stand being ruled by these strong females. Wouldn't the queens help us?"

"The queens rarely help other female demons," Heath said gently. "They are generally ruled by jealousy. I was afraid they would want to destroy Vivienne; she's too lovely."

The vampire queens had once kept the ancient vampires—like Dimitri and Nikolai—as consorts. But like most men given infinite wealth, power, and handsome looks, they proved to be unfaithful. They had betrayed the queens. And so the queens hated them, but they couldn't destroy the strong, ancient male vampires. With Nikolai as his sire, the queens wouldn't want to help him.

They started to trudge uphill toward the exit. It emerged close to the Thames on Dimitri's grounds. Heath pulled Vivi to a stop. In the pitch dark, she couldn't see the iron door just two feet in front of her. "We're at the end of the tunnel."

She reached out and felt the door. "There is no handle."

"Magic," he explained. "It requires an incantation—"

But before the words could leave his lips, the door suddenly glowed red. He pulled Vivi backward as it shot open.

"I thought I should come and fetch you, my dear." Wearing a smirk, Nikolai stood there in the doorway, flanked on each side by giants—men at least seven feet tall, dressed in rough brown tunics. Nikolai smiled at Sarah. "My delightful granddaughter. How splendid. Come, Vivienne, you are safe now. If you do as you are told, no harm will befall you." He waved the giants forward. "Subdue the vampire. He is close to his transformation. We can take no chances. Take my granddaughter from him."

Sarah screamed and Heath moved back, but with Sarah on his shoulders, he couldn't fight. The beast plucked Sarah from his shoulders.

Vivienne leaped forward, but Nikolai raised his hand and she crumpled to the ground. "I—I can't move," she cried.

Heath drove his boot into the crotch of the man holding him—no rules when he was fighting for his life—and then plunged his fingers into one of the beast's eyes. It howled but didn't let go.

A surge of light shot from where Nikolai stood. It hit Heath's chest, hot as fire. Heath tried to lunge for his sire, but his legs wobbled. And he fell.

The giants propelled her, with her hands chained, through Nikolai's lair: the abandoned brothel. Most of the rooms were dusty and tattered, but the one ahead of her, his private study, was opulent and lavish. Men in flowing pants and turbans flanked the doors. They held massive, curved blades. And Nikolai lounged in a huge chair behind a gilt-encrusted desk.

In the carriage, she had tried to speak to her father. She had told him they needed him to protect them from the vampire council. He had promised they would be safe, but then he had commanded her to hold her tongue and speak no more about it. Instead he'd talked to Sarah, happily and politely, as though they were attending a garden party. But when they reached the brothel, Sarah had been dragged away from her and locked in a pretty bedchamber with bars on the windows and no escape.

Her father was every bit as arrogant as any English peer who had ever pursued her. Vivienne had to remember that. She must *use* it.

Nikolai snapped his fingers, and more men in turbans carried a litter into the room from a second door. Heath lay upon it.

Vivienne tried to rush forward. But the guards pulled her back.

"What have you done to Heath?"

He lifted a supercilious brow. "Nothing that cannot be undone." He muttered some words, conjured a ball of swirling light on the palm of his hand, then sent it spiraling at Heath's chest.

Heath's body curled up as the light hit. His eyes flickered open.

Nikolai smiled at her. "Vivienne, you know what you must do. It is your job to seduce Lord Blackmoor."

"No." It came out as a croak. Then she lifted her chin, and shouted, "No!"

Red blazed in her father's eyes. Every instinct told her to cringe. To cower, like her mother used to do. But she straightened and stood as tall as she could. She gazed at Heath, who was covered in wounds from his battle with the bats. He swayed on his feet, and one of the giants gripped him by the shoulder.

"Let him go," she cried to Nikolai. Even though she knew Heath would hate her if she got her wish and he was freed.

"So sorry to disappoint you, my delightful daughter, but I cannot."

She realized Nikolai did not want her to seduce Raine. What had happened to Heath's brother? But before she could ask, one of the turbaned men approached Nikolai. The man made an unintelligible sound, then bowed deeply from his waist.

Nikolai smiled. "Indeed. Open the door and allow him entry."

She whirled around as the servant did his master's bidding. A black hulking . . . thing filled the doorway. The creature ducked its head and waddled slowly into the room. It stood at the same height as the giants, but an enormous pair of wings jutted from its shoulders. The feathered wings wrapped around its body, the tips touching at the front.

The demon opened its wings. Against its chest, it held a small, squirming man. Vivienne's heart gave a lurch. It had only been two days ago that this little gnome of a vampire had given her tea, and hope, when he'd told her Heath could break the curse.

The beast released its grip and Guidon tumbled to the ground with a high-pitched squeal of surprise. Vivienne tried to move forward, but one of the giants grabbed her shoulder and held her. It was obvious from the way Guidon cowered that he had not betrayed Dimitri willingly. His wrinkled face was pasty white.

She had to speak to Guidon. She had to make him tell her how Heath could break the curse.

Nikolai stepped forward. His robes swirled around his long legs, and he moved until his feet were almost treading upon the librarian's gnarled fingers. Nikolai waved his hand and Guidon was lifted into the air and set down on his feet.

"It was very disobedient of you to try to escape the bargain you made, Guidon. You traded your knowledge for your life. I will need you to control the demon. This time I suggest you obey."

Guidon let out a whimpering sound. He met Vivi's eyes pleadingly.

But Nikolai's cold, triumphant voice wrapped around her. "If you do not do as I ask, Vivienne, I will kill Heath. Right now. Right here."

She swallowed hard. "I can't do it. I can't make love to him again. You can do anything to me you wish, but don't hurt Heath."

"You will change your mind, my dear. But it would help if your lover was a little more . . . awake on his feet." He sent another ball of light at Heath, and this one sucked into Heath's mouth and his hands.

Suddenly Heath came to life. He fought against the giant holding him.

"Now, Vivienne, do as I ask. Or you will suffer greatly."

"No," Heath roared. "You don't need to hurt her. Find another woman. I'll make love to her twice in a row, if you bloody well want. Let Vivi and Sarah go."

"Unfortunately for you, Blackmoor, I require Vivienne to unleash the curse. It is the only way I can ensure you will have the power I need you to have. Vivienne has a great deal of strength and power. And the five men she seduced have added to her power. Those men all gave her strength from their unique skills. One was a fighter. Another a fierce lover. One had a quick wit and the courage to take chances in gambling. The other two had great physical strength. And you were the adventurer. You have all made her strong."

"I have no power," she shouted.

Her father's perfectly sculpted face contorted in a sneer. "Do you think I would waste my seed to create something weak? Your power hums inside you. It glows within, like a sun. Over the years, the passion you have taken has stoked that power, like coal fed into flame. But that power has been carefully protected. I had to ensure that, so it could not be detected by other beings—other demons, or the vampires. I made you both to work together. You hold the power that will give him so much strength he could destroy the world. Blackmoor is the only man who can unleash the power hidden within you."

Made for each other.

"That's impossible. I was only made into a vampire a few years ago," Heath said. "Long after Vivi was born."

And Vivienne understood. Her father had planned this since her birth. Perhaps before. "I was created for one reason only, wasn't I? To bring about the end of the world."

Nikolai nodded. "I had to wait to find the right male for the task."

She faced her father, confronting a vampire she knew could kill her. "You created Sarah's mysterious illness to force me to go to Mrs. Holt and pay her price for the medicine. Sarah was never really sick. It was something *you* did to her. Even though she is your *grandchild.*"

She almost felt frost emanate from Nikolai's black, bottomless eyes. "And she did not die, did she? You, my obedient daughter, did as you were told."

"You ensured Heath found and rescued me, didn't you? Somehow you pushed us together, forced us to fall in love."

Nikolai's thick, deep red lips curved. "You are a foolish romantic, child. I only needed you to fornicate with Blackmoor. Which you did. You were like your mother; I could see her infinite need for love when I first stalked her. She was still quite beautiful then."

"You stalked her?" Fear and revulsion echoed in her voice. "What do you mean?"

"I watched. Followed. I felt the light within her. Your mother, Rose, was different than other women I saw. Unique. I had thought about impregnating a woman of a higher class. But not one I saw contained that beautiful golden glow. Such compassion Rose had. When I saw her tend to a boy who had cut his foot badly, despite the bruises she wore from some man's fists, I knew she would be perfect. With her I could create a woman who would be the ultimate temptress."

"And that was me?" His words slipped deep inside her soul. Her mother's beautiful golden glow. "That's what happened to her, that's what made her lose hope and become desperate. You . . . you extinguished that glow, didn't you?"

"I used it to make you, my dear. You took all of Rose's goodness and beauty, combining them with my power and strength. But your birth sucked the soul out of your mother and left her weak. It was why she soaked herself in gin."

Dear God, she had been the one to destroy her mother. Her very existence had done it.

"Stop, Vivi."

The deep, controlled, soothing voice belonged to Heath. "He's trying to bludgeon your heart and soul. He is trying to convince you to do what he asks. Don't listen to him. You didn't steal your mother's life force. If anything, you kept it alive. I believe that. I'm certain of it."

"Silence!" Nikolai shouted. The winged demon drove one of its pointed wingtips into Heath's chest.

Vivienne flinched in horror. "Stop," she pleaded. "Dear God, stop."

"Enough." Nikolai gave a careless wave of his hand.

Blood welled from the wound as the sharp point withdrew. Slowly a trail of blood rolled down Heath's muscles.

Heath did not even flinch. Instead he took advantage of his freedom to attack Nikolai. But the vampire hit Heath with a flash of light, one that sent him reeling to the floor.

Vivienne rushed to Heath's side. She ripped off a strip of her linen shirt and pressed it to the bleeding wound. Heath lay on the floor, his eyes closed, unconscious. Above her, she felt Nikolai staring at her—the way she would be aware of a bug crawling over her skin.

"Why don't you kiss him, Vivienne? Kiss the man you love."

She hesitated. Auburn lashes lay along Heath's cheeks. His mouth was slack, full, soft, and tempting. She yearned to kiss Heath. But she didn't trust Nikolai. And she hated him. He had made her afraid to even give the simplest show of affection, in case it took Heath closer to the transformation.

Instead, she kept pressure on the wound. This was a lifesaving touch, surely this wouldn't hurt him. She looked at Heath, at the man she did love, but spoke to the man she despised. "What is going to happen when he becomes a demon? If you want me to do your bidding, you had better tell me."

"My intentions are very simple. I will control a being that will grow to a height of two hundred feet. A creature that could tear St. Paul's from its foundations with his teeth."

Surely that couldn't be the truth. She turned, and recoiled at the glowing delight in Nikolai's eyes.

"Ah, Vivienne, a beat of his wings could drive a wave of seawater high enough to engulf a town. He would be able to eat dozens of mortals in the space of moments. As a demon, he will be unstoppable. Indestructible."

"But why would you do this to innocent people?"

"What does any man who lives for centuries want? To continue to achieve power. I have decided I will not destroy the world. I will let my demon play; terrify the stupid mortals for a while. Then I will stop Heath from continuing his devastation. What king will defy me when I can have him destroyed with a snap of my fingers?"

He waved his hands. His lackeys darted forward and dragged her from Heath. She struggled but could not break free. Two of the servants dropped him on the litter, which made blood spill from the wound again. They hastened away with him.

"Where are you taking him?"

"To his cell. You will soon be taken to yours."

"You cannot do this to Heath. You cannot force him to kill like that."

"He has already killed."

"You mean—as a vampire."

"And before that, when he carelessly murdered his pretty wife and fragile little daughter."

"That was an *accident*."

"Nonetheless, he took Ariadne from me."

Ariadne? She didn't understand. "You knew his wife. You . . . ?" How could a vampire living in the Carpathians have known Ariadne?

Nikolai stalked to the wall. A tasseled cord was there. He pulled on it, and drapes parted. A portrait, not a window, was on the wall behind the thick crimson curtains.

A blond woman stared down from the canvas. With her pale white-blond hair, her large blue eyes, her peaches-and-cream complexion, the woman glowed like an angel. "That was Blackmoor's wife. The woman whom he drove to her death, because she loved him and he didn't give a damn about her."

Vivienne stared into the large blue eyes of the young woman. Lady Blackmoor looked very much like Vivienne's mother, when Rose had been young, the way Vivienne remembered her, before the harshness of life had battered her.

The softening of Nikolai's eyes, the pain in his tight mouth, was unmistakable. "You loved her. But how could you have known her?"

"Yes," he barked. "I loved her. Adored her. She was the sun I could never have. She was the heaven I could never touch. I resisted my yearning to turn her. I wanted to have her with me for eternity, but I did not allow myself to do that to her. Yet Blackmoor carelessly threw her life away."

"But you lived in the Carpathians."

"I came to England one hundred years ago, Vivienne. After your mother's death, a friend of hers from the slums put a curse upon me, the stupid witch. If I were ever to fall in love with a mortal woman and pursue her, I would die if I did not return to my home country. So I had to leave Ariadne, and I chose not to take her with me. But I could watch her. And I saw him destroy her."

"If you loved Ariadne, what of my mother? Did you also love her?"

His face hardened. "When I seduced Rose, she was very lovely. But she quickly became tiresome, once you were conceived. She clung. She begged. She was desperate and shrill and harsh. And she was weak. Instead of showing pride and spirit, she turned to gin. She grew numb. I never returned to her. I was disgusted."

"How dare you speak of her like that!"

"When I found Ariadne, I understood then why I had become a vampire. I had waited for almost five centuries to find her. I offered her everything. But she was afraid of me. Afraid! When I would have cared for her for eternity. Instead she chose that bastard Blackmoor, and I had to return to the Carpathians."

Nikolai—she could not think of him as her father—strode over to her and grasped her chin. Roughly jerking up her face, he forced her to meet his inky-black eyes. These were the eyes of death, she thought, soulless and eternally cold. "You will make love to him again. If you do not, your daughter Sarah will be destroyed. There. It is as simple as that."

"You—how could you? She's an innocent. She is your grandchild!"

"A man who lives forever has no need for immortality by leaving brats behind. Children are created to serve their parents. And she will serve me this way. Come now, Vivienne, I know I could threaten you with any punishment or pain and you would defy me to protect Blackmoor. You love him. You will have to make a choice. Your beloved daughter or your beloved vampire." He gave her a smile that made her want to vomit. "My dear daughter, I am not worried about being forced to destroy my granddaughter. I know the choice you will make."

Guidon. He knew enough about Heath's curse to believe it could be broken. Would he tell her what she must do? Did he know? But there was no way she could escape this bedchamber and find him. Not with her wrist shackled to the bedpost, and the door locked and barred.

If only she could speak in Guidon's thoughts, the way she spoke in Heath's . . .

Heavens. Vivienne thought back to the tea she'd shared with Guidon. She barely remembered what he'd said to her, she had been so desperate to leave him and go in search of Heath. She'd put down her cup, but Guidon had insisted she drink it. *I made it especially for you,* he had said proudly. *I made it just as I knew you would like it. Almost as though I could read your mind.*

The little gnomelike man had flushed. Even though she was squirming on her seat in impatience, his shyness had been touching. *I hope we will talk again. There is much I could tell you. You have only to ask.*

Could the clever little librarian have thought up another trick? Had the tea contained something that would let her speak into Guidon's mind?

She shut her eyes. *Guidon?* she asked tentatively.

Nothing.

Guidon? Can you hear me? Please say something, if you can. I need to speak to you about the curse. We must stop it, Guidon.

Miss Dare? The vampire librarian's high-pitched, exuberant voice sounded in her thoughts. *You understood, did you, about the tea? I have waited so long for you to talk to me. Since you left me, I have remembered more things—things in the books that I lost. Yes, my dear, the curse can be broken. But it will not be a simple thing to accomplish.*

Tell me, Guidon, she implored in her thoughts. *I will do anything to save Heath, to save all of us. I will tip the earth on its axis if I must.*

No, Miss Dare. This will be more difficult. You must make Lord Blackmoor open his heart to love.

Both my daughter and I told him we loved him. But his wounds aren't healing; it didn't change anything.

It won't work, Miss Dare, until his heart is open.

She knew what Guidon meant. They had told Heath they loved him, but his heart was still closed.

21

The last thing he remembered was Nikolai slamming a ball of light into him to knock him out. Pain lanced Heath's head as he came back into consciousness. His arms were pulled behind him, his legs stretched apart, and all four of his limbs were chained to heavy metal brackets secured to the wall.

Soft rays of light, flushed pink with the dawn, spilled in through the windows of the bedchamber. In an hour, or less, the light would fall on him, burning him to a crisp. . . .

Roses.

The sweet scent of them drifted to Heath. Blearily he took in the sight of feminine bare feet. Black silk shimmered over those feet. The silk rustled and a woman's body came into view as she crouched down to him. Soft hands cradled his jaw, smooth and velvety like flower petals. "What in heaven's name did that monster do to you? Your entire face is a mess of bruises. And you are so weak."

It was Vivi. He knew it. Even though his eyes were failing and he saw only a blurry form. "Vivienne, are you all right?

What has he done to—?" The words died in his throat. "Hell, why are you here?"

The black silk robe slid off her right shoulder, revealing smooth, creamy skin. He glimpsed the deep, tempting valley between her breasts as she got up on her knees in front of him. His breath sucked in hard and sharp.

"He wants me to seduce you," she said softly, in a voice guaranteed to seduce a stone gargoyle. "If I do not, he will kill Sarah."

"Hell and the devil, I'll rip that bastard apart." With her daughter's life in danger, Vivi would not want sex. To force her into a seduction was sadistic and cruel, especially since she had been forced to serve men for so long. He knew what Nikolai wanted and why the monster was using Sarah as a hostage. His sire knew Heath would do anything to save Sarah—including sleep with Vivienne and unleash the demon. And the anger burning inside him at Nikolai would explode when he transformed. It would turn him into the brutal, mindless killer his sire needed.

Black silk pooled around Vivi as she slumped to her bottom in front of him. "I have the key to unlock you. Nikolai believed it would be easier for us to make love if you were free." Her soft-as-sin voice filled with bitterness. "He thought letting us use the bed would be more . . . conducive."

The chains securing his arms rattled. These were not ordinary shackles; he could have easily broken regular iron cuffs. Vivienne fished the key, which hung on a chain between her breasts, and his cock stood up in his dirty trousers so fast, it slapped him in the gut. A soft click sounded, then the shackles dropped away. "I remember locking you up in my carriage, Vivi. Against your will. I'm sorry, love."

She shook her head. "Don't be sorry. I wouldn't have thought to ask you to tie me up, if you hadn't done that."

He gave her a wry smile as he flexed his hand. Vivi was his

sun. Hot, glowing, beautiful. He'd done what he'd hoped to do: opened her to her innate sexuality. He was so furious Nikolai was forcing her to do this, for making sex such a frightening, heartbreaking thing for her.

"I promise you, Vivienne, Sarah will be safe."

"I don't think he will hurt her as long as I do what he says. Or at least, until I do what he says. After that . . . I don't know what he plans to do with Sarah and me. He truly is a monster, Heath. There is so much I must tell you." She leaned over him to fit the key into the shackle on his other wrist. Her breasts brushed his chest, and her puckered nipple drew a line of sizzling awareness across his skin, even through his shirt.

She crouched and released his ankles. His boots were gone. The sunlight seemed to try to nip at her bottom as she bent. Once the cuffs fell free of his ankles he scooped her up and carried her to the bed.

"We're really going to . . . do it?" she whispered.

"We have to. I'll make it . . . easy for you."

"You are going to sacrifice yourself, aren't you? And I don't want it easy." She undid the belt at her waist. And the robe slithered off the crests of her breasts, to fall to her sides and frame her. She was displayed for him: rounded bosom, slim waist, a generous flare of hips. "You don't have to give up. I believe you can break the curse." She explained swiftly what Guidon had said.

"He said you've accepted the curse. I think . . ." She put her hand to her mouth, as though stopping words from breaking free. "Oh hell, I will be blunt with you, Heath. I think you have let the curse control you because it's protected you from love. You are afraid to love again. You don't feel you deserve love. Well, the truth is, Heath, you do not get to chose who loves you. It is what you do that makes people care about you. Sarah and I love you, whether you accept that love or not."

"I don't—"

He broke off as she wrapped her hand around his cock, which pointed hopefully toward her soft, golden nether curls.

"I'm sorry, love," he admitted as she felt how rigid he was. "I know you must be terrified, and I have no right to be aroused. But you do that to me. With your every smile. And with every breath I take near you, every breath that smells of roses and silk and you."

"I believe if you can want love enough, you can break Nikolai's curse. You have to be willing to open your heart." As she spoke, her hands pulled at his shirt.

"No, love. I can do this faster." Given his shirt was in tatters, it proved easy to rip apart. He skimmed his trousers down as quickly. When would the transformation begin? He didn't know. All he knew was he had run out of time.

He rolled over Vivi, bracing himself on his arms. It broke his heart to see how beautiful she was, her eyes shining with hope. He bent and nuzzled her breasts lightly.

"If I can't break the curse," he said huskily, "you have to destroy me."

"Nikolai said you would be indestructible."

"Not possible. Every demon has an Achilles' heel. Ask Guidon and he will tell you mine."

But she shook her head. "There is no need. We will break the curse."

He wanted to. But how could it be possible to do so, just by accepting Vivi's love? He wanted her love. Shouldn't the curse be destroyed then? He licked her breasts. *Exquisite*, he growled in his thoughts, sending the word to her.

She smiled softly. *Every night, I want you to do this. To kiss my breasts.*

She wanted to speak of the future. He fought a spike of fear. He remembered how he used to find breasts, all women's breasts, so tempting. But now only Vivi's interested him. Her pert, soft tits were the most tempting of all. *I promise to kiss your breasts, my queen. In fact, if I work very diligently, I think I can make you come, just by sucking your nipples.*

Her blue eyes went saucer wide. *I don't think I could—*

Relax then, Flower. And let me play.

He licked, laved, flicked, and stroked her nipples. He followed with tweaks, tugs, a teasing nip with his teeth. Then he became serious about his task. He sucked her right nipple and tweaked the nipple of her left. Then he used his vampiric speed to move from nipple to nipple, sucking hard.

She arched beneath him. She clutched at the sheets. Tugged. Ripped them free of the mattress. Bucked fiercely on the bed. And finally let out a wild scream.

Heat blossomed inside him, a fiery warmth that felt like flames licking at his heart. It could be love—or it could be the beginning of his transformation. For the first time in so very long, he might be feeling love, but he couldn't be sure; he couldn't savor it. And he damned Nikolai for stealing that from him.

Forget the curse, idiot, he told himself. Forget everything but Vivi. Forget everything but love.

Panting, she fell back, and she smiled at him, beaming at him like the sun.

Heath, she whispered in her thoughts, *You did make me come. I shall never doubt you again.*

But a voice rumbled up inside his head, a dark, bitter one from his past. A voice that always flayed him with accusations and cold, biting words. *Careless. Irresponsible. Damn fool.* These were the words his father had thrown at him when he was young because his proud, arrogant father had been infuriated by Heath's interest in flora and fauna. It was damn unseemly for the heir to an earldom to go around digging up plants and making sketches in a journal. "*What sort of fool of a boy chases butterflies around a meadow?" his father yelled. "What sort of boy presses flowers in a book? Goddamn, you will turn into a bloody sodomite."*

He had quivered in shame. Even when he'd become the earl, he'd been driven to escape the humiliation and hurt his father had heaped on him, by becoming famous for his books and his studies. He'd had a chip on his shoulder large enough to sink a sailing ship. And poor Ariadne and Meredith had suffered for his stubborn determination to prove his worth to a dead man.

Given all the mistakes he had made, how could he open his heart?

Just try, Vivienne murmured in his thoughts. As though she could read his mind. But he knew, from the faith still gleaming in her eyes, that she had not read his mind, she just knew what he was thinking.

Whether he'd intended it or not, he had fallen in love with Vivi. More than that, he had let her into his heart. He had already done what he had feared the most. When he'd bitten her, he was sure he'd finally pushed her away, lost her. But Vivi was too strong for him. Instead of leaving him, instead of hating and fearing him, she had pulled him back from his selfish grief. She'd offered her love.

"I love you, Vivi." He said it out loud so he could hear it ring out in the bedroom. Even though they were alone on the bed, he'd shouted it out, to ensure the world could hear. "I love you, my angel, my goddess. My light."

I love you, too, Heath. She wriggled against him. At once, he was even harder, and blood surged into his cock, making him rigid as a maypole.

Vivi's trusting smile was like a source of flame, illuminating his past. He'd been afraid Ariadne would mock him as his father had done. He'd been afraid of failing her and Meredith. So he had run away, pretending he was doing it to prove himself. He would never run away again.

He lifted Vivi's hand to his lips, kissed each of her long, slender fingers. She giggled softly.

And his heart—it cracked. It was like the shield he had built to keep out love was an iron door, and Vivi had kicked it down.

"Wait here, my love. There's something I have to do."

She blinked, confused. But she waited. Trusting him. He moved to the center of the room. He had one last throw of the dice, one last chance. One last hope . . . as long as Nikolai and the council proved to be as blindly arrogant as he had been all his life.

Sarah paced in her bedchamber. There were so many emotions boiling inside her, she wanted to keep a lid clamped down firmly on top of them. Fear. Love for her mother and Heath. Love for Julian, who was lost to her forever. Grief. That was the worst one. It seemed to be sucking away at her heart, pulling it apart piece by piece.

All her life, Mother had expected she would marry. Mother had wanted her to fall in love. But she had been afraid to—she knew her mother didn't like men—so Sarah had always been terrified to give her heart to any male. But then Julian had come into her life. A rescuer. He was a vampire, but a gentle one, one who was so good and kind to her. And she had fallen into love so swiftly and so hard, she was surprised the entire world hadn't heard the *thud*. But love was so awful. It made you hurt so much inside.

A rap sounded at her door. Sarah turned away, crossing her arms over her chest and shivering. She was a prisoner. If someone wanted in, they would come inside.

As she expected, the door swung open.

It was him. The vampire called Nikolai, the handsome man who was supposed to be her grandfather. But he was evil and hateful. He wanted to destroy Heath and use her mother to do it. He had locked her in this room. She backed away from him, but he glided toward her as though his feet did not even touch the ground.

Finally he stopped and bowed elegantly. "You lost your great love, little one. I am so very sorry for you."

She recoiled. How could he have known she loved Julian? "I don't want your pity. I want my freedom."

"I came to speak to you, Sarah. You see, I sent the demons to Dimitri's mansion. And I controlled everything they did."

His words snapped something inside her. She lunged forward and grabbed the fireplace poker. With the weapon raised above her head, she felt powerful. For the first time in forever, she felt *strong*.

She swung it at the vampire's head.

Nikolai grasped the poker and jerked it from her grasp. "I can feel the strength of your anger." He smiled. It was hideous how handsome he was, when his heart must be a black mass of garbage inside him. "Finally, the most important part of you has come to life. My dear, Sarah, you are exactly like me."

Her chest heaved with exertion, but not with fear. She hated too much to be afraid. "I am *nothing* like you. You want to unleash some kind of demon to destroy the world. You want to force my mother to do something terrible. And you killed Julian—"

"Shut up and listen, foolish girl," he barked. Before her eyes, Nikolai appeared to grow taller. He glowered at her. "I told you about the demons to explain something to you. I have the power to give your Julian back to you. He is not dead or destroyed. The puff of dust—that was an amusing conceit, I admit. It made it look as though each vampire died. But they did not die. I merely transported them to a sort of prison, using the power of black magic."

Black magic? Her wits whirled. This was the sort of thing in Minerva Press novels. But she had fallen in love with a vampire, and she believed magic truly did exist. "You could bring him back," she repeated. She spoke the words flatly, not daring to hope. She knew what had happened to her mother, even though Vivienne had not been entirely honest with her. Dimitri had told her everything: the fact Nikolai had caused her illness, and about the medicine, and the price her mother had been forced to pay. She knew what sort of a monster this vampire truly was.

"You made me sick," she accused. "You wanted me to die."

He shook his head solemnly. "No, my dear. I would never have truly harmed you. What was draining you was your own stubborn fight against your true nature. The medicine was intended to bring out your vampiric qualities, the ones you inherited from me. But you were afraid of your awakening physical desires, your yearning for adventure, your fascination with the night. I saw into your thoughts. I saw you hide all those things, try to restrain them to please your mother. She wanted you to be a good girl, a proper lady."

Sarah froze. It must be true. How else could he have known? "Do you mean I am a vampire even though I have never been bitten?"

"Let us be direct, shall we?" Her grandfather smiled. The serpent that offered apples to Eve—surely that snake had looked just like Nikolai now. "I will bring Julian back to you, if you let me turn you."

"Turn me? You mean bite me!"

"I mean I will exchange some of your blood with mine and make you a full vampire."

"And that is the price for bringing Julian back. . . . ?"

"Price? It is a gift. Agree, and you can have love, power, freedom. Everything your mother wanted for you. Everything you secretly dreamed of."

Perched on the edge of the enormous bed, Vivienne watched Heath close his eyes, bow his head.

She held her breath. What was he doing? What should she

do? Urge him to come to the bed? The large, four-poster bed was out of reach of the sunlight, but they didn't have long before light filled the room. There were no curtains on the windows to keep it out.

His lips moved, but she couldn't read the silent words. And he said nothing to her in her thoughts. Then he shuddered as though he was going to change, and he snapped his head back to stare up at the ceiling.

She slipped off the bed to go to him. But she took one step and slammed into something warm, hard, yet smooth as velvet: his chest. He'd moved to her so swiftly, she hadn't seen it.

When she had spoken to Guidon through her thoughts, he had explained how she could get Heath to open his heart—in stumbling, halting words. One way to do it was by making love. It might be the only way she could break through the shield around his heart, the only way she could banish his guilt, his belief he couldn't look to the future. Sex would make him vulnerable and then she could try to change him.

Something she'd never tried with any man.

She had to be daring. And saucy and wild. Wearing a wicked smile, she bent forward and took his nipple into her mouth. He groaned, then growled as she gave his erect nipple a light bite.

She'd never been quite *this* daring. Never would she have dreamed of biting.

But his reaction—the way his cock bucked and reared against his belly—gave her confidence. She bit his other nipple gently, and she grasped his cock in one hand and his ballocks in the other and roughly stroked and played.

"God, Vivi, you are going to bring me to my knees," he rasped.

"That," she promised huskily, "is exactly my intention, my lord."

Then, just as in the dream she had about Heath in Hyde

Park, she kissed her way down his cobbled abdomen and lowered to her knees. She was staring at the head of his curving cock. Slowly, she stuck out her tongue. And she licked up the bubbling juices.

Sour. Tart. Wonderful.

His cock told her exactly how much he liked it, by swelling and growing astonishingly larger.

Really, she had no idea how big he actually was, but his erection jutted out and must be far longer than six inches, which was supposed to be average. She had never seen anything so enormous. She loved sucking his cock, but could barely fit half into her mouth. Her lips only coasted partway down, where the shaft grew wide and thick.

She let him out and ran her tongue along the length. Then she whipped his ballocks with her tongue.

His knees buckled.

She stopped flicking, worried he'd fall, but he caught hold of one of the bed's fluted columns. "Your clever mouth is sucking the strength out of me. You are very, very good at this. But I won't last Vivi, if you keep doing this. And I want my orgasm to be deep inside you. After you've come many, many times, of course."

He reached down to lift her, but she darted from his grasp and got to her feet. "You lie down on the bed, Heath. Once again I want you to obey my commands. And trust me."

He lifted a brow. But a heartbeat later he was stretched out on top of the white sheets, waiting for her. His legs were slightly parted, his ballocks hanging heavily between his muscular thighs. His cock rose from its nest of dark auburn hair and stood proud. He put his fist at the base, holding the enormous length straight up into the air.

The sight took her breath away. She wasn't going to lose him. Somehow, someway, she would keep him.

She walked to the bed, aware of the sway of her hips, the jiggle of her bosom. Never had she felt so sensuous. Love made every moment of this breathtaking and beautiful.

"You look like a houri, moving toward me," he murmured. His hand tightened around his thick shaft. Heavens, even his fingers barely touched around the base of it.

Her nerves tingled as she climbed onto the bed. She'd never seen his erection look so large. Could love be making him swell like that? Or was it because he was transforming into a demon?

Obviously he wanted her on top. He'd pillowed one hand beneath his head. He looked far too casual, a dimpled grin playing on his mouth.

Vivi, I feel I've waited a lifetime for this. For you.

Those words . . . she'd heard many pretty words. But his were so special. Real and true and honest. She swung her legs over his thighs and straddled him just below the magnificent prick that would soon be inside her.

But first . . . temptation.

Her quim felt it was steaming with heat. But she planted her palms on his chest, brushed her nether lips lightly along the length of his shaft. Her breasts swung wildly over his face.

His eyes glowed like the moon, silver and bright.

Take me inside. I need this. No matter what happens I know I can't live without making love to you. Even if this is my last day, I want it to be spent in bed with you.

Her heart stuttered, but she forced a smile. *This is going to be our* first *night,* she insisted. *There are too many things I've never dared to do. And I want to do each one with you.*

She clasped her hand around his at the base of his cock. Holding her breath, she brushed the head against her clit. The contact of his firm head to her throbbing, aching nub made her quiver. And her juices flowed so she could play and draw circles and stroke and tease.

She couldn't wait any longer. She knew she should. She must

make this last. To save him, she had to use his desire to make him more vulnerable. And every teasing, agonizing second of foreplay they shared was another moment together.

But this was too good. Her quim pulsed, wanting to hold his shaft and never let it go. Her heart felt so tight. Her ribs were like iron bands. Desire seemed to be making her expand and she couldn't hold in her yearning. They had done so many delicious, erotic things together, but her favorite was having him inside her.

She held him right to the slick entrance of her quim. He surged his hips up and easily slid inside her a good three inches.

Oh God. He was so thick, it was almost *too* much, yet not enough.

She took a deep breath. And lowered. Her tight quim resisted at first, but her juices flowed, and he slid into her. Down, down, down she went. Engulfing him. She had to close her eyes. It was irresistible, delectable agony.

Her moans floated up to the sunlight, to the shafts of sparkling light that fell on the floor by the foot of the bed.

Deeper, please, Flower.

She took him to the hilt, until her quim brushed his nether curls. Her bottom settled on the bulge of his ballocks.

Ride me, Vivi. Tame me.

Tame him? She didn't know what he meant. But she rose and lowered. The shock of his cock nudging her womb made her stop. Made her gasp for breath. She could feel every inch of his erection. Surely it was even larger than the last time it had filled her, stretched her, pushed against her hot, sensitive walls.

She rose, lifting on him until she kept only the head inside her. Then she surged down again until her bottom struck his ballocks and she had to sob with pleasure.

Again and again she did it. Heath smiled, watching her. Enjoying the sight. But he wasn't vulnerable. She needed to do more. . . .

But she was so hot. So tense. So close, she didn't want to stop.

She had to try something else. . . . She had to make him open his heart before he came . . . but she was going to come and she couldn't stop.

He reached out and pressed his thumb to her nether lips as she bounced on him. He shifted his hand, his thumb slid over her clit, and she screamed up to the bed canopy. Stunning sensation blossomed into a delight that rushed through every inch of her body.

He stroked again. Circled, flicked, rubbed, teased, then gave one last hard brush of his thumb that sent her over the edge.

The orgasm slammed over her with a fierce wave of pleasure. Her whole body melted, as though her heart and soul had burst into flames over this man. She collapsed on his chest, coated with sweat, her limbs trembling.

The curse could only be broken if he became vulnerable, if he opened his heart to love. *She* felt vulnerable, but he was chuckling, still in control. Still rigid and thick inside her.

What could she do?

A golden glow poured through the window. The room felt filled with steam, and smelled of lush, rich scents—the sweat of colliding bodies, the juices that slicked their thrusts. Then she saw them. . . . There were no curtains, but the tasseled cords were still there.

She had to make him vulnerable. And now she knew how.

Heath groaned as Vivi lifted off him. Her cunny slid off him, his cock fell out and slapped his belly. She walked swiftly to the window, her lush bottom jiggling. She yanked hard on the curtain ties and tore them down.

He swallowed hard as she approached the bed. He'd loved tying her up. He would love to do it again. But it wasn't to be.

Petal, I can't. I don't know when I might change; I want you to be free to run.

She sucked the end of her finger with feigned innocence. I'm *not going to be tied up.* You *are.*

Arousal hit him like a brick, at the same instant he balked and sat up sharply on the bed. But Vivienne ran the rest of the way to him and scrambled on top of the mattress, anticipation shining in her eyes. She grasped his wrists.

He'd never let any woman tie him up, but he had to admit, the feel of the cords against his skin was erotic. And hell, he'd asked her to do it for him so she could explore her sensuality. Maybe he needed to as well, and if it was the last thing he did before he died, he couldn't complain.

While he'd been considering, Vivi had tied his wrists together with one cord and had run it around a bedpost. She pulled on it, and his arms stretched out behind him. As she leaned over to tie the silken rope to the bedpost, her breasts dangled over his face. He strained up to suck, but soon learned the torture of being tied up. Wanting something, but not being able to get it.

He expected her to bind his ankles with the other cord. Instead, she wriggled down to his hips, and wove the rope around his right thigh. Then the little vixen wrapped it around his balls, securing them in a loop, before she wound the rope around his left thigh and tied a firm knot.

His cock jerked in excitement, and it grew thicker, harder, and throbbed like the devil. He'd never guessed having his ballocks bound would feel so good.

It took everything inside him to fight his orgasm as Vivi sat on top of him and took him deep inside her cunny again. He wanted to hold her hips, he wanted to pump her up and down, but his arms were tied. And each bounce of her curvaceous little derriere tightened the rope around his balls. Pleasure and pain; he hissed through his teeth as he experienced them both. Vivi had found new territory for him, and he was like an innocent, learning how thrilling it must have been for her to explore.

He had to arch his head back as the ropes pulled tight. God, he really was her captive. She could tug on that cord around his balls and hurt him in an instant. The risk made this damned arousing. He had to do exactly what he'd asked of her. He had to trust her.

And she was being wicked on him. She moved her hips up and down so slowly it was sheer agony, then bounced hard and fast and took his breath away. She was so sweet and tight and he was drowning in the hot silkiness of her. He gritted his teeth, willing himself not to come. He wanted this to last forever.

The moment he climaxed he was lost.

She was trying to drive him mad. She put her arm beneath her breasts, which plumped them into large, full globes. With each bounce on his cock, her bosom bounced against her arm. Her nipples bobbed.

His face must have revealed how mesmerized he was. She cupped her breasts, her bounty spilling over her hands. He fought not to spill himself.

Then she got off his cock and scrambled up. His heart raced. She moved along his body, her richly scented cunny coming closer and closer to his mouth. Then she was there, her glistening pink nether lips just out of reach. He strained up to lick her, suckle her, eat her, but she swung her leg over him. Escaping.

Suddenly she tugged at the knots she'd tied, struggling to undo them.

Flower, I was enjoying that.

She winked saucily. "So was I. But for what I want to do now, you must be free."

What could it be? He growled in lusty anticipation. He

jerked his arms apart swiftly and the cord snapped. Then he undid the one around his balls.

Vivi rolled onto her tummy, so her rounded derriere stuck up in the air. *I want you to . . . to go inside my bottom.*

Even in his thoughts, her voice was shy.

You really want me to do that? he asked softly. *We played before with the dildos. . . .*

And I liked it. But this time I want it to be your cock deep inside me.

22

Her words made his prick buck and swell. The rush of blood to his eager, aching cock left Heath dizzy. Vulnerable. He could feel his heart open as Vivienne bit her lip and gazed at him with trusting, bottomless blue eyes.

She lay on her stomach and rested her cheek on the counterpane so she could watch him. Loose and free, her golden hair rippled down her back, reflecting the yellowing light of the sun around the room. And slowly, she parted her legs in invitation. She was so beautiful, he had to take a moment and savor the sight.

But she wriggled her rump on the bed, and cried, "Please, now! I can't wait any longer."

His heart was a tight ball in his throat. He couldn't wait. He knew he wouldn't be able to resist coming now.

But even knowing what he was, what he was destined to become, Vivi trusted him. The way she moaned and lifted her derriere to him was proof. Light spilled behind him. It didn't touch his exposed skin, but the glow illuminated her curves—

the little dip of her lower back, the rise of her voluptuous bottom, the sleek lines of her legs.

She was perfect. In every way. Outside and in. Then she arched her bottom up and turned it in a circle. Heath stared, his throat dry, as she slid her hand down between her legs. Her fingers plied between her glistening lips. Her gasp meant one thing: she was stroking her clit. She was comfortable enough to play with herself with wanton abandon in front of him.

His heart thundered as though he were a nervous virgin. He could feel his cock pulsing with each heartbeat. But this time, each surge of blood into his cock ignited his hunger for blood. Lust was launching his transformation. His fangs were longer. They'd lengthened like his prick.

He should leave her now. Go stand in the sunlight and die. But he wanted to share this—this incredible, intimate moment with her—before he did.

He could control the curse for long enough to pleasure her. And, he prayed, long enough for Vivi to escape this room.

He licked his index finger, soaking it with his saliva, then stroked gently between her cheeks and found her tight little anus.

Vivi squirmed beneath him in pleasure and her hair fell away from her neck. He couldn't stop staring at the long, pale column. His fangs exploded forward.

No. Hell, *no*. This was about sex, not blood. He might be a vampire, but at the core, he was still a man. He wanted Vivi, he wanted his cock inside her, and he wanted to make her come.

Slowly, he manipulated her with his fingers. And she moaned for him. She held her cheeks apart so his finger would finally pop in past the firm ring of her anus. The sight of her fingers gripping her arse, pulling the cheeks open . . . it had his legs feeling as weak as feathers. She did this to him. She humbled him. She made him vulnerable with desire.

I think I will burst into flames if you don't do it now, she whispered in his thoughts. *I love you. I want to be with you forever. But this is . . . I need you right now!*

Indeed, he answering teasingly. *And I need you.* He took hold of his cock and pushed the head against her entrance. Her plump cheeks surrounded his shaft with heat. He sucked in a sharp breath. And eased forward.

She groaned desperately and pulled her cheeks wide again.

He glimpsed her anus—tight, pink, furled, and oh so small. Could he go inside her? He knew he could, but he feared hurting her. Holding his shaft tight, he pushed again, but gently. She opened for him. Enough that he felt the pop, then the scorching grip of her muscles.

God god god . . .

Her fingers worked her clit with fast, hard strokes. He withdrew until he was almost out, then slowly thrust again. Another inch of his cock plunged into fire and pressure.

She moaned and lifted her rump up to him. Together they worked, until he was buried all the way inside her. His pubic hair brushed her bottom, his groin collided with plump cheeks, and his every thrust set their voluptuous bounty quivering.

She arched up to him, gasping, her face blushed pink. Her hand worked madly. Her mouth opened on a silent scream. She came like that, jerking beneath him, crying out without words.

Her bottom surged up, taking him deep, and her muscles pulled at him, gripped him, stimulated him beyond belief. He shut his eyes. *Make it last. . . .*

It was his last thought before his body ignited. A fireball of pleasure swirled around his heart and shot down to his cock. Heat rushed through his jerking shaft, and he knew it was his cum jetting out.

His arms buckled with the intensity of his pleasure. He dropped, but caught his weight on his elbows. He withdrew his cock. Fighting his hunger, he kissed Vivi's flushed neck. She tasted salty and sweet.

He tore off some of the sheets to clean her derriere, and he did it with infinite care. Droplets of his cum rested on her bottom. He swiped those up.

Vivi didn't speak; she was gasping for breath. But suddenly, she arched up, and rolled over on her side, peering at him. "Heath . . ."

His back tensed. His spine arched and his body began twisting and stretching on its own. The heat of orgasm was swamped by a burning fire inside him, by the agony of his body writhing and changing, twisting and distorting.

His right arm jerked beyond his control. *Snap!* The sickening sound filled the room. His shoulder joint had pulled out as his muscles lengthened and stretched apart. With a howl, he grabbed his limp arm, then pushed his arm back in.

"Get out, Vivi. You have to get out of here. I don't know what I'll do while I'm changing. I don't want to hurt you." He tumbled off the mattress, scrambled back to the wall, still in shadow, away from sunlight.

Vivienne struggled to sit up. It was happening now. Pressed against the shadowed wall, Heath was changing. But why? Hadn't that been enough to open his heart?

"Vivi, get away." His voice was hoarse. His body twisted and writhed so viciously, she wanted to be sick. He slid down the wall, his eyes shut, his face contorted. "I love you. I don't want anything to hurt you."

"I love you, Heath. And I'm not going anywhere." She hurried to his side. He rolled away from her, his back facing her. His spine buckled and popped beneath his skin.

Break the curse, she thought feverishly. *Love me. Open your heart. Believe. Believe.*

Hope. Faith. Trust. All the emotions she had tried to tamp

down, all the ones Heath had resurrected in her. They were alive in her now, like a snapping, crackling flame. And she knew he needed to embrace them, too.

But it wasn't working. He had said he loved her. He had wanted to push her away to keep her safe because he truly did care about her. Why wasn't it enough?

Nikolai had wanted to punish him, to make him pay for Ariadne's death. No, the curse had been designed so he could never truly have love. How could he win a woman's heart if he could only make love to her once, then was forced to leave? Perhaps he didn't have to accept love. Perhaps the key to the curse was not that he had to fight it. What if love triumphed in spite of it? What if, despite the curse, he won a woman's heart?

Perhaps the curse had not been broken because she had told him she loved him, but she hadn't *proven* she had given her heart to him. How did she do it?

Her blood had healed him before. Could her blood heal him now? Take away the curse that controlled him? But before, he had barely been able to stop taking her blood.

What if she had to lay down her life to save him? Was she willing to do it? She would have to leave Sarah. But she would save Heath and she knew he would protect Sarah. She knew she could trust him with the most precious person in the world. Was that not proof of love?

She rushed to Heath, where he was writhing on the floor. His spine had distorted and large lumps jutted against the skin of his back. His body was larger. He was growing and stretching and the pain must be excruciating. She pressed her bare wrist to his mouth. Then she shut her eyes tight, winced, and tore her wrist along his fangs. The tips were so sharp, they easily sliced into her skin.

Vivi, no.

She heard Heath's desperate shout in her head, but ignored it. Her blood was flowing.

She had *faith* he would not kill her. She *trusted* him to break the curse and to survive. She *hoped*—and she held hope in her heart the way she'd held Sarah as a baby, with tender, nurturing care. For she would never let the flicker of hope wither and die. Not again.

Without it, she could not live.

The sensation of him suckling at her wrist made her moan. She had to lie down on the carpet beside him. It wasn't the loss of blood; it was the dizzying pleasure rushing through her.

And she didn't hope anymore. She *knew*. She knew what love was. This was it. And she *knew* her future promised to be filled with love. . . .

Vivi's blood spilled on his tongue. Heath swallowed hard, tasting the familiar coppery tang but also her unique flavor. Her blood tasted of cinnamon, vanilla, and something earthy and sweet and special to her.

She shouldn't have done this.

She'd done it to heal him. But a curse wasn't a wound. . . .

Christ, he understood: he had the curse because of his wounds. She was trying to heal a soul he didn't have. He had to stop drinking her blood. But he couldn't. His body was expanding, his mind shutting down. Her blood triggered his most basic senses, and he craved more with a fierce hunger he'd never known before.

His eyes, covered with a red film, struggled to focus. She lay beside him. Her lids were dropping shut. She wasn't moving. And her arm flopped lifelessly against his mouth.

He was killing her.

Damn this curse. He was not going to let anything stop him from saving Vivienne. His body screamed with the need to keep drinking, but he fought it. He eased his teeth from her wrist and held her limp hand. Already, her skin felt cold. Pure terror ran through his veins. With a howl of fury and defiance,

Heath lifted his wrist to his mouth and slashed through his skin with his fangs.

Every instinct howled at him to push her away. Not to protect her, but to leave her, so he could hunt and kill. It was the demon inside him, taking control.

But he struggled to quell it. He got to his knees beside her, his changing body wracked with pain. He pressed his wrist to her lips.

Nothing happened. Her lips didn't move. She didn't suck. She didn't try to take his blood.

Dear God, don't let me kill her. Let her live.

The miracle happened then. Slowly, Vivienne started to drink.

He cradled her against his chest as she did. His unwieldy hands, now tipped with claws, struggled to push the damp hair from her face.

Before his eyes, the claws began to recede. His hands twitched and throbbed as the sharp talons shrank back inside, but he kept his wrist to Vivienne's lips. She needed enough to heal. Far more than he'd given Sarah. It would be enough to change her, transform her into a vampire, but she would be safe and she would live forever.

His back twisted with a jolt so sharp, he almost let Vivi go. But he refused to release her; he refused to hurt her. His spine buckled, then began to shrink.

Was he really changing back from demon to vampire? He couldn't let himself dare hope it was true. . . . No, the hell with it, he *was* going to hope all he wanted. Hope she would survive. Hope for their safety. Hope for a future with Vivienne and Sarah.

"Ow." Vivi moaned softly. "I feel odd. . . ." Her eyes blinked open and the two most beautiful, most sapphire blue, most sparkling eyes stared up at him. "Heavens, I *feel*. I'm alive, and you are, and you're not a demon. And that is the most important thing of all."

He gathered her into his arms, resting his chin lightly on top of her tangled hair. She smelled of sweat, of pleasure, of blood. And his smell was imprinted on her. It flowed through her veins now, marking her. Making her his. But once he told her what he'd done to save her, would he lose her forever? "Vivi, I have to admit something to you. I did something to save you that I had no right to do without asking. . . ."

She had been horrified to discover she was a succubus, and now he had made her into a vampire. He'd condemned her to an existence where she had to do much worse than have sex to steal a soul. Now, she would crave blood as he did. And she would either hunt mortals, or have to endure the endless struggle against her new nature.

He'd saved her without thinking of the consequences, because he loved her so damn much.

He held her, knowing it would be the last time. He kissed her cheek, her lips, the tip of her nose, her forehead, taking every kiss he could, storing them away in his heart.

"Heath, what is wrong? Are you still changing? You look like you are sick with fear—"

"I gave you my blood," he said abruptly. "When you offered me your blood, I took it. It stopped my transformation, but I took too much. . . ." For eternity, she would hate him for what he'd done. "Vivi, I almost killed you. Dear God—"

"But you stopped. You controlled yourself. Heath, it means you did not become a demon." She squared her shoulders. "You never let the curse take control of you. Even as your body changed, in your heart you were still the honorable gentleman I love."

Her words hit his heart like blades. "I had to give you my blood to save you, Vivi. I am so damn sorry, but it was the only way. You would have died otherwise."

She stared at him so innocently, he wanted to tear his own heart out. She didn't understand.

He cupped her cheeks. Gruffly, he said, "It means I've turned you. I've made you into a vampire."

She nodded. Her large blue eyes held his, still filled with love. "I knew I risked dying when I gave you my blood, Heath, but you didn't kill me. You saved me."

Christ. "Vivi, you don't understand. I've made you into a vampire like I am. You will have cravings for blood, and you will either have to spend eternity fighting them or you have to feed from people. And I know you would never want to do that. You can never go out into the sun again."

She would never stroll with Sarah in the sunshine again. Never take her daughter shopping, or to Gunter's for flavored ices, or even to Brighton to see the sea. In his mind, he pictured Meredith running to him across a lawn drenched in summer sun. That was the most beautiful memory of his life, and he'd ached for a decade because he would never experience those feelings again: the caress of the warm light, the smell of flowers and afternoon breezes, the way his daughter looked when sunlight sparkled in her eyes. Now he had stolen Vivienne's chance to fill her life with moments like those.

"I gave you survival, but I've cost you so much—"

Vivi pressed her hand over his mouth. "Heath, I was *already* a demon. You haven't taken things from me, you've *given* me so much. You've given me love. You saved my life." Her gaze slowly caressed him, setting his skin aflame in its path. "Thank heavens, your body has returned to normal. You look . . . well, like you."

"Is that a good thing, love?"

"You are the most wonderful sight I have ever seen—next to Sarah when she was born."

His heart swelled large enough to burst in his chest. "You broke the curse, Vivienne."

"*We* broke the curse. Don't you understand? We have found love, something I thought I would never have. You have given me a treasure I could never have dreamed of having."

He lifted her, though his legs wobbled, his bones ached, and his muscles felt as though they'd been stretched like rubber and snapped back. He rested his forehead against hers. His eyes burned, tears gathering at the corners. He remembered Sarah's teasing words that vampires were not supposed to cry. But a soft tear rolled down Vivienne's cheek, and it dripped to her smiling lips. And he had to blink one from his eyes. Apparently, vampires could cry—for happiness.

He took an unsteady step toward the bed, intending to place Vivi there so she could rest, when the window of the room flew up with such force, the glass shattered. The drapes snapped back and four black shapes flew in.

The council was finally here.

Vivienne screamed as winged creatures landed on the carpet in the bedchamber. At once, Heath set her down behind him. He moved with his amazing speed, draped her robe over her shoulders, and stood in front of her once more.

Her throat dry, she saw the figures that now stood in the shadows. Not more of the batlike demons, but the men of the council themselves. She would not cower behind Heath. She stepped forward to stand at his side. They were partners in this. Heath wrapped his arm around her at once and clamped her securely against his left side. She could hear the slow, heavy beat of his heart.

One of the tall men pushed back the hood that hid his face. Vivienne's heart lurched in terror. It was Adder, the vampire lord who had tied her to the altar, who had intended to rape her, then drink her blood. She had to fight not to shrink back as he prowled forward. His gaze was locked on Heath, but Adder held out his hand toward her.

"All right, Blackmoor," he growled. "We've come as you requested. If you want to protect Miss Dare from Nikolai, you must give her to us."

She froze. Heath had brought the council here? She stared up at him in horror.

Heath stood naked, his arm tight around her. Yet he did not look cowed or afraid. "Nikolai has offered us protection from you. I am not just going to give you Vivienne. You have to give me a reason to betray Nikolai."

"Betray him?" Adder scoffed. "He intends to invoke your curse and use you as a tool of destruction. You are such a damnably soft-hearted idiot you won't want that to happ—" Adder broke off, peered at her, at Heath, then at their tumbled bed. "You were lovers once already, and you have done it again. You damn fool, Blackmoor. The curse—"

"Is broken. It's gone. I did not change into a demon. Vivienne helped me break it."

"You made love and you did not change?" The vampire's face contorted into a startled, blank look of horror.

"As I said, we broke the curse. I no longer need to be destroyed, Adder. There is no need to kill me to protect mortals and vampires."

Adder sneered. "It means you are of no use to Nikolai. He'll stake you and turn you to dust. And use your brother instead."

"So I expect," Heath answered coolly without a trace of fear. "So I have to destroy Nikolai. Yet I know if I help you by killing him, you will repay me by taking Vivienne from me. I won't let that happen."

Adder waved his hand impatiently. "You wish to bargain? There is to be no negotiation. You have found Nikolai for us and brought us into his house. I can destroy him myself right now. With a snap of my fingers, I can summon my demons. How many minions does Nikolai have in this house, a few dozen? I can fight him and win."

Vivienne looked from one fierce, stubborn vampire to the other. Heavens, they'd been plunged into a vampire war. And she had no idea where Sarah was. Sarah would be in danger. Why had Heath done this? She could see the anticipation in Adder's eyes. The man would attack. He was gloating at Heath. Adder believed he could kill Heath, then do with her whatever he wished.

What did he *want* from her? Nikolai had told her she had been specially created to tempt men, to be the first of an army of succubi. But why would a vampire want to destroy humans, when he needed their blood?

The other men—there were five more, swathed in black cloaks—moved swiftly into a circle, so all six surrounded her and Heath. She met Heath's eyes. Silvery-green, they still appeared calm. *Trust me*, he said in her head.

Trust you! They are going to attack you. And we have nothing with which to fight them. I would have to jump over Adder to reach the fireplace poker.

You saved me by giving me hope and love. Keep your hope now. "You can't win against Nikolai," he said softly.

Adder's sharp laugh rang out. "I will. You have nothing to bargain with."

But Heath had her—and if she agreed to go, she could save Heath. Perhaps today she *was* destined to die, and leave him and Sarah forever. . . .

Her thoughts died away as she saw Heath's eyes suddenly widen and the silver-green depths brighten. She knew that look. It was hope. "But you don't want her anymore, Adder." Heath added, "She cannot give you want you want."

"W—what do you mean?" Her voice sounded strange, falling into the sudden silence.

Heath spoke to her, but never shifted his gaze from Adder. "When you helped me to break the curse, it freed you. It makes sense, since Nikolai created you as a . . . a temptation to ignite his curse. You did your job, but by beating the curse, I believe you are freed from your servitude to Nikolai. We destroyed his magic. Which means you are no longer a succubus."

His words astonished her. Heath and Adder locked gazes, like animals pacing, waiting for the moment to attack.

Could it be true? Or was it a bluff? She remembered the rich tang of Heath's blood on her lips. Dimly, she remembered trying to resist, then giving in. It had been so intimate. He had drunk from her and she from him. She felt bonded to Heath now.

Did that mean she would not go to other men in their dreams, or in reality, and seduce them?

But Adder roared. He spun, slammed his fist into the plaster wall, drilling a six-inch hole. "That is impossible, Blackmoor," he snapped. "And impossible to prove."

"You know it is the truth," Heath countered. "She is a vampire now. And she is *mine*."

Heath's possessiveness shot through Vivienne with the force of a bolt of lightning. She ran her tongue over her teeth. She didn't have fangs. But sunlight slanted through the windows, spilling on the floor in front of her. She jerked back instinctively, pulling Heath with her.

Adder gave a sickening smile. "I will need to take her to ensure this is the truth. If it is, then she will be freed, I assure you. And if it is true, you have brought about her destruction. Remember Nikolai holds your brother Raine. Miss Dare was useful to Nikolai if she could ignite the demon in either you or your brother. Now that she is bonded to you, she could have sex with Raine and set off the demon, but she would not give your brother the power Nikolai needs him to have. Out of anger and for revenge on you, Nikolai will destroy her. Let her come with me and I will keep her safe."

The other vampires stepped forward, hands outstretched.

There was no way in Hades she would go with Adder. But how were they to stop six powerful vampires?

Heath wrapped both arms around Vivienne's waist. "Adder, don't be a bloody fool. Nikolai doesn't know Miss Dare is freed from his service. He won't expect it, so we can use it to distract him. If you want to destroy him, that will be your chance. That was why you wanted Vivienne all along, wasn't it? To take her power—and stop Nikolai?"

Heath had no idea if it was the truth. But the way Adder recoiled told him he had guessed right. Adder had needed to destroy Nikolai before the super demon was unleashed. No doubt Nikolai intended to use his demon to destroy the council.

Vivi was Nikolai's child. She was of his blood. If Adder took her blood into his body, her power could give Adder the strength to defeat her father.

Heath's mind stopped in its tracks. There had to be more. Adder could have easily stopped Nikolai's plan long ago by destroying the two cursed vampires, he and his brother.

He grasped at an idea. Vivi's father had been one of the oldest vampires, created by a fallen angel. . . . He quickly posed a question in Vivi's head. *You told me about your mother, Vivi. What made her special to you?*

Vivi looked at him as though he were mad. But her thoughts flowed into his head. *Her name was Rose. She was strong and courageous, and she would look after every woman in the flash-house. She used to make up stories for me, of how one day I would marry a prince. . . .*

He saw Vivi swallow hard, her beautiful throat moving. *I know that mustn't be what you want to know. But it is all I know. She was an ordinary woman.*

She can't have been, he said softly. *She must have been special—different in some way.*

You mean a demon. She said the words flatly. Adder was watching them, trying to fathom the words they were exchanging privately in their thoughts.

No, I don't believe that. Not of a woman who healed others. I believe Nikolai chose her because she must have been like you—beautiful, good, strong—and he knew those qualities would make you irresistible.

Vivienne stared helplessly at him. *You know Nikolai told me my mother had a glow inside her. Could it have been . . . true? Heath, I must tell you: your wife looked exactly like my mother did, when she was young. Nikolai had fallen in love with Ariadne, and that was why he chose you for the curse.*

"Stop!" Adder roared the word. "You will stop speaking in your thoughts or I'll destroy Blackmoor where he stands."

Heath knew he had only moments to figure this out. Had it been a broken heart that had turned Vivi's mother to gin? Had Nikolai compelled Rose to destroy herself, because he no longer needed her? Or had she been drinking because she had realized she was not human, that she had strange powers, and they frightened her?

Was it possible Rose had been just as strong as Nikolai, but her powers had been those of good and healing, whereas his magic was dark and evil?

There was one thing Heath knew about men: the thing they wanted most was usually the most dangerous thing they could have. He had fought his love for Vivienne, his desire to have love and family, because it meant he had to open his heart and risk not just death, but also pain and heartbreak. Was it possible Adder wanted Vivi because *she* held the power to destroy him?

Vivi had stopped him from becoming a demon. Did Vivi have some kind of power that could kill demons—or possibly the power to heal and save them? Could she save vampires?

Had he destroyed her power by turning her into one? Obviously Adder wasn't certain, because he still wanted her.

The council had power only because they were vampires. If Vivi could heal the Nosferatu, if she would return them to their human state, she could end the undead world and leave men like Adder as ineffectual mortals.

Hell, had Dimitri known? No wonder the elder vampire had told him not to bring Vivienne to the vampire queens. If Vivi could "heal" the queens, she would destroy them. They would want her dead. He had to pray he actually had ended her powers by turning her into a vampire. He had to hope Sarah had not inherited the same power. Otherwise they would be hunted for eternity. They would never be free.

But he had to worry first about the here and now. He grinned cockily at Adder, his confidence surprising the other vampire. "I will help you kill Nikolai if you guarantee freedom for Sarah and Vivi. I don't care what happens to me."

What are you doing? Vivi whispered desperately.

I have to ensure they won't pursue you. That you and Sarah will be free and safe. Once Adder gives his word, he will honor it. He has no reason to go after you. He was lying to her now, when she trusted him. When she had faith in him. But he had to, because he was not going to fail Vivienne.

But what about you? I love you. You are going to risk everything for me. I can't lose you.

23

Vivienne tried to stand at Heath's side, but he firmly propelled her back. Then, in front of her eyes, Adder tipped his head back and shouted an incantation of magic. The door seemed to tremble in its frame, it glowed red, then it flew open. Light flashed on blades and Vivienne watched in horror as the two guards charged at Heath with scimitars drawn.

Now she knew why he'd pushed her back. But she had the fireplace poker in her hand and she ran forward. One of the vampire council grabbed her and stopped her.

Heath swiftly dispatched the first servant—he chopped his hand into the man's neck and the body flopped limply to the carpet. The second guard sliced Heath's arm so deeply blood spurted. But Adder pulled the turbaned man back and broke his neck by swiftly jerking the man's head. The snapping sound was unmistakable.

She could hear the slow breathing of the guard Heath had attacked. Heath had spared a man's life; Adder hadn't. The blood on Heath's arm stopped flowing. Before her eyes, the wound healed. More proof the curse had been thwarted.

Suddenly she realized the guards had not come in when the window had smashed. She whispered that into Heath's thoughts. *Didn't they hear anything?*

He shook his head, looking grim. *No, the council must have cloaked their minds. The servants here are not vampires. And it means Adder is stronger than I've given him credit for.*

What are you going to do? She whispered it fearfully.

Use arrogant men against each other, came his cool reply.

They had traveled only a few yards down the hallway when more of Nikolai's servants attacked. The vampire council attacked these men. The guards had treated Heath viciously, but it still broke her heart to see how easily the vampires could kill.

Heath clasped her hand. Was there a way out? Could they escape while Nikolai and the council fought each other? Was that Heath's plan—?

Vivienne, you will come to me. You have failed me. And I have Sarah.

Nikolai's voice, in her head, froze her on the spot. She stared helplessly up at Heath. "Nikolai just spoke to me. He knows what I've done, and he's going to hurt Sarah."

Heath kicked open the drawing room door and ran in, with the council members behind him. Vivienne followed, and the sight before her eyes turned her blood to ice. Sarah stood facing Nikolai. The tall, blond-haired vampire held Sarah's chin and he slowly tipped her head, then brushed her blond hair back to expose her neck.

"No!" Vivienne screamed.

Heath launched forward and slammed his fist into the side of Nikolai's face. The blow would have knocked a mortal man unconscious. Nikolai merely lifted his hand and a blast of white light sent Heath sprawling backward.

"Stop," Sarah gasped. "I—I've agreed to do this. I am willing to become a vampire, because my grandfather will bring

Julian back to me. This way I will be the same as Julian. I can be with him. And Nikolai has promised"—tears welled in her blue eyes—"he's promised he will let you and Heath go free, Mother."

She didn't believe it. And Heath jumped back to his feet, just in time to grab Adder as the vampire ran at Nikolai.

"Bloody hell, don't attack him."

"Very good, Blackmoor," Nikolai sneered. "You don't want me to accidentally hurt my granddaughter because of the council's stupidity." He glared at Adder. "They will want both Vivienne and Sarah dead, because that will keep the council safe."

"I know," Heath said, but Vivienne had no idea what he was talking about. How could she or Sarah hurt the vampire council?

"I have waited a long time to take the blood that was meant for me. In Rose, it was not strong enough. Vivienne has made it stronger; the blood absorbed her courage and fire. And now, in this beautiful child, the blood is filled with the strength of love and courage, and the passion of youth."

"Y—you want our blood?" Vivienne had no idea what he meant. She edged toward Nikolai. He had his attention on the men.

Sarah tried to back away. "You said you would change me."

Nikolai grasped her daughter's wrist tightly. "And I must take your blood first, to do it. I must bring you to the brink of death."

Vivienne saw Sarah's welling fear. Was she now realizing the horrible deal she had made? Vivienne had to prevent him from turning Sarah. She didn't want Sarah to give up mortal life for any reason, even love. Sarah was too young to make such a choice—

A sharp pain shot through her jaw. Startled, Vivienne stumbled back. A knifelike tip almost punctured her tongue. She had *fangs.*

But she didn't hunger for blood. Strength rushed through her body. She was a mother, and it was a mother's duty to protect her child. Suddenly she rose off the ground and she flew at Nikolai. Grasping his shoulders, she pulled him away from Sarah and they both slammed to the wood floor. But she didn't feel the pain of impact.

She pinned Nikolai.

His gaze locked with hers. "How?" he howled. "How did you break the curse?" Then he saw her teeth and his black eyes went wide with shock.

"I broke it with love. And I will save my daughter with every weapon I possess. Including this." She bent and plunged her fangs into Nikolai's throat. She had no idea how to take blood; instinct was guiding her. Blood surged into her mouth. The thought of what she was doing revolted her.

"Mother, no! He was going to bring Julian back. He can't die."

The horrible fear and pain in Sarah's voice stopped her. Her hesitation was enough. Nikolai threw her off and she slid back across the floor. She crashed against Heath's legs and, of course, he paused to help her. In that moment, Nikolai leaped up. Blood flowed from his neck. It wasn't a normal rich red; it was so dark it was almost black.

Heath ran for Sarah, but Nikolai reached her first. Eyes burning with fury, the ancient vampire dragged her terrified daughter hard against his chest. Light from the fire glinted on a blade. Nikolai held it poised over Sarah's throat.

Heath moved forward slowly. In her thoughts she also heard the warning Heath sent to the council. *Don't move. I'll finish him for you. If you attack, you'll kill her. And then I'd kill every one of you. I now know how to do it.*

What did that mean? But she was too sick with fear to care.

"Stop there, Blackmoor," Nikolai barked.

Heath did. But he said softly, "Vivienne made me open my

heart to love. Your curse was not very powerful after all, Nikolai. All I had to do was realize I wanted love more than anything else. That Sarah's love and Vivienne's were worth risking my heart. I had my eyes opened to the real treasure of the world: not power or glory or wealth. But love. And you, damn idiot, have thrown away any chance of love and redemption."

Nikolai hissed like an angry snake. She knew what Heath was trying to do—appeal to the human in Nikolai. But Vivienne saw the blade press to Sarah's throat and she doubted the old vampire had any human emotion left.

Sarah's eyes met hers fearfully. Her thoughts suddenly flew into Vivienne's head. *He lied and I'll never get Julian back. I'm going to die. But I didn't want to be a vampire. I didn't want him to do it. I was too weak and afraid, and I've lost Julian forever.* Heavens, she could read her daughter's mind.

Nikolai had barked a command in a foreign language and the doors burst open. More servants rushed in and his winged demon filled the doorway.

There was no way out.

Heath kept his eyes on the blade Nikolai held to Sarah's throat. He had to be cautious and careful. Behind him, Vivi's heart thundered like cannon fire, and her body quivered in terror. He had to ensure she didn't do anything rash to save her daughter.

He could hear the labored breathing of his maker. Nikolai's face had a blue tinge, his lips almost purple, even though the blood had stopped flowing and the wound had healed.

Nikolai was still growing weaker. Why? Was it because Heath's curse had been broken?

Heath prayed the damn council would wait. But he also noticed the members of the council were moving slower. Laboriously. And suddenly Heath pulled Vivi forward into his arms. Love had given him the strength to break the curse. It had to give him the strength to free Vivi from her servitude to Nikolai. His sire, the vampire council—they were not just ordinary vampires; they thrived on darkness.

He had to keep making them weak. "Don't worry," he whispered to Vivi's startled face. "Sarah will be safe. That is how it will end—with you both safe, free, and living happily ever after."

"With you." She answered, but her voice wavered.

He kissed her. Her lips were hard and unyielding against his, which he expected. She was terrified. But Nikolai let out a growl of frustration. And the members of the council let out howls of pain.

He kissed Vivi's neck, trailed his lips down her throat. Nikolai was shaking now, and Adder had beads of sweat—rare for a vampire—on his head. "I love you," Heath said, over and over, each time he gasped a breath. "I love you, Vivienne, and I always will."

"I love you, Heath. But this isn't—"

He silenced her with another kiss. *Love*. He had been so afraid to hope for it, but it was going to save them all now.

The point of Nikolai's blade had fallen away from Sarah's throat. Heath released Vivi, ran to her daughter's side, and pulled Sarah back. Before her eyes, Nikolai's huge powerful body began to shake. It twitched and writhed, the way Heath had done when he was transforming into a demon.

But suddenly, Nikolai's body began to change. His skin dissolved away from his face, exposing his white skull, with the jaw wide in a grimace of pain. A blinding white light exploded from Nikolai's chest. An explosion rocked the room. And dust flew up into a stream to the ceiling, where it vanished.

"He—he's gone," Vivienne gasped. "How?"

"Because you bit him. Your goodness, your glow began to destroy the darkness in him. But he had nothing but a black heart."

Sarah began to sob, and Vivienne left Heath to hug her daughter. It meant Julian was gone, too, didn't it?

"I couldn't do it, Mother." Sarah sobbed. "I tried to fight my grandfather. I didn't want to be a vampire, but if I hadn't been so scared, Julian would have come back."

Another howl came, this time from the doorway. The winged demon began to melt, then light shot out of its chest, and it burst into sparkling dust and ash. Nikolai's servants dropped their blades and they collapsed to the floor. They were alive, but it was as though they were caught by a magic spell, and Nikolai's death had freed them.

Out of the corner of her eye, Vivienne saw Adder. He was moving unsteadily, like a drunken man, but he managed to pull a wooden stake from beneath his cloak. He jumped toward Heath.

Protective fury took control. She flew through the air, just as she had done to Nikolai. She plunged her fangs into his neck. And an intense warmth passed through her to Adder. His body glowed with a golden light from the inside out. She let him fall, and stumbled back.

Into Heath's arms.

"Have I killed him?"

"No, Flower," Heath murmured, holding her shoulders. "You've brought him back to life."

Adder fell to the ground. He jerked, then groaned. The fangs that hung over his lips retreated. His heartbeat began to go faster.

"You've made him mortal again. You have your mother's special power to heal. And it means you can change vampires back into mortals."

The council members let out a collective howl of fear. They stumbled toward the doorway. But to Vivi's shock, Dimitri stood there now, wearing the immaculate clothes of a gentleman from fifty years before. He laughed at the council. "Too late," he said softly.

And a woman appeared at his side. Then another. And another. One had dark hair piled in elaborate curls, and she wore a stunning gown of scarlet. The second had blond hair threaded with silver and wore black. The third had red hair, which fell free to her waist, and she wore a white, flowing Grecian gown.

The three women, like the three witches of Macbeth, suddenly began to chant. The members of the vampire council stumbled to their knees, cried and pleaded desperately, but then vanished into five puffs of dust.

The blond woman smiled. "There. Those fools have been sent to prison. One in another plane, another realm of this world. Their power-hungry ways are at an end."

Dimitri lifted a brow. "And you, my queens, are not hungry for power?"

"Women only wield power in responsible ways," exclaimed the dark-haired woman.

Vivienne gasped as Dimitri appeared suddenly at her side, but she smiled as he grinned at her. He clasped her hands in his. "My dear Miss Dare, you are truly a remarkable woman. You saved Heath from turning into his worst nightmare, a murderous demon. You destroyed Nikolai with the power of your love. You gave Adder, that pompous brutal fool, the punishment he feared the most by transforming him into a weak, mortal man. And now, I have to repay you for bringing hope and peace to my world."

She blinked. Heath's deep voice saved her. "What are you talking about, Dimitri?"

"With the council and Nikolai gone, I hope to convince all vampires to live in peace. The queens have agreed." He waved his hand toward them. "These are the three most powerful of the queens. They have never allowed any mortals to see them before, but they have come to see your lovely Vivienne. They wish all vampires to set aside quests for power."

"Yes," giggled the redheaded queen. "Dimitri wants all vampires to dedicate their lives to one big, happy orgy."

"Not exactly that," Dimitri said. He nodded to Heath. "Now you must explain to Vivienne what you have learned about her. And then I will tell you all how you can find happiness. But, before all that, we should free your brother Raine. And also Guidon, whom I believe served you well, Miss Dare?"

"I could not have done this without Guidon," she declared. She saw the fear flash in Heath's eyes, and swiftly asked, "Is Raine all right?"

"What's happened to him with Nikolai's death?" Heath asked gruffly.

"He is freed like these other servants are. He is still a vampire, but he no longer carries the curse. Perhaps that means the two of you can put aside your past differences and behave like the brothers you are."

"I want to," Heath said. "I hope Raine is willing."

Two hours had passed and they had all returned to Dimitri's home. The vampire queens now lounged on chaises in the ballroom. Vivienne sat between Heath and Sarah on a large sofa. Guidon sat in a wing chair. Raine was very weak, so he was in a bedchamber, regaining strength.

Dimitri paced between them all. "You see, Vivienne, you will always be at risk because you have the power to turn vampires back into mortals."

She blinked. "But don't vampires want to be changed back?" One look at the queens answered her question. They looked appalled and aghast. "But I would never change anyone who didn't wish it. You must understand that."

The blond queen, Ophelia, shook her head. "It is not that simple. You are a risk. And the queens cannot allow risks to survive. However, you could surrender your power. We can take it from you, if you surrender it willingly."

She looked to Heath. They were both vampires, yet he had told her it was a horrible existence. "Could I not transform Heath and myself back to the mortal state?" Yet, did he want that?

"If it is what you want, Flower, I would be willing. I want to be with you always."

Her heart soared. But it plummeted as the queens shook their heads as one. "You can change one person back. And while you do that, we will take your power away."

"Change yourself," Heath said swiftly. "So you can be mortal with Sarah."

She looked to the queens. "Do you know—is my daughter mortal? I was a succubus. Does it mean she is one, too?"

The dark-haired queen, Cardiamillion, shook her head. "Your daughter is mortal. You can change yourself back, if it is your wish."

But she stood and smiled at the three women. "I would be willing to surrender my power if you can bring back the vampires that Nikolai attacked with his demons. He said they were in some sort of other dimension. Can you rescue them? The vampire I want to change back to a mortal state is Julian."

"Julian Tremaine," Heath added in explanation.

Sarah clapped her hands to her mouth.

Ophelia looked to the others, Cardiamillion and the redhead, who was named Lausanne. "Can it be done?"

Lausanne nodded. "Of course. We have the power to undo any spell cast by a *male* vampire."

The three chanted, and in a burst of golden light, Julian appeared, naked, stunned, and confused. He saw the queens and put his hands over his privates. Then he saw Sarah, and Vivienne knew there was no mistaking the brilliant glow of love in his eyes.

Swiftly, Dimitri explained to Julian what had happened and what their plan was. The lad looked confused. He said slowly, "So I can be mortal again, if I let Miss Dare bite me? And then, Sarah and I can—well, I can court Sarah?"

After all they had been through, the polite term made Vivienne laugh. "Yes," she said. "You have my permission to court my daughter."

Julian met her gaze with shining eyes. "Then change me back, please."

"Raine, I don't want you to spend eternity hating me for the past. I know I deserve your anger, but I also know there's no point in wasting forever spent in rage—whether it's directed at yourself or someone else."

Heath watched his younger brother gaze out the window at the night sky. "I don't hate you," Raine muttered. "I resented you. And Nikolai seemed to cloud my mind. He made me think you hated me. I know it's not true, but I wanted your respect, which you never gave me."

Heath's throat tightened. Hadn't that been what he wanted from his father? But he was destined to never have it.

"Of course I respected you. I loved you."

"No. I could never please you. You always went on at me to do better at school, to drink less, game less. I was always in the wrong."

"Just as I was with our father. Hades, Raine, I went about things wrong. I felt I had to be a father to you, and I had no idea how to do it. All I wanted to do was protect you. I suppose I thought that being a good father meant trying to improve you. I was always a disappointment to Father. I was afraid of failing you."

"I always felt I was failing you, Heath."

Heath moved forward, clasping his brother in a swift, masculine hug. "We were both idiots, Raine. Both fighting demons that didn't exist." He met his brother's silver-green eyes. "I am sorry I turned you into a vampire."

"You saved me, Heath. And I was a bloody fool to listen to Nikolai's poison. Can you forgive me?"

"Funny, I was going to ask the same thing."

They shared a laugh, something they had not done for twenty years. Heath ruffled his brother's hair. "We have eternity to become friends."

"Really?" Raine cocked his head. "I thought we already were friends. Hell, we're brothers after all."

A sense of peace flooded Heath's heart.

"Dimitri explained everything that has happened," Raine said. "About how you searched for me for weeks. About how worried you were over me. And he explained that you have fallen in love. I know it destroyed you to lose Meredith and Ariadne. According to Dimitri, vampires can marry. Not in church, of course, but we take mates for eternity. Are you going to marry Miss Dare?"

"If she'll have me."

"Hades, you haven't asked her yet? Go and propose before some other vampire in here tries to win her heart."

He bowed to Raine. And now he understood the vision in the pool on the moors. It had been the vision of his brother happily accepting Heath's choice of a bride. "Agreed. What in Hades would I do without you, brother?"

And he left. To find Vivienne. He wanted to marry her, make her his mate for all eternity. He wanted her to wear his ring, he wanted to hear her call him her husband. He wanted all the trappings of commitment that went with love. She had said she loved him even though he had made her into a vampire. But she had always wanted independence. How could he propose in a way that would tempt a woman who yearned for independence to agree to marriage?

It was strange to walk beneath the night sky and feel safe and at ease. Vivienne smiled as Sarah gazed up at the spray of glittering white stars. "It's beautiful," her daughter breathed. Then Sarah blushed. "I feel I should tell you I'm sorry. I think I said some unkind things to you."

"I don't remember any," Vivienne said firmly. "And I finally see that you are grown up now. I was trying to keep you as my child, instead of seeing you for the strong and courageous woman you are. You have blossomed into your own, Sarah." She brushed away a tear, thinking of the times she had pleaded with her own mother to change. But now she understood her mother's fall had been because of Nikolai, and that her mother had been a very special woman with a unique power to heal. She felt proud that she had that power, too, even if she had only been able to use it twice. And she knew Rose would have been so delighted by her brave granddaughter.

"You saved Julian's life," Sarah breathed. "He is so happy he is no longer a vampire. And he is so pleased he doesn't have to serve the vampire council anymore. He won't tell me much, but he says they were cruel and abusive masters. Adder was the one who made him a vampire. Against his will."

"I am delighted he is happy now. But he has not gone too far with you, has he?" She arched a brow with teasing fierceness, playing the stern mother. She and Heath had discovered Julian had a strong core of honor.

"Only kisses. Wonderful kisses." Sarah let go of Vivienne's arm to twirl in the moonlight. "If he were to ask for my hand in marriage, would you agree?"

"He was willing to sacrifice his life for you, Sarah. He obviously loves you. I'd be a fool to say no. And I suspect it wouldn't stop Julian anyway. He'd whisk you away to Gretna Green for a clandestine wedding, I fear." And Sarah's deepening blush obviously implied she and Julian had considered a hasty wedding. "I approve of him completely, Sarah. Heath does, too."

"Are you going to marry Lord Blackmoor, Mother?"

Vivienne sighed. She remembered her mother's tales—that one day Vivienne would capture the heart of a rich and titled gentleman, she would be whisked out of the stews, and she would live as a grand lady in a fine house, with servants and dresses and jewels. "He hasn't asked me yet. I don't believe Heath would want to be married again."

"He loves you!" Sarah declared.

"We could have love without marriage. After all, it seems vampires have very unconventional lives." Like the ones in Dimitri's house, who attended orgies. According to Dimitri there were vampire women who were married to more than one man at the same time. Both men were happy to share.

"Do you want marriage?" Sarah asked suddenly. "I know you always insisted you would never marry, even though you hoped I would do so."

"I—I don't know," she had to admit. Ahead she saw long legs striding and the outline of broad shoulders against the moonlit dark. Sarah ran forward, shouting, "Julian!"

Tears sprang to Vivienne's eyes as Julian swept Sarah into his embrace. He kissed Sarah as though she was his sun, a treasure he would adore for the rest of his life. Sarah had found happiness. As a mother, could she have asked for anything more?

"I can't tell if you look happy or sad."

The sensual, drawling baritone set her heart alight. Vivienne turned to see Heath at her side—naked. He had shape shifted and looked the way he had on the night they'd escaped from the vampire council. He looked like a human man but with large wings lazily flapping behind him. She could shape shift, too, and she had tried it several times. But Heath caught her hand. "Don't change tonight. Ride on me instead."

"Ride how exactly?"

His wicked grin made her blood heat, her cunny ache, and her nipples leap up against her shift. "Exactly the way you are thinking," he said.

"If you mean *that* way, then why do you have wings?"

"Trust me."

He eased up her skirts. She gave one worried glance toward Sarah and Julian, but they had strolled across the lawns toward the rippling water of the Thames, leaving Heath and her in privacy. Vivienne held up her frothing hems and moaned as Heath stroked his erect cock against her quim. At once, she was wet with desire, and he slid readily inside. Even after two nights of intense, delicious sex together, this was still new and thrilling. Perhaps because the curse had made this joining so forbidden and therefore precious.

She gasped as his cock slid deep, filling her.

"Wrap your arms around my neck, Flower," he growled.

She did and with a powerful flap of his wings, they rose into the air. Higher and higher they flew, until the ground below was just a patchwork quilt of blue-white moonlight and velvet blackness. Stars winked overhead. Heath shifted position, so he was lying on his back while flying. And she rode him. Daringly she sat up, braced her hands on his chest, and bounced up and down on his magnificent cock. His wings moved slowly, and it felt as though they were making love on a cloud.

They flew over a fluffy one, making her laugh. He launched his hips up and her giggle turned to a sobbing moan.

"Vivi, I love you," he said softly. "Only with you could I soar like this. I wanted to do something exotic and daring, so I could tempt you into madness. So that you would say yes when I ask you to marry me."

She stilled. "Are you—" She was impaled on him, close to climax. Her cunny still pulsed on him even as she didn't move. "Are you asking me to marry you?"

"Yes, Vivi. Will you be my wife? Will you accept me, let me love you for eternity, and lift my heart to heaven with your every smile?"

Laughing, she collapsed on his chest. He held her tightly and twirled them through the air with playful flaps of his wings. "Yes," she cried. "Of course I'll marry you. I love you."

"I cannot believe I'm such a fortunate vampire."

He stopped their gentle spin and she caught her breath. They were still joined. "I cannot believe I just received a proposal while making love in midair."

"Then the best is yet to come." He winked. "Imagine climaxing in midair."

She kissed Heath, tangling her tongue with his. Madly, they shared kisses and nips and caresses, and the tension grew and grew. Until she cried his name in the sky, loud enough for all London to hear it. He arched beneath her. "Vivi!" he yelled. "God, Vivi, I love you."

They came at the exact same instant and clung together, damp with sweat, weak with pleasure, floating on warm spring breezes. Vivienne had never dreamed of a shared climax while flying. But that was the joy of being with Heath: he made the impossible possible.

"To having an eternity of magic and happiness," he murmured as though he'd read her thoughts.

She kissed his beautiful mouth. "To the magic of love," she whispered back. "Now, shall we try for multiple climaxes in midair?"

For more thrillingly seductive erotic romance,
here is a special preview of

DARKEST FIRE

by Tawny Taylor

An Aphrodisia trade paperback on sale in April 2011

1

Sin in stilettos hunted him.

In Drako Alexandre's lifetime, lust had worn many masks—fair and sweet, dark and exotic, male and female—but whatever form it took, it always, without fail, seized its prey. There was no escape. Yet, like the quail in Drako's favorite sutta, "The Hawk," Drako knew he would eventually break free from the predator's grip . . . and shatter its heart.

Tonight, the hunting ground was one of Drako's favorite haunts and lust was a redhead, in an itty bitty fuck-me dress, her mile-long legs bared to *there*, her full tits a sigh away from tumbling out of her dress, and a dozen erotic promises glittering in her eyes. She didn't know it yet, but the hunter would soon be the hunted.

Drako acknowledged her with a hard, piercing stare. In response, lush lips pursed into a seductive pout.

Yes, he'd have this one. But on his terms.

Let the games begin.

Eyes on the prize, expression guarded to keep her guessing, Drako tipped his beer back, pulling a mouthful of bitter ale from the bottle. As he swallowed, the heavy bass of the music thrummed through his body, pounding along nerves pulled tight with erotic need. Red and blue lights blinked on and off, casting everybody in the nightclub, male and female, in an alternating crimson and deep indigo glow.

Her gaze shifted.

His body tightened.

Oh yeah. He liked this place. A lot. He slowly swept the crowded room again with his eyes. Writhing, sweaty bodies, mostly female, packed the small dance floor. Groups of people crowded around tables, the flickering red tips of their burning cigarettes dancing in the shadows.

"I've got the redhead," he announced.

"That's just as well." His brother Talen set his empty glass on the bar's polished top and shoved his fingers through his spiked, platinum hair. "I'm not in the mood for this tonight."

"Not in the mood? Are you kidding me? Look around, baby brother." Sitting on the other side of Drako, Malek shot Talen a bewildered glance. About a dozen women gaped as his shaggy blond surfer-punk waves danced on a breeze.

Drako slid his quarry a heated glance then twisted to flag down the bartender. "Yeah, well, if you spent half as much time working as you do playing, Malek, we'd—"

"Yeah, yeah, I've heard it before, big brother." Malek ordered another beer for Drako then clapped him on the shoulder. "But like I say, life is short. You gotta live while you can." He slipped from the stool, peeled off a twenty, and handed it to the bartender. "Do either of you have a bad feeling about tomorrow's meeting with the old man. . . . ?" Malek stood a little taller, tipped up his chin. "Ohhhh, yes. Talk to you later." Not waiting for them to answer his question, he headed toward the nearest flock of admirers.

"I think I'm calling it a night," Talen said, watching Malek gather a small herd of women around him.

"Okay, bro. See you at home." Drako checked his redhead again. She was still sitting at the table with her friend, but she was looking a little less certain of herself now. One hand was wrapped around a wineglass, the other nervously tugged at a lock of hair.

That was better. An aggressive woman did nothing for him.

Letting the corners of his mouth curl slightly, he lifted his fresh beer to his mouth and waited for their gazes to meet again.

Uh huh. Much, much better.

He held her gaze and everyone and everything else in the crowded bar seemed to slowly drift away, until nobody but his redhead existed to him. Electricity sizzled between their bodies, like heat lightning arcing between storm clouds.

Her tongue darted out, swept across her plump lip, then slipped back inside. She set her glass down and, breaking eye contact, leaned over to her friend. They both glanced his way. The friend smiled and nodded, and then the pair of them stood.

Their arms linked at the elbow, their gazes flitting back and forth between him and the back of the bar, they hurried in the opposite direction, toward the bathroom.

That was an interesting reaction. Nothing like what he'd expected. Was she playing him? Were they both?

Mmmm. Both. Maybe he'd have two women tonight. Two was always better than one.

He dropped a fifty on the bar. And with his beer clutched in one fist, he walked around the far side of the room, taking the scenic route to the dark corridor at the rear. He'd catch them out there, where it was quieter, more intimate.

His timing was perfect. Just as he rounded the corner, they clacked out of the bathroom on a breeze of sweetly perfumed air. They halted instantly, eyes widening, one pair a soft gray-blue, the other a deep brown.

Up close, the redhead lost a little of her charm. It was her friend who demanded his attention now. Her features were different, her almond-shaped eyes tipped up at the outer corners, the uncreased eyelids hinting at her Asian ancestry. Her full lips were plump and freshly coated in shimmering gloss. Her carefully applied makeup emphasized a set of picture-perfect cheekbones, and her slightly mussed hairstyle lengthened a slender neck, a tumble of silky blue-black waves cascading over her shoulders.

He'd seen her before. Where?

"Hi," the redhead said, her voice a deep and sultry siren's call.

He turned toward her again, catching, once more, the sensual promise glimmering in her cool blue gaze. Despite the invitation he read on her face—or maybe because of it—he found himself tiring of her already. His attention snapped back to the quiet woman next to him. An old David Bowie song echoed in his head, "China Girl." "I know this is the world's worst line, but don't I know you from somewhere?"

"I'm not sure." His China Girl stared at the tattoo on his neck, following the curved line up to his jaw. "I think I recognize the tattoo."

"My brothers and I have the identical design, a griffin. It's kind of a family thing. Our mother did the work."

"Your mother? How interesting." The redhead inched closer to get a better look, or so he assumed. "It's very sexy. I'm not crazy about tattoos, at least not most of the ones I've seen. This one's very different. All black and gray and sorta . . . what's the word I'm looking for?"

"Celtic?" The brunette offered.

That brunette was spot on. Their mother had been one hundred percent Irish. There could never be any doubt, with her mane of copper-colored hair and freckles. And the design she'd created for her three sons was as Irish as her maiden name, O'Sullivan.

The redhead scowled. "No, that's not it. I mean, yeah, it is Celtic, but that's not what I'm trying to say. Men with tattoos are a little . . . dangerous."

"Wicked." Something darkened the brunette's expression.

"Yes, wicked." The redhead's white teeth sank into her lower lip. "That's a good word."

Yeah, that was a good word.

He was feeling a little wicked something going on. And he could tell at least one woman was feeling it, too. "Can I buy you ladies a drink?"

"Actually"—the brunette shot the redhead a nervous glance—"we were getting ready to leave—"

"But one more drink wouldn't hurt," the redhead finished, slanting a smile his way. "Thank you. By the way, my name's Andi and this is Rin."

"Good to meet you, Andi and Rin. I'm Drako. Let's go see if we can find a table." He motioned for them to precede him out of the dark corridor. He followed them back into the crowded heat of the bar. As they shuffled and wound their way through the throng, his gaze meandered down the back of Rin's body, from the bouncing curls that tumbled down her back to a nicely rounded ass hugged in a snug black skirt. When she stopped to let a couple pass by, he leaned over her shoulder and whispered, "Maybe we can figure out where we've seen each other before."

A delicate fragrance drifted to his nose. Jasmine. It was refreshing, compared to the cloying blend of cigarette smoke and cheap cologne hanging heavy in the air and making his nose burn.

"Sure. Maybe." She hurried around a couple clawing at each other like bears in heat.

He smiled at her expression as she shuffled past them, her lips parting, cheeks flushing a pretty pink.

Damn, this was a hot place, in more ways than one. It sure

put him in the mood to fuck, with all the gyrating bodies and hard, thumping music. A song he recognized started playing, a slow, sexy number, and taking advantage of the moment, he caught Rin's slender wrist.

She glanced over her shoulder.

"Dance with me." He didn't wait for her to respond, just tugged her gently until her body was flush with his. He looped one arm around her back, splaying his fingers over the base of her spine. He felt her stiffen against him then relax.

She was petite, the top of her head hitting his chest at about nipple level. He liked how small and fragile she felt in his arms, how her little body fit against his.

And how she worked those hips of hers. Damn.

Sparks of erotic hunger zapped and sizzled through his body with every sway. He tucked his leg between hers and rocked his hips from side to side, melting at the feeling of her hips working perfectly with his. Her feminine curves conformed to his hard angles as she pressed tighter against him. He cupped her chin and lifted, coaxing her to look at him, to let him see that beautiful face, to maybe taste her lush mouth.

A second female body crowded against him from behind. A woman's hands glided down his tight thighs. Breasts flattened against his back. Within a second, his prick was hard enough to bust through brick, his balls tight, his blood burning like acid.

Rin's eyes lifted to his, and her lips parted in a natural pout, so different from the practiced expression her friend had donned for him.

That was it; he had to kiss her.

He tipped his head, his entire body tight and hard and ready. But just before his mouth claimed hers, she lurched away. He opened his eyes to catch the redhead slipping into Rin's place as the music changed.

He twisted to find his delicate Rin, but she'd disappeared into the crowd.

"She's my friend," Andi shouted over the music as she undulated against him. "I won't say anything bad about her. But she's just not into this. She's so shy. Sorry." She smoothed her hands up his torso.

He was sorry, too.

There was something about Rin. A quiet sensuality that didn't need to be forced. He hadn't been that intrigued by a woman in a long time. "No need to apologize for her."

"I'm guessing you like your women a little less aggressive?"

"Yeah."

"Got it." Her expression softened. "If you want to be the predator, I can be the prey. Let's play." Giggling, Andi slipped out of his arms and dashed into the crowd.

Now this was getting interesting.

Rin all but forgotten, he set out to hunt down his redheaded quarry in the black fuck-me dress.

Hunter. Prey. It looked like both of them would get what they were after tonight.

The next morning, Drako headed down to the library with a satisfied smile on his face and memories of one lush redhead strapped spread-eagled on his St. Andrew's cross.

Damn, that had been one of the best nights he'd had in a long time. Andi wasn't just a slut; she was a pain slut. The more he gave her, the more she begged. And that insatiability had applied to *everything*.

By the time they were through, both his single-tail whip and his cock had gotten a thorough workout.

He'd sent her home less than an hour ago, taken a shower to wash away the lingering scent of sex from his skin, and was ready to face whatever news their father was about to deliver.

Whatever it was, Drako knew it would be major. The old man had said his good-byes ten years ago, after his brothers and his wife had been buried. He hadn't called, written, or even e-mailed his three sons since. Not that any of them could blame him. He'd paid his dues; he'd earned his freedom. Someday, they'd earn theirs, too.

Until then, duty was duty. It wasn't like they had it bad.

When Drako entered the room, he found the old man sitting behind the desk—the one Drako considered his—hands clasped, waiting, silent, gaze sharp. It was damn good to see that face.

Malek was slumped in a chair next to the fireplace, looking like he'd had a long night, which he probably had. Talen was looking bright-eyed and alert, no doubt because he'd turned in early, like usual.

Drako knew he looked like Talen, but inside, he felt like Malek. Dead-dog tired.

The old man lifted his cool gray eyes to Drako and cleared his throat. "We can begin."

"Sorry I'm late." Drako snagged the closest seat and braced himself for what was coming.

Their father stood, hands on the desktop. "All three of you men know how vital your duty is. You've served well, protecting The Secret faithfully since my brothers and I stepped down over ten years ago. For that, you have earned my respect." He straightened up, crossing his arms over his chest. "But now it's time to prepare for the future." His assessing gaze turned to Drako. "Son, you're my oldest. The leader of your generation of Black Gryffons. You've proven to be an excellent leader—fearless, loyal, responsible, and yet sensitive. I admire the man you've become."

Drako didn't know how to respond to his father's words. It had been a decade since the old man had paid him any compliment, let alone one so great. "As I admire you, Father. You set a fine example, as the firstborn of your generation."

The old man smiled. After a beat, he said, "You've just celebrated your thirty-first birthday. In order to assure your retirement by your fiftieth, all three of you must father sons within the next twelve months. Which means you must take wives. Immediately."

Wives. Children.

Drako had understood this day would come, since shortly after taking his father's place as the leader of the Black Gryffons. Thus, he'd accepted it long ago. It was their fate, their duty, their honor.

But, gauging from Malek's barely stifled groan, at least one of his younger siblings hadn't been mentally prepared for the responsibility of wife and child yet.

"*Must* we all take a bride?" Malek asked. "If Drako conceives three sons, there would be no need for the rest of us to father children."

"Of course," their father said. "There's no guarantee he'll produce one, let alone three."

Malek's shoulders sank a tiny bit. "Okay, but today, marriage and children don't always have to come hand in hand—"

"No bastard child will ever be a Black Gryffon." Their father shook his head. "That's the law."

"I think the law's antiquated," Malek grumbled.

"Doesn't matter what we think." Drako stood, giving his scowling younger sibling a clap on the shoulder. "So what? You have to take a wife. It's not the end of the world."

"Depends on your perspective."

"Hey." Drako glanced at his father. "There's no law that says we have to be monogamous, right? I mean, if our wives know beforehand that we have no intention of limiting ourselves to having sex with just them, then we're good, right?"

Their father shrugged, eyes glimmering with an unexpectedly playful sparkle. "If you can find yourselves wives who are willing to live with that kind of arrangement, then more power to you. Your mother wouldn't. It was hell, giving up certain things, but I could never deny that woman anything." He sighed. "There are some sacrifices that are worth it."

"I hear you," Drako said, knowing full well what kind of agony it had to have been. "Discomfort" was an understatement, but he respected the old man more than he could ever say for his commitment to their mother. Since at least the early eighteenth century every Black Gryffon had practiced some form of D/s, and many of them had multiple lovers. His father had done neither.

In the silent moment that followed, Drako studied the man he had emulated his entire life. The old man's once dark-brown hair was now all silver, and lines fanned from the corners of his eyes, but otherwise in Drako's eyes this man would always be the powerful guardian leader he had respected and admired. His father's body was still heavily muscled, his mind sharp as a blade. Drako guessed retirement hadn't slowed him down a bit.

Only the deep shadow in the old man's eyes hinted at how close he was to passing from their world to the next.

"I miss her, son," their father said. "Your mother loved like nobody I've ever known. The last ten years have been so empty without her."

Drako touched the side of his neck. He could almost swear his tattoo—which had been, ironically, his mother's final gift to him before she died—was tingling. "I miss her, too." Knowing somehow this would be the last time he'd see his father alive, Drako gave the old man a hug then watched as his brothers did the same. It wouldn't be much longer, he guessed, before their father would be reunited with the woman he missed so dearly.

Their father left with a final wave and a smile, and Drako shoved aside the deep sorrow tugging at his heart and forced his mind to the next task he faced as leader of the Black Gryffons.

It was his duty to help his brothers find brides, women who would be willing to live with husbands who, in Malek's case, wouldn't be faithful. And in his own, would accept his lifestyle. It had to be this way, even if it meant it would take longer to find the right brides.

He had to be honest with his future wife, and he expected his brothers to do the same. He would never be able to live with the guilt of hiding the truth. The pain those secrets would cause.

His wife. His bride. Who would she be?

It was a matter of choosing the right woman. A special woman.

A certain set of deep brown-black eyes and sculpted cheekbones flashed in his mind, and it was then that he remembered where he'd first seen his quiet little Rin.

It couldn't be. But it was.

The supposedly shy Rin wasn't who her friend believed. Quite the opposite.

His lips curled into a smile and his heavy heart lifted.

He knew exactly where to find his bride. Rin was one very special woman, and he had a good feeling she'd be willing to listen to his proposal.

In general, people tried too hard to simplify issues. Life wasn't comprised only of black, white, sane, insane, good, bad. There were an infinite number of shades of gray in between.

He had gone to great lengths to find people who saw a full spectrum of gray in the world. Only they could appreciate him, could share his vision.

Someday, every man, woman, and child on the earth would thank him. They would finally appreciate the truth he'd tried to share with them so many times. The simplemindedness that had blinded them wouldn't matter anymore. The truth would be too big and dazzling to deny.

That someday would be soon.

Smiling, he signed the document, ending his voluntary stay

at the hospital. He gathered his prescriptions, medications, and personal possessions and stepped out into the warm, sunny day. The antipsychotic medication left his mind a little fogged and suppressed his emotions, but even with a full dose of Haldol still coursing through his bloodstream, he was ready.

So much work to do; so little time to do it.

A sleek black Mercedes-Benz crawled down the driveway and rolled to a stop in front of the hospital's entry. He waited, unsure whether it was his ride or not. The window rolled down, and a hand waved at him.

When he approached, the passenger handed him a card with no name, no phone number, only a gray-scale image of a chimera.

"Enter," the passenger said, his or her head turned, so he couldn't see the face.

Without questioning the passenger or driver, he got in the car.